CW00502490

Samuel Burr is a TV producer who has worked on popular factual shows including the BAFTA-nominated *Secret Life of 4-Year-Olds*. Samuel's writing was selected for Penguin's WriteNow scheme and in 2021 he graduated from the Faber Academy. He previously studied at Westminster Film School. *The Fellowship of Puzzlemakers* is his debut novel.

THE FELLOWSHIP OF PUZZLE MAKERS

Samuel Burr

ORION

First published in Great Britain in 2024 by Orion Fiction,
an imprint of The Orion Publishing Group Ltd.
Carmelite House, 50 Victoria Embankment
London EC4Y 0DZ

An Hachette UK Company

1 3 5 7 9 10 8 6 4 2

A CIP catalogue record for this book is available from the British Library.

ISBN (Hardback) 978 1 3987 1230 0
ISBN (Trade Paperback) 978 1 3987 1231 7
ISBN (eBook) 978 13987 1233 1

Printed in Great Britain

FSC www.fsc.org
MIX
Paper from responsible sources
FSC® C104740

www.orionbooks.co.uk

For Ann and Andrew,
for everything

The Fellowship Of Puzzlemakers

• MEMBERSHIP REGISTER •

Miss Pippa Allsbrook	Chief Cruciverbalist, Founder and President
Mr Clayton Stumper	Club Secretary and Estate Manager
Mr Hector Haywood	Jigsaw Artist and Deputy President
Mr Earl Vosey	Master of Mazes
Sir Derek Wadlow	Codebreaker
Miss Jean Watkins	Chief Trivialist
Mr Geoff Stirrup	Lead Arithmetician
Miss Nancy Stone	Queen of Quizzes
Mr Eric Stoppard	Minister for Mechanical Puzzles
Mr Martin Dudeney	Metal and Glass Maker
Mr Jonty Entwhistle	Wordsmith and Riddler
Mr Nigel Bentham	Gamesmaster
Miss Angel Webster	Housekeeper

PROLOGUE

1991

LTARDBT ID IWT UTAADLHWXE DU EJOOATBPZTGH!

The shiny brass plaque affixed to the front door was plain gobbledygook to some, but for many who visited this grand house on the outskirts of Bedfordshire, and certainly for the people who resided here, it made perfect sense. It was a basic +11 Caesar shift. Nothing too fiendish at all:

WELCOME TO THE FELLOWSHIP OF PUZZLEMAKERS!

Beneath it, a laminated slip of paper read: *Our buzzer is playing up. Press and hold it, else it sounds like Morse code. Better still, try the knocker. One of us is usually in. No junk mail, please!*

Pippa Allsbrook stood with her back to the house and felt her entire weight collapse against the arched oaken door. She'd pulled it shut the moment she'd stepped outside and clocked the peculiar delivery on the front steps, which had appeared almost out of thin air.

A hatbox.

It looked just like any other with its black leather exterior, gold trim and the letters H.H. embossed in gold on the hexagonal lid. But it was the contents, or more specifically the *noise* coming from the thing, which really confounded her: an insistently high-pitched, piercing sound that, up close, really couldn't be confused with anything else at all.

As Pippa removed the lid – which had been left deliberately unsecured – she was so overcome her legs started to buckle. She reached for the pillar of the porch to steady herself and folded her spare hand against her pounding chest, stealing another glimpse inside.

Surely not.

Tucked inside the flowery paper lining of the box, a beautiful little baby, presumably no more than a few days old, was swaddled in a custard yellow blanket, crying its heart out.

'Oh, my darling. Where the devil have you come from?'

The boy's squalling briefly tempered as Pippa peered down at him, their eyes meeting.

'Aren't you just the most *beautiful* little thing?'

She wasn't used to throwing out such airy blandishments, but the tiny little person looking up at her – a boy if the blue of his romper suit was anything to go by – was perfect in every way imaginable. He had golden wisps of hair whipped on his head like spun sugar, cheeks as plump as a pudding and the palest blue eyes, so piercing they seemed to penetrate her own.

Pippa gathered up her tweed skirt and crouched down on the steps. She reached gingerly inside the box.

First, she wiped away the silvery trail of tears, then she stroked her thumb along the tiny boy's nose, before bopping it once, twice, three times, as if checking he were real, that this wasn't all a dream.

'Boop!' she heard herself say, in a light, sing-song voice. 'Boop . . . boop . . . boop!'

The baby – soothed by the gesture – went very still for a moment.

She looked at him. He looked at her. She felt his tiny hands curl around her finger before his flailing arms suddenly shot upwards.

He was reaching out for her.

She tucked one hand carefully under his head and the other beneath his back without hesitating and hoisted him out of the box. 'Shh, now,' she whispered gently in his ear. 'I've got you . . . I've got you.'

He was so unbearably soft she couldn't help but press their two faces together. With his velvety skin brushing against hers,

Pippa kissed him on the head, his nose, the tiny dimple of his chin. He smelled liked the inside of a milk bottle, of freshly baked bread, and Imperial Leather.

It was only when she nestled the baby boy into the crook of her arm that she caught it. There, in the dense shrubbery either side of the long gravel drive, was a definite flash of something ahead of her. A scampering. It wasn't the faint scuttle of an animal, nor the wind rustling the branches, but a human movement somewhere in the distance. She was certain of it. Someone was out there. Someone was watching.

Step forward, she wanted to say. *Why are you leaving this baby with us?* But just then, the baby's tiny little fist reached out and wrapped around her middle finger and she knew in that moment that their fates were sealed.

'That's it,' she murmured soothingly, gently rocking the boy from side to side in the dappled morning light. Their two pulses were beginning to settle into each other. 'You're safe now.'

For Pippa Allsbrook, in all her sixty-four years on this earth, there had never been a moment as miraculous, nor utterly fated, as this one. It was the the solution she'd spent a lifetime searching for. The missing piece.

PART ONE

C	E	P	O
I	R	N	T
N	A	E	I
O	T	E	N

Chapter One

2016

Clayton Stumper was an enigma.

He always had been, and, now, standing just a few metres away from Pippa's open coffin on the eve of her funeral, he feared he always would be.

He could barely bring himself to look.

From the other side of the old billiard room, he caught a glimpse of her hair, a silver cloud of perfectly coiled perm, and clocked the padded shoulders of her favourite Givenchy dress protruding from the long pine box, which was lined with pink velvet and adorned with a bright display of purple and white gerberas. She had asked for the floral tribute on her coffin not to read *MOTHER* or *FRIEND* or *PRESIDENT* but *TSILABREVICURC*.

It had taken some explaining at the florist, but that was what she had requested, and Clayton was determined to follow her instructions. She was still challenging her friends even from beyond the grave.

The wake was being hosted in the largest and most formal room at the Fellowship of Puzzlemakers. There were mottled brass candelabras affixed to William Morris walls and, along the long end of the room, two bay windows, encased with elaborate tasselled draperies, looking out over the parterre. Over the years, this was where the Fellowship had hosted all their formal events – puzzle tournaments, special lectures, product launches – but now the space looked more like the communal lounge of a nursing home. Where there was once immaculate decorative baroque furniture there were now reclining winged armchairs, jigsaw tables and crossword-setting boards, all angled towards the early evening.

Guests weren't due for another hour, so Clayton had come to spend some time with Pippa. He didn't like the idea of her being on her own. But instead of going straight over and keeping her company, he found himself hovering at a distance, trying to pluck up the courage.

All week he'd been putting on a brave face, pretending he was just fine, when really the bottom of his world had fallen out and he didn't know where to turn.

It had started around the time Pippa had fallen ill. A new impulse had started to consume him: a compulsion to find out the truth. To discover exactly where he came from, who his biological birthparents were and why they'd chosen to leave him here, on the steps of the Fellowship, twenty-five years ago. It hadn't felt as urgent before – he'd always had everything he needed here, had never gone without – but the moment he'd realised that Pippa, the woman who raised him as her own, wasn't going to live forever, Clayton had started to feel untethered.

He distracted himself by sorting through the games cabinet in the corner of the room. This glass repository was where they kept their various puzzling consumables: compendiums, counters, marbles and ball bearings. Even though he'd stuck a notice on the door asking residents to return the items where they'd found them, nothing was ever in the correct place.

Beside this cluttered cabinet was a green-felt-lined mah-jong table, and next to that an enormous freestanding blackboard, which, if examined in the correct light and from the right angle, revealed half a century's worth of chalked inscriptions: riddles and nonograms, patterns and grids. The faint scribblings of some of the sharpest, most brilliant minds in all the British Isles.

Clayton cleared his throat, tried to say *hello* to her, but couldn't quite manage it.

The room was so unbearably quiet.

The only noise was of the colossal grandfather clock opposite, its swinging pendulum emitting a faint but authoritative *tick, tick, tick*. Clayton tried to block it out. He didn't need to be reminded of the time, and how little was left for everyone here at the Fellowship.

If only he could press pause, he thought, keep things exactly as they were forever.

As he reached the foot of the coffin, he took his first proper look at the woman inside.

Pippa Allsbrook.

The pioneering cruciverbalist. The polymath. President of the Fellowship of Puzzlemakers and Chairwoman of the British Crossword League.

Clayton had to admit, even in death she looked quite spectacular. At the foot of the coffin were some of her most treasured personal effects: her favourite pearl-plated compact mirror, a battered, leather-bound copy of Sam Loyd's *Cyclopedia of Puzzles*, and a bottle of her favourite Dom Pérignon, which she always kept a case of in the back of her wardrobe, ready to pop at special occasions.

She was eighty-nine at the end, as everyone kept reminding him. *We shouldn't mourn, we should celebrate. What a life, what a legacy!* Of course, that was all true, but . . . for Clayton, it didn't make her loss any less devastating.

He gripped the edge of the coffin and, before he could change his mind, leaned over so he was just inches from Pippa's face.

'Hey, Pip . . .'

Silence.

'It's only me.'

Her waxen skin wasn't just pale but watery, almost see-through, like a sheet of gelatine. He could count the creases that sprang from the corner of her eyes like a sunburst, could see how the funeral directors had rouged her hollow cheeks, lined her lips, painted her eyelids – a darker shade than she would usually wear.

It took every effort to raise his other hand and reach inside the coffin properly, lifting Pippa's frail wrist folded across her lap and inserting his hand gently under hers, but when he did, the weight of it lying on top of his, the coolness of it, felt familiar to him. It warmed him somehow.

Before he turned to leave, Clayton reached into his back pocket and took out that day's *Times* crossword (No. 27,122), slipping it inside the velvet lining near her feet. He'd considered having a go at filling it in but couldn't quite bring himself. The grief had left him groggy and, even at the best of times, the cryptics were usually beyond him.

He was not a puzzlemaker himself, of course. Unlike everyone else, he hadn't chosen to live here; he had been gifted to the Fellowship by someone. There were so many questions now, so many things he'd wished he had quizzed Pippa on, but it was all too late for that.

Just like the unsolved grid he had just slipped inside the coffin, he was never going to get the answers he needed to fill himself in. To make himself complete.

Chapter Two

Downstairs

The Old Queen's Head, Islington

TUESDAY, 7TH AUGUST, 1979

Pippa was dying for something bubbly.

Standing at the bar, she tried to catch the eye of the young barmaid who had a perfect swirl of platinum blonde hair on her head like ice cream on top of a cone. The woman was wearing the largest gold hoop earrings she had surely ever seen; three in each ear, they chimed like tiny church bells as she shambled up and down the line doing an excellent job of ignoring Pippa's expectant gaze.

'Next!' the lady barked, looking straight past Pippa to the handsome young man who'd just appeared behind her. 'What can I get you, my darlin'?'

Pippa sighed and tipped her head to the ceiling in despair as the man stepped round her.

Ever since she'd hit the half-century, Pippa was beginning to feel as if she were a figment of her own imagination. She was becoming invisible to the world.

'May I order a drink, please?' she asked. 'I can see you're busy, but I've been waiting a little while now.'

'Be with you in a sec, doll,' the woman responded, without even glancing up from the pump.

Pippa took a deep breath.

For the past ten minutes she had been keeping an anxious eye on the mirrored section of the bar in front of her. The door leading to the upstairs lounge was reflected in the space between a bottle of Bombay Dry and Bell's. She'd caught at least ten people slipping through while she'd been waiting to be served. Each time, relief had flooded through her. Despite the initial wave of interest, she was worried about whether people would actually show their faces. That was the trouble with puzzledom – it did rather attract the introverted types.

UPSTAIRS FUNCTION ROOM
RESERVED FOR PRIVATE BOOKING.
7–TILL LAST ORDERS.

A landlord suddenly appeared beside the barmaid: a portly chap with a swollen gut like a giant marble, so perfectly contained, it appeared as if it might shoot down and pop out one of his trouser legs if he sneezed.

Pippa tried to catch his eye, lifting herself up on tiptoes to make herself even taller but he was focused on emptying a bag of halfpennies into the cashier tray, whistling the theme to Ski Sunday.

If I stood on this bar in just my undergarments, she wondered. *If I removed every stitch of clothing, or, better still, dressed as a man, with a fake moustache and bowler hat, perhaps then I might get a bloody drink.*

The only person who had acknowledged her presence was an older gentleman a few bar stools down.

He was immaculately dressed in a grey double-breasted pinstripe suit and a brown felt fedora hat, and was carrying a battered leather briefcase, pipe and paper. She'd been watching him out of the corner of her eye, plucking coins from a leather purse and lining them up along the bar as if preparing to play backgammon.

He ordered himself a barley wine and a packet of dry-roasted peanuts, the exact money – fifty-nine pennies – already counted out in front of him.

She couldn't quite place him but was certain she recognised him from somewhere. His cologne – an assault of exotic spices and woods – seemed familiar too. It was Fabergé Brut. The same scent that Melvyn Prado-Lee, an editor she'd assisted at the *Telegraph*, would spritz himself liberally with, usually after heading out for a lunch meeting and coming back smelling of his mistress.

She'd been twenty-one years old, fresh out of Cambridge University with great prospects and even greater aspirations when she'd first met Melvyn – a man she would go on to encounter many times in her life – and she had yet to come across anyone she loathed more. She'd anagrammed his name once – something she liked to do when someone provoked a strong reaction in her. Some of her favourites over the years:

Eric Clapton. *Narcoleptic.*

Clint Eastwood. *Old West Action.*

Margaret Thatcher. *That Great Charmer.*

For Melvyn Prado-Lee, she'd conjured *Pervy Old Man Eel.* Couldn't have been more apt.

The old fellow beside her lifted his barley wine from the bar, and in doing so revealed a small blue badge pinned to his lapel. A globe emblem wrapped in a laurel wreath, topped with the Crown jewels and the letters *GCHQ*. She knew it was an honorary badge that the top-secret intelligence organisation gave to all retired personnel, which meant that its owner was none other than Sir Derek Wadlow, the legendary codebreaker and international chess master himself. She had been to a cryptology lecture he gave at the Savile Club years ago. He was part of the team that cracked the Enigma machine at Bletchley Park.

Derek – now surely in his mid-eighties – tramped away from the bar, shuffling at an inordinately slow pace, as if he had dropped something very small and was scanning the ground for it. When he eventually reached the back of the pub, he slipped through the door leading to the function room upstairs.

Pippa couldn't quite believe it.

Sir Derek Wadlow wanted to join her puzzle club? He was a veteran of Bletchley Park, a man who'd helped decipher enemy code, surely one of the most acclaimed cryptologists in

Britain, perhaps even in the world. What a coup, what a terrific endorsement, and before they'd even got going, too.

The ambition behind her society was simple: to bring together like-minded puzzlers – cruciverbalists, enigmatologists, logicians, trivialists, riddlers – for a regular meet-up in the pub. Not just professionals, for they were few and far between – but enthusiastic amateurs, anyone who revelled in, and had the mental capacity for, fiendish games and challenges.

Ever since she'd become a professional compiler, Pippa had developed quite a following. Or at least the alter-ego she'd created for herself had. These days, there were dozens who would write to *Squire of Highbury Hill, London*, enclosing clippings of grids torn from the paper, marked with start and end times to show their varied competencies. Sometimes they'd even post hand-drawn puzzles of their own with cryptic clues for her to appraise, enclosing stamped-addressed envelopes for her to autograph their work, like a royal seal of approval.

A few weeks ago, she had posted out a dozen invitations to a select circle of celebrated puzzlers to join the inaugural meeting of the society. She'd encouraged them all to share the word with their own contacts – everyone was welcome, she had insisted. Or rather, Squire of Highbury Hill had insisted.

Murray Salter – the crossword editor at the *Express* – responded by return, promising to circulate the details to all his freelance compilers; Clement Banks – UK Scrabble League Champion 1967–1972 – said he'd be sure to get the details printed in the programme of the next tournament he was in. Before long the invite had made it into periodicals and journals across the country and the RSVPs were flooding in.

'Have you seen all the oddballs heading upstairs?' Pippa heard the barmaid mutter to the landlord. 'Who did you say they were?'

The landlord shrugged. 'I just take the bookings, Pam.'

Pippa coughed lightly into her fist.

'But they've got a name, haven't they?' the barmaid went on, oblivious. 'The Federation of something or other.'

Give me strength, Pippa thought. *Or a glass of Asti Spumante at the very least.*

'And did you see that old boy counting out his coins just now?' the barmaid continued. 'Looks like he'd been saving up for weeks.'

He's a millionaire, Pippa wanted to say. *The man is a multimillionaire because he helped saved this country with his brain. One of his little toes is cleverer than you two twerps put together.*

The landlord was squinting at the bookings sheet he'd lifted from beside the till. 'The Fellow . . . Ship . . . Of . . . Hang on, I need my readers.'

'The Fellowship of Puzzlemakers,' Pippa snapped, and the two of them turned to regard her.

Suddenly they saw her. She gave a flash of her hand as if to say hello, here I am.

'Sorry, what was that?'

'The Fellowship of Puzzlemakers,' she reiterated. 'It's my society. It's our inaugural session. And it starts . . .' She glanced at her wristwatch. 'In two and a half minutes. Now, could I *please* trouble you for a glass of something? I really ought to shake a leg and get up there.'

Pippa unclipped her bag and pulled out her purse. She hated to be ignored, worse still to be ridiculed, but it was her nerves that were also getting the better of her.

'I didn't mean no offence nor nothing,' the barmaid said. 'We usually have darts on Tuesdays, that's all.'

'This one's on the house, ma'am—'

'*Miss* . . . please,' Pippa corrected before she could stop herself. 'And that's very kind. Do you have anything sparkling?'

The barmaid lifted her soda gun and pointed it at her. 'I've got tonic or soda. Whatcha fancy?'

Moments later, steeling herself at the foot of the narrow, carpeted staircase, clutching a complimentary Campari and soda she didn't really fancy, Pippa Allsbrook lifted her flannel skirt and ploughed her way up the stairs and into the next chapter of her life.

Chapter Three

An hour into Pippa's wake and Clayton could honestly say he'd never seen the place so full. Amongst the melee were all eight of the current residents: Geoff Stirrup – their lead arithmetician – was showing Jean Watkins, Top Trivialist, and Earl Vosey, Chief Mazemaker, something out of his portfolio. It was a battered tan leather thing that he carried everywhere and contained all his latest mathematical musings, scrawled hastily on slips of green-gridded paper, which he would stuff inside in a very haphazard fashion. Clayton would occasionally find these little notes dotted about the house, covered in numbers, arrows, blank boxes and barely intelligible instructions. They made little sense to him but usually they'd end up appearing in one of the Fellowship's quarterly pamphlets, on their blog, or in the external publications Geoff regularly contributed to. People seemed to go mad for them.

Both Jean and Earl looked totally nonplussed at whatever Geoff was demonstrating but were nodding vacantly. It was sometimes best to play along, otherwise you could get stuck with him for hours.

Dotted about the rest of the room were the others: Eric, Nigel, Martin and Hector – all chatting to the various guests. They included several illustrious puzzle champions, former Mensa committee members, clients, sponsors, cleaners, gardeners.

They'd all come to pay their respects, to honour the woman who'd established this society and turned it into a thriving commune where, in its heyday, it had been the biggest independent producer and distributor of puzzles anywhere in Europe.

Everyone seemed to have a glass in their hand, so Clayton was happy enough. So long as they were all enjoying themselves.

He pressed his back against the swinging service door into the scullery and re-emerged moments later bearing a silver tray of hors d'oeuvres: stuffed celery sticks, crab filo cups, cheese and pickled onion sticks.

Everyone had insisted they should get caterers in, but he wouldn't hear of it. It had been a welcome distraction, if he was honest, pulling the spread together.

He placed the tray on the ottoman and poured himself a sherry from the trolley – a good one, not his usual Harveys Bristol Cream – then slid a cube of Cheddar from its cocktail stick and chewed the warm, moist chunk of cheese until it coated the insides of his mouth.

'Hey,' came a voice behind him.

Clayton turned to regard a young woman who had wedged herself into the corner of the room. Her face was faintly illuminated by the phone in her hand.

'Oh, hello there,' Clayton replied, lifting a finger and wagging it quizzically at her. 'It's Amy, isn't it?'

'Amber,' she corrected.

He snapped his fingers in defeat. 'Almost got it. I've always been dreadful with names. Forgive me.'

The young lady gave a tight grin.

She was wearing a black T-shirt with the words *Hotel California* emblazoned on the front and jeans slashed, presumably fashionably, at the knees.

Clayton had overheard the girl, who was granddaughter to Eric Stoppard – the wooden-puzzle master – explaining to someone earlier how she'd just got back from a year backpacking in Australia. She'd been working on fruit farms and at a surfing school and getting blind drunk almost every night. He couldn't think of anything worse.

Standing in the corner, the two of them were, by at least fifty years, the youngest people in the room.

Eric Stoppard lived on the top floor of the Fellowship and largely kept himself to himself. He was a former mechanical engineer – sharp as they come – and a fine creator of all their wooden interlocking puzzles that always did particularly well at Christmas. The perfect gift for an uncle you barely knew.

At seventy-nine years of age, Eric had only recently been assigned the role of Minister for Mechanical Puzzles, when Tony Hargreaves, the previous occupier of the position, had moved to a luxury retirement home on the Costa Del Sol. Tony still sent postcards monthly, much to everyone's dismay.

'It must be kinda weird,' Amber announced, sipping from a bottle of Babycham and pulling a face as if it were poison. 'Living here with everyone at your age.'

'Not really,' Clayton shot back. 'What would be weird about it?'

'Well . . .' she began, casting her eye over his shoulder, gesturing to the scene going on behind them. A small group had congregated around the chesterfield, playing a lively round of Fictionary – one of Clayton's favourite parlour games – while her grandad Eric had his head out the window, smoking a cigar.

'I guess it depends what you consider weird,' he replied, with a shrug. 'It's perfectly normal to me, and everyone else who lives here.'

'But aren't you, like . . . *young*?'

Clayton gathered the edges of his jacket, secured a button into the wrong hole. 'I don't know what that's got to do with anything.'

The girl shrugged. 'No reason, I suppose.'

He was beginning to feel uncomfortable. Amber was looking at him in the way a historian might study an old coin, examining every inch, from Brylcreem to brogues.

'Thanks for coming anyway,' he said, keen to get on. 'Lovely to see you, Amy.'

'Amber.'

'Amber, sorry, yes. Take care now, won't you.'

As he made his way over to his friend Earl, he passed the Fictionary group. Someone shrieked out the word 'coddiwomple' but he couldn't make out the rest, and while he'd usually be the first to join in, he wasn't in the mood for games today. As he made his way past the group, he saw the middle-aged lady, whom he didn't recognise, but who had been staring at him all evening, perched on the arm of the sofa. On the top of her head was a black hat that looked a bit like the tyre of a small car. As he glanced back at her, their eyes briefly locked before she looked away again.

When he reached Earl, he muttered quietly into his ear, 'Who's that woman back there? The one with the hat on, over my right shoulder?'

Earl turned very deliberately in his seat, lifting the spectacles off his head to inspect the row behind.

'Don't make it *too* obvious, Earl.'

Earl flashed his hand at the lady. When he turned round, he was beaming. 'That's Nance! Smart as a whip that one. She's looking well.'

'But who is she?'

'Nancy? She lived with us for years, right up until . . .' He closed his eyes briefly. 'Oh, must have been shortly before you turned up.'

Clayton felt himself sit more upright. 'They were close? Pip and her?'

Earl scoffed. 'Thick as thieves.'

'And what was her name again?'

'Nancy Stone. They used to call her the Queen of Quizzes.'

Clayton glanced behind but their view was now obscured. Someone had started clinking a glass as if to make a speech, and the congregation of Puzzlemakers were starting to huddle round their former president in her velvet-lined box.

He wondered if he might catch Mrs Stone afterwards, if it was worth seeing if she remembered hearing anything about the day he'd arrived at the Fellowship. It couldn't hurt to try.

As he approached the coffin, he was pleased to see his friends holding a coupe of champagne in one hand and an egg-custard tart folded into a napkin in the other. Those were Pippa's favourites.

'We're falling like dominoes, aren't we?' Hector quipped, gesturing his orange juice towards the casket and splashing some inadvertently on the body inside.

'This one's really knocked me for six,' Earl added, still by Clayton's side. 'It's hard to comprehend, isn't it?'

Hector Haywood puffed out his cheeks in response. 'Another one bites the dust.' The man was barely five feet tall and had a thick military moustache under his nose like a strip of Velcro. He would usually be wearing a paint-splattered flannel work-shirt and pair of slacks, but that evening he'd opted for a tatty charcoal suit.

'Not just another one, though, is it?' Clayton heard himself say.

Everyone turned in his direction, shuffling to allow him to enter their circle.

'What's that supposed to mean?' Hector asked.

'Well . . .' Clayton began, feeling himself colour. 'If it wasn't for Pip, none of us would be here, would we?'

Jean and Earl – two of his closest comrades in the house – looked kindly towards him, lifting their drinks in agreement, but Clayton noticed Hector quietly scoff to himself, arching his fierce white brows to the ceiling.

The funny thing about Hector Haywood was that he wasn't a puzzlemaker at all, not in the purest sense. He was an artist. His extensive range of jigsaws were, to several fellow residents' great frustration, the Fellowship's best-selling line to date. These technicolor paintings depicting coastal village scenes, baskets of yarn-tied kittens and kitsch corner shops had been reproduced on millions of jigsaw pieces and were mostly sitting unsolved in the back of wardrobes all over Britain. But while Hector's jigsaws were always cheery, the man himself was the biggest misery going. He was permanently irritated by something or other, his conversational patter limited to an endless stream of negativity. In the last few weeks, following Pippa's death, Clayton had started to find the man almost insufferable.

'Well, while I've got everyone . . .' Hector began again. 'We do have to start thinking about what's next for the Fellowship.' He leaned on his lacquered cane, drawing himself up to his full height. 'I know there's talk of cancelling our spring fayre, but I really think we should press ahead.'

For a while no one issued a word. Instead they dipped their heads and stood together in considered silence around the coffin.

A frail hand Clayton recognised as Jean's curled around his side, pulled him into an embrace, and he could almost taste the Elnett hairspray as she rested her head briefly on his shoulder.

Jean Watkins was Chief Trivialist, had a plaque on her bedroom door upstairs saying so. She looked after all trivia-based products, was as sharp-minded as she was softly dressed, always bundled in a bright chunky jumper or cardi and usually found hovering by the tea urn in the dining room, offering to pour anyone a cuppa, while testing out some of her questions.

Clayton noticed Jean's swollen feet were encased in sequinned pumps – her party shoes – and he felt a thickness creep into his throat. She was ready to dance, to celebrate a life well lived, and who could really blame her. His chin began to tremble and he scuffed the tip of one brogue against the floor to stop himself from embarrassing himself, really digging down into the pile of the vivid carpet. It was the colour of cough medicine.

'Come on, everyone,' Earl announced. 'Pippa wouldn't want us moping around, would she? Shall we raise a little toast?'

'What a good idea,' Jean said, beaming at him. 'She'd be three sheets to the wind by now. Let's have a bloody drink.'

'Shall we pop that Dom?' Hector asked, peering into the coffin where the bottle sat between Pippa's feet. Before anyone could stop him, he started peeling off the foil wrapping of the Dom Pérignon. 'Shame to waste it,' he said, opening the bottle and charging the glasses while everyone stared down at their friend, who appeared, to Clayton at least, as if she were taking a brief nap in the middle of a party. She'd be back with them any moment, surely, she would.

'To our cryptic queen.' Earl made the toast because Hector didn't drink. 'The doyenne of crosswords.' He pointed at the gold Fellowship pin on his lapel.

VENI, VIDI, SOLVI.

The Latin slogan emblazoned on the badges also appeared on all their branded stationery: the headed paper, compliments slips and invoices.

I CAME, I SAW, I SOLVED.

Clayton glanced around the circle. Every single person was wearing their pin proudly on their lapels. Clayton had yet to be presented with one, and today was simply a reminder of the fact.

Everyone here had earned their membership, except him.

'On behalf of us all at the Fellowship,' Jean announced, stepping forward in her sequinned party pumps, her hand loosely covering her mouth to stop herself from bawling. 'Thank you for all you've done for us. You were not just our leader, but our landlady, our confidante, our muse, our friend.'

Clayton raised his glass. 'And the most extraordinary mother a boy could ask for.'

'To Pip,' they clinked.

Chapter Four

Upstairs

The Old Queen's Head, Islington

SESSION 1

Entering the function room, Pippa was struck not only by the number of people gathered there – nearly a dozen at first glance – but also how unbearably quiet it was. Most people were hovering in the corners of the room, staring into their drinks, not knowing quite where to look or what to say.

She moved towards the trio of gentlemen congregated around the oche of the dartboard, one of whom was Derek Wadlow. From a distance, the excessive plumes of tobacco smoke billowing above their heads made it look as if they were on fire.

'Evening, chaps.'

She lifted her glass to Harry Benson, a fellow Mensa committee member, who had his hand inside a packet of scampi fries, and whose eyes briefly flickered towards Pippa at her greeting. He was standing beside a chap in a sheepskin jacket she didn't recognise but who caught her attention immediately. He stood an easy six feet two and had long blonde hair that fell to his shoulders. Handsome beyond question.

'I don't know about you gentlemen,' Derek went on, oblivious to Pippa's presence, 'but I'm finding the *Telegraph* a tad predictable these days. All those double definitions. It's a bit humdrum, don't you think?' He took a quick slurp of his brown drink. 'As far as I'm concerned, no one tops that fellow in *The Times*. His Sunday grids are quite tortuous.' Derek tipped his head to the Artex ceiling and clicked his fingers. 'They've even given him a name . . .'

'Squire,' Pippa answered, stepping forward and offering her hand.

'Squire, that's the bugger!' Derek cocked his head in Pippa's direction, taking her hand with some hesitancy.

'Sorry, dear, what was your name?'

'No, sorry,' Pippa said. '*I'm* Squire.'

He looked at her as if she'd gone out of her mind. 'I'm sorry, lovey, you've lost me now.'

'It's my pseudonym.'

She pulled a cigarette from her purse and sparked up, blowing a thick ring of smoke between them.

'So, hang on a second,' he snapped. 'You're telling me that *you're* the one who writes those demon clues that drive men like me potty? You're . . . *Squire*?'

'That's correct,' Pippa replied, her voice entirely flat and even. They'd started her off on Mondays to begin with – the easiest slot in the week – but she'd quickly risen up the ranks and, within a year or so, she was headlining. They didn't usually credit the setters at *The Times* – but her grids had caused such a commotion they'd decided to make an exception. If nothing else, solvers knew who they should address their complaint letters to.

Pippa tipped her head a bit higher, pleased to finally unveil herself.

'I've never officially revealed myself as a woman. Everyone just assumes I'm a man.'

She noticed several craned necks around the room, others beginning to clock on.

Derek scoffed. 'I've heard it all now. And how long have you been getting away with that?'

'I'm just about to set my four thousandth grid,' she explained, reaching into Harry Benson's packet of scampi fries and helping herself. 'You'd be hard-pressed to find a compiler anywhere in the country, at any of the broadsheets, male or otherwise, who's reached that milestone.'

Pippa didn't mind tooting her own horn when she needed to. She was used to having to assert herself, especially in circles like this. It could be exhausting at times, but she relished any opportunity to confound people's expectations of her. To catch people by surprise.

'Is that so?' Derek said, visibly irked by this apparent deception.

'My real name is Pippa. Pippa Allsbrook. Squire is my sobriquet. I use it interchangeably, like a stage name.'

She'd chosen Squire because it meant, among other things, a shield-bearer of a knight. A protective veneer. A defence. It was the second identity she hid behind.

Derek looked at her in vague disbelief, shaking his head as he necked the rest of his drink. She noticed how the dashing chap in the sheepskin jacket standing next to him had taken a small sidestep away from the man. Hopefully he wasn't such a chauvinist.

'And correct me if I'm wrong,' Pippa began. 'But you're the famous Derek Wadlow, formerly of GCHQ?'

He lifted the flat of his hand. 'Guilty as charged.'

'Your reputation precedes you, of course.'

'That's right. My *own* reputation, not someone else's.' Derek took a deep inhale of his cigar, grinning at the two men either side of Pippa as the smoke poured from his nostrils.

She couldn't help but smile.

Of course, the real issue here wasn't anything to do with the fact she used a pseudonym (that was a *Times* crossword tradition, after all), it was the fact she was a woman, operating in a man's world, excelling in it, even. By not alerting everyone to her gender, she was simply affording herself the opportunities she would have been granted if she'd been born with one X chromosome rather than two. This was a man's world. She was simply levelling the playing field.

'Derek, are you planning on joining us regularly or—'

'It's *Sir Derek*, if you don't mind. Not Derek.'

Pippa pulled her cardigan together.

'Very well,' she responded, finding herself mildly amused, but not at all surprised. Not only did he smell like her old boss, but he was beginning to sound like him too. What a pity, she thought. A man she'd so admired.

'Well, thank you again for coming, Mr Wadlow.'

'You're welcome, Mrs Allsbrook—'

'*Miss*, actually,' she corrected, taking a slow drag on her cigarette and smiling playfully at the other gentlemen in earshot to make sure they heard – especially the handsome chap in the sheepskin coat, to whom she gave a little wink.

Pippa was beginning to wonder if she might need to ask the barmaid for more chairs. There were another four late arrivals while everyone made their awkward introductions and took their seats, bringing the total number of attendees to fifteen.

As she might have predicted, the room was exclusively male, and entirely middle-aged, except for Sir Derek who was, frankly, well into the winter of his years, along with another chap who, upon hauling his way up the staircase, slumped into one of the armchairs by the fire and nodded off before anyone could catch his name.

Pippa clapped her hands theatrically above her head.

'Gather round, everybody,' she bellowed. 'I thought we could kick off with a little housekeeping.'

There were to be weekly sessions every Tuesday, she explained, with guest speakers and themed challenges, plus members would be invited to present specific puzzles they'd been working on for critique and workshopping within the group. The next session would open with a discussion on palindrome sequencing and everyone was encouraged to bring along a related puzzle of their own to stimulate the group. Mr Grantham – a renowned lexicographer in the back row – had kindly offered to host a seminar on the history of lipograms and univocalics.

'If things go well, perhaps we might work towards producing puzzles on commission, start selling limited-edition runs at the fairs and conventions.' She waved her hands in front of her. 'Let's see how we get on, who knows where it might lead us.'

The next quarter of an hour was spent sparring with a particularly obtuse spoonerism that featured as yesterday's seven-across in the *Guardian*, before Pippa turned to a fresh sheet on the flip chart.

'Now, I'd like to ask you all something,' she declared, and wrote the word *Puzzleology* at the top of the page.

'Why do we partake in puzzles, would you say? If we draw up a list of words then we can use them to establish our club's code of conduct, the principles that this special society will stand for.'

Suddenly everyone had found something interesting to look at in their laps.

'Anyone?'

'For me,' Derek Wadlow called out, 'cracking codes isn't a game. It's what I was born to do.'

DESTINY, Pippa scribbled on the sheet behind her. 'Thank you very much, Mr Wadlow.'

'I'm a man of routine,' Eric Stoppard – a stellar engineer of mechanical puzzles – chipped in from the middle row. 'Once I've had my supper I head to my workshop, mess around in there till it's time for bed.'

RITUAL, Pippa added to the page. 'Very good. I'm just the same with my crosswords, Eric. I set my grids in the morning with a cuppa and solve at night in bed with a cocoa, or something stronger if it's been one of those days.'

The handsome man with the sheepskin coat and luscious blonde locks lifted his hand in the front row. 'For me, I enjoy seeing what my mind is capable of. And showing others what's possible if you really apply yourself.'

'And remind me,' Pippa asked, reaching to touch the side of her hair. 'What was your name and what do you do?'

'Earl Vosey. Master of Mazes, according to this month's *Country Life* magazine anyway,' he answered proudly. 'I've been obsessed ever since I was a little boy. I designed the one at the Godsley estate last year. Sending people round in circles. I've made a career of it.'

There was a ripple of laughter and Pippa nodded at the gentleman, even more taken with him. She wrote the word *INSPIRE* behind her, then waited to see if Earl had anything else he wished to add, quite happy to listen and look at him all day if he didn't mind.

'And the other thing is,' he went on, tucking his hair behind his ear. 'It's my way of escaping. Once I'm thinking about mazes, my mind goes somewhere else entirely. All my troubles melt away.'

RESPITE, Pippa scribbled. 'I know exactly how that feels,' she said.

There was something truly captivating about the man, and it wasn't just his ravishing looks, but something else she couldn't quite put her finger on.

Earl Vosey. Pippa reshuffled the letters of his name in her mind, appreciating the perfect mix of vowels and consonants.

Easy Lover.

Perhaps it was an augury, with any luck.

She rattled through the other hands that had started to shoot up, keen not to leave anyone out.

Other words that ended up on the sheet were:
STIMULATION, RAPTURE, ERUDITION, TRADITION, HEALING, MISCHIEF.

For Pippa, summing up exactly what puzzles meant to her was nigh on impossible. For as long as she could remember, she'd treasured words more than words could ever describe.

Having lost her mother shortly after she was born, Pippa's childhood was best described not just as grief-stricken, but uprooted. Her father, Clarence, had been a prominent serviceman in both wars, first as an RAF pilot, then a group captain, so she'd been sent to live at her unmarried aunt's in Broadstairs where she became accustomed to keeping herself entertained. She'd learned to use her intellect to occupy her time with fiendish word games she'd concoct all by herself, as well as the crosswords her aunt Grace would cut from the back of *The Lady*, her token attempt at childcare.

It was during these troubled formative years that Pippa retreated into her love of language. She would play with words as if they were putty.

These days there was still nothing quite as thrilling as setting a grid, or, for that matter, solving one. The process of compiling a crossword was not unlike cooking a very elaborate meal. First, you had to assemble your ingredients – the words – and then you had to cook them, to marry the flavours and textures, align them in perfect harmony, until it became one delicious plate of food. A perfect meal, or crossword for that matter, could be devoured, but never scoffed. It should be appreciated one mouthful at a time.

'And may I suggest another reason we might puzzle?' Pippa announced, squeezing the word *CONSCIOUSNESS* onto the page. 'Sometimes I feel that solving puzzles is a way of connecting with a consciousness other than our own. It's a way of making sense of the world around us, if that doesn't sound too grand.'

She looked at the audience who were hanging on her every word, gazing up at her as if she held answers not just to today's *Times* cryptic, but to life itself.

Suddenly it was as if she'd found her light. Here, Pippa Allsbrook was beginning to feel she could be herself – wholly and without reserve. And more importantly, she realised, so could everyone else. She felt a bubble of excitement rise inside her.

She quickly scrawled the words *BELONGING*, *INCLUSIVITY* and *ACCEPTANCE* behind her before she forgot.

'What I'm trying to say is, puzzling doesn't have to be just about finding connections, but *making* them. Human connections.'

Several members shuffled awkwardly in their seats at this notion, but it was unquestionable: puzzles brought people together.

She was beginning to make it sound like some awful social club, but before she could elaborate, a chap in the back row called Geoff Stirrup, who wore a sleeveless geometric sweater and bottle-top spectacles, and who'd barely uttered a word all night, slowly lifted to his feet.

'That's why I've come tonight,' he croaked, clearing his throat behind his fist. 'I've always been a bit of a loner, to be honest, never had a great deal of friends. So I thought I'd bite the bullet, come along and say hello. I guess . . . what I'm really looking for is a sense of . . .'

'Fellowship!' Pippa answered, pointing her pen at him. 'A sense of fellowship, am I right?'

Flushing, Geoff nodded and slumped back into his seat.

Pippa smiled her thanks to him.

She knew there was a good reason she'd come up with that name. That's why they were all here. It wasn't just for the puzzlemaking, which was usually a solitary endeavour, but the *fellowship*. It was the most important component of all. Of course it was.

Geoff had taken the words straight out of Pippa's mouth, although they were words she'd never dare speak aloud herself.

She was embarrassed by the fact that, at fifty-two years of age, she was beginning to feel a bit lost in the world, a bit alone. She had always been an outsider, always wrestled with her need to flaunt the exceptional parts of herself with her desire to fit in with the world. It was one of those disappointing facts of life Pippa had reluctantly come to accept. Success in life amounted to fitting in, not standing out. Everyone was looking for the blank box they could conveniently slot themselves into. They were all just unsolved clues in the world's most mundane crossword.

'I couldn't agree more, Geoff,' she said. 'A room full of extraordinary minds. Imagine what we could achieve together.'

Chapter Five

Clayton had been on his feet all day. Several hours into Pippa's wake and having topped up everyone's glasses with a fresh bottle of Dom, replenished the bowls of Bombay mix, and tipped an obscene number of profiteroles into a glass fruit bowl, he really just needed a moment to himself. A bit of fresh air.

It was almost midnight when he entered the hedgerow maze.

It had always been his favourite part of the grounds. He had walked its serpentine path so many times he didn't need to look up from his feet crunching gravel in the darkness below or see the identical green walls that wound round and round, in and out of themselves. The once complex route was now so ingrained his legs just led him there.

The specific design was known in the puzzle circuit as a three-dimensional labyrinth, which meant there was a single path leading to its core but many other tracks that twisted in and out of each other, going nowhere. Over the years Clayton had been taught to consider these surplus corridors – the dead ends and false turns – as simply part of the fun. The magic was always in the solving, never in the solution.

These days, the Fellowship survived off the royalties of over two hundred individually licenced products, which sold in the UK and internationally. On their own, each puzzle turned over modest sums but collectively they amounted to quite a decent figure, enough for them all to live comfortably. This cumulative approach to business was everything the Fellowship was about. One of their favourite many mottos:

To go further, go together.

When he finally made it to the core of the maze, Clayton sat with his head in his hands on the picnic bench under the weeping willow. Its thick canopied branches curled at such an acute angle they appeared to almost be folding their arms around him.

Before long the sound of another person's footsteps could be heard in the distance. They scuffled softly against the winding gravel path, then faded to nothing.

'Earl?' he called out. 'Is that you?'

'Clay, old boy,' came Earl's faint, breathless voice. 'Give me a sec, son.'

If anyone would come looking for him, it would be the mazemaker, Earl Vosey. They were as thick as thieves, always had been.

Earl had taught him to ride his first bicycle just the other side of these hedgerow walls – a red Chopper everyone had chipped in to get him for his fifth birthday. He'd taken Clayton to his first cricket match at Lord's and bought him his first shaving set at fourteen – a proper chrome-handled brush and a cut-throat blade from Taylor's of Old Bond Street. Several years ago, he'd even encouraged Clayton to apply for BTEC diploma courses after his GCSEs. Clayton had left Bedford Polytechnic a few years later with no firm friends to his name, but a distinction in hospitality and catering, and a knack for turning out perfect shortcrust pastry.

'Are you coming in, Earl?'

The crunching of gravel could be heard once more, but the tread was slow, less sure at each step.

Clayton started to wonder if he had imagined the voice entirely.

Earl was surely the world's greatest living labyrinthian. There were several dozen hedgerow mazes of this epic scale all over the world in his name. He was a master of his craft, a legend in his field.

'Clay?'

'Yes?'

'I can't find my way. Can you remind me?'

Clayton opened his mouth to speak, then closed it. He squeezed his eyes at the bowed branches above, wondering how on earth the man could possibly be lost in a maze he had created himself, that he was famous for.

'What are you talking about?' he shouted. 'You know the way, of course you do!'

Just put one leg in front of the other, he thought. Forty-six strides to be precise – he had counted them once. But then Earl's voice bellowed again, louder this time, more alarmed.

'I'm lost, Clay. I can't remember the way, son.'

Clayton felt a lump forming in the back of his throat. He pushed himself up from the bench.

'Take your time, Earl. You've probably had too much fizz, that's all.'

There was silence. The man had frozen still. He could be anywhere.

'Go back to the start,' he shouted, feeling his voice catch in his throat. 'It's a right, left, left. Then it's left, right, right, left.'

He waited for the sound of footsteps to approach, some assertive strides after a momentary lapse of cognizance, but there was nothing.

Eventually he traced his own directions in reverse and found the acclaimed mazemaker with his back in the opposite direction of where he needed to be, scratching the side of his head. He looked small and scared, almost childlike, like a little boy lost in a supermarket.

'It's this way,' Clayton said, linking his arm through Earl's, clamping him close to him. They walked in step together, ambling deeper into the maze's core, and at various junctions – or nodes, as they were officially known – he went in one direction and Earl the other, their arms tugging against each other.

'Here we go,' Clayton said brightly as they reached the centre, easing his friend down onto the bench as if he were made of something very fragile. 'You shouldn't have mixed. I told you to keep on the shandies.'

'I'm losing my mind, Clay. That's what happens when you get to my age.'

'Rubbish,' Clayton shot back. 'You're only eighty. There's still plenty of snap in your celery.'

The muffled sound of Sinatra's 'My Way' could be heard a way off in the distance. When he listened carefully, Clayton could just make out the lyrics being bellowed by a group inside, imagined the legs punting the air, arms draped lovingly around each other.

He folded his arms across his stomach, recognising that same unsettling sensation building inside him, realising he had never felt more lost or lacking in direction.

Earl placed a hand on his knee and looked at him with a serious expression.

'Clay, I think it's time you started thinking about what your future might look like—'

'I'm not having this conversation again,' Clayton cut in. 'I'm perfectly fine here. You've got nothing to worry about with me.'

Earl was shaking his head. 'You know what your trouble is, young man? You've grown old before you've grown up. You've lived your entire life backwards, missed out on so much.'

'Nonsense.'

'You know more about dying than living!'

'You're being ridiculous now.'

'I'm sorry, Clay, but none of us are getting any younger. It's a fact of life. The one thing you cannot solve. *Vita incerta, mors certissima.* You know what that means, son?'

'Please, Earl. I can't right now.'

'The most certain thing in life is death.'

For a while both men were silent. Of course Earl meant well, but sometimes Clayton wished he'd temper his words. The eventual demise of this place was inevitable, of course, but so was it utterly frightening. The death of the Fellowship was also the death of Clayton. He was no one without them.

'Earl, towards the end, . . . when Pip didn't have long left.' He raked his hand through his hair, briefly closing his eyes. 'I mentioned that I felt ready to try and find some answers. To work out who left me at the door all those years ago.'

In Pippa's final few days, when she'd been sent home from the hospice with a palliative-care nurse, Clayton barely left her side. From dawn till dusk, he sat on a fold-out chair next to her bed, sometimes resting his head on her quilt while she slept, but otherwise chatting to her constantly, even when she didn't have the energy to speak herself. It was as if by keeping the conversation going, he might just be able to keep her alive.

'And how did she respond?' Earl asked. 'Did she say anything to you?'

'She squeezed my hand,' Clayton replied and as much as he tried to stop himself, hot tears welled in his eyes and he started to cry.

'Oh, Clay.'

The noise that came out of his mouth was ugly and despairing, but he found it difficult to contain. It spluttered out of him like the air escaping from an untied balloon.

Earl pushed a silk hanky into his lap, folded an arm around his shoulder. 'She really wasn't saying very much towards the end, was she?'

'She was listening, though.' Clayton wiped the hanky under his nose. 'She was listening to every word, I'm sure of it.'

Earl smiled kindly at him. 'Yes, I'm going to miss our chats – she loved a good natter, didn't she? I found myself revealing all sorts to her over the years.'

'About what, Earl?'

Earl's mouth was pursed as if he was about to say something. Eventually he just smiled and looked down at his brogues. 'Oh, it doesn't matter. Nothing important.'

Somewhere in the branches above, an owl made a shrill screech, and the leaves sighed to each other in the wind. It was early summer and the air was only just beginning to chill, the sky a velvety midnight blue.

'The thing that I don't understand,' Clayton began, 'is why so little is known about where I've come from?'

'You stumped us, didn't you?' Earl replied with a shrug. 'You're the mystery we've never been able to solve.'

'But is there anything you remember from that day?'

'What do you want to know?'

'Anything!' The word came out more eagerly than Clayton had intended. 'All I've ever known is that I appeared on the front step one morning in a hatbox. But there's got to be more to it than that, hasn't there? I didn't fall from the sky.'

'I thought you weren't interested in finding out about your birth parents?' Earl replied. 'You always said Pippa was your mother, that you never needed anyone else but us—'

'And she is! She . . . *was*. But now she's left us . . .'

The truth was, Clayton hated the idea of Pip thinking he wanted anyone other than her. She'd given him everything. And by looking for whoever his biological mother and father were, by upsetting the equilibrium here, he risked damaging his relationship with the one thing that had always been there for him. The Fellowship.

'It might have seemed ungrateful, Earl. If I'd made a fuss about finding my parents when the two of you, everybody here, had showered me with more love than I could ever possibly need.'

Earl's arm reached out and squeezed his knee. When he spoke, Clayton couldn't help but notice a drop in tone.

'Are you sure you want to go digging, Clay? You never know what you might find.'

'I'm certain,' he replied, his voice surprisingly strong, resolute.

'Please rack your brains, Earl. What do you remember from back then? Even the smallest clue might help.'

Earl adjusted himself a little in his seat.

He tilted his head to the sky and the bench creaked with his weight as his eyes suddenly went very far away, as if the memory might be written in the stars above them.

'I'm sorry, son,' he eventually said. 'I can't remember anything at all.

Chapter Six

TUESDAY, 18TH DECEMBER, 1979
SESSION 5

The legendary code-breaker, Sir Derek Wadlow, was stationed by the pub's overhead projector, about to deliver that week's warm-up exercise.

Since their inauspicious introduction, Pippa had registered a change in the man's behaviour. He looked at her not in the same sneery manner as before, but as a fellow puzzling legend, an equal.

That evening, she positioned herself in the back row, feeling a creeping sense of pride as everyone took their seats. Even if she said so herself, The Fellowship of Puzzlemakers was off to a promising start. Just four months in and they had their core membership of sixteen – still exclusively male, much to Pippa's regret – but otherwise everything was going great guns. Everything that was, except the fact that Earl Vosey, the handsome mazemaker in the sheepskin jacket she had taken such an instant hankering to, had revealed himself to be off limits.

It turned out that Earl lived in Ealing and was married to a woman whose lineage traced back to Salamanca in Spain, of all places. She imagined his wife, Rosa, to be incredibly beautiful, serving up spicy bean stews at home, clacking castanets at the stove. She tried not to think about it too much.

'Take one and pass it on, if you will.'

Derek issued a wad of photocopied handouts to the person closest to him, Hector Haywood. He was relatively new to the Fellowship, making his debut just a few sessions ago, and for the past couple of weeks Pippa had noticed that he was wearing the same paint-splattered flannel shirt and tatty pork-pie hat. He was a funny little man, with eyebrows that were so severe and untamed they might have been painted on as a joke. They gave him a permanently grave expression, as if something appalling had just happened.

When Hector entered the room, there was always a faint odour that followed him – one of stale, malty crumbs at the bottom of a biscuit barrel.

Pippa had noticed that people avoided sitting next to him. By all accounts, he didn't claim to be a wordsmith, an academic, a scientist, an engineer or a historian, like the others. He didn't claim to read particularly widely, pretend to have any interest in philosophy or tuck that day's cryptic into his breast pocket, folded like a checkered pocket square, like so many of the others. In fact, she wasn't certain if he did *The Times*' crossword, or even could. Instead, the quiet, moustachioed man who sat at the back of the room was supposedly a figurative artist, or illustrator, as he preferred to be known.

Other than these small clues, Pippa was really none the wiser. She wasn't sure what Hector was doing here.

Derek shuffled over to the door to switch off the lights. He lifted his drink and had a quick slurp before sliding an acetate onto the screen:

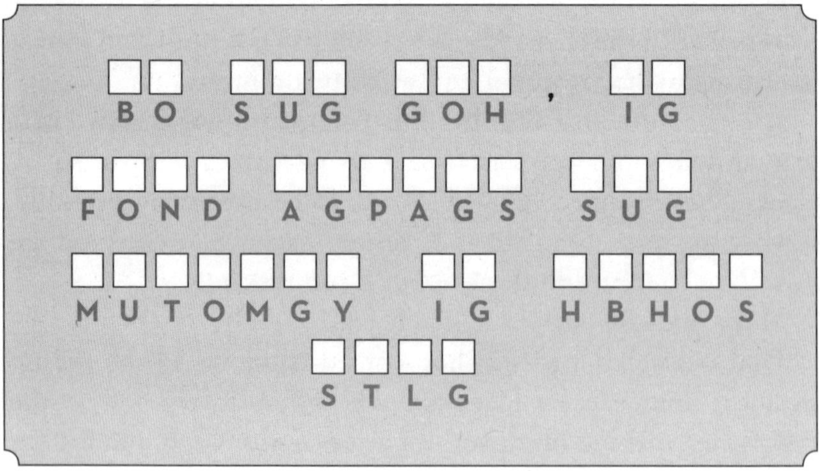

'Cryptograms,' he said. 'Or *quicktograms* as I like to call them, require not just logic and creativity but *risk-taking*. This one here is dead easy. It's been coded using a substitution cipher.'

Derek had been absent from the past few sessions due to his increasingly hectic schedule. It had become clear that despite his advanced years, the man never stopped. He was routinely giving after-dinner speeches, lectures for the WI and making appearances at museums and educational institutions all over the UK, and the world. He'd just returned from a twelve-night cruise around the Baltics where he'd delivered a series of lunchtime lectures on World War II. The cruise company had put him up in an ocean-view deluxe suite and paid him for the pleasure.

'It's a case of deploying frequency analysis skills,' Derek continued. 'Or in other words, studying patterns in text – the frequency of specific letters used in the English language. Look at the way the words are formed, the rhythm and shape of the letters in front of you. Once you've started filling in some of the gaps, take a punt! Half of codebreaking is mere guesswork, not that I'd tell anyone that, of course.'

Pippa was pleased to have finally nailed the format of their sessions.

Every Tuesday evening, a few minutes after seven, they'd kick off with a ten-minute exercise around the projector, then they'd move on to workshopping someone's latest puzzle creation (in recent weeks, Eric Stoppard's exquisitely crafted range of interlocking wooden toys had charmed them and Nigel Bentham's take on solitaire with hand-blown glass marbles the size of snooker balls had blown them all away).

The final forty minutes of their weekly conclave was reserved for members to announce any commissions they had won, share upcoming competitions, swap industry contacts and generally have a natter about the ups and downs of puzzledom, and life itself. This was the part Pippa most looked forward to. Others seemed to agree, as it had started to take up more and more time, the rest of the agenda shrinking to accommodate their casual fraternising.

Last week she'd spent almost the full hour in a corner chatting with Earl Vosey about his ambition to turn his giant labyrinths into pocket-sized puzzles, with the help of Eric Stoppard who had offered to collaborate with him.

Pippa glanced around the room. Earl was strangely absent this evening.

'What does ETAOIN mean to you all?' Derek asked.

Everyone went silent.

'Pippa, might you be able to enlighten us?'

'It's a mnemonic device,' she answered. 'A word made up of the most commonly used letters in the English language, written in order of frequency. E being the most common letter, then *T*, then *A*, then *O*, et cetera.'

'That's correct,' he confirmed. 'So, if we look at this particular cryptogram in front of us, which consists of forty-one coded characters, does anyone notice anything?'

'The coded letter *G* is written nine times,' Geoff Stirrup called out. 'It features more than any other.'

'Excellent work.'

Hector Haywood gingerly raised his hand in the air. 'And *S-U-G* appears twice,' he added quietly.

Everyone turned to look at him. It was the first time they'd heard him speak.

'It's in line one and line two,' he said. 'So, if we assume *G* equals *E* – the most commonly used letter – than it's a fair bet the word might be a common three-letter word ending in *E* . . . like *THE*.'

Derek smiled at the artist in his paint-splattered shirt. Everyone was suddenly scribbling in their notepads, their faces creased in concentration as they tried to decode the eleven-word phrase in front of them.

'I'll give you all thirty seconds for this one.'

Twelve seconds later and Earl Vosey burst through the door. His long blonde hair was dripping with rain, his white shirt sodden, clinging to his torso.

He tiptoed across the room, searching for a place to sit.

'I think this one's free,' Pippa said in a hushed voice. 'You can sit here if you like?'

Earl winked at her, taking the seat she'd been keeping her bag on.

No one could dispute the significance of his contribution to the group. For the past few months, he'd been focusing on pushing his life-size labyrinths to country houses and stately homes across the country. He'd just received an enquiry from the custodian of a palace in Vienna, of all places. A Mr Brandstätter wanted his family crest, featuring a mythical sea creature, to be used as inspiration for the design. These days, Earl was not only capable of incorporating symbols into his work but secreting words in the route paths of his designs too.

'I got caught in those roadworks up in Holloway,' he muttered.

'Time's up!' Derek called. He looked across the room as he prepared to pick a volunteer. 'Miss Allsbrook, would you care to show us what you've got?'

Pippa's heart lurched. Her mind had evidently wandered during the exercise.

She made some excuses under her breath and filled in what she had on the board, embarrassed at her lacklustre attempt.

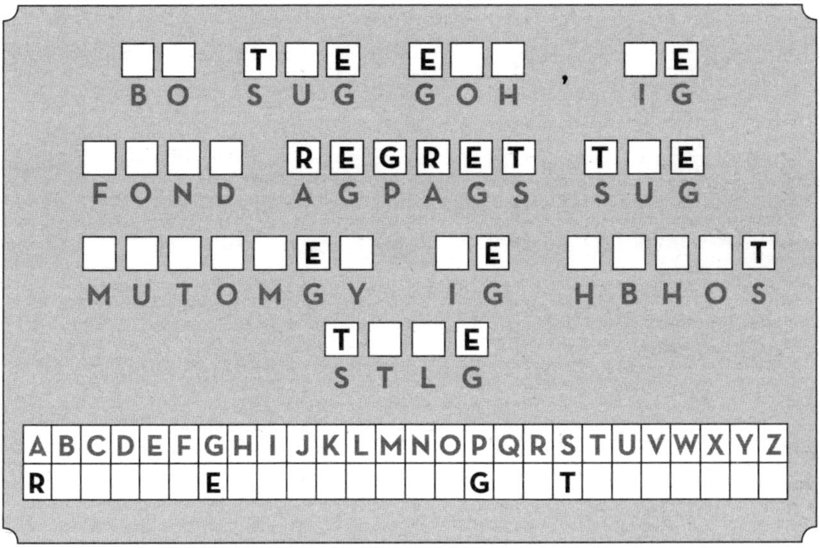

'Anyone care to fill in the rest?' Derek asked, visibly unimpressed.

Before he'd even finished asking, a short, portly chap by the name of Maurice Dobson lifted his arm in the air. He was a renowned professor of theoretical physics at Imperial and had a penchant for calcudokus, a grid game similar to sudoku that had an additional mathematical component to it. He trudged his way to the front looking rather pleased with himself.

'Fourteen point two-five seconds,' he boasted, showing the stopped clock on his Casio watch to Derek. Then he filled in the squares:

IN THE END, WE
BO SUG GOH IG

ONLY REGRET THE
FOND AGPAGS SUG

CHANCES WE DIDNT
MUTOMGY IG HBHOS

TAKE
STLG

A	B	C	D	E	F	G	H	I	J	K	L	M	N	O	P	Q	R	S	T	U	V	W	X	Y	Z
R	I		Y		O	E	D	W			K	C	L	N	G			T	A	H				S	

They skipped the workshop that week in lieu of Geoff Stirrup's surprise birthday celebration. Geoff was a numbers man who, ironically enough, didn't wish anyone to refer to it being his fiftieth.

Pippa wasn't much of a baker, but she had seen Delia Smith make a marmalade cake on television that didn't seem too much bother, so she'd given it a go and, even if she said so herself, the results were not unpalatable. She'd even gone to the trouble of piping the letter *L* on the top (if Geoff didn't want anyone mentioning it was his big Five Zero, she'd write it in roman numerals instead) and put twenty pounds of her own money behind the bar and encouraged everyone to join Geoff for a celebratory drink. It didn't sound as if he had any birthday plans.

She was just heading down to join everyone at the bar when their new member, Hector, cornered her at the foot of the stairs.

'May I have a quick word, Mrs Allsbrook?'

She gathered the edges of her cardigan, feeling as if she was about to be told off. 'Firstly, it's Miss. But of course, Hector. How may I help?'

Hector offered a tight grin, gesturing for her to join him in the corner of the pub. 'I was rather hoping, Philippa, that you might be able to help me fulfil an ambition of mine.'

'Oh, yes?' she asked, shooting a look over her shoulder where Earl looked as if he was getting ready to leave. 'And what's that then?'

'Jigsaws.'

'Sorry?'

'Jigsaw puzzles. It's quite a market, you see, and I've been looking to get my foot in the door for a little while. I really think my oeuvre might lend itself to the medium.'

'I see . . .' Pippa said, suddenly realising why he'd joined their puzzle club after all. He was after a contact.

'I'm an illustrative painter, so I wondered if you might know anybody in that world? You seem to know everyone, if you don't mind me saying.'

'Let me see what I can do,' she said. 'I'll make a few calls, see if I can pull some names together. I take it you have a portfolio if anyone asks?'

'Oh, yes,' Hector replied. 'I've been painting since I was a young lad.'

'Leave it with me.'

'Thank you.'

'I can't promise anything but—'

'No, I mean, *thank you*,' he said, and suddenly his hand was grasping her forearm quite tightly. 'For setting up the Fellowship. It's nice to have somewhere to come each week. I'd be lost without it.'

Pippa faltered. *Somewhere to come each week*? It was an odd thing to say, she thought, but standing this close to the man, there was also something about the dark rings under his melancholy eyes and that unpleasant smell, which was beginning to concern her.

'I'm so glad to hear that, Hector.'

She had a sudden urge to wrap her arms around the lugubrious figure in front of her, to ask if everything was all right.

'You only regret the chances you didn't take,' he declared pensively, staring into the middle distance.

'What was that?' Pippa asked.

'That encrypted phrase earlier,' he explained. '*You only regret the chances you didn't take.* I was rather taken with the sentiment.'

'Yes.' Pippa nodded. 'Yes, I think you might be on to something there.'

Chapter Seven

Clayton was woken by a velvety purr.

Dame Klotski's limp, arthritic limbs rarely journeyed to the fourth floor of the house. But on the morning of Pippa's funeral, she must have climbed the forty-six steps to Clayton's room, nudged open the door and sprawled out on his patchwork quilt, because as the first light of dawn seeped through the blinds, she was there, staring at him.

'Good morning, darling.'

In human years Klotski was almost as old as Clayton, but in cat years she was really pushing her luck. Well past one hundred and looking every day of it, her pink jellybean paws were cracked like old ladies' feet, her eyes as piercing orange as the day he found her. The colour of burnt butterscotch.

The alarm clock on Clayton's nightstand wailed like an air siren, blinking the date and time on an extra-large panel display.

FRIDAY MORNING
08:15
CLOUDY WITH A 50% CHANCE OF SHOWERS

As Clayton reached over to bash the snooze button, the cat curled herself into a croissant in the warm spot where he'd been lying.

He was five years old when he'd found her. He'd been playing on the grass verge of the driveway with his favourite toy, a sliding primary-coloured block puzzle, when he noticed the suspicious cardboard box by the iron gates. When he went to retrieve it, he noticed that someone had punctured holes in the side and written, *SORRY. SHE'S VERY SWEET BUT WE CAN'T HANDLE THE SCRATCHING. PLEASE TAKE CARE OF HER* in black marker on the lid. As he lifted the flap of the box, two glassy marbles blinked up at him. The little creature, primed on its haunches, opened its mouth and let out a faint cry.

'Aren't people just wicked?' Pippa declared after Clayton ran inside with the box to show her. 'Imagine abandoning a living thing like that at our door. We are not an orphanage!'

Everyone had turned to look at little Clayton, who was lost in his toy puzzle, perched on a stool at the top of the table. An awkward silence had hung in the air.

The mystery of his parentage had barely dawned on Clayton at this point. It wasn't as if he didn't have a mummy or daddy – he had lots of them. On his first day of school, he'd been asked to paint a picture of his family and he hadn't hesitated, telling his teacher that the army of bodies he'd rendered in thick red crayon in front of a big yellow palace were all his family. 'Of course, we'll adopt her,' Pippa announced, moving to stand behind Clayton and drape her arms lovingly around the boy. 'Always room for one more in this place. Isn't that right, Clay? The more the merrier.'

'She'll need a name,' Earl announced. 'What shall we call her, son? Any ideas?'

As if on cue, the kitten padded over to where Clayton was sitting at the table and collapsed inside the wooden tray of his puzzle toy.

Clayton cocked his head in consideration, enjoying the sense of responsibility.

'Klotski!' he offered, referring to the name of the puzzle in front of him.

Eric Stoppard had picked up the thing at a toy fair in Stockholm a few months earlier and Clayton had barely kept his hands off it ever since.

'Well, I think that works!' Hector remarked. 'Little Klotski the cat. Klotty-dotty. Lady Klot.'

'*Dame* Klotski, I think is more appropriate,' Pippa cut in. 'Look at her!'

The cat had sprawled out like Barbara Cartland on her famous chaise-longue, her furry legs folded queenly in front of her.

'Dame Klotski,' Clayton confirmed, and everybody laughed.

So that was that, the decision was made. Dame Klotski the cat was the Fellowship's newest recruit and Clayton no longer their youngest member. The two of them had been inseparable ever since.

The alarm was wailing again. Clayton reached over his dozing cat to turn the damn thing off.

He couldn't have had more than a few hours' kip. As soon as the final guests had left the wake the previous evening, he'd been struck by an uncontainable urge that had kept him up half the night.

He *had* to find the hatbox he had been delivered in.

He was sure he'd seen it before, but perhaps that was because the image had stayed with him: a large, black, hexagonal box with a pretty floral paper lining and some gold letters etched on the lid. He knew it was the sort of thing Pippa would have kept, but after scouring the attic in the early hours then tearing through one of the storage sheds outside, he'd found nothing.

He dipped his bare feet into the moccasin slippers next to his bed. He could tell that some of the residents were already awake. The house creaked and groaned like a tired old body these days; there was the piercing squeal of shower pumps pushing hot water around the house, the swill of antique copper pipes flushing it all away.

Downstairs, Clayton set a catering pan of water on to simmer before plunging in eighteen eggs from two family-sized boxes and twisting the timer the moment the shells were submerged. He took great pleasure in preparing Friday breakfasts, which were always eggs and soldiers, unless it was a bank holiday, or someone's birthday, in which case he'd do pancakes.

He adjusted the robe of his dressing gown and glanced at the whiteboard on the wall. Today's schedule was marked with an ⋆*AR*⋆ meaning 'All Required'. Firstly, there was *Pippa's Funeral Service at 10.A.M.*, followed by *Pippa's Bedroom Clear-Out – The Alphabetibox Suite, Third Floor.*

As if they didn't know which room she occupied, Clayton thought. That was Hector all over – being overly officious about everything. It was his idea to get everybody together, to sort through Pippa's things as soon as they got back from the crematorium, so that any items of sentimental value could be shared between them and anything that held monetary value could be sold off.

If truth be told, there had been a few occasions – particularly when Pippa was bed-bound – that Clayton had taken the opportunity to riffle through some old papers stashed away in her bureau and rummage through the boxed files marked *CONFIDENTIAL*. He wasn't quite sure what he was hoping to find – some formal evidence of his life, he supposed, some receipt of his birth or at least a record of his entry into this world. But he had discovered nothing at all. It was as if he never existed.

The timer chimed at three minutes-fifty and Clayton spooned the soft eggs out for Earl, Martin and Jean. Their viscous yolks would coat the back of a spoon like liquid candle wax, just as they liked it. Thirty seconds later he retrieved the semi-soft eggs from the pan for Hector, Geoff and Nigel. Their orange centre would just be set around the edges. Finally, forty seconds later, he lifted the lone medium-hard egg out for Eric, who would only eat one if his yolk was chalky and crumbled with the touch of a teaspoon.

He lined up the eggs in their Denby cups on the tray, then dispensed the various tablets from the pill organiser onto the draining board and wrapped small bundles of prescribed medication and supplements in Post-it notes, labelled with individual names, so he knew whose was whose.

He was not a fully qualified carer by any stretch but when he was studying for his catering diploma at the local polytechnic, he'd particularly enjoyed the nutritional science module. Ever since, he'd taken a keen interest in creating healthy meals for the Fellowship. He knew that spinach boosted immunity, oily fish was good for the brain, and eggs were meant to reduce the risk of strokes and heart disease.

He was willing to try anything to prolong the inevitable. To keep them all on their feet and around for as long as possible.

They all arrived back from the crematorium a few hours later, soaked from a thunderstorm. As everyone rushed into the staircase hall, Clayton shook his umbrella at the door, feeling numb.

Listening to Hector run through Pip's life in the Eulogy, he'd realised how much of her past he'd never heard about before.

There had been talk of Pip working as a secretarial clerk at a conveyancing firm in the City under a chauvinistic boss she'd despised; a year living in Luxor, Egypt; a master's in sociolinguistics from King's College; a star appearance on a BBC documentary called *For the Love of Crosswords*. She had lived his life twice over – and then some – by the time he'd appeared at their door.

He couldn't help wondering what else he might not know about Pippa's colourful past – and the others' lives, for that matter – who *else* might have secrets they'd never shared.

He followed everyone up to the Alphabetibox suite, climbing the stairs with Earl in silence.

'Now, listen, son,' the mazemaker said, as they stopped outside the room. 'You have first dibs, OK? So if there's anything you want, you just shout.'

Clayton nodded blankly.

He hesitated before pushing open the door.

It had been exactly three weeks since he'd last entered Pippa's bedroom. He'd felt altogether like a different man back then, when he had shouldered his way past the threshold at seven forty-five in the morning, balancing a tray with a toasted muffin smeared with lashings of lemon curd, plus a well-brewed lapsang tea with sugar and a lick of blue-top milk, in Pippa's favourite bone-china cup. Seconds later and his entire world had been turned upside down.

As Clayton passed the threshold of the Alphabetibox suite, he was instantly struck by the sudden drop in temperature. The room was piercingly cold. Someone must have switched off the radiators to preserve the energy for the rest of the house. It was a constant battle in this place, trying to keep everyone warm without the bills going through the roof.

'Listen up, everyone,' Hector bellowed, standing on the green velvet chaise longue. 'No one is to lift a thing from this room without it being logged in the inventory first. Is that understood?'

Everybody nodded agreeably but were clearly desperate to crack on with the treasure hunt.

Pippa's bedroom was the largest of all the suites in the house, split across two levels, with large sash windows adorned with prawn-pink curtains looking out over the parterre.

The various mirrored wardrobe doors that ran along the long end of the suite were a series of built-in closets; behind every door was endless designer apparel, each organised into their respective concessions, not unlike the ladieswear floor of a department store. Hosiery and underwear; dresses and eveningwear; costume jewellery, silk scarves and designer handbags.

Pippa wasn't exactly known for her organisation by any standard, but she arranged her clothing quite particularly, just like she did her crossword clues. Opposite the wardrobe there was a row of filing cabinets where she'd archived them alphabetically. Someone had worked out that she'd compiled over seven thousand grids, written over a quarter of a million clues, across her career.

The other end of the room was all bookshelves: Pippa's countless volumes of clothbound dictionaries, classic literature, journals, encyclopedias and maps, plus, on the very top shelf, the complete works of her favourite novelist, Danielle Steel. All one hundred and nine of her books were drawn in a line like the Great Wall of China.

'This is not a boot sale,' Hector continued, glancing at Jean who had several laundry bags open at her feet, ready to gather her haul. 'And I dare say, there are likely things here of great value and etymological significance. You know what she was like, hoarding stuff away.'

Hector continued instructing the group. There was talk of a man from the British Library coming to look through Pippa's catalogue of univocalics and chronograms; the digital archivist from London coming to scan the notebooks so they could be published on the Fellowship's blog. But Clayton had long switched off; instead he was concentrating on Hector's shoes. There was a streak of polish now smudged across the fabric of the chair. A smear on the immaculate green velvet.

A cardboard box jabbed against his ribs.

'Shall we?' Earl asked, gesturing towards Pippa's bureau. 'Why don't you see what you can find over there?'

As Clayton moved towards the desk, he passed Jean at the wardrobe trying on a dress.

'How do I look?'

She'd inserted her head through the hanger of a shiny, lamé number that looked a bit like a toffee wrapper.

'It's Yves Saint Laurent,' Jean explained, shimmying. 'I think she'd probably want me to have this.'

At the bureau, Clayton's hand went straight to Pippa's Rolodex, the system she used for all her contacts. It was something he remembered playing with as a child – the hundreds of tatty index cards affixed to a spiral binder were quite fun to flick through, to imagine stories of the people your finger stopped on. It was amazing how many people she'd known, how many lives she'd had an impact on. He'd learned in recent years that the majority of these acquaintances were, in fact, people she'd befriended in the third act of her life. There was once a time – although Clayton found it hard to believe – that Pippa had been lonely. She'd confessed to him that she hadn't had many friends at all in her earlier years. The Fellowship had gifted Pip this enormous circle. Puzzles had united them all.

His fingers were flicking through the names without realising it, just like he used to as a little boy. He'd been meaning to pick out the details of the strange white-haired lady who'd caught his eye at the funeral, the woman who'd supposedly been a former resident, a close friend of Pippa's. There was something about the look she'd given him – as if she knew him, somehow – that had been playing on his mind.

'Nancy . . . Stone,' he muttered under his breath, scanning each crumpled card before moving on to the next.

Nancy Stone, Nancy Stone, Nancy Stone.

There was a *Mr SANDERS* with the faintly pencilled words *SEXIST PIG – AVOID* under his name; a *Mr George SCOTT-STANLEY* who she claimed was a *TIGHT-WAD*, and then there was a *Mr Norris STEVENS* who, to all intents and purposes, was no use to anyone anymore because he was, supposedly, *DEAD*.

There were a couple of *SCOTTS* and plenty of *SMITHS*, but no *STONES* at all. Nancy Stone was nowhere to be found.

Clayton sighed.

He was feeling disheartened but then, at the sight of Pippa's typewriter lurking under its protective cloth cover, he felt all his breath leave his body.

He lifted off the cover and just admired it for a moment. Of the many items cluttering up her bedroom, it was this one that he most closely associated with her. A Remington Rand Deluxe Model Seventeen. He sank his fingers into its concave keys, pressed down into their smooth, dipped shapes. The sight of the machine alone, the feel of its keys, the sounds it made – *click-clack-click-clack-dinnng-ziiiip* – instantly conjured memories of Pippa frantically scrambling to meet deadlines for the papers, racing to type up her clues in time for the press.

'Clay!'

'Clay! Come and look at this.'

Although he had his back to everyone, Clayton had sensed the commotion going on behind him.

He returned the protective fabric sheath to the typewriter, tucking it in at the sides, and before he turned around, somehow he knew what he was about to be faced with. He could feel it in his bones.

Pippa's ottoman bed had been pushed up on its mechanical arms, revealing the storage space below it.

Everything had gone very still all of a sudden, as if all the air had been sucked from the room.

Earl and Jean were peering in. Nigel, Geoff and Eric looked frozen on the spot. Hector and Martin were watching them, watching him, smiling thinly.

'We've found something, son,' Earl explained. 'Something I think you've been looking for.'

Clayton felt a tightness building across his chest.

He took a steadying breath, then moved cautiously towards them, feeling both compelled and reluctant to lay eyes on what he knew he was about to be confronted with.

When he was close enough, he placed his hands in his pockets and leaned over to peer inside.

There were various vacuum-sealed bags filled with summer clothes, spare bedding and towels, plus countless jigsaw boxes and board games. But in the centre was something black, lacquered and hexagonal. The sight of it sent a ripple through his whole body.

Clayton got down on his knees and reached inside to wade through the items and get a hold on the thing.

The hatbox was larger than he'd imagined. He felt his throat constrict as he lifted it out from under the bed. There were a series of ornamental symbols on the side, and on the lid, two swirly letters in gold foil.

H.H.

There was a collective gasp in the room as he stood there, now a grown man, twenty-five years old, gripping the famous vessel in which he'd first arrived.

H.H.? Clayton thought.

He tipped the thing left and right, then up and down, while everyone looked on speechless.

'I'll make a note on the spreadsheet,' Hector remarked, 'that you're taking the hatbox.'

Clayton ignored the comment and, before turning to leave, nodded a courteous thanks to everyone in the room.

Someone held the door open and he slipped out onto the landing, gliding down the seemingly endless corridor as if he were sleepwalking – dreaming – all the time holding the box tight to his thumping chest.

He didn't want to examine it in front of the others, didn't want to prise open the lid or peer inside while they all watched, and not just because this was something intrinsically linked to his identity, to where he'd come from.

He shook it gently first, then rattled it over and over until he was certain of what was inside.

The flutter of paper, like a little bird flapping its wings, desperate to escape.

A letter, he hoped.

A letter with all the answers.

He prised open the lid and, reaching inside, pulled out a wax-sealed envelope nestled in the flowery paper lining of the box.

Slipping his nail under the lip, he tore the thing open in one forceful swipe, pulling out the typewritten note inside.

Dearest Clay,

And then there were eight. You know it's always best to leave a party before it's over, don't you?

Now, time for one last crossword.

I've been compiling this for as long as I can remember.

Everything I've learned during my life forms part of this, the clues to your future.

Listen very carefully now, Clay.

Life is more complicated than any challenge I could set.

Each of the solutions that make up this grid are the foundations of a fulfilling life, a happy life.

So don't just solve these clues, seek them out, experience them.

There is, of course, another puzzle you'll need to solve one day. Your past. When you feel ready, all the answers are waiting for you. To begin that quest, you'll need to locate a clue that features in a line of this letter.

Easy? Like all great puzzles they'll get harder as they go, don't worry. You'll need your passport, so don't forget that.

Enjoy it, Clay, and whatever comes next. If there's one thing I can promise you it's that life won't always be straightforward, but nothing worth solving ever is.

Love always and forever, Pip x

ACROSS

1 One may turn up to put one in (10)
7 Zilch at Wimbledon (4)
8 To gain knowledge (5)
10 Windows to the soul (4)
11 Uncover or divulge (6)
13 A large amount of something pleasant (6)
15 French bread (4)
18 _______ one's stuff (5)
19 You may have two before noon (4)
20 Daring exploits (10)

DOWN

2 Surgical instrument (5)
3 Again, in a different way (4)
4 Joint forces (6)
5 A hungry desire (5)
6 A faintest notion not to be ignored (7)
9 Gnawing pain of conscience (7)
12 Courage to carry on (6)
14 Risked or braved (5)
16 Dangerous emotion (5)
17 Gusto, relish (4)

Chapter Eight

TUESDAY, 9TH SEPTEMBER, 1980

SESSION 52

The Fellowship was flying. As well as increasing their membership, they were beginning to make inroads with the commercial side of things, to build a name for themselves on the circuit.

Pippa was spearheading the society's move in offering their services for hire. She'd just secured a long-term contract with Whizz Kid Media, who published magazines such as *Puzzler's World*, *Word Play* and *Tea Quizzes*. The society was due to deliver a portfolio of word-based games to them every quarter. And just the other week, Eric Stoppard – the gifted wood-whittler – had presented a prototype for a set of Christmas-themed wooden brain teasers he was looking to sell at a toy fair. They were interlocking shapes cunningly engineered to be slotted together in a unique sequence, resembling a robin redbreast, a decorative wreath and some jingle bells. Pippa couldn't help thinking they would be quick and cheap to reproduce for the mass-market. The perfect stocking filler. But that wasn't all she was excited about.

'Hector Haywood, would you come up here, please.'

That evening, on a blisteringly cold Tuesday in mid-September, the awkward illustrative painter in a brown sleeveless sweater, red corduroy shirt and cream slacks, clambered his way to the front of the function room through a fug of tobacco smoke, looking mortified.

It turned out Hector's paintings (for that was how Pippa referred to them despite the creator insisting they were merely *illustrations*) were luscious, seductive, dreamlike images. Every little detail had been turned up a notch and improved upon, made that bit more perfect than real life. They were ideal to be turned into jigsaws – to be broken down and put back together again, admired, piece by piece.

'We have some rather good news to share,' Pippa announced. The room hushed as she went to the back of the room and retrieved a canvas she'd tucked behind the jukebox.

'This marvellous picture here of Little Venice in London has just sold to Gibsons, one of the largest jigsaw manufacturers in the country. Isn't that right, Hec?'

Hector nodded, then looked down at his shoes.

Pippa thought she caught his moustache twitch with embarrassment. She'd urged him to bring the picture along that evening, desperate to share the exciting news with everybody. The painting in her hand featured a series of narrowboats waiting by a lock. The vessels, all adorned with colourful folk art, were reflected in the Grand Union Canal. The names of the boats read: *Knot So Fast*; *Over the Hull*; *Float Your Boat*.

'And not only that,' Pippa went on, 'but Gibsons were so enamoured by Hector's talent, they've commissioned him to paint half a dozen others. On a bi-monthly basis, he'll be delivering a different jigsaw design to be sold all over the country.'

'"Kitten Chaos",' he explained, entirely deadpan. 'That's the first brief they've given me.'

'Many congratulations,' Earl Vosey called out. 'Pleased for you, mate.'

There was a smattering of applause as everyone commended him on the news.

'Thank you, everybody.'

He was clearly mortified by all the attention and desperate to get back to his seat but instead of shuffling away as Pippa expected him to, he lifted his finger in the air to shush everybody.

'I just wanted to say . . .' he began, stuffing his hands inside his pockets. 'That I wouldn't have had this opportunity if it wasn't for Pip introducing me to Gibsons in the first place—'

'Nonsense!' Pippa cut in, although that was, in fact, emphatically true. 'As well as being our Prince of Pieces, Hector, you're an *artist*. This is all because of you.'

He grinned.

As well as painting, it had come to light that Hector was also a skilled woodworker and glassblower who created elegant hourglasses to order, cradled in bespoke wooden cages that he whittled himself, then assembled and varnished with his own hands. He had brought one to the pub a few weeks ago – when they were testing out the complexity of some wooden tangrams Eric was experimenting with – and she had been so enamoured of the artistry in the glasswork that he had gifted it to her at the end of the session. It took pride of place on her mantelpiece.

'I've been wondering how I might say thanks,' Hector announced. 'And I'd like to donate a proportion of my future fees directly back to the Fellowship—'

'Oh, Hector, that's really not necessary,' Pippa said.

'I think we should establish a Fellowship kitty,' he went on. 'Some of us need a bit more help than others – to buy materials, test out prototypes, that sort of thing. So perhaps we can start a little seed fund, support each other in our individual puzzling pursuits . . .'

Pippa found herself a bit choked.

It was a genius idea, of course. It would mean that their individual successes weren't just advantageous for the esteem of the group, but financially beneficial, too. They were all in this together. Their mission to turn out the best puzzles in the land was now a collective one.

'That's most generous of you, Hector. Are you really sure—'

'A noble gesture if ever there was,' Jonty Entwistle declared. 'What wisdom exists that is greater than kindness, eh?'

Hector waved his hand humbly in front of himself as everyone continued to congratulate and thank him. 'Don't mention it,' he muttered, and shambled back to his seat, his cheeks glowing red.

That evening, as the members were saying their goodbyes, Pippa asked Hector if he wouldn't mind helping her stack the chairs.

'Have you parked by the church again?' she asked.

'I have, but let me walk you to your door,' he answered. 'I'm heading in that direction anyway.'

They took slow strides together. Hector held onto Pippa awkwardly as they shuffled along the slippery pavement, her arm looped through his as they advanced along the winding path that cut through the park.

'I take it you don't have children, then?' Hector asked. 'A family?'

Pippa found herself wrapping her quilted coat a little tighter around herself. She had pursued an intellectual life, rather than a family one. It wasn't a decision she'd consciously made, more a series of life turns that had led to that particular outcome. It was something she thought about daily; deeply regretted sometimes, too.

'How would I have time for my crosswords if I had children?'

Hector chuckled. 'That's certainly true.'

When they reached the entrance to the church, Pippa squeezed the man's arm and said, 'Thank you, Hector. I'll be fine from here. You head off home now.'

She offered him a quick hug and his face glowed pink.

Pippa turned and walked as if she were heading home. But once she'd crossed the road, she fumbled through her bag as if she'd forgotten something. Hector had reached the far end of the car park, stopping by a canary-yellow campervan, which was tucked to one side. He opened the side door and clambered inside.

After a few moments she darted across the road and crouched behind a Ford Cortina, careful to obscure herself in case he looked back. She waited and waited but the lights of the vehicle never came on, the ignition never fired, the vehicle never moved.

Several minutes passed and Hector still hadn't moved from his parking space, hadn't switched on the ignition and started on his way home, and now she realised why.

Hector Haywood was living out of his van.

Chapter Nine

Clayton had pored over every line in Pippa's letter so many times that the words had melded into a dizzying, unintelligible blur. Never mind the clues to his *future*, he thought. The crossword could wait. It was the past he needed to solve. But why did everything have to be a game? Life was complicated enough. Clayton didn't need to be challenged further.

In what line of the letter was there a clue to his past? What was the quest that she referred to? Where were the answers waiting for him?

He rubbed his eyes and glanced at the alarm clock, realising he must have drifted off at some point. It was approaching 3 a.m. and there was a whistle from a window somewhere; the squeal of outside being let in.

He swung his legs over the bed and padded across the floor for his slippers. And it was then, somewhere in this sleepy, barely conscious haze, that the answer came to him.

You'll need to locate a clue that features in a line of this letter.

Pippa always used to say that if a solution didn't jump out at you, you should take some time away from it. That the brain did so much work without you even realising.

He grabbed the letter and jabbed his forefinger down each first letter in every paragraph. It was there, written out *in a line*, not a literal horizontal line of the letter, but a vertical one, stretching down the left-hand margin of the page.

The capital letters that began with *Dearest Clayton* and ended *Love always and forever, Pip x*.

It wasn't a straightforward letter, of course it wasn't: it was a puzzle itself. An acrostic.

D ....

A ....

N ....

I ....

E ....

L ....

L ....

E ....

S ....

T ....

E ....

E ....

L ....

Danielle Steel.

There was a jolt of something hot that surged through Clayton and sent him to his feet. He thought back to everyone clearing her room, tried to picture the bookcases, the top shelf filled with Pippa's favourite romance novelist, the embossed gold of the author's name flashing in his mind. The paperback books had been left totally untouched by the others, as Pippa had known they would be. She must have secreted something among the novels.

Before he knew it, Clayton was wrapped in his blue flannel dressing gown and fumbling for a battered old torch from his chest of drawers. It was what he used when they had a power cut, but the batteries needed changing and when he pressed the button, the torch emitted a pathetic shaft of flickering light.

With one hand squeezing the door handle, and the other directing the torch, he stepped onto the landing, being careful not to wake anyone as he moved stealthily towards Pippa's room.

At the door to the Alphabetibox suite, Clayton drew his robe tighter around himself and then crept inside. He went straight to the bookcase, sliding the ladder along the rail till it was beneath Steel's immense back catalogue.

Clambering up the thin steps, he was staggered by the number of books the woman had written.

They were all sandwiched together, the spines wrinkled, bent back, broken; the pages well thumbed, folded over, yellowed with age. These were stories that Pippa didn't just read but devoured. She'd get through one a night sometimes.

He flicked through a few that caught his eye, knowing Pippa preferred Danielle's earlier work.

Zoya featured a faded image of a ballerina on the cover. *Second Chance* had an unusual image of a pair of red boxing gloves tied to two engagement rings.

He went through another batch of them, riffling through the pages as quickly as he could, to see if anything had been hidden between them, inside them, underneath them, on top of them. The pages, as he flicked through, smelt sweet, like vanilla and almonds.

It was only when he stopped and leaned back on the ladder that he caught it.

Lodged between a novel called *Secrets* and another called *The Ring* was something that wasn't a book at all. It wasn't even paper. It was wood.

There was something oblong in shape, almost identical in dimensions to a standard paperback book, that was the odd one out on the shelf. An intricately decorated wooden box.

As Clayton slid the thing out from between the books, he knew exactly what it was.

It was one of Pippa's puzzle boxes. The Alphabetibox her room was named after.

Holding it aloft, examining it from every angle, it was one of the most beautiful things he had ever held in his hands. The box was about the size of a tissue box, made up of a patchwork of wooden panels, with thumb-sized holes in the base, square panels that could be pushed inwards, screws that could be turned clockwise; there were four rubberised legs on the four corners that rotated anticlockwise, and, on the front, the initial *C* had been carved on a shiny gold disc.

C for Clayton?

Most prominent of all, however, were the lettered columns on the lid.

Four of them could be moved up and down in various formations to spell, presumably, a word or a phrase.

This box had been made especially for him. He was meant to find it, to solve it, and retrieve the answers inside.

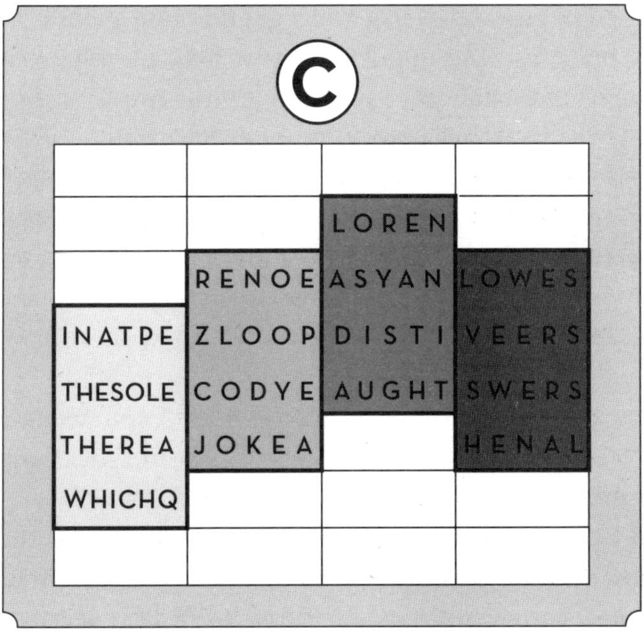

Chapter Ten

MONDAY, 8TH DECEMBER, 1980

It wasn't supposed to be raining.

Pippa was outside Waterloo Station, cowering under a shelter in the forecourt, failing to hail a cab. She was heading to *The Times* offices, ready to file her latest run of cryptics, and carried with her an orange valise bag and a gentleman's leather briefcase. The bag bulged in the middle where it held her typewriter and the battered old briefcase was hulking with reams of the yellow ledger paper she always used to type up her clues.

As was customary when she had a deadline looming, Pippa had spent a few days tucked away at The Lodge, her tiny, vine-embowered cottage in Sherborne, Dorset, and was returning to the city with more than a hundred new clues, ready to set her grids. She'd bought the modest little retreat with a share of her father's will.

When her father had died in the war, a fourteen-year-old Pippa – being his only offspring – had become sole beneficiary of the family estate.

She'd been sent to live with her aunt Grace in Broadstairs by this point, and the proceeds of the endowment were secured in a trust until her twenty-first birthday. She'd later learned that a proportion of this money had gone into a separate fund for her aunt. A form of payment for her selfless wartime childminding, no doubt. But the majority of the inheritance remained in Pippa's name and when the sum was finally unveiled to her seven years later, it was significantly greater than Pippa had ever anticipated. In fact, the wealth had not come directly from her father at all, but from her grandparents, and the recent sale of Creighton Hall, their ancestral estate in Bedfordshire.

The money had been more than she'd known what to do with.

She wouldn't go as far as to say it was a burden, but it had certainly brought with it a sense of responsibility.

She'd made a couple of charitable pledges almost immediately – to the British Red Cross and the Women's Institute, initially – and the balance she kept, on the advice of Mr Hugo Chapman, her financial advisor, in stocks and shares. As an ardent feminist fresh out of Trinity College, Cambridge, Pippa had made it a prerequisite to invest in firms with at least fifty per cent women on their board. This was against the guidance of her FA, who'd insisted it would limit their options and stunt the growth of her portfolio. That was a given, of course, but it also wasn't really the point.

'Taxi!' Pippa yelled, waving her arm above her head like a loon.

Pippa had schlepped halfway across Westminster Bridge in the drizzle by the time a black cab finally took pity on her, screeching to a halt beside her.

The moment she opened the door she tossed the briefcase onto the back seat and it bounced off the vinyl onto the floor. The metal clasps snapped open and suddenly there were reams of loose yellow papers strewn across the floor of the taxi.

'Blast!'

On her hands and knees in the cab, Pippa started to reorder the clues, realising her system of typing out the ACROSS clues and DOWN clues on separate pages was entirely mindless, especially when she hadn't stapled them together.

'Everything all right back there, m'love?'

Pippa waved an inch of yellow paper above her head. 'Splendid, thank you. Just getting myself together. Don't mind me at all. *The Times* offices, if you don't mind. It's on—'

'Fleet Street,' the driver cut in. 'I know the one.'

It took a moment to register the voice as a woman's, but when Pippa did, she gathered up her bits and angled herself in the seat to get a proper look. It was rare thing: a female cabbie in London. In fact, she couldn't say she'd ever been picked up by one before.

The lady was wearing a steel-blue bucket hat, which from the pavement Pippa had assumed was a man's bowler hat, but was actually quite an elegant thing with a black bow on the side. She had a ciggie lodged between her lips, an arm extended towards the half-open window. Whenever she flicked the end of her fag, the cinders were blowing straight onto the back seat, directly into Pippa's lap.

'Weekend away, was it?' the lady asked as they pulled up at the lights.

'Something like that,' Pippa replied, brushing ash from her new tweed skirt.

'And what is it that you do?' the driver enquired. 'If you don't mind me asking.'

Pippa gritted her teeth. It was usually at this point that she might make up something dull about a solicitor's office or legal firm, giving the – conventionally male – cab driver a sense that she was neither a mother nor a housewife, but a professional woman with her own middling career that needed no further scrutiny.

'I work for a newspaper,' she answered, hearing a sense of pride creep into her voice. '*The Times*, in fact.'

The lady turned round in the driver's seat. She was wearing pink horn-rimmed spectacles, dangly silver earrings, and had a string of pearls draped across her neck. She had a softer face than Pippa had imagined and was younger than her gravelly voice suggested, perhaps early thirties or so.

'So, you're one of those journos, then?'

'Close, but no cigar, I'm afraid . . .'

The two women briefly locked eyes.

'Although you could say that I write about the world,' Pippa mused. 'Try and make sense of it, in my own little way.'

'You've lost me, I'm afraid.'

'I'm a professional crossword compiler,' she explained. 'In fact, as of last month, I've set more cryptics than anyone else in the country.'

As the lady turned to take her in, the car swerved recklessly across the road, narrowly missing a white builder's van beside them.

'You're having me on!'

Before Pippa could affirm this fact, the driver who'd just avoided being slammed like a dodgem started winding down his window.

'Sweetheart,' the man shouted, his bald head glowing red with rage. 'You wanna look where you're pointing that thing. It's not a bloody shopping trolley.'

Pippa seethed as the chap sped away. 'Do you get that often?' she enquired.

'Several times a day.'

In the rear-view mirror, the two women issued each other a resigned grin.

Pippa wondered how a woman might deal with such persistent misogyny. She got off quite lightly in her current role, hiding behind her sobriquet.

The cabbie tossed her ciggie out the window, narrowly missing a motorcyclist wearing highly flammable PVC leathers.

Pippa smiled. She couldn't help but be charmed by the woman. She scanned the car for clues as to who she was. Propped up on the dashboard was a tiny portrait of a silver-haired man wearing a cravat, encased in an equally tiny portrait frame. She couldn't quite make him out but he was too old to be her husband, surely. Her father, perhaps?

'Who's that?'

The woman cackled as her eyes swivelled to where Pippa was pointing. 'That's my Les.' She stroked her finger along the oval image, as if caressing the man's face. 'Leslie Phillips, from the *Carry On* films? I'm the secretary of his fan club, have been for years. Always liked a silver fox, me. What I wouldn't give to have a night with that man.'

'I'm not familiar with his work,' Pippa replied, making a mental note to look him up in the *Actors' Handbook* later. Her knowledge of comic actors wasn't exactly one of her strong suits, and it was important to keep abreast with popular culture to ensure her clues remained relevant.

'They say puzzling is good for the old noggin,' the driver declared. 'Stops you going doolally when you're old.'

'You're not wrong there,' Pippa replied. 'It engages both sides of the brain – the analytical on the left and the creative on the right. Puzzles are a real mental workout.'

'I was a contestant on *Brain of Britain* a few years ago, and Mother and I do all the TV quizzes together,' the driver replied.

Pippa was getting a good sense of the lady – she was on the cusp of finding herself alone in the world, perhaps twenty years behind her.

'You might not believe this,' the driver went on, lowering her voice as if she were about to confess something shameful. 'But I've actually got a photographic memory.' She turned and tapped the middle of her forehead. 'Ever since I was a little dot, whatever goes in there never comes out. Too clever for my own good, my mother says.'

Pippa found herself sitting on the very edge of her seat. An idea was beginning to formulate in her mind. If this cabbie was capable of memorising twenty-five thousand London street names, and one hundred thousand points of interest across the capital – as Pippa knew the Knowledge exam demanded – then surely she had the capacity to dabble with a bit of quiz setting. Perhaps she might help establish a trivia division at the Fellowship. Pete – the landlord at the Queen's Head – had been pestering her for months to run a quiz night.

But before she could enquire further, the woman started dishing out her entire life history, prompted occasionally by Pippa, who chipped in with the odd question, intrigued by the woman.

She lived with her mother in a council house in Leytonstone. It turned out she'd been driving a cab for thirteen years, making it onto page five of the *Romford Recorder* in 1967 when she became the second woman ever in Britain to pass the Knowledge, aged just twenty. A former secretarial clerk called Shirley Preston had pipped her to the post, only four days earlier.

'If I can help it, I try to get home for tea. Mother expects me to cook the supper. And then we do the crossword together.'

'I'd be thrilled if you would consider joining my puzzle club one week,' Pippa said. 'No commitment required, of course. Just pop along and see what you think.'

'Puzzle club?'

'That's right. We're called the Fellowship of Puzzlemakers, and we meet every Tuesday.'

The driver looked at her a moment, as if seriously considering the invitation.

'I'll have to see what Mother says.'

Pippa sighed. She couldn't help but pity the woman. Although both her parents had died way before their time, she really couldn't bear the idea of someone breathing down her neck like that.

'She's rather keen on me finding a fella at the moment,' the lady remarked, as if reading her mind. 'Keeps telling me I'm going to die a lonely old spinster unless I pull my finger out.'

Pippa rolled her eyes.

She couldn't help thinking that if the driver's romantic tastes did lean towards the more mature gentleman, there was no shortage of single, silver-haired chaps on offer at the Fellowship.

'I'm thirty-three next month,' the lady revealed. 'If you're not married or with kids by now, it's inevitable. You're going to die alone, with cats, if you're lucky . . .'

Pippa felt a quiver in her stomach. She pulled herself up straight, briefly catching the eye of the lady in the rear-view mirror.

'Gosh, I'm sorry.' The driver pressed her hand to her mouth, as if shoving the words back in. 'That was careless of me. I didn't mean to—'

'That's quite all right, dear.'

'You don't have children, then?'

Pippa painted a tight grin across her face, ready to deliver her stock response. 'How would I have time for my crosswords if I had children?'

The lady looked relieved as Pippa turned and looked wistfully out of the window. Life certainly runs away with you sometimes, she thought, and before you realise it you haven't achieved the things you'd always dreamed of. To meet a man, to fall in love, to start your own family. All things that most people took for granted, but, for Pippa, things that had seemingly passed her by. Like lots of other women her age, she'd had to decide between building a family or a career, unlike men, who miraculously managed to have both.

When they eventually pulled up outside *The Times*, Pippa settled the fare and was about to head inside when the lady lifted her hand to stop her.

'Where does your Fellowship meet, then?'

Pippa beamed. 'Let me jot down the details.'

'No need. Like I say, I've got a photographic memory.'

Pippa let out a squawk of laughter. 'Oh, yes, how funny. I almost forgot.'

'Our next session is tomorrow, upstairs at the Old Queen's Head in Islington. And if you need to ask at the bar, my name's Pippa Allsbrook.'

The lady blinked at her, then repeated it all back without so much as a pause. It was as if she were simply reciting a recording in her mind.

Pippa smiled and extended her hand through the window. 'I didn't catch your name, my love . . .'

'Nancy,' the lady shot back, sucking on another fag. 'Nancy Stone. Ta-ra, love.'

TUESDAY, 9TH DECEMBER, 1980
SESSION 60

The fellowship arrived in dribs and drabs the following evening, shaking their umbrellas by the door.

'I suppose we ought to get going,' Derek said.

The men scraped their chairs towards the projector but Pippa was distracted by the bright lights of a black cab beaming through the greasy windows of the Queen's Head as it manoeuvred into an impressively tight parking spot outside.

Pippa's heart leapt. 'I think . . . we may have a guest joining us this evening,' she announced breathlessly to the room. 'Everyone on best behaviour, please. This one's a real cracker.'

It wasn't every day that she met someone like Nancy Stone, and she'd spent the last twenty-four hours hoping that the plucky female cab driver might show her face. She peered out of the window and watched as a woman sprang from the driver's seat in a purple silk blouse, suede skirt, and a green velvet cloche hat, tottering in pink kitten heels across the pavement and into the bar downstairs.

A few minutes later Pippa felt an unusual rush of pride as the function-room door swung open and in strolled Nancy Stone, handbag in one hand, gin and orange in the other.

'Good evening,' she said hesitantly. 'Is this the . . . Fellowship of Puzzlemakers?'

Before anyone could answer, Pippa had hotfooted it over to her, embracing the woman in an enormous hug, almost lifting her off the ground she was so happy to see her.

'I'm so glad you made it. Come and sit down,' she urged. 'We're having a quiz this evening.' She turned to face the room. 'Everybody, it is my pleasure to introduce you to the Fellowship's latest recruit . . . a woman of exceptional mind who is smarter than most of us put together.'

An hour later and Pippa was lifting Nancy's hand above her head at the bar in front of everybody. 'You're looking at our first Queen of Quizzes—'

'Oh, I don't know if that's true.'

'It is,' Pippa confirmed. 'You wiped the floor with us all. And we're no idiots.'

'So, come on then,' Hector said, his head tilted in curiosity at her. 'Why is it you know so much?'

They were all huddled around the woman in wonder.

Nancy shrugged. 'Oh, I don't know. I've always just had this thirst for knowledge, can't get enough of facts. I just soak it all up.'

'And what's your specialism?' Pippa asked. 'If you had to pick just one.'

'You won't catch me out on capital cities,' Nancy answered. 'I know all one hundred and ninety-five of them.'

The room suddenly went quiet as everyone tried to summon the most minor country they could think of.

'Belize?' Pippa offered.

Nancy smiled back at her. 'Belmopan.'

'Montenegro?'

'That's easy. Titograd.'

'The Marshall Islands,' Earl threw in.

'Is that even a country?' Pippa asked. 'It's part of Fiji, isn't it?'

'No,' Nancy said. 'It's one of the smallest countries in the world – between Hawaii and the Philippines. The capital is Majuro.'

Pippa couldn't help but laugh. Not only did the woman know every street in London, she knew every capital in the world, too.

Nancy glanced at her watch, gave a pained expression. 'I'm afraid I should probably get going.' She leaned towards Pippa and whispered. 'Mother thinks I'm on a date with a mystery man. If I'm not back before ten, she'll think we're engaged . . .'

Once Nancy had said her goodbyes, Pippa walked with her to the door.

'Forgive me if this is presumptuous,' she began. 'But surely you're entitled a night to yourself?'

Nancy's eyes went very big. 'If I told Mother I'd joined a puzzle club she'd shriek. She'd think all of this was just an indulgence. Frivolous fun!'

'Well, we both know *that's* not true,' Pippa replied. 'If there's one thing that puzzles aren't, it's frivolous *or* fun. This is serious business!'

The two ladies laughed.

Nancy elbowed Pippa playfully in the ribs. 'What about you and that tall fellow, anyway? Earl, is it? The maze man. You like him, don't you?'

Pippa tried to feign ignorance, but it was pointless – Nancy could see straight through her already. 'How can you tell?'

'You sort of light up, when he talks to you. Your voice goes all high like a little girl. And your face flushes.'

Pippa scoffed. She didn't think that was entirely true but, to her embarrassment, she could feel her cheeks colouring anyway. 'Well, sadly, he's off limits.'

'Why's that?'

'He's . . . *married*.' She said this as if she might have made a move otherwise. Pippa knew there was little chance of her ever establishing an intimate relationship at her age. She could flirt with the best of them, but when it came to anything more serious she tended to back away. Romance was not her forte.

'The handsome ones usually are,' Nancy sighed, beginning to root around in her handbag. 'Either that or they're homosexual. And if life has taught me anything, it's that there's little point pursuing either. Here, let me fan you. You've gone awful red.'

'Menopause,' Pippa whispered.

Even though Nancy was much younger than Pippa, she gave her a sympathetic grin. 'I'd say it's love, this time. Not hormones.'

Pippa leaned against the wall as Nancy opened the pages as wide as the creased spine would allow and started wafting the thing in front of her face. A surprisingly strong flurry of cool air soon enveloped her.

'What is that anyway?' She gestured at the book in Nancy's hands.

'This? Oh, it's one of Danielle Steel's. Just something I read when things are quiet in the cab. Passes the time.'

'I don't think I've read any of hers before.' Pippa reached out for it. 'What's it called? *Full Circle*?' She stared at the glamorous image of a blonde woman and a rather dashing man on the front cover. 'Nance, can I borrow this when you're done?'

Nancy pushed it into Pippa's hands and began to walk towards her cab. 'It's yours. I've read it four times. A real bonkbuster that one is.'

Pippa flicked through the well-thumbed pages. 'I dare say it's about as much sex as I'm going to get these days . . .'

Inside the cab, Nancy rolled down the window and let out an almighty cackle before tooting her horn and driving off into the night, shouting, 'See you next week!' as she rounded the corner.

Pippa turned to head back into the pub. She was beginning to feel that in Nancy Stone, she'd not only bagged herself a fellow female member, but also the makings of a great friendship.

Chapter Eleven

Why must everything be turned into a game, Clayton thought.

If there was something Pippa wished to tell him, if there were answers to his past waiting for him, then why couldn't she just write it down. He shouldn't have to compete to claim it with a locked puzzle box. This wasn't information to be won. It was his birthright, surely.

The first light of dawn was beginning to seep through the gaps in his slatted blinds, sending thick shadowed lines across his bedspread like a zebra crossing. It was unlike Clayton to deny himself sleep, but he couldn't even think about laying his head on the pillow when he was potentially on the cusp of uncovering something so fundamental to his identity, to his existence on this earth.

After several hours wrestling with the Alphabetibox, aligning the lettered tiles in hundreds of different combinations, he'd eventually given up and taken a hammer to the thing. He felt awful about it now and would likely never know what the coded phrase was meant to be.

Clayton pushed the claw hammer to one side as if pretending it had never happened, then brushed the tiny shavings and bits of splintered wood from his quilt, before gathering them up again and placing them in his wastepaper basket – out of sight, out of mind.

He'd tried to damage as little as he could, just so he could get under the lid. The top of the box was mostly busted; the surprisingly shallow inlet tray underneath, with its green felt liner, not unlike a snooker table, now partly exposed. And there was something else just visible under the lid.

When he held the box under the anglepoise lamp on his bedside table, he could see something grey and metallic reflecting back at him.

He broke off one last panel to get a hold on the thing and carefully extracted the contents like a surgeon removing a precious organ from a patient's body.

It was an ornate skeleton key. An elaborately decorated key with a latticed filigree head – the letter *H* prominently carved into the swirly design, and teeth that were intricate and slightly worn, suggesting that while the item looked pretty, it served a purpose too. It wasn't ornamental or symbolic. It unlocked something.

But what exactly? Surely there was more to go on, another lead to help him on his way, a destination to reach? Clayton was missing something, he knew it.

The solving is always more important than the solution.

That familiar phrase of Pippa's was ringing in Clayton's ears. The quest she referred to in the letter, the answers to his past that were apparently waiting for him – this key was just the beginning of it.

It was all part of her relentless plan to get him to engage with the outside world. To step outside the Fellowship. She'd set a puzzle trail to somewhere, to someone; an adventure, of sorts.

She wouldn't have conceived of this quest unless she'd thought it was the best way for him to find out the truth. There was a reason she couldn't tell him what she knew about where he'd come from before she died. Clayton was certain of that.

He wasn't afraid to ask for help when he needed to, but because he'd already decimated Pip's puzzle, he felt compelled to try and crack the rest himself. That's exactly what Pippa would have wanted.

He just needed to concentrate, to focus, to rest.

Perhaps if he got his head down for a few hours, he might wake up with an answer, like he had done with the acrostic earlier.

He reached behind him and plumped his duck-down pillow, tucking the key safely underneath it, then adjusted the quilt so it sat flush against his duvet. He removed the batteries from his alarm clock, and, as he settled cosily into bed, felt curiously convinced of something.

It was about time he did something for himself. By himself.

He'd show them all what he was capable of, he thought. He'd solve the puzzle of his past, the mystery they'd never been able to solve.

Clayton pulled the duvet up to his neck and before long, was blissfully asleep.

Was there a greater pleasure on this earth, Clayton wondered, than dipping under the covers on an afternoon and sleeping without an alarm. When he awoke several hours later, he felt like a different person. But when he rolled over to face the Alphabetibox on his bedstead and the key sitting beside it, his heart sank. He still had no idea how to solve Pippa's puzzle.

Clayton pushed himself up in bed and switched on his reading lamp. He took the box in his hands once more, turning it over slowly under the light. There was something troubling him about the flash of green interior underneath the lid. It appeared slimmer than the total height of the box, which was at least three inches or more. He dipped his small finger through the lid, trying to gauge the depth before deciding that, like its own optical illusion, it was definitely shallower than it needed to be. The box was either strangely engineered to obscure the majority of its interior, or there was something lurking underneath. A hidden chamber.

Clayton's pulse started to run away from him and he tipped the box on its head, registering the various push-in panels and suspiciously manipulable screws that turned like the knobs on a cooker and, with the thrust of a forceful pinkie, or a pen, pushed in and out like buttons.

He shook the thing in front of him, but nothing.

He lifted the box to his ear, and only then when he jiggled the thing like a cocktail shaker, and listened very carefully, could he hear the faintest whisper of something inside.

★

Forty minutes later and having exhausted endless manipulations of the box's various moving parts – squeezing the loose panels on the side, pushing in all of the screws at once, isolating them in turn, rotating them all at forty-five degrees, ninety degrees, one hundred and eighty degrees, before doing the same all over one by one – Clayton finally hit the jackpot.

He'd been jotting down the formations he'd tried so he knew which ones to avoid replicating, and the one that had done the trick involved four particular manipulations:

LEFT PANEL IN > RIGHT PANEL UP > REAR-LEFT SCREW IN > FRONT-RIGHT SCREW TURNED 90.

There was a satisfying *ker-plunk* sound and the underbelly of the thing popped open, the contents spilling into his lap.

Clayton felt a rush of something, a tingling surge shooting through his body. Adrenaline. Pride. It wasn't something he was all that used to.

What had plopped out of the thing was another nicely weighted, cream-coloured envelope, wax-sealed with the Fellowship crest.

It was almost identical to the letter he'd received inside the hatbox.

Clayton felt his hands begin to tremble as he picked it up and gently slipped his finger under the seal until it came away.

There were two items enclosed in the envelope.

First, he retrieved a folded sheet of A4 paper. The plain white page was filled with just two lines of typewritten text.

CLUES TO UNLOCKING YOUR PAST, PART ONE.
A VISIT TO SOMEONE VERY SPECIAL.

Clayton swallowed hard and placed the sheet to one side. He reached inside the envelope for the remaining slip of paper, feeling his heart thumping wildly in his chest as he touched its perforated margin.

It was the missing index card from Pippa's Rolodex!

Miss Nancy STONE
31 Cheviot Street,
London
QUEEN OF QUIZZES.

Pippa was sending him to meet Nancy Stone.

Chapter Twelve

TUESDAY, 21ST APRIL, 1981
SESSION 78

Pippa had nominated Derek Wadlow to lead the innovation challenge that was taking place at this evening's Fellowship meeting.

He flicked the switch of the creaky projector the pub had lent them and the back wall of the room lit up with the brief.

Sequential & Combination Puzzles:

(I)

A puzzle that is solved by achieving a particular combination starting from a random/scrambled combination.

(II)

A set of pieces that must be manipulated in a specific sequence to complete or progress further into the challenge.

There was a nervous rustle of carrier bags as people examined their work one last time.

Derek reminded everyone that in order to score highly in this challenge, a submission needed to fulfil both aspects of the brief, with five points up for grabs for each. And for any submissions that delivered a new or surprising element, a total of five extra points were available. Any puzzles that scored above the threshold of seven and a half were automatically eligible for seed-funding out of the Fellowship's kitty.

'We were rather hoping that at least one product could be put forward for the Spring toy fair in Stockholm,' he announced. 'With the Fellowship's royal seal of approval.'

Eric Stoppard offered to go first. He presented an icosahedron sphere, about the size of a grapefruit, which had been spliced into twenty sections that turned on a central axis. The idea was to rotate the various sections in order to line up six colours. It was dizzying to look at and even Eric struggled to arrange the pieces in front of everyone, which he claimed there were more than twenty septillion combinations for.

Next, it was Pippa's turn.

She leaned down and pulled the cloth shoe bag from under her chair – the box nestled safely inside.

Hector – sitting beside her – patted her arm as she rose from her seat. 'Good luck, Pip,' he whispered. 'You've got this.'

She smiled back at him. Pippa wasn't quite sure how it all happened, really. A man she had once felt nothing but sympathy for, Mr Haywood – the vagabond artist turned jigsaw designer – was now the person she shared her home with. A week after she'd seen him clamber into the back of his van, she had casually dropped into conversation that she was looking for a lodger. She wasn't, of course, but she couldn't bear the idea of him living like that, especially when she had two perfect rooms upstairs and, if truth be told, a secret need for a bit of company of an evening.

Three months in and they still hadn't spoken about his former housing situation. Pippa couldn't help thinking that somehow, he knew that she knew. Whether or not this was the case it seemed impertinent to ask. She just hoped that one day he might feel comfortable revealing what had happened, what had led him to being temporarily homeless.

The biggest breakthrough, however, was learning that Hector had once been married. From the sounds of things, his relationship with a lady called Elizabeth hadn't lasted very long, but Pippa couldn't help trying to join the dots in her head. Perhaps the breakdown of his relationship had led him astray, she wondered. Perhaps that's what resulted in him going off the rails, becoming something of a hermit, living out of his campervan.

She tried not to let her curiosity get the better of her. Whatever had happened in Hector's past, the pair were rubbing along quite nicely and their arrangement, while never formalised, looked set to continue. He was her new lodger. She was his landlady. But more importantly, they'd become rather good friends.

Pippa took her place in front of the projector and took a swig of her Campari and soda, then loosened the drawstring bag and revealed her puzzle box to a chorus of caught breaths.

'I'm proud to present the *Alphabetibox*.'

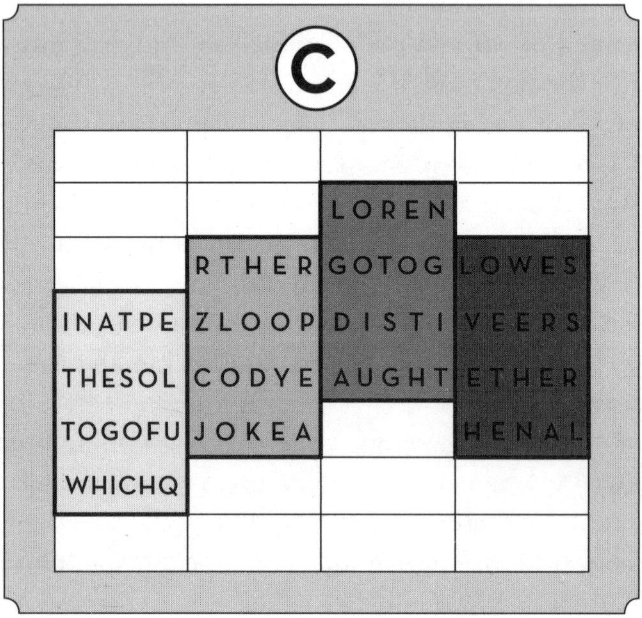

Pippa rotated the box – polished to a sheen – in the dusty light, quietly admiring the way she had put it all together. She was particularly fond of all the ironwork inside – the various hasps, clasps and brackets, which Hector had helped her engineer. She handed the box to Geoff Stirrup beside her, asking him to pass it around, before explaining how she'd been inspired to create a wooden combination puzzle that was also word-based, and could be entirely personalised to whoever was going to solve it.

The lettered tiles on the front of the box were in fact interchangeable, so you could spell out your own twenty-one-character phrase. Just like its own combination padlock, users could set the secret code – or in this case, the *words* – that would release the lock.

No one was listening to her. Instead, they were glued to Dickie Langley – an ex-Navy commander – who now had possession of the box, trying desperately to get inside it.

A few people got out of their chairs and crouched by him, offering their own suggestions.

'Perhaps there's a magnetic latch and that's what the hole on the side is for.'

Pippa stood with her back pressed to the wall. She took sips of her drink and before long they were grappling over the box, jostling for it, desperate to get their hands on the thing.

'What does the *C* mean at the top?' Nancy asked. 'It looks hand-carved, certainly deliberate.'

A crucial component of such lock boxes were the obligatory red herrings, designed to distract and divert the attention of the solver. Pippa had gone to town on those. There were several pointless additions to the design, including deliberately loose-fitting side panels, which wiggled by touch, some etched hieroglyphics on the lid that were purely decorative, and some screws at the base that she'd hammered in entirely willy-nilly.

'No, we can't ignore the letters,' Earl announced. 'That's clearly the key to it. Look at all the trouble she's gone to. Pass it here.'

Looking over Earl's shoulder, Pippa saw that the letters on the lid, so far, had been aligned:

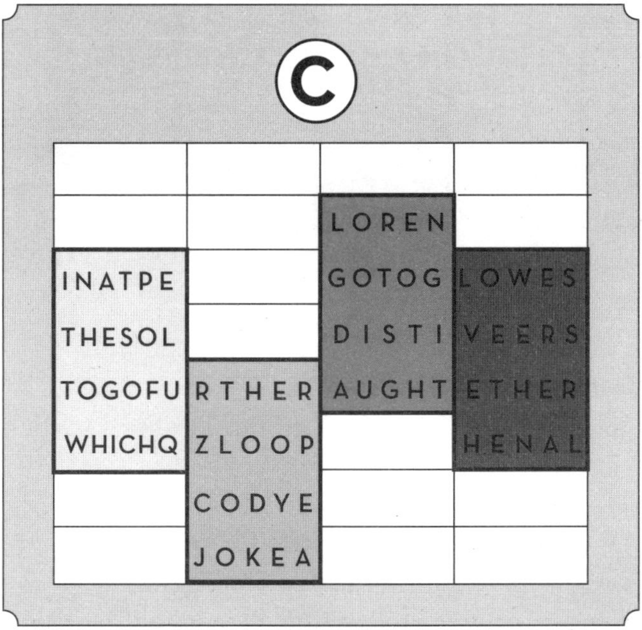

Getting there, she thought.

She took her empty glass towards the stairs, suddenly feeling the effect of the alcohol she'd been quaffing at a rate of knots ever since she'd arrived. She turned in the doorway with a smile on her face.

'I'm going to get a drink. I'll buy two in fact and give the second to whomever manages to complete the box by the time I'm back.'

She took her time at the bar, chatting aimlessly to the landlord, Pete, about all the endless rain they'd been having, and by the time she returned she was met with scattered applause.

'We've cracked it,' someone announced.

They held the lid open to her and she examined the letters on the front:

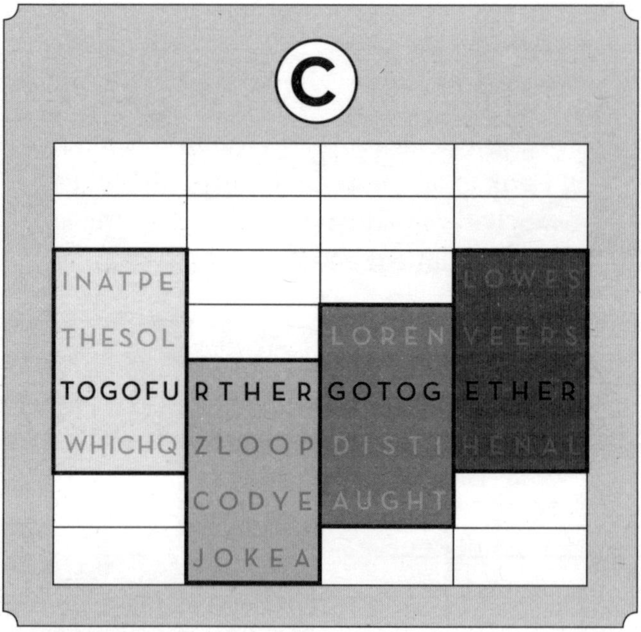

'Congratulations, everyone.'

Earl had the 'Save the Date' card she'd popped inside the box. It read simply:

OUR HUNDREDTH SESSION
'To Go Further, Go Together'
22.09.81

The box itself was now in the hands of Derek Wadlow, who was judging it for himself, examining something on the base, and he didn't lift his gaze as Pippa stood in front of the group.

'Do you like it then?' she asked everybody.

'It's marvellous, Pip,' Ian said. 'So the *C* on the top is a Roman numeral? Our centenary session, is that right?'

'I must say I'd lost track of the dates,' Earl said. 'Our hundredth session, is that right?'

'Do we have any plans, Pip?' Nancy asked. 'A party, perhaps?'

'It's not finished,' Derek called out.

The room quickly went silent.

'It's two puzzles in one,' he continued.

All eyes moved towards Derek and his fumbling hands.

'You mean there's more?' Nancy asked with her hand on her chest. Derek raised his finger in reply, consumed by the task at hand. A few seconds later, he had cracked it. Everyone watched as he reached inside the box and presented a scroll, tied with a red ribbon. Their mouths were open as he lifted the box up to show them the secret compartment he'd unearthed inside.

'How did you find that?' someone asked. 'Did you have to squeeze the sides?'

Of course, it wasn't just a case of unlocking the lid of Pippa's box but finding and figuring out how to open the secret compartment at the base. The first hidden chamber they had found was almost three inches in depth – two inches shorter than the total depth of the box.

Derek read from the unfurled sheet. '"Our hundredth session will be taking place out of London – an anniversary gala will be held at a hotel in September, all expenses paid for by me."'

There was a burst of applause as Pippa handed Derek the glass of barley wine she'd bought from downstairs. If anyone was to find the secret second compartment, she knew it would be Mr Wadlow.

'Where are we going, Pip?' Earl asked. 'Somewhere nice, I hope.'

Pippa lifted her finger to quiet them all. 'We're going . . .'

she began, feeling a bubble of excitement rise inside her before clasping her hands together. 'To Bedfordshire!'

The silence that followed was so stark it made the hairs on Pippa's arm stand on end.

She fumbled with the brooch on her blouse, glanced around the room for some assurance, eventually catching Earl's eye.

'*Bedfordshire?*' he repeated, with his face all screwed up, as if she might have said the Outer Hebrides instead. 'Why Bedfordshire, Pip? Of all places?'

'Why on earth not?' she answered swiftly. 'I've booked us all a lovely hotel in a village called Marston Moretaine. We have the whole place to ourselves.'

'The whole place?'

'That's right. I'm quite certain you're going to love it. They're giving us access to the conference suite and supper is thrown in at no extra cost. A buffet, no less. How could I say no?'

Of course, it wasn't any overnight at a hotel. They were attending a sales viewing. Pippa was taking them to her former ancestral home, the place she had set her heart on buying, the first headquarters of the Fellowship of Puzzlemakers. It was the place that, with any luck, they'd all soon call home.

Over the last few months, Pippa had begun to feel as if everything in her life had been building up to this moment. Subconscious or otherwise, Pippa had kept the bulk of her inheritance to one side because she knew that one day she was going to do something extraordinary with it. Of course, over the years, she'd spent some frivolously, she'd be the first to admit, but once she'd bought more silk scarves than anyone could possibly ever wear, splashed out on some extortionate costume jewellery, and ticked off all the countries on her bucket list, she knew that the rest of the money ought to go towards something more meaningful. The money she'd set aside was a clue to the third act of her life, a precursor to something truly momentous to come. She just hadn't realised what that was.

Until now.

Chapter Thirteen

In the boardroom at Creighton Hall, Clayton sat alongside the surviving members of the Fellowship around a long, lacquered-walnut conference table, in a long, wood-panelled room on the ground floor of the house, trying to look interested.

'And now,' Hector announced. 'Let us move onto Any Other Matters. Turn to the next page on the agenda, everybody.'

Everyone flipped the page of the committee's agenda and issued a collective sigh, noticing all twelve further topics of discussion. What was usually a thirty-minute assembly at the start of the week had been going on for an hour and twenty minutes and showed no sign of concluding.

As far as Hector Haywood was concerned, it was business as usual, but Clayton – the assigned secretary – was having difficulty concentrating.

'Clay, you *are* writing this all down, aren't you?'

Clayton swiftly picked up his pen and nodded, but in truth his mind had drifted entirely. Hector's voice had become an unintelligible drone to his ears. He'd barely got down a word.

He'd been responsible for taking the committee minutes ever since he was fifteen years old, and had continued to perform the role with diligence and dedication. His tools – a gold-plated tortoiseshell fountain pen and a nicely weighted jotter's pad inside a black leather portfolio – were the same he'd used in every meeting ever since. He enjoyed the ritual of it, the sense of duty. He also liked listening to each of the puzzlemakers discuss their various projects, learning how their extraordinary minds worked.

That week, though, he was finding it difficult to think about anything other than what he'd uncovered the day before – the box, the key, the details for Miss Nancy Stone.

'Your pen isn't touching the page, Clay. So I can only assume you're missing what I'm saying.'

'Sorry,' Clayton replied, shaking himself awake. 'What were you saying?'

'I was *saying* that this year's fayre is bound to creep up on us . . .'

Clayton nodded blankly at him.

'Write it down! For goodness' sake, write it down, boy.'

It was Hector's first meeting chairing as President, and he was going through the discussion points with all the thoroughness and earnestness that they'd all come to expect from the man. So far, he'd raised the subject of a faulty printer in their workshop, as well as announcing an opportunity for all wordsmiths to pitch in as freelance contributors to a new magazine launching in the autumn.

Now Hector was explaining how they'd have to pick straws unless someone wanted to nominate themselves as this year's fayre co-ordinator.

It was a Fellowship tradition – a cross between a community open day and village fete. Historically, it was a chance to sell products direct to consumers in the marquee they erected in the grounds, but it also helped attract potential new members and residents. People would travel from all over the country to spend the day with them, to get a taste of life at Creighton.

Clayton tore a bit off his paper, scribbling, *Meet you in the maze when this is all over?*

He pushed it discreetly towards Earl opposite, who took one glance, flipped it over, and scrawled his response. *If I haven't expired with boredom, certainly.*

'So what are you going to do?' Earl asked.

'I'm thinking.'

Clayton was huddled in the middle of the garden maze under the dripping branches of the willow tree with his closest companion.

He had just confided everything he'd uncovered in the last twenty-four hours to the mazemaker. It had left him feeling a little lighter, certainly, if not more apprehensive about things.

Clayton was beginning to feel daunted at the prospect of what might lie ahead. He wasn't just worried about what the puzzle might uncover, but whether he had the necessary skills to complete it.

'What if I can't solve it, Earl? What if this whole quest goes nowhere?'

Earl took Clayton's hand in his. 'You have us, Clay. We'll always be here for you. You can ask for help at any time.'

Clayton nodded in agreement, feeling instantly calmer, but he knew this was something he needed to solve himself.

After noticing Nancy at the funeral, and then uncovering her contact details inside the puzzle box, Clayton had done a little digging. He'd gathered some scant details about the woman via a couple of discreet conversations with the residents.

Nancy Stone was a top trivialist; she had the answer to everything apparently. She'd joined the Fellowship a year into its inception, when they were still convening in the room above the London pub. She was supposed to be considerably younger – twenty years or so – than most of the other members at the time. There was talk of a slightly troubled domestic life – a controlling mother at home who never approved of her daughter's pursuits. She ultimately became known for her highly elaborate quiz books, especially a bestselling series that Clayton had heard of over the years: *The London Cabbie's Quiz Books*. They were a sort of treasure hunt across the capital, made up of fiendishly obscure questions and ordinance survey maps.

'I'm baffled,' Earl said, 'by why Pip might suggest you get in touch with Nance. You don't think she might actually be linked to your . . .'

Clayton looked down at his feet. Of course, it was something he hadn't been able to stop thinking about.

'I guess time will tell.'

Earl adjusted himself on the bench, as if shaking off the notion. 'I wish I'd had a chance to catch up with her, Clay, after the funeral. There were so many people, I didn't quite manage to—'

'She left immediately after the service.'

Earl glanced at him in surprise. 'She didn't stay for drinks?'

Clayton shook his head.

After the funeral, they'd all gone to the pub, where there'd been a few hundred quid behind the bar, bowls of crisps, a few platters of sandwiches. But Nancy had dashed away before Clayton could introduce himself.

'Well, that *is* curious,' Earl replied, looking quite perplexed. 'Nance would never turn down a free drink.'

For a while, neither man spoke, both lost in deep, serious thought.

Clayton's insides churned. He eventually peeled Pippa's crossword out from his pocket and unfolded it in front of him, pressing it into Earl's lap.

He had already explained Pippa's note about how the eighteen crossword clues were supposedly the clues to his future – while the Alphabetibox, the key, and Nancy Stone, were somehow linked to him unlocking his past.

'So the crossword was in the hatbox?' Earl asked. 'Those are the solutions to a happy, fulfilling life?'

Clayton nodded.

'Pick a clue for me, Earl. Any clue.' He reached inside his jacket pocket and pulled out his tortoiseshell fountain pen, whipping off the cap. 'I'll start solving it now. The perfect distraction.'

Earl smiled at him. He lifted the sheet and ran his finger very purposefully along the clues, taking his time, moving from DOWN to ACROSS, then back again, before tapping his finger heartily on the sheet on a clue that read: *Daring exploits (10).*

'Start at the bottom,' he suggested. 'Start at twenty across, son.'

Chapter Fourteen

TUESDAY, 22ND SEPTEMBER, 1981
SESSION 100

The Fellowship of Puzzlemakers were, for the first time, on the move.

Crawling their way out of London in Gary's Wheels – a coach Pippa had hired from the *Yellow Pages* – they were en route to their special centenary gala at Creighton Hall Hotel, Mid-Bedfordshire.

Earlier that day, Pippa had instructed everyone to meet outside the Queen's Head at three o'clock sharp. The crowd that had assembled on the pavement as Pippa made her way up Essex Road looked different to the usual bunch who gathered of a Tuesday evening.

Some had turned up in casualwear – summery polo shirts, stonewashed jeans and dazzling white training shoes, like teachers on a school trip – while others were dressed more formally for the occasion. Linen suits, elasticated braces, polished brogues. They really were a sight.

'Let's hit the road,' Pippa declared at a few minutes past three, ushering everyone onto the bus.

She watched the cream of the British puzzling community climb on board before settling into a space at the back, beside Nancy.

From her seat, Pippa did a quick head count.

It had become something of a tradition to leave a spare chair at the pub for their resident cryptologist, Derek Wadlow, who had a habit of arriving later at the sessions. On the coach that afternoon the spare-chair custom continued, though they all knew the famous codebreaker wasn't joining them. Someone had even placed a trilby hat on the seat in honour of the man.

Derek had passed away three weeks after Pippa had secretly met with him to discuss her grand plans for the Fellowship.

'It's going to be murder around Highbury Corner at this hour,' Nancy said. 'He should head along Holloway Road if he has any sense.'

Pippa gave a tight smile. She felt an attack of the collywobbles coming on. It was the anticipation of the evening ahead. The surprise pitch she was going to make to them all. She'd barely slept these last few weeks worrying whether she'd be able to drum up enough support.

As they inched along a congested Holloway Road, Nancy whipped out the latest Danielle Steel saga – *Kaleidoscope* – while Pippa tried to distract herself with Eric Stoppard's latest creation. The Sudokube. It was a meticulously engineered cuboid, a little larger than a Rubik's, that featured a 3x3 grid. She was still fumbling with it as they passed through Highgate, before giving up on the thing, finding that the numbers were beginning to blur.

Nancy had a concerned look on her face. 'You're not going to puke, are you?

'Gosh, no,' Pippa insisted. 'Nothing like that.'

'Because I'll ask the driver for a bag if you think—'

'I'm fine. Just anxious to get there, that's all.'

The two ladies gave each other a smile, then Pippa glanced out the window, drumming her fingers against the arm rest. In truth the nerves were making her feel a bit queasy. Here she was, leading everyone back to her ancestral home without them realising. The trouble was, you couldn't keep secrets within the Fellowship – everyone spoke. And so Pippa decided to pitch to them all at the same time, once they'd seen the place with their own eyes and realised exactly what was on the table.

There was, however, one person she felt confident confiding in. One person she was certain would be willing to make the big move, because he already lived with her.

Pippa's lodger, Hector, was the only other person who knew what tonight was really about.

As they got onto the M25, she found herself edging out of her seat and scooting down the aisle of the bus. She just wanted to get a sense of an ETA.

'*No* talking to the driver,' Gary snapped, pointing at the laminated sheet on the dashboard.

DO NOT DISTRACT THE DRIVER UNDER ANY CIRCUMSTANCES.
KINDLY CONSULT THE COACH GUIDE IN YOUR SEAT POCKET.
ALL REASONABLE QUESTIONS ARE ANSWERED THERE.

Pippa rolled her eyes.

Gary might well be 'The Most Reliable & Responsible Driver in the Home Counties' as his listing in the directory promised, but so was he the 'Most Curmudgeonly'. The second they'd boarded he had explained, in no uncertain terms, that sick bags were exclusive of rental costs and would be charged at fifty pence a pop. He'd also encouraged them not to use the on-board lavatory unless it was absolutely necessary. There'd been an incident overnight on a trip to Liverpool with a hen party and, as much as he'd tried to crank the cistern, he couldn't clear the deposit.

'He's a charmer,' Pippa remarked, as she clambered back into her seat.

Nancy was rummaging through a tin of boiled travel sweets, lining up all the yellow ones on her tray table.

'Pear drops are my favourite,' she explained. 'The blackcurrant ones make my tongue itch. Do you want one?'

Pippa shook her head.

'Raspberry?'

Pippa waved her hand and smiled affectionately at her friend who proceeded to pull two giant knitting needles, the size of drumsticks, from her bag, and got to work on a new woollen seat cover for her cab.

Pippa was thrilled she had decided to join them on their first official outing.

For a while her friend had been down as a question mark. Predictably enough, her mother wasn't too thrilled about her heading off on a weekend getaway but, at the last minute, she said she'd join them. Pippa sensed a newly acquired rebellious streak emerging in her friend and couldn't help wondering if her own wilful spirit was starting to rub off on her.

Even so, it was cherished members like Nancy who Pippa now feared alienating with her secret proposition. The woman was only thirty-four years old, the youngest Fellowship member by at least forty years, if not fifty in most cases. Unlike the rest of their membership, her retirement days weren't even a distant glimmer ahead of her. Why would she ever consider joining this enterprise at this stage of her life? Nancy was still young enough to settle down, to start her own family, should she ever meet a man.

Pippa picked up the Danielle Steel book wedged between the pair of them, pushing the concern to the back of her mind. For the past few weeks, these books had become her solace. A total balm for her brain. She'd devoured twelve editions from Nancy's collection – *The Ring* being her personal favourite – and she'd put her name down for this new one too.

'You know, the funny thing about these novels,' she announced, tapping the bright teal cover. 'They're not romance stories at all, are they?'

'No?' Nancy asked.

'They're fantasy. No man would ever behave like this.'

Nancy rolled her eyes. 'Oh, you're such a cynic, Pip!'

'A realist, more like.'

'You'll be swept off your feet one day, just you wait.'

Pippa laughed. The thought of it, at her age, was absurd. She'd achieved lots of things in her life, but securing any kind of serious relationship had never even been remotely on the cards.

Beside her, Nancy continued clacking away with her knitting needles and Pippa couldn't help but turn and smile dotingly at her. Even though she often gave her stick for it, it was her friend's unshakeable optimism that Pippa admired the most. It was clear

Nancy still kept the faith that one day she'd fall hopelessly head over heels. She wished she shared Nancy's sunny disposition, sometimes.

'That reminds me,' Nancy began. 'How are things going with you and the jigsaw artist?'

Pippa turned to look at her friend.

'Any chance that friendship might develop into something more . . . serious?'

Pippa made a horrified expression. 'With Hector? I shouldn't think so.'

'Oh.'

'He is my *tenant*, Nance, a lodger, nothing more than that. Don't be getting any ideas now.'

In truth, the pair had become much more than just housemates. She realised now – several months into the arrangement – that she had needed his companionship as much as he had needed a roof over his head. And not only that but she trusted the man. She wouldn't have confided in him about her secret plans for the Fellowship otherwise. And yet, despite their growing closeness, there was still a sense that she was yet to fully understand the man. Whatever had happened in his dark past, whatever had left him so isolated, so lost in the world, she would likely never find out.

'Apparently you enjoy making his lunch,' Nancy went on, clearly enjoying this acquired knowledge. 'And when he's painting in the afternoon you bring him a selection of biscuits and a cup of tea—'

Pippa's mouth opened before she spoke. 'Only if I'm sticking the kettle on for myself!'

Nancy was holding in a laugh. 'You make a mean ham-and-cress sandwich, apparently.'

'Well, I do,' Pippa exclaimed. 'It's hardly haute cuisine.'

There was a beat.

She quickly checked Hector was out of earshot. He was four rows in front with Geoff Stirrup, a retired accountant turned numerical puzzle master. Everyone called him the Calculatrix.

'And what *else* did he say?' she went on, feeling unusually exposed.

Before answering, Nancy draped her hand over hers, which she hadn't realised were gripping the fold-out tray table in front of her.

'That it's a shame you've never got married, because you'd make a wonderful wife . . . or a mother.'

Pippa rolled her eyes, mortified but also quietly flattered.

She was less sure she'd make a perfect housewife, but she'd always known she'd had a strong maternal streak. At least *someone* was reaping the benefits.

Several junctions up the M25 later and Pippa – struggling to sit still with anticipation – started handing out a photocopied agenda for the evening ahead, delivered as a series of cryptic clues.

The Fellowship of Puzzlemakers
Centenary Gala

5.30 p.m.
Initially, a round door really introduces new knowledge slowly (6)

7.00 p.m.
Buff etcher contains a spread (6)

10.00 p.m.
To be announced . . .

Settling back into her seat, it wasn't long before the coach turned a sharp bend into Marston Moretaine.

Pippa hadn't seen the place in almost fifty years, but it was every bit as enchanting as she remembered. The village was surrounded by fields and farmland and just as people started to comment on its quaintness, Creighton Hall was suddenly there, perched atop a hill.

What was remarkable was how the property managed to

appear both deeply imposing and distinctly unkempt at the same time. A vast Victorian edifice in pale yellow sandstone, there were two peeling pillars set either side of the impressive oak door, which you had to climb a set of stone steps to reach.

Hector caught Pippa's eye as they pulled up outside the grand house. He looked entirely dumbstruck.

She felt an odd liquid flutter in her stomach that wasn't just nerves, or even excitement, but a creeping sense of guilt too.

The hoteliers who owned the property – the Barclays – were waiting for them as the coach doors hissed open. Until now, Pippa had only ever communicated with them by letter and telephone. She'd asked them not to disclose the nature of their conversations to any of the guests.

Francis Barclay was in his mid-thirties but had fairly priggish, catalogue clothes on: a yellow golfing jumper and red needlecord trousers. He had the most perfectly manicured handlebar moustache and hair waxed to such a shine it reflected like a puddle in the afternoon sun.

'Welcome to Creighton, Philippa . . . *at last*,' he declared, giving her a wink that wasn't the least bit subtle.

His wife, Jocelyn – a dainty thing in a clingy maroon twinset – lingered next to him like an ornament.

'We're so pleased to have you all,' Francis declared, his arms outstretched to them. 'Leave your bags and we'll see to those.'

All of a sudden, a young, rather busty woman appeared, wearing a royal-blue tabard. She was dragging a chrome luggage trolley noisily across the patio.

'Are you sure?' Pippa asked. 'We really don't mind carrying our own.'

She had her knapsack in one hand, a briefcase in the other, and, at her feet, a battered old suitcase, covered in foreign-flag stickers.

'Oh, yes,' Francis answered. 'Our housekeeper will handle all of that. She insists on it.'

The weariness in his tone did not go unnoticed. Indeed, the housekeeper wouldn't take no for an answer and started flinging everyone's belongings on the trolley in a very slipshod manner before anyone could stop her.

The lady had a shock of unnaturally dark, almost witch-like hair, tousled on her head like an abandoned bird's nest. And as she got closer, Pippa realised that on her feet were not practical work shoes but sandals that appeared to have been crocheted. Not only that but draped around her neck was a hefty gemstone of some kind, hung not on a dainty chain but a loop of fraying rope. It swung against her ample bosom like a wrecking ball.

'I'll take that,' the woman demanded, pointing to Pippa's things. Pippa found her feet shuffling together, clamping around the suitcase.

'Madam, let me have it, please.'

'It rather seems you've got your hands full,' Pippa replied politely. 'I can carry my own things, no bother at all.'

The woman smiled. 'No, I'll take it. It's my job. And I'm very good at it.' She grabbed the case at Pippa's feet, then prised the briefcase from her hand, and the knapsack from the other, throwing both smaller bags casually over each arm like a milk maid.

'Heavens,' Pippa muttered, watching the woman in fascination.

The housekeeper lobbed the case on the heavily loaded trolley and started shouldering it towards the house like a contestant on *World's Strongest Man*, looking very pleased with herself.

A few seconds later and the wheels of the thing caught on an uneven paving slab, sending the whole trolley toppling over. Everyone's luggage spilled out over the drive, the impact causing a thick cloud of gravel dust like a bomb had just gone off.

'Christ's sake!' the housekeeper spluttered. 'Stupid bloody thing.' She was waving her arms about as she appeared from the billowing debris, like she was emerging from a fire.

Pippa sensed Francis was looking at her, as if checking if she'd noticed the commotion going on. He contorted his lips into a rueful grin.

'That's our housekeeper, Angel,' he explained. 'She certainly tries her best.'

Pippa grimaced.

There was a strip of red carpet leading up the stone steps towards the front door, which she headed towards, waving everyone to follow. The carpet squelched underfoot with last night's rain. Either side of the central stretch of carpet, she noticed there were little white flowers poking out of the cracks in the stone.

Pippa was suddenly struck by a vivid memory of making daisy chains on these steps as a young girl to escape her aunt during the holidays. She used to sit quietly on her own making friendship bracelets for some of the girls at school, which she would keep in a trinket box under her bed. By the time she came to presenting these gifts, the flowers had mostly wilted and the petals had started to come away.

She felt a sense of melancholy entering the grand old house all these years later with new friends. Her new family. Ready to start this new chapter in her life.

Chapter Fifteen

20

DARING EXPLOITS (10)

Clayton didn't own a suitcase of his own. He had never needed one until that day.

He retrieved a brown leather valise case from the attic decorated with jauntily placed foreign-flag stickers and slogans from far-flung places Clayton could barely pronounce, let alone pick out on a map. *QUEBEC: LIVE IT TO BELIEVE IT*; *BHUTAN: HAPPINESS IS A PLACE*; *ALBANIA: GO YOUR WAY!* He laughed to himself at the irony of the last one: *ECUADOR: ESCAPE YOUR WORLD.*

It had obviously belonged to Pippa; she had travelled halfway around the world by the time she was his age.

Clayton stood in the middle of his room – the case flung open on his bed – wondering what to pack for his last-minute jaunt down to London to find Nancy Stone.

He had decided to tackle Pippa's puzzle quest exactly the way he thought she'd intended – with as much guts as he could muster. In other words, just the way she did everything in life.

He'd googled the actual definition of **adventures** in the *New Oxford Dictionary* shortly before booking his hotel on Trivago – just to be sure. *Stories of astonishing miracles and heroic adventures. Unusual, exciting or daring experiences.*

If this wasn't that, then he'd be blowed.

Earl had obviously pointed him to this clue first because he knew he needed that extra nudge. Earl was always encouraging him to step out of his comfort zone, to break away and do something for himself for a change.

At twenty-five years of age, Clayton knew it was ridiculous, embarrassing even, but he had never gone away on his own before, never boarded a train so spontaneously, never travelled without knowing exactly where he might end up, nor when he might return.

He'd decided he wasn't going to rush the crossword. He was going to take each clue at a time, make sure he embraced every little part of it, that he didn't let Pippa down.

'Pants . . . socks . . .' he said to himself, rummaging through his drawers.

For some time, Clayton had been aware that his boxers had lost their elastic. Now was as good an excuse as ever to purchase new ones, he thought. He'd pick some up from the M&S at the station.

Clayton swallowed his anxiety, reminding himself that, with any luck, he'd be back home in just a couple of days, and if anyone needed him he was only at the end of a phone.

Spontaneity wasn't something that came naturally, and already he was beginning to build a mental list – a schedule, even – of things he might do while he was away to fill the time, if say, Nancy wasn't home when he first knocked. He didn't have her number so just hoped whatever time he popped in would be convenient for a chat.

He wondered about getting cheap seats to a show – there were websites for that sort of thing. Or perhaps there'd be time for a visit to the British Museum.

He moved to the wardrobe. The rail held just a dozen pieces of quality clothing and, unsure exactly what Pippa had in store for him, he opened his arms and bundled up the whole lot, throwing everything inside the case, before taking it all out and folding it neatly. There were his two favourite jackets (one twill, one wool); his favourite Aran sweater; four shirts (two button-down, two cotton casual) and his best-fitting black corduroys. In the drawers below, he put in an old pair of jeans he wore for gardening, a waterproof cagoule, a Cuban-collar shirt, a roll-neck, cable knit, vest tops, socks and underwear.

He had been to London many times before, of course. There had been a thirtieth anniversary gala at Claridge's a few years ago, and for the past four years, at least, he had escorted Pippa to the Harrods' January sale, not to mention their quarterly mid-week matinees at the theatre: *The King and I*, *Fiddler on the Roof*, *Calamity Jane*, his personal favourites. As well as sharing a love of musical theatre with Pippa, the two of them shared a mutual appreciation of art and would occasionally attend exhibitions together in London, even up until just a couple of months ago. The Hayward – on the South Bank – was their favourite. They had a joint membership. It expired at the end of the year.

Before closing his suitcase, he went to the corner sink and gathered up his toiletries – his cologne, comb and shaving bits. In the unit below the basin there was a tea tray with a porcelain cup and saucer, sugar sachets, UHT milk, a glass barrel of his favourite all-butter shortbread, and a tiny travel kettle. Sometimes he liked to make tea for one, not eight.

He picked up the kettle and popped open its lid – an act he performed periodically. Stuffed around the coiled metal element was his inheritance money. It was made up of the cash that several residents had accumulated and passed on to him after they'd gone. There was almost ten thousand pounds, all rolled up in rubber-band-bound notes. He took a few bundles and slipped them inside a pair of brogues in his case.

Chapter Sixteen

THE FELLOWSHIP OF PUZZLEMAKERS
5.20 P.M.

Pippa entered the swirly moquette-carpeted cocktail lounge of Creighton Hall Hotel – in the room where her grandfather once hosted regular poker parties – and immediately did a double take. Where she was used to seeing a mahogany card table there was now a tatty snooker table, and at the far end of the room, where there was once an extensive record collection and golden gramophone, there was now a small but fully-stocked cocktail bar.

Earl Vosey was alone at one of the stools, dressed in what could only be described as a classic three-piece morning suit. He wasn't one for shirtsleeves or tailored trousers; she'd never even seen him in a smart jumper, come to think of it, let alone shiny dress shoes.

'Don't you polish up well, Mr Vosey?'

Pippa perched on a needlessly high bar seat beside him. He was having a Moscow Mule. There was a brief silence as she adjusted herself and the two of them took each other in, dressed in all their finery.

'Is it a bit much, Pip? Do I look silly?'

'Not at all!' she replied, leaning over and straightening his dicky bow. 'You're the spit of Robert Redford in *The Great Gatsby*. Ravishing.'

'I just thought I'd go for it. As it's a special occasion and all. I don't get many chances to dress up these days.'

'Well, I think you look very handsome. Surely the most handsome man in Mid-Bedfordshire.'

Earl smiled, pressing the back of his hair down. 'Thanks, Pipster. That's very kind.'

From her lobes hung her favourite garnet-and-pearl earrings. She'd bought them that spring in Paris. The antique jewellers in the Marais district must have seen her coming. She left with four different pairs.

'You look nice, too,' Earl said, after a moment's pause. 'Very . . .' He gestured across her bejewelled outfit as he tried to find the word. 'Glittery.'

Glittery? she thought, feeling a tad dejected. It wasn't exactly what she was going for, but she supposed she'd take it.

She was in Dior – a mauve, lavishly embellished off-the-shoulder number she'd picked up a few weeks earlier at Harrods. It was a quarterly ritual of hers: to pay a pilgrimage to her favourite shop in the world.

She ordered herself a Tia Maria and adjusted her balloon sleeves, sensing Earl was looking at her. His steel-grey-blue eyes were like the high beam on an articulated lorry – you didn't have to be facing them to know when they were fixed on you. To her shame, she felt an instant ripple of pleasure through her entire body.

'You look lovely, Pip. You really do.'

She felt herself beaming. 'Oh, you're just saying that.'

'No, *no*, you're a very beautiful lady. You do know that, don't you?'

Pippa could feel herself going pink again.

Beautiful? she thought. It wasn't a word she'd naturally associate with herself. Intelligent – yes. Impulsive – of course. Iron-willed, often too. But she wasn't sure she'd ever considered herself *beautiful*.

'It's always boggled me,' Earl went on, 'how a lady as wonderful as you hasn't been snapped up already.'

'Oh, stop talking such nonsense now.'

'It's true!'

'Earl! Pack it in!'

'Surely the men must be queuing round the block!'

Pippa, smiling ear to ear, shook her head in protest, as if she wanted him to stop.

Show me these admiring men you speak of, she wanted to say. In fact, show me a single man who's ever considered me anything other than a handful. She was too intelligent, too impulsive, too iron-willed for most.

'Perhaps I've just never found the one.' She took a quick gulp of her Tia Maria.

Frank Sinatra was playing faintly on a speaker somewhere and the two of them listened to the pleasant, crooning music. Pippa glanced at her watch. Still a few minutes till cocktail hour officially began. They'd all arrive on the dot, no doubt.

Perhaps it was the generous pour going to her head, or being unusually alone with the man, but seeing Earl sipping his drink, Pippa had a sudden urge to lean in and press her lips against his, to let him take her whole body in his arms. Instead, she pulled herself up straight and angled her stool a few degrees away from him, reminding herself the man was happily married. Plus, Hector had just entered the room.

Pippa watched as he came towards them and hauled himself clumsily onto the spare stool with all the grace of a small child mounting a donkey. The poor chap, at five feet two, almost needed a stepladder to get up there.

'It's a good job I don't have vertigo,' he said in an unusual display of good humour. 'Who designed these bloody things anyway?'

'Just let me know when you need a hand down,' Pippa quipped. 'I don't want you spraining an ankle.'

She lifted her hand to catch the eye of the barman. 'Another round, please. And Hector will have . . .'

'Just a tomato juice for me.'

'Nothing stronger?'

Hector shook his head.

He'd never been a drinker. In fact, now that she thought about it, Pippa had never seen him touch a drop of alcohol, ever since they'd known each other. An allergy, perhaps.

He was in his usual flannel shirt. No paint splatters that evening, though, and it looked like his moustache had been tidied up and those pesky nose hairs had been taken care of.

'Can't help feeling a tad underdressed,' he said, adjusting his collar. 'This is all right, isn't it? I gave it a good wash.'

'You look lovely, Hector.'

Pippa suddenly realised that it was unlikely he owned anything smarter than his collection of plaid shirts and some rather bobbly woollen jumpers. Perhaps she should have bought him something to wear for the occasion. Left it in his room without making a fuss about it.

'How's Rosa doing, Earl?'

Hearing Earl's wife's name slip out of Hector's mouth gave Pippa a start.

As much as she had developed her own unrequited feelings for Earl, she knew that he would remain a castle in the air, forever off the cards. On the few occasions she'd heard him speak of Rosa, he'd done so with such deep affection and devotion it had made her melt. He was clearly besotted with the woman.

'Earl?' Hector repeated. 'Is everything . . . OK?'

Earl was looking at his dangling feet. When he finally looked up at them he gave the most pained expression, which sent shivers down the back of Pippa's neck.

They'd all known for some time that his wife had been having tests. He'd missed a session recently taking her to hospital but he'd made it sound so routine.

'We got the results last week.'

'And?' Pippa said, leaning in towards him, and then Hector took the words straight out of her mouth.

'Nothing serious, I hope?'

'It's cancer.'

They all froze. Pippa felt her heart sink.

'We thought it was just fertility issues,' he went on. 'We've been trying for a while now, to no avail . . . but in fact it wasn't that at all.' He took a sip of his drink, his eyes suddenly large and searching.

'Incurable.'

Hector struck his hand against the bar, making their drinks rattle.

Pippa was lost for words.

'*Oh*, Earl,' she heard herself say. 'We really had no idea . . .' She felt her hand press against her chest in disbelief.

'It's malignant. She'll probably have a few years, maybe a bit longer if she responds well to treatment. Time will tell.'

Pippa shook her head at the bleakness of it all, the unfairness, and suddenly she felt her throat clam up, as if she might cry.

'I wasn't going to come today, but she forced me out the door. She'd already packed my bag and hired this suit for me.'

The silence that followed was so heavy it was palpable. It only lifted when Hector raised his finger loftily in front of them.

'Nothing is certain in life but the unforeseen,' he proclaimed.

Pippa turned to him, stirred by his words, and Earl did the same.

'I'm just not sure how I'll be able to . . . go on, Hector, you know?'

'If I've learned anything over the years . . .' Hector replied, tilting his head as if the words he was searching for were ball bearings in one of Earl's miniature maze toys '. . . It's that you'll be amazed what the human spirit is capable of, even when you think you can't go on. Resilience is at the core of our existence, Earl. You'll surprise yourself. Just you wait.'

The mazemaker nodded in appreciation, briefly squeezed the man's arm in thanks.

Pippa was momentarily mute, wondering where Hector's words had come from, from which part of his life he was speaking of. It was rare to hear him speak so candidly, with such profoundness and warmth. She'd never quite determined why his life had gone so off the rails, how he'd ended up living out of his van, how his marriage had ended. She didn't feel it was her right to pry. But judging by this outpouring, perhaps there had been some incident in his past, some trauma – a personal loss of his own – that he had yet to share.

Seconds later and Earl brandished a slip of paper he'd drawn from his wallet.

'Rosa has made a list of all the places she wants to see before she . . .' His words trailed to nothing and he slid the note towards them.

Pippa leaned over the bar to unfold it.

A bucket list.

Tea at the Ritz, Climb the Eiffel Tower, Tour the Colosseum, Swim in the Dead Sea.

She was no graphologist, but somehow she could interpret this lady's handwriting, and she could tell from the exaggerated swirls and playful loops of her unshrinking hand, that, in another life, she and Rosa might have been very good friends.

'The whole world is out there, Earl,' Pippa declared. 'Go and explore it, before it's too late. Do you hear me? Go with your heart. Go with Rosa. Have adventures together. Your own adventures.'

Chapter Seventeen

Clayton's bag was packed. He was lugging his suitcase down the corridors of Creighton Hall when he noticed the door to Pippa's old room was slightly ajar. He nudged it open with his foot, glancing at the emptiness inside, feeling a mournful ache as his eyes landed on the space beside the ottoman bed where, for several weeks, he'd sat holding Pippa's hand.

Before he realised it, he'd dropped his case and was making his way inside.

During the final stretch of Pippa's life, when she'd been sent home from the hospice with a palliative-care nurse, it had been here that Clayton had kept vigil.

He'd sit on a fold-out chair, sometimes resting his head on her slippery, navy satin quilt while she dozed. The nurse would be in the corner, flicking through a magazine, and he'd known she was listening to every word, but he hadn't minded.

'Shall we play a game?' he'd asked one afternoon, a few weeks before she'd slipped away. 'That might be fun, mightn't it?'

Pippa's eyes were half closed but he could tell she was still awake, like an old flickering bulb about to go out for the final time.

'Jubble?' he suggested, rummaging through the games shelf beside the bed.

Pippa didn't say anything, but her hands emerged from under the duvet and started to rub together with glee.

'I thought so,' Clayton said. 'Right, let me get it set up here.'

He gathered up the pile of books on her bed to make space.

Jubble was one of the Fellowship's bestselling word-tile games, featuring a purple velvet bag of beautifully etched letters on a series of polished, hexagonally cut stones. The aim was to come up with as many words from the letters as possible within the timeframe. It was accompanied by an electronic pocket watch

– the Second Shaker – which when jiggled – or Jubbled – three times, generated a randomised time in which you had to complete each round.

Usually, they'd take it in turns to pick letters from the drawstring bag, but given Pippa's recent lethargy, Clayton drew them himself, dipping his hand inside the bag and hearing the familiar crunch of the stones rubbing up against each other, like pebbles on a beach, before laying them out in front of them.

He shook the timer above his head and Pippa stirred in bed, pushing herself up a little against the headboard. She looked pale and drawn, but her hair was immaculate, as it always was.

'Two minutes!' he announced. 'We should be able to do something with that, shouldn't we? All set? Three, two, one . . . and we're off!'

He stared at the arrangement of tiles, hoping the words might leap out in front of him, but they did nothing. In fact, the letters just became senseless shapes and his mind started to drift.

There was something he'd been meaning to ask Pippa for a few weeks now.

'Pip,' he began breathlessly. 'I know this isn't something I usually like to speak about but . . .'

The words he'd rehearsed a thousand times had completely disappeared from his head. For years he'd got used to diverting the conversation whenever it got on to the mystery of his parentage. He never liked to ask too many questions. It was as if there was a self-protective cut-off point in his head, a boundary he knew not to cross, a sense that, if he strayed beyond it, he might not like what he found.

'But . . . I suppose what I'm trying to say is, I'm old enough now. So if there's anything you know about how I came to live here . . . where I came from . . . then it's probably time I know. In case it might help me, you know, feel a bit more . . . complete.'

Pippa's razor-sharp focus shifted from the letters to him, like a spotlight.

He wondered if she could see his heart pounding beneath his jumper. Whether the rash he could feel crawling up his neck had appeared above his jumper.

'Even the smallest clue,' he added. 'It might give me something to go on, you know . . .'

He glanced at the stopwatch. Still sixty seconds to go. Usually this game went quickly.

'Patience,' Pippa said quietly.

'What was that?'

'Eight letters,' she murmured. '*Patience*.'

'Oh . . . right, yes, very good,' he said, jotting it down on the score sheet. 'That's a good one.'

'Protection,' Pippa called out a few seconds later, and then, before Clayton could even find his pencil, '*Contrition*'.

Patience.

Protection.

Contrition.

Clayton made a note of the words on the scoresheet, wondering as he did, with a sinking feeling inside him, whether they weren't just answers in the game, but a response to what he was asking. He wouldn't put it past her. Was she really asking him to wait until she died before he went digging? Was she hinting at the fact she'd been cushioning him from some sort of truth?

If she had, then perhaps she felt a sense of remorse about the whole affair.

The time had run out.

'I've only managed a five, I'm afraid,' Clayton muttered, realising he was probably talking to himself. '*Panic*.'

He reached over and took Pippa's hand and, shocked by how cold it was, folded his spare hand on top, sandwiching it tightly to try to keep it warm.

Please don't die without telling me anything you might know.

'I hope you don't mind my asking,' he said quietly. 'You'll always be my mother, of course, but I need to know where I've come from, who I am. I'm ready for the truth.'

At this, a tiny, tentative smile crept into her face, and Clayton felt her hand squeeze his before she drifted off to sleep.

Chapter Eighteen

THE FELLOWSHIP OF PUZZLEMAKERS
7 P.M.

'Why don't you all line up over there?' Pippa suggested. 'I have some prizes to dish out.'

The buffet had opened in the dining room a short while earlier and now everyone was not just stuffed, but at risk of nodding off.

To start they had tuna loaf with cucumber sauce or prawn cocktail; for mains they could pick between mackerel fillets or braised turkey in cider, with sides of creamed parsnips, sautéed green beans, potato gratin and peas amandine. Everything had been sprinkled liberally with chopped parsley to give a feeling of real fine dining. And for pudding – arctic roll or chocolate-mint mousse – they'd all been handed little plates with the words *100th SESSION* piped in raspberry coulis, like you might get at the Dorchester.

What Pippa found most surprising about the spread was the fact it hadn't been prepared by a team of catering staff but the eccentric housekeeper they'd met earlier on. Apparently, despite Angel's slightly manic entrance earlier, she was a scrupulous cook and catered many of the hotel's private events. Perhaps that was one reason the Barclays kept her around, she thought.

As everyone took their positions along the white wall of the hotel's conference suite – which had been converted from the old stables – Pippa couldn't help thinking she was being confronted with the most unlikely identity parade of criminals. A rag-tag bunch of offenders if ever there was. It made her heart soar and her head dizzy with pride seeing them all stood together like that.

Earl was first to be presented with the Fellowship's first membership badge. It featured their society's unique crest: a playful yet ceremonious motif that looked a bit like a pink cloud but was in fact supposed to represent a brain. Plus a rather natty motto, she'd decided on herself.

OFFICIAL MEMBER OF
THE FELLOWSHIP OF PUZZLEMAKERS
VENI, VIDI, SOLVI.

Given the conversation they'd just had at the bar, Pippa found herself getting slightly choked up as she attached the shiny pin to Earl's suit jacket while he stood proudly in front of her with his hands folded behind his back.

'There we go,' she said, tapping his broad chest, blinking away the emotion. 'Suits you.'

I CAME, I SAW, I SOLVED.

'I know it's only a badge,' he said, running his finger along the emblem. 'But I can't tell you how much it means. Belonging to something, feeling you're a part of something bigger than yourself? It's special, isn't it?'

Pippa nodded but inside she felt rotten.

She hated the idea that the new direction she was taking the Fellowship in might push people like Earl away.

'Earl, whatever happens later on this evening,' she began, 'I want you to know there'll always be a space for you at the Fellowship. Do you understand?'

He stared at her, bemused, but she had already moved on to the next person in the line – Eric Stoppard, the crabby craftsman who made fiendish little games out of wood.

'Try not to make *too* big a hole,' he said as Pippa fumbled with the pin. 'This suit's hired from Moss Bros.'

Next it was their mathematician, Geoff Stirrup, who wanted his badge not on his lapel but inside his coin purse so he could keep it on his person at all times.

Beside him was a giddy Nancy Stone. She had somewhat overdone the cocktails.

'Stick it on my boob, Pip. Perhaps I'll catch someone's eye.'

As Pippa stepped in front of her, the Queen of Quizzes thrust her ample bosom towards her. She was wearing a very revealing cocktail dress accessorised by a little silver purse slung over her shoulder, especially for her Marlboro Lights.

'Do you know . . .' Nancy took a quick puff on her cigarette while she waited to be inaugurated. 'When I passed the Knowledge when I was nineteen, I showed my mother my taxi badge. Proud as punch I was. You know what she said?'

Pippa dared not guess.

'That's for *men*. Women don't drive taxis.'

'Oh, Nance, I am sorry.'

'There I was thinking I was breaking barriers. She took the wind right out of my sails. I'm not going to let her spoil this one.'

Pippa kissed her lovingly on her cheek. 'Don't.'

Once everyone had received their badges, there was a special associate prize for their numbers guy, the Calculatrix, Geoff Stirrup. He'd surprised everyone in recent months with a string of major publishing deals, including several of which he'd generously donated back to the Fellowship purse in full, to help other puzzlers get their work off the ground.

For the final award, Pippa projected a photograph of Derek Wadlow on the screen and dimmed the lights.

'As you all know, we lost a dear friend and fellow Fellowshipper a few months ago. I know Derek leaves a great hole in our society.' She gestured towards the spare seat in the middle of them. 'Both literally and metaphorically.'

Everyone spoke of his death as coming out of the blue, how sudden it all seemed, that he was here one minute, sipping his barley wine and extolling the virtues of cryptology, and then, gone. But Pippa had taken comfort from knowing that Derek had somehow known his time was up. He had foreseen the whole thing before anyone else, of course.

Just four days before he passed – of what turned out to be a haemorrhagic stroke in his sleep – Derek had requested to see Pippa at his apartment in Fitzrovia.

Pippa had thought he'd looked weary that afternoon in his armchair and yet after their brief tête-à-tête, she had learned that the following day he'd attended an appointment at his publisher's in Bloomsbury (he had just delivered the fourth instalment of *Mr Wadlow's Cracking Codes* puzzle-book series), delivered a lecture at a warfare studies symposium at King's College, and even shown his face at a drinks reception at the Wellcome Trust.

The man never wasted a minute on this earth. He went out at his zenith.

'So, tonight we celebrate in his honour,' Pippa went on. 'And this commemorative glass trophy here – designed especially by our own Martin Dudeney – will be dedicated in Sir Derek's name and awarded annually to someone who deserves some special recognition for their contribution to the group. We'll call it the Wadlow Prize.'

There was a smattering of applause.

'The first recipient of this award will be announced . . . right now, in fact.'

There were whispers from the assembled crowd and everyone shot glances at each other, trying to work out who the lucky recipient might be.

'Hector Haywood, would you step up here, please.'

He looked completely flummoxed as people started congratulating him. 'Me?'

When he eventually made his way to the front, Pippa presented him with the glass trophy and everyone let out a cheer. He'd recently started producing his own line of puzzles – *Haywood's Jigsaws* – which were already stocked in several department stores across the country. He insisted on donating a share of proceeds straight back to the Fellowship.

'Congratulations, Mr Haywood. You are an exceptional artist, a fine jigsaw maker, and the Fellowship's greatest advocate.'

His eyes welled with tears. 'Thank you, Pippa. Are you sure?'

'I'm positive.'

'I've never won anything before.'

'Never?'

'Not once.'

'Not even for your artwork?'

Hector shook his head. 'I wouldn't say I'm an artist, Pip, I'm just a—'

'I won't hear it. You *are* an artist, Hector. Just because you are painting jigsaws doesn't make you any less of one. And let's not forget, if it weren't for you donating that sum of money all those months ago, we wouldn't have started the kitty. Perhaps we wouldn't all be here right now . . .'

She looked quickly over her shoulder and muttered as quietly as she could in his ear, 'And I might not be about to make the announcement I'm about to make.'

He grinned at her.

'But if we're going to pull this thing off, Hector,' she went on. 'I'm going to need someone to help me run this operation.'

'Go on?'

'I'm talking senior board-level support.'

'Do you mean . . . *President*?'

'Of course *not*,' Pippa blurted. '*I'll* be the president. You'll be my . . . deputy. How about it?'

'It would be an honour.'

'That's a deal then.'

10.00 P.M.

It's a risk of a commercial undertaking (9)

A NEW ___________

She had written the final cryptic clue on an acetate and projected it onto the wall of the conference suite, and there followed an abrupt silence as the puzzlemakers – many of whom were three sheets to the wind – tried to crack it.

'One last thing . . . as promised.'

With her back to the assembled audience, Pippa paused to take a deep breath. She could feel her pulse running away from her and her legs started to quiver, sending ripples down her sequinned dress. She went to take a last sip of her fizz before realising it was empty. The bottle next to it was drained as well.

It was time to come clean, to reveal the truth about why she'd dragged them here in the first place.

She gestured towards the projected words on the wall. 'Who's solved it, then?'

Six gentlemen raised their hands, then a seventh, who changed his mind and lowered it a few seconds later.

'Help me out, boys,' she said, taking a marker pen and turning her back to them all at the projector. 'Spell it for me, if you will.'

The gentlemen looked cautiously at each other, waiting to see who might show their hand first.'

'A,' Earl called out.

'Correct.'

'D-V,' he continued.

'Very good, Earl.'

The other men joined in with, 'E-N-T-U-R-E.'

It was a classic charade clue. Commercial (referring to an 'AD') and Undertaking (a synonym of 'VENTURE') made up ADVENTURE.

She picked out the *Collins English Dictionary* she'd carried from home in her suitcase and took her time leafing through the pages, angling the book towards the white light coming from the projector.

'"Adventure. Noun. A daring, hazardous undertaking . . ." Are you ever too old for one?' Pippa asked. 'That's a question I've been asking myself these past few weeks. And tonight feels as good a time as any for us to decide . . . together.'

A few people shuffled uncomfortably in their chairs.

'I wanted to make a proposition to you all. None of us are getting any younger, are we? And I'm sure I'm not the only person wondering what retirement will look like. Especially when so many of us aren't married, don't have kids, even live alone . . .'

There were some affirmative grumbles among the audience, which settled Pippa's nerves a little.

'So, I wondered what you made of this place?'

She slapped her hand on the panelled wall behind her, tapped her foot on the vinyl flooring. 'This hotel, Creighton Hall.'

'What do you mean?' Eric asked.

'It's ours if we want it. This could become our new headquarters, our residential home. I've got the deposit in my briefcase upstairs.'

'Pipster,' Earl said. 'What on earth's got into you? Are you drunk?'

'The Barclays want this place sold,' she explained. 'It's a total cash drain, sinking money left, right and centre. Who holidays in Bedfordshire after all?'

'We do apparently,' Eric quipped. 'I might have guessed something was up.'

'If I can secure enough interest,' Pippa said. 'We can take this place off the market first thing in the morning. It can become the Fellowship of Puzzlemaker's first headquarters. Our place to produce our finest work yet. A place for us all to live. To be together.'

'A commune?' Nigel Bentham asked.

'A *utopia*, Mr Bentham. We could corner the market, start churning out puzzles, all while living under the same roof. None of us are getting any younger, are we?' she went on. 'And I don't know about you but . . .' she lowered her voice, as if she didn't want to be heard, 'it terrifies me . . . being on my own, when I'm old.'

Several people in front of her gave small nods of the head. Clearly the prospect of completing the final lap of life alone was something in the back of their minds too.

'But how on earth could we ever afford a place like this?' Geoff the Calculatrix asked, forever crunching the numbers. 'The stamp duty alone, Pip, the upkeep costs. It would cripple us.'

'This house once belonged to my grandparents,' she explained.

'Until it was sold off after the war. When my father died the equity of the sale was placed in a trust fund – for my twenty-first birthday. Presumably they thought I'd have settled down by then, that I'd need a house to raise my family in, but sadly I never did.' Pippa paused, finding herself momentarily choked up. 'Until now that is.'

There was a collective mumbling between the assembled audience.

'I promise we can make it work,' Pippa added. '*I'll* make it work. I will shoulder most of the investment myself, with my inheritance cash. Plus . . . an anonymous donor came forward a few weeks ago.'

Suddenly everyone straightened in their seats.

'Who?' Nancy asked.

Pippa took a breath before answering.

'Our dear Derek.'

There was a collective gasp and people started mumbling to each other.

The truth was the late codebreaker's posthumous grant had given Pippa the endorsement she needed. He had no living relatives so he'd split his considerable assets between three organisations: the GCHQ Charitable Trust, the Bletchley Park Foundation and the Fellowship of Puzzlemakers. Combined with the money Pippa had sitting in the bank, she was certain she could pull it all together.

'My mother died of thrombosis shortly after I was born,' Pippa announced to the group, trying to keep her voice steady. 'I'm not sure if you all know that?'

Several of them shook their heads, even her lodger Hector looked slightly taken aback.

'Not a lot of people do. I tend not to speak about it, but I was sent to live with my Aunt Grace – my father's sister – when I was only a few months old. Grace was a tyrant, a bully. She hated children and wanted nothing to do with me. I was simply a burden to her. It wasn't a happy childhood, and, even when I was just a little girl, I dreamt of the day that I might run a house of my own, and raise a family, where everyone felt loved and cherished. That they would never feel the way I . . .' she tailed off, a lump in her throat.

She looked out at the faces in front of her and felt the most overwhelming sense of fondness, even love, towards them all.

Nancy had got to her feet. 'We *are* a family, aren't we. You've shown me more kindness than my mother ever has.'

'So you're considering it then?' Pippa asked, feeling the words catch in her mouth, the prospect of her friend taking the leap and joining her suddenly overwhelming. As much as she wanted it to happen, Pippa was conscious that Nancy was at a completely different point in her life.

Nancy tipped her head to the ceiling in consideration.

'Don't decide right now, Nance. Take some time to think about it. But what about the rest of you? I can't do it on my own. No man . . . or woman is an island. It's the essence of a commune, isn't it, and fellowship. *To go further, go together*—'

'Count me in!' Hector blurted, with his hand extended stiffly in the air.

Pippa smiled. She appreciated the public voice of support, though of course it was hardly a surprise. But before she could say another word, Geoff Stirrup's hand shot up, followed by Nigel Bentham's and then several other hands began to cautiously sprout upwards until Pippa counted eight people with their arms in the air.

Pippa felt like she might implode on the spot with excitement and then, to her extended delight, Nancy Stone lifted her hand above her head.

'I'm in, too,' her friend said. 'I need a fresh challenge. An excuse to move out of the house. It's exactly what I need.'

'But what about the cab, Nance?' Pippa asked. 'And your mother?'

'In all honesty, I'm starting to lose my love of it,' she answered. 'All that road rage, the misogyny. Plus my mother needs to learn I've got my own mind. I'm not going to live under her thumb forever.'

Pippa felt a lightness in her chest.

Despite the countless glasses of champagne she'd knocked back that evening, she suddenly felt completely clear-headed, as if she could see her entire future. The final act of her life would be shared among the extraordinary people who'd just bravely lifted their hands in support of her idea. The Fellowship would be her swan song.

As she cast her eye across the room, she couldn't help noticing that Earl Vosey had his arms folded tightly in his lap, his gaze lowered to the floor. He looked completely devastated.

Pippa felt an immediate churn of guilt turning her stomach. No sooner had Earl received news that he was going to lose his wife, then Pippa was announcing that she was taking his beloved puzzle club away from him too. Her life, and the mazemaker's, were about to go in very different directions.

Chapter Nineteen

'I'm off!' Clayton shouted from the staircase.

Earlier that day he'd asked Earl to let the rest of the Fellowship know what Pippa had left behind for him – and that he was taking the first steps on her meticulously planned adventure.

Now, everyone had come to wave him off. Even Dame Klotski seemed to have got wind of the news, padding her way through the crowd and nudging against his shins.

'Goodbye, Klotty,' Clayton said.

He bent down to stroke his doddery cat behind the ears and her tail instantly curled at the tip, becoming a question mark above her.

'I'll be back soon. It's just a little holiday.'

Please don't die before I get back.

Clayton scooped her up and she extended her body into his, lifting her stiff limbs gaily in the air.

'You're off then, son?' Earl asked, appearing in front of him. 'You're really doing it?'

Clayton put the cat down. He nodded, trying to look casual about the whole thing with his hands slipped inside his pockets.

Earl looked at him a long moment, then his arms were out and he was grabbing him, clamping him to his chest. 'That's m'boy,' he said softly into his ear. 'I'm sure whatever Pip has to share with you, there's a good reason she didn't tell you before.'

Clayton was surprised at how tightly his old friend's grasp was, how long it took before he was finally released.

'I'll only be gone a few days, Earl. You'll barely notice I'm away.'

He was saying this to the mazemaker but also to himself. *It will be fine*, he was saying. *There's nothing to worry about at all. Everything is going to be absolutely fine.*

Hector rattled his van keys impatiently. 'We should get going, if you want to catch that train.'

Clayton nodded, then picked up his case.

The clapped-out yellow campervan had been the Fellowship's main mode of transport for as long as he could remember. Hector insisted on driving everywhere in it, the van operating like a complimentary shuttle bus to all the residents' usual haunts – the chemist, the surgery and the hairdresser – at least a couple of times a week. Hector had even extended his taxi service to driving a teenage Clayton to school, much to the derision of some of his peers, who nicknamed it the banana bus. Yet another reason he'd opted for a home education in the run-up to his GCSEs.

'Call us if you get into any bother,' Geoff said. 'You know where we are.'

Clayton smiled, then bowed his head, not wanting to read their expressions or let them catch his.

'I hope you find whatever you're looking for,' Jean said, her head tipped sympathetically to one side. 'We all do.'

'Godspeed!' Nigel added, slapping him on the back.

Clayton passed through the enormous arched wooden door he had arrived at all those years ago and made his way down the steps with an increasing sense that whatever he was about to uncover, whatever he was about to learn about his arrival all those years ago, about the people or person who abandoned him, it was unlikely he would return feeling the same about himself, or the place he was leaving behind.

From the passenger seat, Clayton watched Hector insert his fingers into a pair of leather driving gloves behind the wheel.

In the rear-view mirror, he could make out various faces by the front door. Jean was waving manically with both hands above her head as if she might never see him again. The sight of it made Clayton turn away, to look into the footwell of the car.

It was then that he spotted the bundled object beneath his feet, wrapped in a tea towel.

'What's this?'

Hector switched on the ignition and glanced over at where he was pointing. 'Oh, that's just something we thought you might like to take with you.' He slipped into first and they manoeuvred across the gravel drive.

Clayton picked up the mysterious object at his feet, unfolding the towel in his lap to peek at the item inside.

It was a beautiful miniaturised hourglass suspended in a wooden cage – one of the bespoke pieces he'd seen Hector working on the other day.

'Thank you,' he said hesitantly, unsure of its significance but touched all the same.

It was only as they made their way through the wrought-iron gates and out onto the main road that Clayton realised what he had in his hands.

The grains of sand were coarser than usual, darker than they normally used – charcoal in colour, almost black.

And then he realised. It wasn't sand at all. It was ashes.

'Pippa always gave us her time . . .' Hector remarked beside him. 'So it felt appropriate. We got a few hours out of her in the end . . .'

Clayton nodded, lost for words.

'. . . Everyone's got twenty minutes each.'

He rotated the hourglass and watched the tiny particles funnel through, a constant steady stream of Pippa counting him down.

As Creighton receded from view and the van streaked through the winding country lanes, he felt a surge of something, a bolt of energy pulsing through his body. So he wasn't going to be travelling alone after all.

PART TWO

SOLVE THE MAZE TO REVEAL THE MESSAGE

Chapter Twenty

TEN YEARS LATER
THE FELLOWSHIP OF PUZZLEMAKERS
TUESDAY, 8TH JANUARY, 1991

Creighton Hall, now officially listed in the Yellow Pages as *the headquarters of the Fellowship of Puzzlemakers, est. 1979*, was bathed in a watery pool of mid-winter light.

It was a Tuesday morning, a few minutes past nine, and Pippa was outside, tucked inside the telephone box in the walled garden, a low blanket of milky fog surrounding her, as if she were suspended in a cloud.

The trouble with the phone inside the house was the signal. The wood-panelled, lead-lined walls of the old house didn't help, but the actual positioning of the former rectory – in a clearing of the Forest of Marston Vale – meant that the line was usually disturbed. A tête-à-tête on the house landline was, for this reason, a stimulating auditory puzzle in itself.

And so it was here, tucked in a quiet corner of the grounds, that Pippa liked to make her calls.

She removed the receiver briefly from her ear and could just catch the familiar bumblebee-like hum of the machines in the workshop and printing room opposite. Through the glass panes of the red antique booth she smiled towards the house and various outbuildings, comforted by the thought of everyone inside, busying themselves with their various puzzle projects: Geoff Stirrup alone in his study quietly constructing his calcudokus and jigsums to the sounds of Bach on his Walkman; Hector tucked away in his treetop studio painting his latest jigsaw collection based on a series of iconic European cityscapes, entitled *Continental Scenes: Cities of Dreams*; Nancy in a cloud of cigarette smoke setting questions for her weekly quiz at the Old Queen's Head. She'd been a tad distracted with her pub-quizzing duties recently, as she was in the process of delivering a new general-knowledge game: Quizioms. It was an exciting collaboration with Jonty Entwistle, one of the Fellowship's newest recruits. Jonty was a retired lexicographer, or dictionary compiler. He and Nancy had become close companions, despite the fact there was twenty-five years between them. Together they were co-devising a game that tested the players' ability to identity obscure idioms and adages from plain gobbledygook.

'Tell me, Earl,' Pippa said into the receiver. 'Do you still enjoy a Moscow Mule?'

There was a small laugh down the line. 'Do you know . . . I haven't had a cocktail in years.'

The routine phone chats to Earl on Tuesday and Friday mornings had started around the time his wife passed, eight months earlier. Pippa had grown concerned her friend was losing his usual joie de vivre.

'Well, I'll soon see to that. We'll get the bar fully stocked ready for your arrival.'

'Oh, please don't go to any bother, really I insist—'

'Not at all! I actually quite fancy one myself.'

Pippa couldn't wait to welcome him. It had become a comforting ritual in her week, retreating to the garden with her morning tea and, sometimes, a hot water bottle tucked under her coat to call her friend.

Inside the booth, there was a pen dangling by a piece of string, some notepaper, and, for extra authenticity, someone had gone to the trouble of affixing stickers with details of some local sex workers. Hector, in his typical humourless way, had attempted to tear them off, of course, but the remnants of one advertisement remained and the name *Miss Behavin'*, the words *Busty Blonde Bitch* and a pair of exposed nipples were still there for all to see.

'We're so looking forward to welcoming you,' Pippa said, beaming at the enormous, faded breasts in front of her. 'Even if it is just for a few days. I bet you won't recognise the place.' She tugged at the coiled cord of the phone, releasing a kink. 'Earl, You are going to come, aren't you?'

There was silence down the receiver.

'You're not going to change your mind again?'

The mazemaker cleared his throat and, in a low, furtive voice, said, 'I've already packed my case, Pip. I've set the lights on timers, cancelled the papers. I'll be there tomorrow, don't you worry.'

'Oh, *smashing*.'

Pippa let out a breath. She was beginning to fear the man was becoming a recluse.

'A change of scene will do me good,' he added. 'You're right. As usual.'

After the call, Pippa ambled back to the house with a spring in her step, feeling something warm rise inside her, despite the crisp air. A chat with Earl always did that to her, even when he wasn't feeling on top of the world.

The lawn was tipped with frost and crunched beneath her slippers. Climbing the steps to the terrace, she noticed the Rebus suite – a vacant bedroom on the third floor Pippa had earmarked for their guest – had both its windows flung open. There was a sheepskin rug draped over the ornamental iron balconette, and then, from nowhere, Angel appeared, beating it over the railings with a hockey stick.

Miss Webster – the walking disaster of a housekeeper – had been left behind by her erstwhile employers like a forgotten box in the attic.

Without the heart to let her go, Pippa had half expected, hoped even, for the young lady – now in her early thirties – to take the initiative and leave by her own accord, but instead she had remained firmly in position. It left Pippa, as an ardent feminist, and Angel's reluctant employer, somewhat conflicted. She couldn't help wondering if there was another profession she'd be better suited to, another life she could be living.

She waved at her from the terrace, but Angel was oblivious, striking the white oval of wool as if the poor creature was still alive and trying to break into the room.

At the breakfast table a short while later, Pippa helped herself to the last two boiled eggs in the pan marked *semi-soft*.

'Morning, Hector.'

The jigsaw artist lifted his hand at her, a triangle of toast between his teeth. It was unusual to see him at this hour. Usually he'd be up at the crack of dawn and would take a cup of tea and rack of toast with him up to his garden studio. Pippa quietly admired the man's tenacity, his commitment to his craft. She would often remind herself that, without the regular income that was generated by his ever-expanding jigsaw range, the Fellowship finances would be even more precarious than they already were.

'Another chilly one,' he remarked.

Pippa offered something about the sky being clear enough that it would soon warm up. She settled herself at the table, broke the lid off her first egg.

As well as being her favourite meal of the day, it was a particularly enjoyable word to clue. 'Jumbled RAF basket meal', for example.

'Jumbled' being the indicator word to unscramble the next part of the clue – 'RAF basket' – which was, of course, an anagram of a 'meal'.

'Breakfast'.

There was something about the ritual of a leisurely morning feast – and especially eggs, which Pippa had always thought of as brain food – that made her heart lift.

As far as she was concerned, it was something people didn't do enough of: to take a few moments to yourself, when your mind was at its clearest. To reflect on the endless possibilities of the day stretched before you. To spoil yourself before the world spoiled you. She swore by it.

Pippa snapped open *The Times* in front of her. Tuesday's grid was compiled by Hypobulia (the alias of Colonel Sedgewick – former Chairman of the Illustrious Society of Eccentrics) whom she'd always admired. He was particularly deft with his spoonerisms.

'Four across,' she called out. '"Footwear for pack animals." Five.'

She lowered the paper slightly to see Hector's face furrowed in concentration.

She had the answer already – of course she had – but she wanted to give Hector a chance. He had his head angled towards the window, where two blue tits were jostling for the excess crusts left on the sill. He opened his mouth before closing it again, just as there was a clattering sound in the scullery next door.

Nancy appeared, poking her head through the serving hatch, a cigarette hanging out her mouth. '*Mules*,' she answered, then slapped the little window closed.

Hector tutted. 'Oh, for crying out loud. I could have easily got that!'

Pippa swallowed a smile.

She pencilled the word into the grid, trying to pick the next easiest clue so as not to irk the man any further.

Three dips into her second yolk and four clues later, Pippa pushed her chair out from the table and dashed towards the landing. She'd just remembered their housekeeper upstairs, preparing Earl's room, and dreaded to think what she was doing up there.

Standing in the threshold of the Rebus suite moments later, still chewing the last of her toasted soldiers, Pippa was lost for words.

The room was unrecognisable.

The walls – once a perfectly pleasant sage green – were now the colour of Colman's mustard.

'You've painted the room?'

Angel, hunched over on all fours, turned and nodded gleefully.

'But . . .'

'You said the man needed to recharge,' Angel replied. 'To have his spirits lifted?'

'Well yes, but . . .'

Angel was dabbing the floor liberally with Shake n' Vac, Tropical Breeze. She paused, looking at her expectantly, as if wondering what exactly the issue was.

Pippa took a deep breath. 'A quick run round with the Henry and some fresh sheets would've done the job.'

Angel shook her head. 'Yellow – Mrs Allsbrook – is the colour of optimism and happiness. It encourages mental function, freedom to be oneself.'

'Is that right—'

'It clarifies your spirit, inspires the soul.'

'Does it now.'

The housekeeper nodded cheerily. 'Just what this chap needs, by the sounds of things.' She heaved herself from the floor with a grunt.

In a strange way, Pippa couldn't help admiring the woman. She was a rare bird, a free spirit, lived life entirely by her own rules – not unlike a younger version of herself in fact. But on a day-to-day level, there was no denying it. Angel was a nightmare.

'Who is this guy anyway?'

Pippa waved her hand in front of her. 'Oh, just an old friend from the pub days.'

The corners of Angel's mouth had lifted into a smirk.

'What is it, dear?'

Angel gestured somewhere above Pippa's head. 'I like your new hair.'

Pippa, immediately self-conscious of her newly set, voluminous perm, folded her hand against the side of her head. It was about time she had a new look.

'Thank you,' she replied, turning to face the other side of the room.

From the four posts of the solid mahogany bed hung a series of Angel's handmade dreamcatchers – odd feathery things that had started to pop up all over the place. She crafted them from old embroidery hoops and decorated them with purple amethyst crystals mail-ordered from America. They were meant to reduce negative energy influences and induce a deeper sleep, apparently.

'And is the new hair-do for our guest?' Angel asked, making

a circular gesture with her finger around Pippa's head. 'It suits you, I think.'

'Earl's wife passed last summer,' Pippa explained, feeling oddly defensive. 'We're simply offering him some respite, Angel, a chance to consider his future—'

'With us?'

Pippa pretended she hadn't heard.

She turned to run her hand across the top of the antique pine drawers. Covered in dust, just as she'd predicted.

'I trust everything is to your satisfaction?' Angel asked, untying the strings of her apron, looking very pleased with herself.

'Yes,' Pippa replied, smiling thinly at the woman. 'Thank you, dear. You've done more than enough.'

Chapter Twenty-One

19			

YOU MAY HAVE TWO BEFORE NOON (4)

Clayton had always been a stress eater. After arriving at the Lancaster Court Hotel too late to properly digest his dinner, he'd gone to bed without having a proper meal – just a packet of crisps and a cereal bar he'd brought from home.

He'd woken ravenous.

Standing in line at the hotel's dining room for breakfast, having reluctantly added the £19.99 surcharge to his room, he watched the man behind the egg station in a ludicrous toque hat and chef whites prepare his made-to-order breakfast.

The solution to Pippa's second clue had made him smile.

Eggs.

She was always going on at him, telling him he should make time for breakfast. 'To spoil yourself, before the world spoils you,' she used to say.

Moments earlier, when the chef – a rather severe, unsmiling chap – had asked how he'd wanted his eggs, Clayton had struggled to decide. Usually it was *him* cooking the eggs and rarely did he bother making them for himself. So in an unusual display of impulsion, he'd asked the chef for all three. He hoped the man wouldn't judge, but, really, when was he going to get this chance again?

Clayton swallowed a yawn as the chap made a start on his fried egg.

He'd barely slept all night, which wasn't like him, and the quivery, twisting sensation in his stomach wasn't just hunger.

Today was the day.

He was going to pay a visit to the mysterious Nancy Stone, to find out what role she played in his story, whether it was her who'd left him at the door of the Fellowship all those years ago.

The thought of it made him grip the edge of the egg station.

'Excellent job,' he commented, as the chef handed him the warmed plate with all the charm of a verruca. 'Very grateful. That will definitely keep me going.'

Clayton picked his way across the dining room to a small table in the corner set for one, balancing on his tray the three eggs, plus a pot of natural yoghurt, a shot glass of grapefruit juice, and a peculiar-looking slice of rubbery cheese that he'd regretted as soon as he'd picked it up but didn't feel he could put back.

He'd chosen this particular hotel because it was a stone's throw from Hyde Park, which in itself wasn't a million miles from Nancy's address.

To get there, he didn't even need to jump on the Underground – which he always found a bit stressful – just walk along the Regent's Canal, three quarters of a mile or so.

Tucking into his feast, Clayton realised he felt guilty at the luxury of it all. Not just the buffet breakfast – which was delicious – but all the endless possibilities of how he might spend some time in London. He couldn't remember when he'd last had a couple of days to himself, time to spend so selfishly, devoid of any responsibilities or commitments to others.

He was wondering about ringing home to check in on everyone, when his phone chimed a cheerful marimba melody in his pocket.

> DeaR ClaY HOW RU hAVU SEEN NANC YeT NE THING SHE REMeMBER? HOPE U R HAVIN GR8 HOL/ D On'T 4GET 2 CALL IFU GET IN2 NE BOTHER ! V BEST WIshES. EARL

Earl's Motorola V220 handset had no touch screen, but instead those big, rubberised buttons designed for old, arthritic hands. Clayton had taken him to Argos to buy the device a few years ago, taught him to send an SMS message, showing him how to jab the keys in the correct sequence in order to select the desired letters. Earl had quickly got to grips with the basic concept, likening the tap-tap-tapping of buttons to composing Morse code. His texts certainly had a ring of encryption about them, especially when he wasn't wearing his readers.

An hour later and having freshened up in his room and responded to Earl –

> Morning! All good here. The room is clean and breakfast hearty. No need to worry. Heading to Mrs S. now actually. My love to everyone x

– Clayton had pushed his way through the revolving door of the hotel, out into the thick, polluted air of central London.

He felt at once overwhelmed and sick with too much of everything: eggs and nerves and the noise of the city. As he made his way northwards, winding his way through the congested streets, it wasn't long before he started to sweat – too warm under his cagoule, thick Aran knit and cotton shirt. He was just removing the waterproof, tying it around his waist, when a bright red double-decker bus screeched past and he had to stop himself from flattening his body against the side of a nearby building.

Once he'd connected to the towpath, he assumed things would become less stressful, but he kept having to stop to allow cyclists to pass – all of whom whizzed by in their Lycra without so much as a thanks – so it wasn't the pleasant amble he'd imagined but more like taking a stroll down the middle of the Tour de France.

He was also disappointed to find the water strewn with bits of litter, covered in a luminous-green slime and smelling sulphurous, like dank drains. He'd imagined it being quaint, like in Hector's jigsaw puzzle (*#018 - A Lock to Like: Little Venice, London*) but it was nothing like his painting at all.

Finally exiting the towpath, Clayton found himself pulling up a few streets from where he needed to turn off for Nancy's.

Eventually, just half a mile from his destination, he made a slight detour into a nearby gated square for a sit down.

He just wanted to take a moment. To think about whether this next step was definitely something he wanted to do. Because once the door opened, he knew there would be no going back.

He looked at the two benches immediately in front of him. A sweet older-looking lady – in her seventies or so – was having her lunch. He launched himself towards her.

She looked at him with panicked eyes.

'Sorry, didn't mean to startle you. You don't mind if I sit down?'

She nodded, but the look on her face suggested she wasn't so sure. She budged up to the very end of the bench, as if Clayton wasn't the eleven-stone waif of a man that he was, but someone five times his size.

Clayton took a deep breath as he reclined in the seat.

It was gorgeous out – a balmy, blue-skied day – and he tipped his head to the midday sun trying to calm himself. He glanced at the lady beside him.

She had a Tupperware box in her lap and her hand was inside a packet of Mini Cheddars. She was wearing a red polka-dot silk scarf tied around her hair to make a hood. At her feet, a scrappy Yorkshire terrier with a pink bow in its hair was sitting on its haunches, snarling at him.

The lady soon began stuffing her crusts inside her lunch-box.

'Oh,' Clayton said. 'Don't feel you have to go.'

The lady was already halfway out of her seat. She looked him up and down, giving him the once-over, then let out a sigh. 'It's not like I have anywhere to be, I suppose.'

She slumped back into her seat and Clayton smiled at her, looking ahead at group of hooded young men on bikes who were doing wheelies and blasting angry music from a speaker.

'It's trying to rain,' the lady declared, almost excitedly.

Funnily enough, a cloud had appeared above them, though nothing serious.

The lady angled her nose towards the sky, as if she could smell it. 'Just you wait. Any second now. I can feel it coming . . .'

'Oh, I think we'll be all right,' Clayton replied. 'Do you have far to go if we get caught?'

'Up there,' she answered, pointing to a rather squalid high-rise block towering over the gated square; a grey, joyless abomination of a building with tiny cell-like windows.

He forced a smile at the place. 'Well, at least you haven't got far to walk. Do you come here often?'

'Every day,' she answered. 'Ever since he died.' She pointed to the memorial plaque on the bench, stroking her hand gently along the faint inscription.

IN MEMORY OF LEONARD MILLINGTON

HE LOVED HAVING A PACKED LUNCH HERE.

1939–2015

'Oh, I'm sorry,' Clayton said, suddenly sitting upright.

The woman had draped her arm along the top of the bench as if she were embracing the invisible man between them.

'It must be nice, though,' he added. 'Having somewhere to come and remember him?'

The woman nodded, smiling wistfully ahead.

Clayton tried to do the maths – her husband must have been seventy-six, seventy-seven years old? No age at all, really.

'The thing is, young man . . .' She was sitting so close now that he caught the scent of her heady perfume. It was synthetic flowers, like the air freshener in the loo at home. 'You get to this point in your life and, if you're not careful, all the people you've ever known have either drifted away, gone doolally, or they've died. Now my Len's gone I'm completely alone. I'm invisible to the world. When you came over to me just then, I almost couldn't believe it. You start to wonder if you actually exist. Whether people can still see you. Sorry if I'm rabbiting . . .'

Clayton felt a lump in his throat and tried to swallow it.

'Do you know . . .' she went on, lowering her voice to almost a whisper. 'I ring the speaking clock sometimes, just to hear a voice.'

Clayton's insides ached. 'I'm sorry to hear that.'

'I never thought it would come to this, but then who would? I suppose that's what happens when you haven't got family, you know. Not that you've got anything to worry about, of course. Your whole life is ahead of you.'

He knew the woman was desperate to talk, but he wished she would change the subject.

'It's my birthday tomorrow . . .' she explained, 'and I've got no one to celebrate with. I'll be eighty . . .'

Clayton adjusted himself in the seat.

'I certainly don't feel eighty,' she continued. 'I still feel young, like a thirty-year-old. Getting older without getting old. Now that's the secret. You must think I'm mad!'

'No . . .' Clayton replied.

She was just trying to expend as many words as she could while she had the chance. They were tripping off her tongue as if they might be her last. '. . . No, I don't think you're mad at all, actually. It doesn't matter how old you are, does it? Bodies age, but souls don't.'

She tilted her head, as if she were examining him in a new light. 'Who taught you that?'

'It's something I've always known, growing up.'

'Well, anyway,' she concluded. 'Never get old, my friend. I wouldn't wish it on my worst enemy.'

He'd seen the reports on the news, of course, read the headlines in the papers about the loneliness epidemic, but he'd never actually met anyone who suffered from social isolation themselves. That was what the commune stood for, after all. Fellowship.

'My name's Clayton, by the way. Clayton Stumper.'

'Cilla,' she declared, taking Clayton's hand when he offered it. 'Cilla Millington.'

'It was lovely to meet you, Cilla. I'm sorry I have to head off.

I've got to go and visit a lady who lives not a million miles from here.' He glanced over his shoulder, trying to get his bearings. He could check on his phone, but he had memorised the route in his head before he'd set off and he'd soon find the way.

'You're not turning up empty-handed, I hope.'

'Excuse me?' he asked.

'You're going to someone's house and you haven't even got a bunch of flowers.'

'Oh . . . yes.'

She was right of course. He didn't think flowers were appropriate, but he should take something with him.

'Good idea, Cilla. I'll pick up something en route.'

She smiled as he put his jacket on, watching him with a curious look in her eye. 'I can't say I've met a Stumper before,' she said. 'Where does it come from?'

Clayton wanted to laugh. 'Your guess is as good as mine, Cilla.'

'You mean you don't know?'

'I haven't a clue!'

And with that the two of them laughed.

He made his goodbyes, turned and headed in the direction of Nancy Stone's house, determined to finally find out.

Chapter Twenty-Two

THE FELLOWSHIP OF PUZZLEMAKERS WEDNESDAY, 9TH JANUARY, 1991

Angel's Vauxhall Cavalier swung round on the gravel shortly after four o'clock and Pippa darted straight to the front door to welcome their special guest.

Through the letterbox she could just make the mazemaker out.

She hadn't seen Earl in ten years and for a moment or two, as she watched him haul himself from the passenger side of the car, then lift a battered leather duffle bag from the boot, she wondered if there'd been some dreadful mix-up and Angel had collected the wrong passenger entirely.

The man she had always had such a hankering for, the chivalrous and smart and inexplicably handsome Mr Vosey, was surely not this fellow making his way towards the house with what appeared to be a full, grizzled, grey beard. The way he carried himself on the short walk across the gravel, it was as if he was missing a piece of himself. But as he padded across the gravel and up the steps, she caught the trademark brown sheepskin jacket, a flash of his long hair catching in the mid-afternoon light, and she knew.

Earl Vosey – *Easy Lover* himself – was back.

Clutching the door handle, Pippa felt a coil of unexpected nerves twist through her body. A decade ago she'd invited everyone to what was then a struggling hotel and now she had another secret motive up her sleeve. A proposition she couldn't wait to put to Earl. She was at it all over again.

The truth was, they needed Earl, as much as he needed them.

The Fellowship – as a commercial enterprise – had been operating at a fairly modest level ever since it had been established, taking moderate but regular sums for their freelance work (the paper-based puzzles they delivered to national newspapers and magazines year-round) and more substantial royalties for their licensed retail output – but mazes were big money, especially if they could encourage Earl to start constructing for the country houses again. They could clean up.

'Mr Vosey,' she declared. 'Back at last.'

She opened her arms and they embraced while Angel stood to the side eyeing them both. Pippa inhaled the familiar, woody aroma of his cologne, and while they had their arms around each other, she couldn't help feeling the suede of Earl's jacket, almost patting him down to check what was left of the man inside. He was slimmer than she remembered.

'New hair?' he asked.

Pippa touched the side of her head self-consciously. 'Oh . . . I've had this a little while . . .'

He clutched her elbows. 'Well, you look as lovely as ever.'

'Thank you,' she replied, conscious her cheeks were colouring and Angel was holding in a laugh.

'And you're looking very . . .' She lowered the spectacles perched on her head to get a better look at the man. '*Well*,' she managed.

He grinned thinly. 'Oh, I don't know about that.'

'Well, anyway, welcome to the Fellowship. Or welcome *back*, I should say.' She turned sharply into the house. 'Come in, come in,' she said, more as an order than an invite, and Earl, insisting Angel go ahead of him, trailed the ladies inside, tripping on the step and scuffing the top of his scalp on the door frame.

'Mind your head now.'

Earl spent the next quarter of an hour being bombarded by everyone.

Martin Dudeney and Eric Stoppard cornered him first in the billiards room, offering awkward hugs and extending their condolences, then Geoff Stirrup appeared, issuing a manly slap to Earl's back and asking how he was holding up, while Nancy was so giddy with excitement, she squeezed him like a soft toy. Of course there were others who didn't know Earl from the pub days, but were equally pleased to welcome the mazemaker, given his reputation.

He was the Fellowship's special guest of honour. For two nights only. Or so Pippa had led the residents to believe. If she had anything to do with it, they'd all be seeing a lot more of the man in the coming months.

'Let me show you to your room,' she suggested, peeling him away from the fawning crowd.

She pushed the secret door concealed within the William Morris wallpaper of the parlour and they climbed the carpeted steps towards the living quarters. There were a few ground-floor rooms available for those who couldn't hack the stairs, but Pippa was determined to keep her suite on the third floor, even when in years to come her creaking joints would think otherwise. She knew this was a mark of her stubbornness, her refusal to let her age dictate how she lived, but she couldn't see that ever changing.

Earl heaved his bag up the steps behind her, all the way to the third floor, pausing occasionally to catch his breath.

'You all right back there, dear?'

'How many more stairs, Pip?'

'Oh, just a couple.' Earl's huffing-and-puffing had reached marathon levels when a minute later, she announced, 'Here we are. I'm down there by the way.' She gestured to the bedroom along the hall with its engraved plaque on the door: *Alphabetibox Suite*. 'And Hector is opposite . . . in Whimsies.'

The name was in reference to the whimsy jigsaws he'd become known for in recent years, made up of uniquely shaped pieces. A series of interlocking leaves in a blustery autumn park scene, for example.

'How's he doing anyway?'

'Oh, he's ticking along just fine,' Pippa answered, leading him down the hall. 'In fact, he's the perfect deputy, I must say. We'd all be lost without him. And his beloved jigsaws.'

It was true. Not only were the thousand-piece puzzles that

Hector created by far the Fellowship's biggest seller, it was his impeccable work in the back office that they also relied on.

While Pippa oversaw the Fellowship's product development, the licencing and finances and so forth, it was Hector who took care of the day-to-day stuff – tracking orders, the deliveries and stock fulfilment. Everything that actually kept the place going but bored Pippa to tears.

'You know he's got his own assistant now?' she explained. 'Angel – the housekeeper – is his apprentice? She cleans his palettes, helps stretch his canvases in the studio outside?'

'No?'

Pippa nodded. 'You should have heard the fuss he made when I floated the idea.'

Earl scoffed. 'I bet.'

'The thing is, I had to distract her with *something* . . . to save her running amok in the house.'

Outside the Rebus suite, she handed Earl his key, dangling on a miniaturised version of their Sudokube, another of their popular lines, available from all good stockists.

'Crikey,' he said, as he opened the door. 'What is that *smell*?'

Pippa found herself shielding her mouth with her cardigan sleeve. It reeked like a dank old church. She followed him inside and headed straight to the window. 'That'll be Angel's incense. She's mad for it . . . and assumes we all are too. Apologies.'

Moments later, perched on the end of the bed waiting for the air to clear, Pippa watched Earl unpack his things, feeling entirely at ease in his close company, despite their many years apart.

'I'm pleased you made it here anyway . . .' she announced, twisting a pearl on her necklace between her fingers. 'I know it's not been easy, since you lost . . . your wife.'

Earl had a pair of grey underpants in his hands as he turned. He looked completely diminished, a shadow of himself.

'I've never told anyone this,' he replied softly. 'But there was a time, in the days and weeks after she passed, when I wasn't sure if I could . . . go on.'

'Oh, Earl.'

'I even considered . . . you know . . .'

The words trailed to nothing but the way his eyes dropped helplessly to the floor gave Pippa the answer, and made her stomach churn.

'Gosh. I wish you'd said something.'

She wanted to swoop him up there and then, to tell him everything was going to be all right, that she would make sure nothing like that ever entered his head again.

After Rosa's diagnosis, the couple had enjoyed ten years together. When she eventually passed away a few months ago doctors said it was miraculous how she'd managed to fight it for so long, though Earl surely could think of another word.

'It was shattering,' he announced, staring vacantly at nothing. 'Just watching my future smash into pieces like that. I'd started to get my head round the fact I wasn't going to become a father, that one day I'd become a widow. But after Rosa died, a part of me died too. I didn't know who I was anymore.'

'You will always be Rosa's husband,' Pippa answered without hesitation. 'And the finest mazemaker in the land, as far as I'm concerned.'

Earl gave a small grin.

'I would have loved a child too,' she heard herself say. And now it's too late, she thought, feeling desperately sad all of a sudden.

'. . . I suppose I've just never been lucky enough to meet anyone—'

'Or someone wasn't lucky enough to meet *you*. That's another way of looking at it.'

She grinned.

There was a silence that hung heavily between them.

Pippa had just shared something she didn't like to admit to herself, let alone anyone else, and she couldn't help but feel a trifle awkward.

She almost wanted to pluck the words from the air and put them back into her mouth and pretend the whole conversation had never happened.

'I've never told anyone that before either,' she added. 'Not a single soul.'

Earl gave a grateful nod.

'I can't say I'm surprised,' Earl said. 'You've always had a caring streak.'

Pippa beamed, pleased that he'd noticed.

'Just because I've never washed a man's clothes,' she announced, 'doesn't mean I wouldn't make a terrific mother.'

He was looking at her differently. She was sure of it. His head tilted slightly to one side as if it was the first time he'd laid eyes on her.

'Still, there's no point dwelling on the past, is there?' she added, pushing herself up from the bed, trying to look chipper. 'We should live for the present, Earl. Who knows what's around the corner. Adventures are to the adventurous, and all that.'

Earl's eyes narrowed on her. 'What's that supposed to mean?'

'Oh, nothing,' she replied breezily. 'You must be starving. Shall we have a spot of something downstairs?'

As they entered the conservatory for Earl's welcome afternoon tea, Hector was already at the window table, as planned.

'Hector, you remember Earl.'

'Mr Vosey,' Hector said, offering his hand like an insurance salesman over the starched white cloth. 'Pleasure to see you again. And please accept my condolences.'

Earl smiled gratefully. 'It's very nice to be back. I can't believe what you've done with the place.'

First, Pippa had shown him all the communal rooms, then led him outside to Hector's treetop art studio, followed by the printer room and workshop where they'd recently had a series of coil-binding machines fitted, an engine-fuelled lathe, and a special die-cutting machine so they could print and dice up the jigsaws rather than subcontracting the work out.

'I believe Angel's prepared a little something for us,' Pippa announced. 'Speak of the devil . . .'

The housekeeper emerged through the swinging service doors,

pushing a heavily loaded cocktail trolley towards them at breakneck speed. It jangled as she navigated around all the spare tables.

'What's all this then?' Earl asked, as Angel pulled up beside them. She handed out the cocktails, which were sitting on top of the trolley, already made. A simple tray would have sufficed, Pippa thought.

'It's not a Moscow Mule?'

She nodded at their guest.

'You remembered?'

How could she forget.

'Are the others not joining us?' Earl asked, looking around at all the spare tables as he took a sip.

'We thought not,' Pippa answered swiftly. 'There'll be plenty of time to catch up with everyone. But it's just the three of us for now. And our housekeeper, Angel, of course.'

'Oh, yes,' Earl replied, and they all watched Angel retrace her journey back to the bar with the trolley. 'She seems quite a . . . character.'

Pippa made a face. 'You know she's into tarot cards, spirituality, that sort of thing?' She carries all these crystals in her pockets. They're meant to bring her good fortune. No sign yet.'

Earl laughed.

'The trouble is,' Pippa added, 'for someone who's meant to help us, she creates an awful lot of work—'

'She just needs very clear instructions,' Hector said. 'We can't accuse her of not trying.'

'You're right.' Pippa relented. 'It's just, sometimes I wish she'd try . . . a little less.'

Once they'd all smothered their scones in seedless raspberry jam and clotted cream and had the necessary debate about which should be applied first, Pippa glanced at Hector – who had just taken a bite of a cucumber sandwich – and nudged him with the heel of her shoe.

'Mr Vosey,' he began, in a tone that made Earl sit a little taller in his seat. 'We were rather hoping you might . . . consider something for us.'

'Oh?' Earl scraped the excess cream from his knife against the plate.

'We wondered if you might be up for a challenge.'

'A . . . *challenge*?'

'We'd like to commission you,' Pippa said. 'To build your biggest, most elaborate garden maze yet.'

He blinked at them both.

'There's acres of lawn outside, Earl. I've already staked out a section for you—'

'But, Pip, I've *retired*.'

'Oh, I know, but . . .' Pippa's heart sank as she realised how sapped Earl looked, how jaded he sounded.

The plan she'd discussed with Hector was to entice Earl with a project he could get his teeth into, then see if he might consider joining them, as a full-time resident.

Earl dabbed his napkin on his lips. 'You know I don't muck around with games anymore. I'm too old for all that nonsense. No offence or anything.'

Pippa allowed the remark to go straight over her head. She knew he didn't really mean it.

'Well, don't decide just yet,' she replied brightly, reaching for the jam. 'Puzzles are in the air here, don't forget. I'm sure the muse will return once you've spent a few days with us. Just you wait.'

Earl didn't look so sure, and Hector's disappointment was written all over his face, but Pippa wasn't worried at all. Give it a couple of days, she thought, then you'll find your spark again. We'll get the old mazemaker back. Earl would find himself again. She was certain of it.

Chapter Twenty-Three

1									

ONE MAY TURN UP TO PUT ONE IN (10)

Clayton was a few hundred yards from Nancy's, passing a parade of shuttered shops along the busy Harrow Road, when a lorry hurtled past at such speed the tailwind almost blew him sideways.

After his chat with Cilla in the park, he was beginning to feel his nerves settle. Plus, he'd followed her advice and popped into a corner shop so he didn't turn up empty-handed. He'd settled on a box of York Fruits – the crème de la crème of fruit jellies – which he was sure anyone would be grateful for.

Turning onto Cheviot Street, Clayton was comforted by how quaint it was, how beautifully maintained, with tall sycamore trees lining both sides of the road. The houses – all Victorian terrace cottages – were relatively small but perfectly proportioned with stucco brickwork and shuttered sash windows. Away from the bustle of the main road, the area had a safe, neighbourly feel.

He pulled out the index card from Pippa's Rolodex to check, once again, that he had Nancy's correct address, before he approached.

She lived at Number Thirty-One.

He crossed to the side of the street with all the odd numbers and as he walked along the pavement, his heartbeat matching his steps, he studied each house he passed. Number Twenty-Five was clearly a young family's home, with children's drawings in the front window and a pink plastic trike in the garden. Number Twenty-Seven had beautiful purple wisteria framing the porch. Number Twenty-Nine had all its shutters drawn and a *BEWARE OF THE DOG* sign on the gate. And then he was outside Thirty-One.

The light was on upstairs.

Clayton felt dizzy all of a sudden.

He rested his hand on the wheelie bin outside, taking a few steadying breaths as he glanced towards the house.

Nancy's door wasn't like the others on the street, which were mostly painted white or cream or grey. Nancy's door was pillar-box red, just like the telephone box at home.

He let himself through the tiny iron gate. It squeaked as he pushed it closed, setting off the dog next door. A brown bear of a German Shepherd leaped at the window, its jaws wide open, slobbering the glass.

Clayton's hands were shaking so much, the pressure he put on the bell wasn't enough to make it ring and he had to jab at it three times until it sounded.

A few seconds later and there was the noise of someone moving inside.

Clayton pressed his lips into a friendly smile, scraped his fingers through his hair while he collected himself on the front step. He didn't quite know what to do with his hands, so stuffed them in his pockets, then behind his back, until he caught the rattle of a chain being released from the door and suddenly it was inching open and there was a young man, a tall, string-bean of a man, looking back at him.

He flashed his hand. 'Hello there.'

The chap in front of him – presumably Nancy's son – was perhaps a few years older than himself. He was bearded and bespectacled with an impressive triangle of chest hair poking out the top of his V-neck T-shirt.

'Hi,' the man replied. 'Can I help you?'

Clayton blinked at him.

'I hope so,' he answered. 'Is this where Nancy lives? Nancy Stone?'

The man looked at him quizzically. 'Yeah . . . why's that?'

'I was hoping to have a quick chat. It's about something quite important. Nothing . . . serious. Well, I suppose it's not un-serious . . .'

The man ran his hand under his beard, his eyes fixing on him. 'Is she expecting you?'

'Now that I can't answer. But I hope so. Her friend sent me, you see.'

'Well, she's not here at the moment.'

Clayton let out a sigh. So he'd built himself up for nothing. Perhaps it was a sign, perhaps he wasn't meant to speak with her after all.

'But she should be back any minute,' the man added, glancing at his watch. 'You can come in if you like?'

If you made an **appearance** simply by turning up, then Clayton had already succeeded in the next crossword clue. But as he trailed the man inside Mrs Stone's house, he thought that appearances were also how people presented themselves, how people judged each other, so he cast his eye about the place trying to get a measure of the woman.

Nancy's home smelt of stale cigarette smoke, like an old pub.

In the hall, there was a well-worn but slightly psychedelic patterned carpet that extended throughout all the ground-floor rooms and made Clayton, who was already feeling giddy with nerves, go slightly lightheaded as he followed his host into the front room.

Inside, there was a framed black-and-white picture of Trafalgar Square hanging on the wall. A knitted Beefeater sat on the mantelpiece along with what must have been a dozen silver quizzing trophies, plus her range of quiz books – the London Cabbie's Quiz Books – which Clayton's curiosity drew him towards, until his host gestured towards the sofa.

'Take a seat,' the man said.

'Thank you.'

Clayton settled down on the edge of the sofa – a beige leather two-seater – and folded his hands neatly into his lap, pressing his feet together as if trying to make himself as small as possible.

There was a moment's pause. The young man had the air of someone who didn't wish to engage in small talk.

'I'm Clayton, by the way.'

'Neil,' the man replied. 'Do you want a tea or anything?'

I would murder for a cup, he thought. 'Oh no, don't worry. I'm good.'

'Sure? I'm putting the kettle on. It's no bother.'

Clayton smiled, pressing his hands together in his lap. 'Milk and one sugar, please.'

He watched Neil disappear into the kitchen and there was a clatter of cups, the sound of a fridge door opening and closing.

'Mrs Stone usually finishes work around now,' came his voice through the walls. 'She shouldn't be too long.'

Clayton sat a little taller on the sofa. He'd assumed his host was Nancy's son – but he'd just referred to Nancy not as Mum, or Mother, but *Mrs Stone*. He'd wondered if the name might have changed since Pippa had entered her details into the Rolodex, but clearly not.

'Sorry,' he said, when Neil reappeared carrying a tray. 'I hope you don't mind me asking but . . . do you live here or . . .'

'I'm a carer,' he answered. 'Mrs Stone's husband is upstairs. He's bedbound – had a stroke a few years ago.'

'I'm sorry to hear that.'

Perhaps she didn't take his name, he thought.

Neil placed the tray with a mug and plate of Jaffa cakes on the coffee table in front of him.

'I start at midday when she's heading out for work. Speak of the devil . . . Here she is now.'

Clayton turned to look out the bay window.

A London cab had just pulled up outside. There were two fluffy dice dangling from the rear-view mirror.

The door to the driver's seat flung open and out clambered a short but fearsome-looking lady in her sixties, wearing a pillbox hat – similar to the one she'd worn to Pippa's funeral only a week ago, only in sweetcorn yellow today, rather than the jet black.

She stood for a moment by the car, puffing on an e-cigarette.

He wasn't sure if she could see him through the dense vapours that surrounded her, or indeed the glare of the afternoon sun blaring through the front-room window as she approached the house, but he smiled at the lady nonetheless.

As the front gate squeaked closed, Clayton couldn't help noticing a flash of recognition in the lady's eyes, a resigned, slightly pained expression on her face as she clocked him standing in her front room.

She knew who he was. She knew why he was there. She'd been expecting him all along.

Chapter Twenty-Four

THE FELLOWSHIP OF PUZZLEMAKERS
THURSDAY, 14TH FEBRUARY, 1991

Everyone's toast was cut into hearts that Valentine's Day.

As Pippa entered the breakfast room in her dressing robe, she was lost for words.

There were heart-shaped helium balloons tied to each dining chair, heart-shaped bunting draped from the curtain poles, and on the table itself, heart-shaped confetti sprinkled in glittery pools over the lace cloth. As was customary at this time of year, Nancy had assumed her role as resident Cupid with great aplomb.

In the hall, the customary Cupid Box (an old copy-paper box wrapped in red crêpe paper) had appeared on the console table, ready for everyone to post their Valentine's cards. It was a tradition that had started during the first few years of them living together. Notes tended to be sent anonymously and somewhat cryptically. They were often mini puzzles themselves, the solutions being sweet declarations of gratitude, respect and friendship, everything the Fellowship stood for. This year, the contents would be handed out at a dinner-dance Nancy had booked at the Mid-Beds Golf Club. The event was open to the entire Fellowship, not just full-time residents, so they were expecting quite a crowd.

'Morning, gentlemen.'

Pippa pulled out a chair, joining Hector – partly obscured behind *The Times* – and their wordsmith, Jonty Entwistle, both with two boiled eggs cooling in front of them.

'And a very happy Valentine's to you both.'

Hector rolled his eyes. 'Load of old nonsense, isn't it?'

'Speak for yourself, dear boy,' Jonty shot back, pulling a comb from his breast pocket and running it through his newly dyed hair. It smelled like gasoline. 'Love is a despot who spares no one. Am I wrong?'

Pippa blinked at him.

It was too early for Jonty's proclamations. She needed some coffee first.

While she sometimes enjoyed the grand ramblings of the man, most of the time it was incredibly irksome. However, there was one thing she'd always admired about Jonty. He had the most impeccable dress sense.

That morning he appeared in his usual suavity: a maroon tweed suit, double-breasted with a scarlet hanky poking out the jacket pocket, its silk folds resembling a red rose, presumably to mark the occasion.

'I'm sorry,' Hector said. 'But it's the worst of consumerism.' The jigsaw artist tore his toasted heart in two with his teeth. 'The very worst.'

Pippa swallowed a smile. She'd just realised the man had red glitter on his forehead, but hadn't the heart to mention it.

In truth, she rather liked the fuss that Nancy made.

Ever since Jonty had arrived at the Fellowship three months earlier, she'd known her friend was entirely smitten, despite the hefty age gap. The pair were never out of each other's pockets, even when they weren't collaborating on their new Quiziom game.

'I don't know why you let her get away with it,' Hector went on. 'I really don't.'

'Oh, it's only a bit of fun,' Pippa replied. 'Why should we deny her that? If it makes her happy. And besides, I suspect a few of us might be harbouring secret crushes this year . . .'

Pippa turned her gaze towards Jonty, and the man – reddening slightly – flicked his wrist theatrically in reply.

'A gentleman never tells.'

'Where is our quizmaster anyway?' Pippa asked. 'I refuse to believe she's working. Her deadline isn't for another three days.'

Nancy was due to submit her latest round of questions from her pub-quiz league for their next installment of their best-selling trivia books.

'She's popped into town for a blow-dry,' Jonty explained. 'Apparently we won't recognise her when she's done.'

Pippa rolled her eyes and reached for the coffee pot. 'Answer me this, gentlemen,' she began, pouring a cup. 'Why is it men find it so difficult to show their feelings? Why does romance . . . challenge you so much?'

She was addressing them both, but really Hector, who was a closed book in that sense.

'It doesn't *bother* me,' he replied. 'I just think . . . we're too *old* for all of this.'

'For love?'

He sighed. 'You know what I mean. This palaver!'

'Well, speak for yourself,' Pippa replied, feigning indignation.

She'd never allowed any man to tell her what she was too old for, even if on this occasion she tended to agree with him.

Later that evening, Pippa was joined by Nancy at her dressing table as they got ready for the dinner-dance. They were staring into the mirror, giving fake eyelashes a go. It was Nancy's idea – not something Pippa would usually partake in – and she wasn't haven't much luck with them at all.

'More fizz?'

Nancy, without breaking her gaze with herself, reached for her glass without blinking. 'Wouldn't say no, love.'

Taxis to the Mid-Beds Golf Club were due in forty minutes and already some associate members had arrived downstairs ready to set off for the venue.

'You don't mind if I have a quick spritz?'

Before Pippa could answer, Nancy was already reaching for her perfume in front of the mirror: a sweet floral Estée Lauder fragrance she had been wearing for years. Presumably she hoped the scent might allure Jonty, but she was dousing herself in it as if it were insect repellent and she were off to the wild jungles of Papa New Guinea.

Pippa covered her glass.

It hadn't escaped her attention that her friend had been

borrowing the fragrance recently. Perhaps she could leave it in Nancy's room, buy herself a new one the next time she popped to Harrods. No reason why they couldn't both wear the same.

'It's funny, when you think about it . . .' Pippa said, shaking her head. 'We were just strangers, weren't we? All those years ago.'

'All great friends were strangers once,' Nancy replied, and folded her arms around her.

Pippa topped up her friend's glass all the way to the lip, allowing the bubbles to fall, before going again. Nancy was in a preposterously shiny, gold lamé number, while Pippa had been persuaded to wear a rather busty velvet maroon frock from Dior. Nancy said it showed off her figure, though why she'd want to do that was anyone's guess.

'So, how are things with you and Jonty?'

At the mention of their resident lexicographer, Nancy plucked a cigarette from her purse, sparked up and exhaled a ring of smoke. 'What do you mean?'

'You're spending a lot of time together, that's all.' Pippa tried to make the remark sound casual, when in truth she was a little worried, protective even, of her friend.

Not only was she concerned about the hulking age gap between the two of them, but she'd noticed that Jonty had quickly befriended all the ladies of the house within weeks of his arrival, including Angel, who he regularly took to the pub and for country walks at the weekend. There was no sign that his relationship with the housekeeper was anything other than platonic, for now, but as far as Pippa was concerned, he was a certified womaniser. And yet, despite multiple warnings from her, and others, to stay clear, Nancy couldn't be dissuaded. She had fallen for him.

'I hope he's treating you nicely?'

Nancy dragged on her cigarette. 'Of course. He's a gentleman. Still hasn't kissed me, mind.'

'He *hasn't*?'

Nancy shook her head, looking downcast.

Pippa *was* surprised, though that probably explained why

you could cut the tension with a knife whenever the two were together.

'Perhaps tonight you'll get lucky. Or *he* will, I should say.'

She was about to fetch another bottle when she realised that Nancy's face was tilted in contemplation at her.

'And how's *your* gentleman caller?' Nancy asked. 'If we're talking about men.'

At the mention of the mazemaker, Pippa found herself sitting a little taller on the stall.

Earl's visit a month earlier had gone better than she could have dreamed. After the clumsy proposal she'd first made, the rest of his time at the house had gone without a hitch. By the time he'd left, not only had he promised to consider the maze commission, but he'd asked when he might return for a second stay. Just as she'd predicted, a few days at Creighton Hall had given Earl everything he needed. Stimulation. Purpose. Fellowship.

'What are you getting at, Nance? Earl's a friend, a dear friend, that's all.'

'But you've been in that phone box more than ever since he left. Anyone would think you two were . . . up to no good.'

Pippa shook her head in protest. It was true their calls were more frequent now, more intimate too. But not in that way.

It had become a form of talking therapy, for the pair of them. They were friends, yes, but they were something more than that, too, something she hadn't yet put her finger on. Tucked away in the red booth, lost in private conversation, they continued to share all manner of insecurities to each other, picking up where they'd left off in Earl's room. For Pippa, it was often things she hadn't quite processed herself until she heard the words come out of her mouth: her regret at never experiencing love, never starting a family of her own, and her own frustration at admitting this to herself so late in her life, and as a fiercely independent lady, conscious they had no bearing on any woman's position in the world but craving them none the less.

'Yes, I suppose we've grown a little closer, in a platonic sense, of course,' she answered casually. 'But most importantly, I'm pleased to report he had one of the best weekends of his life. I knew he would.'

'You always know best, Pip.'

She waved off the remark. 'What makes you ask anyway?'

'Oh, no reason.'

'What is it, Nance? What are you playing at?'

'Nothing!' she said with a slight smile in her voice, and she pushed herself up from the chair and moved towards the door with a cheeky glint in her eye. She turned and leaned against the door frame. 'You're a very beautiful lady. You do know that, don't you?'

Pippa scoffed. 'Are you drunk, Nance? You've only had three glasses.'

Nancy shook her head. 'I'm not at all drunk. I mean it.'

Pippa gave a grateful smile to her friend and returned her attention to the mirror.

She didn't feel beautiful.

She had just managed to glue the lashes to her right eye, but the ones on her left just weren't playing ball at all. They were all askew, and clinging on for dear life, like a spider trying to climb into her eye.

'You know what Jonty said the other day?

Pippa spun herself around.

'Good character is real beauty that never fades. And you're completely beautiful to me. Remember that this evening, won't you?'

Before Pippa had a chance to say anything, Nancy threw a wave over her shoulder, then darted down the corridor, leaving in her wake an asphyxiating cloud of perfume and an unsettling feeling in Pippa's stomach.

Whatever Nancy was up to made her nervous.

Chapter Twenty-Five

8

TO GAIN KNOWLEDGE (5)

Nancy sank into an armchair that was so well cushioned it looked almost inflatable. She gestured for Clayton to sit, too.

The lace curtains from her front room were casting a dainty, filigree shadow across her pale, fine-boned face. He perched on a wingback chair that had such a well-sprung base he almost shot straight back out of the thing the moment he sat down.

'The thing is, Clayton . . . can I call you Clayton?'

'Please.' He gripped the sides of the chair to keep himself in place.

'The thing is . . . Pippa was my friend. My very good friend. I trusted her implicitly but . . .' She pulled a cigarette from a crumpled packet in her lap and sparked up. 'But she wasn't without fault. Do you know what I mean?'

'No,' Clayton replied, without any hesitation. 'No, I don't know what you mean, sorry.'

Nancy took a deep, thoughtful drag on her smoke. She was wearing a pink cable-knit jumper when she arrived, with a string of chunky pearls draped across her neckline and a pair of large, pink, horn-rimmed spectacles that magnified her intelligent grey eyes. He tried to search her face for any clues to their kinship. She had a thin, tidy nose, his was big and broad. Her hair was pale, much like his own, but he suspected it was dyed, so could have been any colour originally.

If Clayton had to guess, he'd say she was in her early sixties, but it was hard to know for sure. Much like the lady he'd met earlier on the bench in the park, Nancy had the spirit of someone a great deal younger than the lines on her face suggested.

As soon as she'd arrived home, she had removed her coat and stowed her dainty hat on a stand in the hall that held several other smart-looking pieces of headwear – then dug around in the back of a pine chest of drawers, retrieving a packet of cigarettes and a box of matches. She'd just finished her daily cabbing shift so apparently now was as good a time as ever to have this conversation.

'Well . . . none of us are irreproachable, are we?'

'No,' Clayton replied hesitantly.

'And I suppose the position she was in at the Fellowship. She became almost . . . untouchable.'

'Right.'

He still wasn't used to hearing someone talk about Pippa in this way, in the past tense, not as the beating heart of the Fellowship, and the centre of his own world.

There was now a dense cloud of cigarette fumes floating between the two of them. Clayton found himself breathing through his nose to avoid choking. His impromptu visit had obviously driven his host to break her abstinence. He couldn't help but wonder if she was feeling as he was.

He reached for another Jaffa cake before stopping himself. 'Sorry,' he said, pushing the plate away from him. 'I'm nervous. I always eat when I'm nervous.'

'There's nothing to be nervous about.'

'There isn't?'

Nancy smiled. She shook her head, then reached for another cigarette, explaining she had only gone four days smoke-free, but would try again next week.

He really wanted to blurt out the question on the tip of his tongue then. *So are you my birth mother? Is that why I've been sent here? Did you dump me at the door before you left?* But he couldn't quite bring himself. It felt clumsy, almost impertinent, to accuse a stranger of such a thing when he was sitting just five feet from the woman in her front room, picking away at her Jaffa cakes like a glutton.

'I'm not sure if you're aware,' she went on, 'but we'd recently reconnected, Pippa and I.'

'You did?'

Nancy nodded, lifting out of her chair to open the sash window an inch and Clayton, removing his hand from his mouth, breathed a sigh of relief. 'Must have been six months ago when Pippa's first letter arrived. She was stuck in bed. I think she'd had a fall?'

Clayton nodded. He remembered that first fall the previous winter as if it were yesterday.

'I can't tell you what it meant,' Nancy continued. 'To hear from her again after all those years. It felt just like the old days. We slotted right back into place, but then that's true friendship, isn't it? When it feels like time never passed.'

Clayton smiled. He took some comfort from the fact that Pippa had reconnected with an old friend before she died, but he was still none the wiser as to why Nancy would have stepped away from the Fellowship in the first place.

'She posted this to me.' She held up the back of her hand. 'A ring that I left at the Fellowship, when I returned to London.'

Clayton squinted at the thing. It looked like two rings pushed together – one silver, another gold.

'She kept it for me, all those years.'

'Why did you leave?' he asked, trying to bring the conversation back to why he was there in the first place.

Nancy twirled a lock of her hair. 'That's . . . complicated.'

'Well, I need to know why she sent me here,' he replied, surprised at his own directness. 'I need to . . . I want to know what she was hoping I would find here. Whether you're . . .'

She was looking at him, bewildered. 'You think I'm the solution?'

Clayton's heart sank. 'You're not?'

Nancy's arms folded tightly around herself. 'Well, that's for you to decide, isn't it?'

'But—'

She pushed herself out of her chair, moving towards the

mantelpiece where all her trophies were lined up in order of height, like they were her own children.

When Nancy had first walked through the door, before Clayton had taken his seat opposite her, he'd glanced quickly at one of the silver plaques out of curiosity.

They were, of course, awards from her pub-quizzing days. She was the chairwoman of the National Pub Quiz League, but she competed in events herself too, and, by the looks of things, she'd had great success.

'It reminds me of what Pippa used to say . . .' Nancy went on, looking pensively at all her awards, one hand curled to her waist. 'The pleasure is always in–'

'The *solving*,' Clayton finished. 'Never in the solution.'

Nancy spun round, beaming. 'That's it!'

Clayton looked unsure. 'I'm not following.'

'Pippa's set this trail so you can find out where you've come from, yes, but also where you're *going*. Who you want to be.'

'But why has she sent me to *you* specifically?' If he was going to tick off the next clue on Pippa's crossword, he would have to **learn** why on earth he'd been sent to meet Nancy and not someone else who'd left the Fellowship before he'd arrived.

Nancy shrugged. 'Perhaps she thought I could teach you something?'

'And can you?'

She laughed. 'There's lots you can learn from me, young man. Maybe she wants you to step beyond the Fellowship, to embrace the world, and your own independence, just like I did when I left all those years ago. Maybe it's not that at all. But I can't give you any answers until you ask me the right questions.'

Clayton wished Nancy wouldn't be so cryptic about it all. 'Well, if this is just the first clue from Pippa, then what should I do now? Where do I find the next one?'

Nancy's eyes lit up. She pointed her finger in the air. 'Now that's something I can help you with.'

And then, to Clayton's surprise, she turned and dashed out of the room.

'Pippa wanted me to give you this,' she shouted from the hallway, returning a few moments later brandishing a small padded envelope.

As he took the package, Clayton immediately clocked the inimitable stamp of Pippa's desk – the red wax seal on the back, stamped with Pippa's monogram, just like the crossword had been – and felt an overwhelming sense of relief all of a sudden. Of course this wasn't the end. It was just the beginning. He'd got past the first hurdle, that was all.

'She sent you this?'

Nancy nodded, her eyes suddenly glassy.

'It arrived with the final letter she posted to me,' she explained. 'Just a week before she passed. The instructions were that I should hand it to you. Whenever you turned up. *If* you ever turned up.'

Clayton folded his arms around the envelope, pressing it tightly to his chest. 'Thank you.'

Nancy's head was tilted sympathetically at him. 'Clayton, could I give you a hug? Would that be strange? Are you a huggy person?'

He felt his body go slightly stiff.

'Because I am, and, well, it looks like you could do with one if you don't mind me saying—'

'Yes,' he heard himself say. 'Yes, if you don't mind. That would be nice.'

Suddenly Nancy had extended her arms and seized him, clamping him so tightly that he wasn't so much as being hugged by the woman, more wrestled.

Clayton felt her string of pearls digging into him and then her hand was suddenly on the back of his head, stroking his hair. He allowed his head to fall briefly on her shoulder, realising, in a moment of overwhelming clarity, that she smelled just like Pippa. She was wearing her favourite perfume. Estée Lauder's *Beautiful*. He closed his eyes.

'Shh, now,' she whispered in his ear, although he hadn't said a word.

They remained like this for a few more seconds, until Clayton heard someone descending the stairs. Neil, the carer, was finishing his shift.

'I should get going,' he said, finally peeling himself away.

'Well, you know where I am,' Nancy replied. 'If you ever want to speak again. And if there's anything I can do to help.'

Clayton nodded and moved into the hall to collect his things, placing Pippa's envelope safely inside his coat pocket, deciding he'd open it as soon as he got outside.

Neil slipped his shoes on beside him. The two men were heading out to leave the house together.

'Are you off, love?' Nancy asked. 'Thanks for staying on a bit. Make sure you arrive half an hour later tomorrow, OK?'

'Thanks, Mrs Stone. And no worries at all. I'll see you again tomorrow.'

Standing next to each other in the cramped hallway made even smaller by the large mahogany hatstand and matching side table, Clayton moved to open the door, just as Neil did the same.

'Whoops,' Clayton said. 'After you.'

'No, you go ahead . . .'

'No, no.' Clayton blushed. 'Please.'

Neil hesitated, and then just as Clayton moved forward, Neil did the same so the two of them crashed into each other. Clayton was relieved to see that Neil was turning a similar shade of puce.

'Gosh, sorry,' Neil said. 'Let me get it.'

Nancy was watching with a faint smirk on her face as the two of them contorted themselves around each other and finally through the door.

Clayton turned and flashed his hand on the step. 'Thanks again now.'

'Goodbye, Clayton,' she said. 'It was nice meeting you.'

'See you tomorrow, Mrs Stone.'

'Thanks, Neil, love.'

Outside, the day was coming on and the two young men were bathed in a radiant, late-afternoon light that dazzled through the sycamore trees and made everything appear brighter, less subdued than before.

Clayton strode confidently through Nancy's garden gate, holding it open for the carer behind him, keen to avoid any more awkwardness.

'We made a right meal of that, didn't we?' he remarked, and Neil, slipping past him, made a funny noise that he assumed was a nervous laugh.

'A little bit, yes. Anyway, it was nice meeting you, Callum.'

'Clayton.'

'Sorry! *Clayton.* I'm bad with names.'

'Me, too. Nice meeting you, Neil. Which way are you heading?'

They'd reached the end of the road and Neil was putting his headphones in. 'I'm going left. You?'

Clayton looked left then right, trying to get his bearings. 'Umm . . . I've got to get onto the canal—'

'Right.'

'I thought the towpath was *left*,' Clayton replied.

'No, I just mean right, we're heading the same way.'

'Oh, right.'

The two of them laughed. Neil removed his headphones and Clayton slipped his hands inside his pockets, not knowing what to say, until he asked, 'You don't mind if I walk with you for a bit?'

There was the trace of a smile creeping around the man's eyes. 'Sure, if you like.'

Chapter Twenty-Six

THE FELLOWSHIP OF PUZZLEMAKERS
14TH FEBRUARY, 1991

'Did you see that?' Nancy asked, as they clambered out of the taxi in the golf club car park. 'The way that driver looked at me. Like I was some . . . old dear!'

They had just arrived for their Valentine's dinner-dance, having split a couple of cabs between them all. It worked out all right in the end. Not only were they eligible for the group discount, but the concessionary rate, too.

Pippa found herself sandwiched in the back of one car with Hector and Nancy's homme-du-jour, Jonty Entwistle, while her friend sat up front, regaling tales of her own black-cab days in London to the driver – who was barely out of his teens and clearly couldn't care less.

'What was it all for, Pip?' Nancy asked.

The ladies were leading the charge towards the clubhouse, arms linked like a silver chain, while the others trailed them. 'I'm already starting to feel not as important, or interesting, as I was when I was younger woman.'

Pippa gave a sympathetic shake of the head. 'You were a trailblazer, Nance. A pioneer. No one can take that away from you. And you're hardly old – wait till you get to *my* age.'

'But why?' Nancy asked. 'Why does it have to be so . . . awful.'

'Because it's a fact of life,' Pippa concluded. 'The world sees you differently when you're old. If they see you at all, that is.'

The clubhouse was a rather squat, single-storey building positioned perilously close to the course's eighteenth hole, so much so that some of the red bricks had shrapnel pockmarks where stray golf balls had struck. It gave the building a vaguely menacing quality, as if it were under siege. Arriving at the venue, guests were encouraged not to loiter and instead head straight for the safety of the vestibule. Likewise, when leaving, there was a notice stuck to the door which read:

HEAD STRAIGHT FOR YOUR CAR. LOW FLYING BALLS.

Inside, Pippa and her puzzlemakers were handed a Bucks Fizz by two teenage waitresses, then escorted to the club lounge and into the private dining room where velvet curtains were partly drawn in an attempt to obscure a smashed windowpane.

Entering first, Pippa was surprised to see someone already at their table, obscured behind the pages of the *Daily Telegraph*.

'Who on earth's that?' she asked, with creeping dread. 'Oh, for crying out loud, it's not a stripper, is it?'

She instantly regretted giving Nancy free rein of the event.

The mystery guest lowered the paper and, in an instant, Pippa felt something hot pulse through her body.

'*Earl!*'

He flashed his hand casually at them all. 'Good evening, everyone.'

While they all rushed over to welcome him, Pippa just stood there, frozen to the spot. Her hand went to touch her new lashes, to make sure they were still attached.

Earl was in a cream linen suit, looking nothing like the man who'd visited them a month ago. His hair – previously greasy and unkempt – had been washed to a shine and slicked back just like the old days. And the unkempt beard she'd recoiled at? Now trimmed to a stylish goatee.

She stepped forward. 'How *lovely* to see you again. And looking . . . so well, too.'

She angled her face for a kiss, and felt his warm lips press against her powdered cheek.

'I had no idea you were coming.'

'No?' Earl looked surprised. 'But Nance invited me.'

Pippa forced a grin. 'Of course. I remember her mentioning it now.'

She shot a fierce look over her shoulder at Nancy, who was frantically laying the place cards on the boardroom-style table set for sixteen.

Of course, their resident Cupid was trying to set her up. That's why she'd insisted Pippa wear those ridiculous fake eyelashes and this increasingly warm, clingy dress. She just couldn't help herself.

They mingled with drinks and crudités for a while as Nancy carried on fussing, placing the Cupid Box in the middle of the table with a few spare blank cards and pens for anyone who'd yet to dispatch their notes.

After returning from the toilet, Earl offered his arm to Pippa. 'Shall we take our seats?'

They circled the table looking for their place cards. Pippa felt an odd sense of appreciation towards Nancy in that moment. It didn't take a genius to work out who she was going to be sitting with.

She was beside Earl, with poor Hector the third wheel on her other side, while Jonty and Nancy sat opposite them. The visiting wives of their associate members were all stationed alongside their husbands, naturally, while Ruth and John Gibbon, a couple of renowned trivialists from Stoke, were granted top-table seats, as they were celebrating their fortieth wedding anniversary later that week. The other single ladies of the house, Janet Richardson (retired headteacher of forty years, divorced, without kids, now heading up the Fellowship's kids' division), Jean Watkins (former postmaster, widowed, with a penchant for logic puzzles), and their housekeeper Angel (perennially single, part-time staffer and attuned to the moon's cycle, with no interest in puzzles whatsoever) were sandwiched between all the surplus men, presumably in case sparks were to fly.

Once everyone was settled, Nancy reached over the table to get a grip on the Cupid Box. 'Now then. Let's see what we have, shall we?'

Several gentlemen around the table let out audible groans as she whipped off the lid and tipped the thing upside down, the contents spilling out in front of her.

'Give me strength,' Hector grumbled under his breath. He'd already angled his chair away from the scene. Any second now and he'd be off for a smoke on the terrace, Pippa was certain of it.

'Look at all this!' Nancy exclaimed. 'A record turnout at the Cupid Box this year.'

She began by distributing a couple of cards to a sweet man called Larry Towles.

'Goodness,' he said quietly. 'All for me?'

Larry was in his early eighties and had an undeniable charm, a kind, handsome face and, most unusually for a man of his age, a full head of thick brown hair, which Pippa had always assumed was a 'piece' until she'd caught him stepping out of the bathroom one time. His fringe was stuck to his forehead like the wet tail of a dog.

He raised his little haul of love letters. 'Much obliged, ladies.'

Next, there were cards for John Gibbon from his wife, Ruth – and vice versa, rather predictably – while Lesley and Jean both received a couple of cards each, looking rather pleased with themselves.

Finally, pausing for effect, Nancy leaned over the table and presented Jonty with a small red envelope, accompanied by a suggestive wink.

Everyone watched in anticipation as he peeled out the card and read the enclosed message.

'*Don't* read it out loud,' she urged.

Jonty scanned the first few lines. 'N-no. I certainly won't.'

'And this must be for me?'

Nancy had a small envelope in front of her, and something else folded into her hand.

She tore open the card first, scanning the words inside with an expectant look on her face, which Pippa noticed soon fell away, leaving her friend looking confused; hurt, even. Nancy turned her attention then to what she had in her hand. A gift.

A ring box.

Dear God, no, Pippa thought.

'I thought we said no presents this year,' she called out. 'What is it, Nance? What have you got?'

Please don't let it be what I think it is. She really wouldn't put it past the man. She had yet to put her finger on it, but there was something about their relationship that didn't quite add up, and it wasn't just the age.

'I'm not sure what it is,' Nancy answered, holding up a gold and silver ring.

'It's a puzzle ring,' Jonty explained. 'There's a man in Chester who makes them on commission. Two metal bands that slot together. Very natty little pieces. I had a special message inscribed on the inside.'

Nancy squinted at the inside of the ring. 'What does it say?'

'That's for you to work out,' Jonty answered sheepishly.

Nancy's face completely lit up. She glanced over at her admirer, then kissed two fingers, pressing them to his cheek.

After a moment's awkward pause, she continued dishing out the final few cards. 'Angel,' she called out next. 'There's one here for you, love.'

Nancy passed their housekeeper a small envelope.

'How sweet,' she remarked, passing the card between her hands as if it were a hot stone before slipping it into her lap, unopened. 'But whoever you are I hope you're a Capricorn because my sun rises in Aries, so anything else and it'll be a disaster.'

There were several laughs around the table.

It wasn't unusual for Angel to join the Fellowship's social events. Despite the fact she was half their age, it had become patently clear that, other than the occasional trips into town to attend a sound bath or get her chakras aligned, there was very little going on in the woman's life.

That evening, she was in a black smock dress that exposed not a single square inch of her skin and was wearing two prominent drop earrings (meant to activate the heart chakra, apparently). She'd styled her newly cropped hair with what looked like a gentleman's pomade, the dark fringe moulded to her head like the overflowing wax of a candle.

'And Pippa,' Nancy said. 'This one must be for you.'

'For me?'

Pippa cautiously reached for the envelope from Nancy and turned it playfully in her hand, holding it up to the strip lights above her, as if scrutinising a precious ancient relic. It wasn't unusual for her to receive the odd card on Valentine's Day, usually a harmless note from one of the men who wanted to thank her for something or other, but the letter in her hand felt different somehow. It had been marked boldly with the letter P. The inscription of the pen was fine and there was no hard indentation, no shine to the ink, so she figured the secret correspondent had used a ballpoint to inscribe her initial on the front. She lifted it under her nose and gave a deep inhale.

'Well, they're a smoker, that's for sure.'

Pippa glanced at all the men enjoying an after-dinner cigar at the table. Larry, opposite her, stubbed his out immediately.

She swiped her fingers under the seal and slipped out the card inside. It was one of the generic, plain ones that Nancy had left on the table. A last-minute dispatch.

Inside, someone had written:

P,

You'll never know what you mean to me, for I shall never be able to express it, but please accept this as a small gesture of my appreciation for everything you've done, and continue to do, for me.

'What does it say?' Nancy asked. 'Don't be shy, come on.'

Pippa felt a tingling inside her.

The handwriting was small and tight but perfectly readable; neat, even. 'Nothing,' she beamed, returning the card to its envelope, placing it out of sight in her lap. 'It just says . . . Happy Valentine's Day, from your mystery admirer. Very sweet. Who's next?'

Only when the group had turned their attention to someone else did Pippa glance in acknowledgement at Earl.

She knew it was just a platonic note, certainly no hint of anything romantic, but it was the thought that most touched her.

'Thank you,' she said, in a low voice. 'That's very kind of you.'

Earl shuffled a little awkwardly in his seat. 'Sorry, Pip—'

'Nothing to apologise for. I'm very touched that you—'

'No,' he said. 'I mean, I'm *sorry*, I didn't write that.'

She looked at him a moment then, realising she'd got the wrong end of the stick entirely. Instant shame flooded through her, matched only by a sudden, bitter disappointment. 'Of course. Silly me.' She leaned back in her chair, completely mortified, and turned her head towards the jigsaw artist sitting the other side of her.

Hector was beetroot.

He gave a terse, affirmative nod at the card she clutched in her hand. Pippa grinned at him and watched as he pushed himself up from the chair, taking his pipe in the direction of the smokers' terrace.

Of course, Hector had chosen that evening of *all* evenings to deliver a formal note of appreciation via the Cupid Box, she realised.

She reached for her champagne and knocked back the whole thing in one breathless gulp, wishing the whole evening was over with already.

Dinner was haute cuisine. This meant there were four courses rather than the usual three: an appetiser, second course, entrée and dessert. By the time their puddings arrived – a chocolate roulade with raspberry cream – most people were stuffed, too full even to dance.

Pippa had just excused herself and was heading to the ladies' to re-powder her nose when she felt the footsteps of someone behind her.

'Pip!' Earl called out.

She turned with one hand on the door to the toilet.

'I wanted to give you this . . . when you were on your own,' he explained.

'Oh?' Pippa ran a quick hand through her hair.

He looked nervous as he reached inside his linen jacket to pull out something small, oblong, made of paper. 'I hope you don't think I've overstepped the mark.'

Pippa's pulse started to race as she extended her hand for the envelope he was holding. So he *did* have a Valentine's card for her after all.

'The thing is,' Earl went on. 'I've been thinking about what we've been talking about. About that unfulfilled ambition of yours . . .'

Pippa – with a quizzical expression – slipped her hand inside the envelope and pulled out the contents. Inside wasn't a Valentine's card at all, but a pamphlet.

LOVE MAKES A FAMILY

Apply today to change a child's life for the better.

Earl stepped towards her. 'A long time ago, when Rosa and I were struggling to conceive, we looked into a few options . . . so I wanted to share them with you.'

'Adoption?' she asked.

'Foster parenting,' Earl said. 'I hope you don't mind me suggesting it. Only they're crying out for people, and I think you'd be perfect.'

Pippa's eyes went to the floor, feeling at once overcome with emotion.

'But, Earl. Surely I'm too . . .?' Her voice caught in her throat as she tried to align what exactly she was thinking. 'I'm too . . . old, am I not?'

'Fostering is *temporary* guardianship, Pip, so your age is mostly irrelevant. So long as you've got a safe home and can steer a young person towards the right path in life.'

Pippa bit her bottom lip, stifling the sudden well of tears pooling in her eyes.

'Think of what you could offer a child, Pip, what we could *all* offer them for that matter. All of these brilliant minds. There must be a thousand years between us all—'

Pip lifted her hand. 'What do you mean *us*?'

Earl gave a sheepish grin. He moved a few paces down the corridor and disappeared through the door that led to the locker-room, where they'd been storing their coats. When he reappeared a few seconds later he was wheeling a large suitcase.

Pippa's hand went to her mouth.

'I was wondering if you might accept me on a trial period,' he said. 'A few months to construct the maze, then we can decide if I should stay on . . .'

Pippa stood frozen on the spot, not sure what to say but feeling a tingle of something warm ripple through her.

'I can't thank you enough, Pip, for helping me out of my rut, reminding me you're never too old for a bit of fun.'

Before she had even realised, her arms were wrapped tightly around the man.

Allies, she thought. Not just friends. That's who they were to each other. They had each other's backs, were there to protect each other, to encourage them into becoming the best versions of themselves. She had done just that for him, and now he was doing the same back.

'Thank you, Earl,' she said softly in his ear.

'No, thank *you*,' came the reply, and the two of them remained outside the ladies' loo for a short while longer, entwined in each other's arms.

Chapter Twenty-Seven

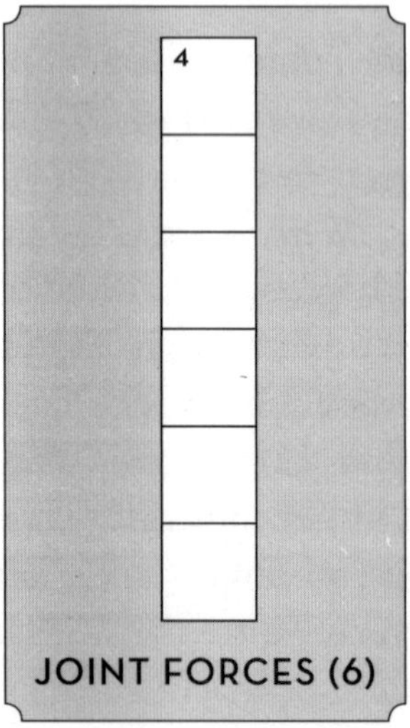

As was so often the way, the next crossword solution had popped into Clayton's head as he made his way back to his hotel with Neil at his side.

It wasn't the first time Pippa had prompted Clayton to make some friends his own age. And not just friends but **allies**, as she so often referred to her own closest circle. A good friend should build you up, she always used to say. They should help you become the best version of yourself. In that sense, forging a friendship was akin to finding a soulmate. But how on earth did you go about finding someone like that?

Clayton had been walking with Neil for what felt like a few hours, but was in fact ten minutes, when the carer finally opened his mouth to speak.

'So that's why they called you Stumper?' he asked. 'Because you just turned up there one day? And they don't know where you came from?'

He felt an overwhelming sense of relief as the questions hung between them.

'That's right,' he answered. 'I'm the mystery they've never been able to solve.'

At this, Neil gave a proper laugh – a silly, sudden snort – which took Clayton by surprise.

'Sorry, but that's quite good.'

'Yes,' he replied. 'Yes, I suppose it is.'

He'd been itching to open the padded envelope inside his jacket pocket ever since leaving Nancy's, but, so far, had resisted. He'd open it on his own as soon as he got back to the hotel.

Right now, he was using Neil as a guinea pig, practising his social skills out on the man. In his attempt to introduce himself, he'd rattled through quite a lot, explaining how he lived with a group of ageing enigmatologists – or puzzlemakers; how he'd recently lost someone incredibly close to him, the lady who'd raised him as her own; how this had encouraged him to find out who'd abandoned him there all those years ago; how that search had led him to London, to visit Nancy, and how he was now following a trail, of sorts. A puzzle trail.

At this point, Clayton feared he'd been rabbiting or, worse still, boring Neil with his life story, but perhaps the man was just a very active listener.

'I had no idea . . .' Neil said, shaking his head, 'that Mrs Stone lived anywhere like that. She's never mentioned it.'

Clayton turned to look at him, surprised. He'd barely looked up since they'd started walking together, his head tipped bashfully to the ground.

'I know she hosts the quiz nights at the pub. She invited me once.'

'You didn't fancy it?' Clayton asked.

Neil shook his head. 'Nah, I don't really go out very much.'

'Oh.'

'I'm not a hermit or anything. I just don't mind my own company, you know.'

'Yeah,' Clayton said, turning and briefly catching the man's eye. He'd used that excuse before himself. Easier to stay at home, to keep to yourself.

'I love puzzles though.'

'You do?' Clayton asked.

'Doesn't everyone?'

Clayton tipped his head thoughtfully. He supposed, in a way, that was probably right.

From the second he'd left the Fellowship, he'd seen puzzles in various guises wherever he looked. In the waiting room at Bedford Station, a baby in a pushchair – no more than a year old – had been mesmerised by a shape-sorting toy; on the train he'd sat opposite an older chap who was tackling a sudoku, the *Metro* newspaper folded across his knee, while he chewed the end of his pencil. There were maze motifs decorating the tunnelled walls of the London Underground and on his walk to Nancy's, he'd seen a woman gazing into the back of a removal truck, wondering how she might contort the boxes to fit in the last few possessions she had at her feet, like some sort of tangram game. Puzzles formed a part of everyone's lives, not just his own.

'I used to do jigsaws with my grandparents,' Neil said. 'My mum died when I was young and my dad . . . well, he wasn't really around very much. So they brought me up instead.'

Clayton discreetly eyed him. He'd been wondering what Neil's story was, where he'd come from.

'You've probably solved some of our jigsaws then,' he said. 'They're the most popular in the country, made by a man called Hector Haywood. We call him the Prince of Pieces.'

'Not Hancock's Jigsaws?' Neil asked. 'No . . . what are they called? Haywood's . . . *Haywood's Jigsaws*?'

'That's right,' Clayton said. 'He's made over a thousand of them now. If you tried to solve them all, you're talking a million pieces.'

Neil puffed out his cheeks.

'So whereabouts do you live, Neil?'

He pointed at the brown expanse of canal leading their path. 'About two hundred yards that way. I've got a houseboat—'

'You haven't!'

Neil grinned.

'Like a *proper* narrowboat?'

'Yeah.' He was blushing a little. 'I'm moored in Little Venice at the moment. I try and stick around West London if I can. It's nice and quiet around here.'

Clayton realised he was swinging his arms while he walked. There was a lightness in his step all of a sudden. It was the most relaxed he'd felt since he'd arrived.

'Must be lovely to have your own space,' he remarked. 'To be so independent . . .'

'It is,' Neil agreed. 'I tried a houseshare in Wembley once. Lived with three others – it wasn't for me. Too much noise and mess.'

Clayton scoffed. He knew all about that. 'I live with quite a few people. There are nine of us – sorry, eight – there's eight of us now.'

Neil turned to look at him.

There was the slight softening of his features – a sympathetic smile – that made Clayton's stomach lurch slightly.

'They do enjoy a party,' he went on. 'And they're always playing games and drinking till the early hours, which can be a bit annoying, especially when I'm trying to sleep.'

Neil blew out his cheeks. 'Not for me, thank you very much.'

They were walking under a flyover somewhere near the Harrow Road, which was emblazoned with an oblique line of graffiti: *ALL WE NEED IS MORE LIKES*. Another puzzle, Clayton thought. A riddle, of sorts.

'So, what's your boat called?'

Neil bit his bottom lip, looking hesitant.

'Go on,' Clayton urged.

Neil cleared his throat. '*Serendipity*.'

They glanced sideways at each other.

Clayton felt his neck prickle slightly. 'That's nice.'

'Really?'

'Yeah, I like it. What made you choose it?'

'Oh.' Neil waved his hand in front of him. 'That's a long story.'

Clayton looked at him in anticipation. *Go on then*, his eyes said. *I'd like to hear it*.

'I'm heading down there.' Neil pointed over his shoulder.

Clayton's stomach dropped a little. 'Oh, right.'

They were standing where the canal divided in two. Paddington Basin was to their right, and on their left, over a footbridge, another stretch of water, presumably where Serendipity was tied up.

'Well, that was . . . nice,' he said. 'Chatting, I mean. I hope you didn't mind me . . . hijacking your commute.'

'Yeah,' Neil replied. 'I mean, no, I didn't mind. It was nice actually.'

Clayton smiled, rubbing the back of his neck.

He'd walked much further than he should have. He was going to have to go back on himself, try to find where he should have turned off for his hotel. He'd been so distracted by the conversation that, for a minute or two, he'd forgotten Pippa's parcel tucked inside his jacket – the next clue on this strange quest.

'I bet it was the last thing you wanted,' he remarked, before he could stop himself. 'Some strange man telling you his life story when all you wanted was to get home—'

'No. No, I didn't mind actually. It was . . . very interesting. And I don't think you're strange at all . . .' His cheeks instantly coloured and he looked down at his feet.

'Well, nice meeting you . . . Clayton.'

They gave each other a knowing look. He'd got his name right this time.

'It's Callum.'

Neil looked horrified. 'I thought you said—'

'I'm joking!'

Neil pressed his hand to his heart in relief as Clayton let out a laugh, a big, throaty laugh, for the first time in weeks. He didn't want to say goodbye yet. He wanted to keep talking. To find out more about the man, to see if they had anything else in common, whether they might even become friends.

'Bye then,' he said, and offered his hand, hoping it wasn't too clammy from his pocket. 'Pleasure meeting you . . . Nigel.'

They both sniggered.

Neil shook his hand and Clayton couldn't help noticing how satisfyingly strong and soft it felt folded around his own.

The man eventually returned his hand to his pocket, turned and headed over the bridge and out of his life, unlikely to ever be seen again.

Back at the Lancaster Court Hotel, Clayton felt oddly deflated, like all the air had gone from his balloon.

He'd placed the envelope Nancy had given him on his bed and was looking at it warily from the other side of the room while waiting for the tiny kettle to boil.

The kettle clicked off but he continued staring ahead, not moving from the spot.

In truth, it wasn't just Pippa's surprise gift from the grave that had sent him into a daze, but something, or *someone* else entirely.

He hadn't been able to stop thinking about Neil ever since he'd left him.

He couldn't remember the last time he'd met someone new, someone his own age, someone he seemed to genuinely get on with. But was he just imagining it?

Perhaps it was Pippa's fault – *the crossword's fault* – for making him believe he'd formed a bond, made a connection – an ally – when it was nothing more than a friendly, fleeting exchange with a stranger.

But isn't that what Pippa always used to say?

All best friends were strangers once.

He thought, too, of his chat with Cilla on the bench earlier that day. The lady who was turning eighty tomorrow and had no one to celebrate with. The thought of it made his insides churn.

Realising the water in the kettle was beginning to cool, Clayton finally poured himself a tea, then moved towards the bed. He picked up the envelope, examining it under the unnaturally bright lights of his hotel room, before ripping it open with such e the tiny waxed seal disc flew to the other side of the room.

Clayton's hands were shaking as they slipped inside and pulled out a slip of typewritten paper.

Dear Clayton,
Me again. Ready for part two? You're flying now.
<u>The key</u> to this cryptogrid is simple. The questions get easier as you go. So perhaps try answering in reverse?
If you need a little geographic help, I'm sure there's someone who would be happy to lend a hand, to help you unlock part three. . .
If there's one thing I've learned in life, Clayton, it's that you should never be afraid to ask for help.
With love, as ever.
Pip x

T	K	U	T	Z	P	A	A	S	Y	B	V	O	Q	W	L	A	N	U	E
D	O	B	M	V	O	T	E	G	I	H	W	F	A	T	D	V	G	I	B
S	H	Q	U	U	Q	N	F	O	Q	Z	P	P	B	E	M	H	N	T	Y
F	W	N	O	R	A	T	Y	V	D	E	X	I	X	Q	A	E	A	C	H
N	O	V	Q	Q	Z	U	N	C	H	G	E	J	P	N	C	R	O	W	K
Y	S	K	L	F	N	P	V	N	G	U	B	Q	Q	U	V	X	K	I	Y
V	B	D	G	I	D	U	S	O	I	H	M	N	O	G	Z	P	G	U	Y
I	C	N	J	S	V	Z	I	J	L	G	M	V	W	Y	R	E	H	Y	D
P	I	F	W	L	Z	M	I	C	M	I	G	Y	P	C	K	Z	W	J	G
N	G	Q	B	N	X	I	B	T	T	L	V	S	M	C	K	K	L	D	F
K	L	M	T	H	U	R	U	V	I	H	N	X	H	C	W	X	I	R	V
Q	K	W	D	Y	V	D	P	C	L	O	M	L	B	I	A	L	I	Q	I
G	J	T	Q	N	A	W	Q	H	L	S	G	Y	T	T	Q	D	Z	N	V
Q	W	Z	L	I	M	L	G	K	N	L	I	Y	L	A	O	I	S	W	S
I	C	U	B	X	P	X	X	D	M	F	H	K	L	Z	D	M	O	J	R
B	L	X	T	X	Z	O	D	O	P	K	N	N	I	O	S	L	P	O	N
Q	N	E	U	L	X	G	W	Q	D	K	F	H	T	L	O	W	E	P	J
U	S	N	Z	Z	L	G	V	D	I	S	N	P	N	G	B	M	H	J	X
O	E	G	Y	X	J	P	R	Q	U	D	E	K	P	A	U	L	W	A	Y
F	G	C	H	J	J	K	G	M	N	S	W	S	M	Z	Z	O	I	B	B

Clues to the four entries in the grid:
1. S: Basement (10)
2. S: 87-135 (7)
3.W: Oratory, Uruguay, Bunch of Grapes (8-4)
4.N: The greatest city in the world? (6)

Clayton gripped the edge of his bed, feeling a fresh wave of panic flood through his body. The one that he'd found inside the wooden puzzle box. The one with the elaborate H carved into its design.

Noticing that 'the key' had been underlined, Clayton went to check the inside pocket on his jacket to feel for the gold skeleton key he'd brought from home.

So the enclosed grid was linked to the key somehow? Perhaps it would finally reveal what the key unlocked.

Clayton had seen this type of puzzle before, though he'd never attempted to tackle one himself. Cryptogrids were a Fellowship invention. And they were notoriously tricky. A famous cryptologist called Sir Derek Wadlow had started making them years ago, before the commune had even been founded. They were similar to wordsearches in a way, but to make things more difficult, they involved a layer of encryption. So, it wasn't just a case of finding a set of words but answering a series of questions, then working out how the answers might be coded in the grid.

Clayton took a deep breath and downed his tea. It was going to be a long night.

Chapter Twenty-Eight

THE FELLOWSHIP OF PUZZLEMAKERS
THURSDAY, 28TH FEBRUARY, 1991

Pippa didn't tend to smoke unless someone else was, but that morning she found herself alone at her desk, encircled by a billowing cloud of Benson & Hedges, struggling to make heads or tails of the Fellowship's balance sheet.

She would be lying if she said she hadn't been distracted recently. She'd been too consumed with Earl's return, and the exciting fostering idea he'd proposed, to address the mounting pile of bills on her desk.

The morning after the Valentine's dinner-dance she had nipped outside to the telephone booth and made some enquiries with the council.

The only person who knew about this development was Earl, because a few days later she'd been summoned to the council offices to have a preliminary chat with one of their social workers.

The whole distraction had diverted her from the one thing she'd known for some time needed fixing. The Fellowship's bottom line.

The trouble was, she had a brain for words, not numbers, and while she was smart enough to recognise this, she still wasn't prepared to relinquish control of the finances, to ask for advice, or to delegate the task to someone more equipped – like mathematician Geoff Stirrup, who would have no trouble interpreting the figures. Disappointing people, not living up to the expectations of those closest to her, had always been Pippa's biggest trauma, ever since her father had walked out on her as a little girl and she'd spent years wondering if it was her fault.

No, Pippa wasn't going to let anyone down. She just needed a bit more time to get her head around it, that was all.

She bent down and yanked the bottom drawer of her pedestal, setting the whole thing tumbling forwards with the weight of its contents. Inside was yet more paperwork – receipts, purchase orders, utility bills – but lurking at the back was an old Buchanan & Lyall tobacco box, a rusty red tin no less than a century old.

She ran her fingers along the dents in the sides, which gave it a mottled, almost mosaic finish. The metal lid had contorted with age and she had to prise her thumb under the corner lip, which was slightly raised, to wrench the thing open.

Seeing the gold-plated skeleton key with its long, slim stem topped with the letter *H*, nestled on its paisley pocket square, still made her heart beat that bit faster.

It had once belonged to her mother, but it wasn't until her father passed away that the key had come into her possession.

It had taken her several months to work out its significance. Such was the disorder of her family's personal affairs that no formal documentation was assigned to the item; no written instructions had been left to help her crack this particular puzzle. It had come down to plain detective work in the end, establishing what the sorcerous-looking key actually unlocked, what the *H* on the top symbolised.

Perhaps now it might help her out of this sticky position she found herself in, she wondered. Before she made any rash decisions, she'd go over the numbers once more, she determined. The trouble was she'd never been brilliant with money, had always grown up with more than enough to spend, had never had any cause to worry about where the next installment was coming from or how to best spread costs, cut back, avoid creeping into the red.

These days it was different. She was no longer responsible for only her own finances but also those of the Fellowship's, and everyone who called it home. There were bills to pay, expenses to cover, upkeep and repair costs to settle and, in recent years, quite a few debts to clear.

'What the devil is that?' Earl blurted behind her.

Pippa leaped out of her skin. 'Christ on a bike! Where on earth did you come from?'

She'd been concentrating so sharply on the key in front of her she hadn't noticed Earl creep into her study behind her.

He was pointing at the ceiling, pulling a face at the strange pattern above them. 'Looks like you've got a serious leak on your hands.'

Pippa scoffed. 'Why is it *my* leak?'

'Because you're in charge!'

'Nonsense. We're a commune. No one is in charge here.'

'Is that right?' Earl said, hiding a smile.

'It is. We share responsibilities.'

Of course, that was exactly the sort of thing that fell into her remit, as President, and landlady of the house. She couldn't deny that there were elements of her role she neglected for more interesting tasks. General household maintenance often got shunted from her to-do list.

'You'll need to get someone out,' he added, shaking his head at the marbled pattern above her, which, Pippa couldn't deny, looked quite ominous. She'd noticed a few weeks ago that it had started to turn a funny colour but had failed to do anything about it. The damp marks were now large splodges, like a strange atlas of the world taking shape above them.

'I keep meaning to ask,' Earl began. 'Any word on the fostering?'

Pippa shot a look over her shoulder. 'Keep your voice down, will you!'

'Sorry,' he whispered.

The two were in cahoots on the application. For now, Pippa had determined to keep the conversations she was having with the council between themselves. If things were to progress, she knew she'd have to get everyone on board, but she was worried how people might react to the idea, and couldn't decide how best to broach it.

Earl had started rummaging through the papers on her desk. He glanced at the balance sheet, swiping it from the desk.

'Hands off that.'

Pippa leaped to grab it back, but Earl lifted it playfully in the air.

'Pass it back, Earl. That's private.'

'Nothing's private in a commune,' he replied with a cheeky glint in his eye, waving the yellow paper above his head like the flag of Brunei. 'You're meant to share everything.'

The pair ran a circle around the desk, then again in the opposite direction, like children, before Pippa lunged at him, snatching the paper back.

'Not the balance sheets, we don't.'

'How's that maze coming along anyway?' she asked, stuffing the paper in her drawer.

Earl's pressed his hands together, almost in prayer. He had just started breaking soil in the grounds, staking out the route. 'It's going to be a doozy, this one, Pipster. Just you wait.'

She pulled up a chair. 'I never doubted it. Here, if you want to help, open the post with me.'

There was a mound of unopened letters sitting in her in-tray as usual.

She liked to start with the most recent post, the logic being that anything older would soon be chasing her anyway.

Earl reached for the first letter from the pile and Pippa lifted the second, as if they were drawing playing cards.

The moment she peeled open the manilla envelope in her hand, Pippa felt her mouth open in shock.

'What is it?' Earl asked.

'The council,' she answered in a hushed voice. 'They're sending a social worker . . . to carry out a house assessment.'

'You're kidding?'

He reached for the letter and she passed it to him.

'I've been fast-tracked, Earl.'

He glanced up from the page. 'But this is in a week, Pip?'

She nodded grimly. 'It's getting awfully serious all of a sudden.'

A few long seconds stretched between them and Pippa turned towards the window, looking out at the sullen sky, wondering out of everyone in the house, who might possibly object, how she might win them round.

'Try not to get your hopes up,' Earl suggested. 'Until you've got the nod from everybody here.'

'I'll need *everyone* on board, won't I, Earl?'

He gave a reluctant nod.

'And if one person objects . . .'

'Then you'll have no choice but to abandon the plan.'

She gave a resigned sigh.

Of course, she knew this already, but to have it confirmed by someone else, someone like Earl, only confirmed the matter. It would only take one person – a single voice of dissent – to shatter this dream of hers.

The trouble was, once Pippa had set her sights on something, once an idea had started to form in her mind, she found it almost impossible to let it go.

Chapter Twenty-Nine

A LARGE AMOUNT OF SOMETHING PLEASANT (6)

As Clayton made his way through Queen's Park with a birthday balloon tied to his wrist, he spotted the red flash of Cilla's silk headscarf on the memorial bench and breathed a heavy sigh of relief. She was a woman of routine, just as he'd predicted. He'd timed it all perfectly.

He had plans for the afternoon: a particularly demanding cryptogrid in his wallet to nail, a mysterious gold key that unlocked something, somewhere, and an idea in his head about how he might go about finding out. The questions beneath the grid were London-themed, he'd decided, and he'd been sent to Nancy because she was perfectly positioned to help, should he come unstuck.

Clayton wasn't afraid to lean on others when he needed to. That was something Pippa had instilled in him from an early age: being smart wasn't always about raising your hand with the answer. Sometimes the cleverest thing to do was to ask for help.

But before he requested the expertise of the cab driver, there was something else he had to do. Someone else he wanted to see.

He couldn't bear the idea of Cilla spending her eightieth birthday alone, without anyone acknowledging the occasion.

'Cilla!' he called out. 'I'm back!'

He lifted his hand to her but she hadn't clocked him yet. Her prickly Yorkshire terrier had, though. He could hear the furious little mutt as he got nearer, yipping and barking at its owner's heels as if he were coming at them wielding a blood-stained axe, not a Bag for Life full of well-meaning gifts.

As well as carrying the card and balloon, he'd brought **oodles** of treats with him: some overpriced cupcakes from a concession stand at Paddington Station – Strawberry Sundae and Midnight Mint – plus two tins of gin and tonic he'd picked up at M&S, along with a bunch of cheering pink freesias and a packet of Schmackos dog treats. Anything to win the dog over.

'Many happy returns,' he announced once he was in earshot, and Cilla squinted at him against the midday sun.

'Remember me, Mrs Millington?'

'Oh,' she replied, finally recognising him. 'Yes. Yes, of course. Stumper, isn't it? Clayton Stumper? How could I forget that name.'

The look of mild surprise on her face turned to something closer to astonishment as she spotted the large, foiled balloon he clutched in his hand.

Clayton untied it from his wrist and passed it carefully to her.

80 YEARS YOUNG, it read on one side. And on the other: *TIME TO PARTY!*

'Hold on tight now. We don't want to lose it.'

'What's on earth's all this?'

He opened the carrier bag and presented her with the card, the cupcakes and the dog treats. Anyone would think he was handing her solid gold bullion, the way she was looking at him.

'It's nothing much,' he said, removing his coat and draping it across the seat. 'Just a few bits to mark your special day.' He slipped the flowers between the rungs of the bench as he took his seat, so they were sat proudly between the two of them. 'We all deserve to be fussed over at least once a year, don't we?'

Cilla had angled herself away from him all of a sudden, and he heard a strange snuffly noise. His heart sank, wondering if he'd got this all wrong. Not everyone liked celebrating their birthday – back at the Fellowship, Hector would spend the whole day in hiding to avoid being presented with a cake and candles. Clayton had never understood why anyone would pass up an opportunity to eat cake.

She turned back towards him, her eyes watery, and the corners of her mouth twisting into a smile.

Clayton shifted on the seat, unsure what to do. He was tempted to put his arm around her, but he knew it would only make it worse.

'I don't know what to say . . .' she croaked.

'You don't have to say anything.'

'Bless you.' She gripped him quite tightly by the arm. 'I can't tell you what this means. Really.'

Of course, Clayton knew it wasn't the gifts she was moved by. It was the fact he'd remembered her. That he'd seen her. That's what the gifts said. She wasn't so invisible after all.

'My family throw me a big party every year,' he explained. 'I pretend I don't like the fuss, but secretly I love it.'

Every year, on the anniversary of his debut at Creighton Hall, Clayton was spoiled rotten. Pippa would write in every birthday card, every year, that he was the greatest gift she'd ever been given. The residents would don paper party hats, taking it in turns to bake him ever-more-elaborate cakes, and dance to his favourite music in the library. Clayton had never felt unappreciated, or unwanted, on his birthday. And now, he felt compelled to return the favour. To someone who was less fortunate.

'Whoever brought you up,' she said in a trembling voice. 'Well . . . they must have done a fine job.'

Clayton smiled and rubbed the back of his neck. 'They did all right, I think. I've been lucky, really.'

A few moments later and they'd both unfolded a tissue from Cilla's handbag across their laps and were tucking into their cakes while the dog munched happily on his treats.

Cilla proceeded to divulge her life story, pausing only to lick icing from her fingers.

Clayton learned that she was London-born and bred, raised a few miles away in Edgware. She went to a comprehensive a few streets away, but left when she was just thirteen.

'I was diagnosed with peritonitis,' she said. 'I was quite poorly for a while. Doctors thought I might not make it.'

'Is that why you left school?' Clayton asked.

She nodded.

'I was meant to go to a top private school in Barnet. I'd won a scholarship. But I was too ill to go in the end.'

'So you were clever then?' Clayton asked.

'*Too* clever,' she quipped. 'Little girls were supposed to know their place back then. Not to outshine the boys. But a teacher came to see my parents one day, told them he thought I had something about me, you know? Mr Phillips was his name, a lovely man; he reckoned I had a sort of . . . spark. A bit like you, really.'

'Me?'

She nodded. 'You're clearly very . . . bright.'

He wanted to laugh.

'No,' he pleaded. 'No, I'm no genius, that's for sure.'

She shook her head dismissively as if he were being modest.

The truth was, growing up at the Fellowship, Clayton had never felt especially clever. How could he, when the rest of the residents were always ten steps ahead of him. But for the few years that he'd attended the local school with kids the same age as him, he'd realised he was quite normal, really.

He was quick to pick things up, had a knack for memorising mundane things like TV schedules, grocery lists and prescriptions, plus he played a musical instrument to a fairly competent standard, which surely counted for something. Grade Six on piano by the time he was eleven. He could still play 'My Old Man's a Dustman' now, even with his eyes closed.

But no, he didn't possess any of the special intellectual qualities of his friends. He wasn't exceptional in any respect.

Forty minutes after he arrived, Clayton glanced at his watch.

'I'm sorry but I've got to run again.' He reached for his coat behind him. 'But with any luck, Cilla, we'll talk again another day.'

He had already written his mobile number in her card – which she'd yet to open – saying she was welcome to ring whenever she fancied a chat, that he was only at the end of the phone.

'I hope you enjoy the rest of your birthday—'

Cilla's gloved hands were clasping his all of a sudden. 'Thank you,' she said, eyeing him with such deep affection he felt a flash of something warm run up his spine. 'Thank you so much, young man.'

Clayton left the park behind and headed south into West Kilburn. There was something about the prospect of a trip to Nancy's that made him pick up the pace and at various points on the way, he wasn't so much walking as cantering like a horse.

As well as looking forward to seeing the Queen of Quizzes again, there was someone else he hoped to see. He figured if he arrived the same time as yesterday, there was a good chance he might just bump into Neil.

Perhaps he had misread the situation, but he was sure he'd sensed the same hesitancy from Neil when they'd parted ways the previous evening, a reluctance to say goodbye for good.

As he approached Cheviot Street, he strode towards Nancy's house as if pulled towards it by some sort of strange magnetic force. Despite the fact he was simply retracing his steps from yesterday, things felt very different somehow. Clayton felt different.

He let himself through the squeaky gate once again and the German Shepherd next door started its usual hoopla at the window. This time, he tried not to let it throw him.

On Nancy's front step, he quickly spritzed himself with the Paco Rabanne atomiser he kept in his pocket and ran his hand through his hair.

Remembering how yesterday he'd struggled with the bell, he pressed it extra firmly until he heard its chime inside the house, before taking a step back, running a hand through his hair again.

A few seconds later and the door opened, but this time it wasn't the carer who greeted him, but Nancy, her shock of fair hair pushed back by those pink horn-rimmed spectacles on her head.

'Hello again,' she said, touching her pearls. 'You're back.'

Clayton couldn't help glancing at his watch. 'You've finished early.'

Nancy looked puzzled, and then the corner of her lips lifted into a faint smile. 'Expecting to see our lovely Neil, were you? I'm afraid he left a little while ago. I told him to head home—'

'Oh.'

'Because he stayed late for us yesterday.'

Clayton gave a pained smile, nodding. 'Of course. That makes sense.' *It makes perfect sense. Why didn't I factor that into my timings?*

'Did you need him for something or—'

'No, no,' he blustered. 'Not at all. Nothing like that.'

'You sure?' Nancy asked. Her inscrutable gaze was fixed on him. 'You look a little . . . disappointed?'

'No,' Clayton lied. 'No. I mean yes, I'm sure. Do you mind if I come in, Mrs Stone? There's something I wondered if you could help me with.'

Nancy smiled and gestured for him to step inside. 'Let me stick the kettle on. Do you fancy some more Jaffa cakes . . .?'

Chapter Thirty

THE FELLOWSHIP OF PUZZLEMAKERS
SUNDAY, 17TH MARCH, 1991

The spring showers that year were relentless, coming down in thick melodious blankets, a drumroll against the slate roof of Creighton Hall, day and night.

The weather had been so inclement, all of Earl's groundwork on the garden maze had been for nothing. The route he'd started staking out was all sludge, the trenches he'd started digging just days after his arrival, now ravines of rainwater. He was going to have to start over. And to make matters worse, the leak that Pippa had failed to stop in her study appeared to be getting worse. A piddling trickle was now coming down the middle of the crystal chandelier in the hall, which Pippa kept meaning to get sorted.

She'd put down a Tupperware bowl to catch the drips as a temporary fix and asked everyone not to worry. She'd get someone out soon to come and have a look. In all honesty, the reasons she'd avoided ringing an expert was because she was worried what they might find. The last thing she needed right now was another great bill to pay.

In the old billiard room, the needle had just come up on Dusty Springfield and a palpable silence filled the air.

Pippa had summoned all the residents around the waxed leather chesterfield to make her big announcement. Even Angel had turned up, perched on the tea trolley in the corner of the room with her sandaled feet dangling in front of her.

Pippa took a steadying breath.

She wasn't one to suffer from nerves, but the magnitude of what she was about to share with everyone had been weighing on her for days, weeks even, ever since she'd started talking to the council about the prospect of becoming a foster parent.

She took some hesitant steps towards the fireplace, rested her drink on the mantelpiece, and turned to face the assembled crowd.

If it wasn't for Earl sitting on the studded arm of the sofa, coaxing her on with his kind, pleading eyes, she would have been sorely tempted to make her excuses, to pretend that whatever she'd meant to share with them all really didn't matter anymore.

'I need to let you all know something,' she blurted out, her voice strangely high and scratchy. 'And that is . . .' She took a deep breath. 'I am in the process of applying to become a foster carer, and in two days' time a social worker is coming from the council to carry out a house assessment, to see if the Fellowship is a suitable place to help raise a child.'

The words had tumbled out of her mouth like a commentator at Royal Ascot.

Manic, incoherent and entirely without measure. It wasn't how she'd intended to pitch it at all, but the nerves – and the champagne she'd been quaffing all evening for Dutch courage – had left her babbling.

But as a deafening silence rose up to meet her, she almost wished she'd continued talking. The only noise was the steady drip-drip-drip of the leak in the hallway, sploshing into the Tupperware bowl. It sounded even louder than it had earlier.

Everyone was gawping at her as if she'd gone out of her mind. Geoff Stirrup's jaw had gone so slack he was in danger of losing his dentures. Beside him, Hector seemed perplexed. And perhaps most surprising of all, Nancy looked almost affronted. She stared at her from the sofa with a narrowed glare, a lit cigarette dangling forgotten from her fingers.

'Does anyone wish to say anything?' Pippa asked, the desperation in her voice as loud as a bell. 'Some of you have gone a funny colour—'

'A *child*?' Hector repeated, as if Pippa might have said a Siberian tiger instead. 'Living with us . . . *here* at Creighton? Did I catch that right?'

'It's something I've always longed for,' she explained. 'Something I didn't even believe was possible until very recently.'

She caught Earl's eye, and he nodded at her encouragingly.

Silence.

Nancy raised her hand. 'I want to know how long you've been plotting this? And did anyone else know?'

Pippa adjusted her silk shawl, wrapping it tightly across her shoulders. 'I only sent the application off a few weeks ago, Nance. I never expected them to even consider me . . . but if you want the truth, raising a child has been a lifelong ambition of mine.'

'So why have you never mentioned it? Not once in all these years we've been friends.' Nancy took a slow, contemplative drag on her cigarette and Pippa, considering her reply, shifted her weight from one hip to the other.

'Because . . .' She took a deep breath. 'Because that would involve admitting that I've failed at something . . .'

'Sorry,' Hector said. 'But what exactly have you *failed* at?'

'Well . . . I suppose . . .' Pippa faltered, trying to summon the word. 'I've failed at love, haven't I?'

Suddenly the eyes of everyone in the room softened on her.

It all felt so personal, so soul-baring, so unlike her. 'I've never been a great one for accepting defeat,' she went on. 'But the truth is, romance is a puzzle I've never quite cracked. I've never been in a *loving* relationship where I've felt able to bring a child into the world. Everything else in my life, I've done on my own.'

All the time she'd been speaking, Earl's eyes had been fixed eagerly on her, his lips pressed together in a reassuring smile, but now she couldn't help noticing his gaze had lowered to the carpet.

Pippa's dating history wasn't something the two of them had ever discussed. In fact, it wasn't something she talked to anyone about. Even with Nancy. Certainly, she'd never told a soul that she'd only had four proper kisses her entire life.

The first probably didn't count – she was eleven at the time, and the boy hadn't so much kissed her as run his tongue along the inside her mouth as if probing for something; the second and third had been bona fide, shared with a quiet but personable chap in her study group at Cambridge. She'd got close to falling for Terrance Pressfield, until she'd learned he had three other girls on the go at the same time. And then there was the fourth and final kiss. Again, she was hesitant to include it because it also didn't quite qualify. It being an entirely unwelcome move.

A boss of hers at the conveyancing firm had cornered her in the stationery cupboard, gripping her rear with his cold, bony hands. She'd booted him directly between the legs and reported it to HR but it had all been brushed under the carpet. She could still taste his stale coffee breath. She'd been twenty-one at the time.

'The world is different now, of course,' Pippa explained. 'There are all sorts of ways to bring up a child if that's something you wish to do. Families take all shapes. I'm only beginning to realise that.'

'But I thought *we* were your family,' Nancy replied. 'That's what you always said the Fellowship was to you. No?'

'Of course you are,' Pippa insisted. 'We *are* a family!'

'But we're not *enough*?' Geoff called out. 'Is that what you mean?

'*No*,' Pippa replied. 'No, nothing like that at all.'

'You told us all *this* was your dream,' he went on. 'This house, this commune, and we all took the leap with you. Now you're after something else.'

Pippa could feel her defence falling apart in front of her eyes.

He was right. When she'd pitched the idea of the commune all those years ago, when the house was still a hotel, she'd omitted one crucial detail, even to herself. Pippa didn't just want to be part of a family. She didn't just want to run a household. She wanted to raise a child. And now she needed them all on board for this adventure, too.

'This isn't about starting a new family,' she pleaded. 'It's about expanding the one we've already got.'

There was a weighted silence, save for the leak in the hall that was beginning to sound less like a trickle, and more like a steady stream.

'So how old would this kid be, then?' Hector asked, with a troubled look on his face. 'Are we talking a baby, a toddler . . .'

Pippa lifted her finger. 'Assuming I pass the assessment, Hector, the social worker has advised that – due to my age, no doubt – a slightly older child might be more suitable, particularly given it's my first placement. It's unlikely to be a newborn, put it that way. There's even talk that it might . . .' She hesitated. 'It might be a teenager.'

Hector looked slightly relieved, but everyone else seemed horrified. Eric tipped his head to the ceiling in disbelief. Jonty shook his head then reached into his purple suede jacket and removed his notepad, starting to take the minutes on the Fellowship's behalf.

'I know what you're all thinking,' Pippa went on. 'That it's mad for someone *my age* to attempt something like this. And I know that my decision will affect all of you, if the placement does happen.'

The faces of the crowd in front of her seemed to agree.

'But I really think it could work . . . and if age is just a number like we always say it is, then why should it matter how old the Fellowship's next member is?'

Pippa made a few steps towards them all, softening her voice as she continued. 'If creating the Fellowship has taught me anything, it's that it's never too late to pursue an ambition. We're all put on this earth for a reason, aren't we? And perhaps this is it? Perhaps my upbringing, and everything that's happened since, has led to this opportunity right now.'

She could feel her cheeks glowing and was worried she'd said too much, conscious the drink had made her sound sentimental; mawkish, even.

'I'll be in my office tomorrow,' she concluded. 'That's an open door to anyone who wishes to raise an objection. And rest assured, I won't be pursuing this without everyone's approval. This house is yours as much as it's mine and—'

Before she could finish, there was the almightiest crashing noise, which made everyone jolt upright in their seats. It was the sound of a hundred crystal glasses being lobbed off the top of the stairs.

Pippa winced at the noise.

She didn't need to rush out to the entrance hall with everyone else to determine what had just happened. She'd realised immediately and felt a pang of guilt so severe she could do nothing but reach for the mantelpiece to keep herself from sinking to the floor.

The leak that everyone had been pestering her about for months had finally done its worst.

The crystal chandelier had just plummeted to the floor. The ceiling had caved in. And it was all her fault.

Chapter Thirty-One

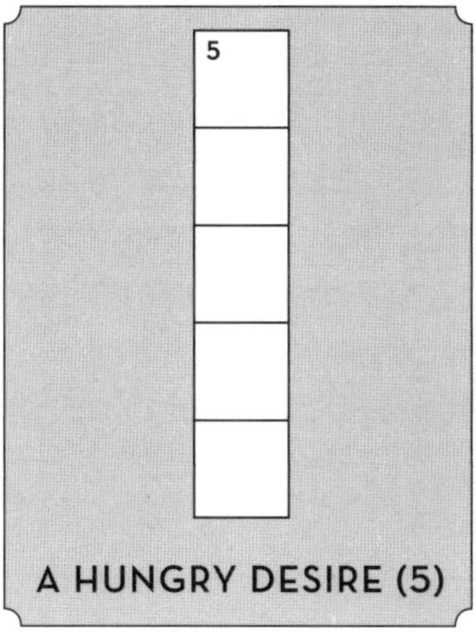

Clayton was perched on the trampoline of a wingback chair in Nancy's front room, watching the Queen of Quizzes study Pippa's cryptogram with a magnifying glass pressed right up to her face. He'd already shown her the H key, which she claimed not to recognise at all, but hopefully she'd be able to help him find the answers in the grid. He'd only managed to solve and locate one so far.

While studying the puzzle last night, he'd decided that Pippa's suggestion to try answering in reverse was actually an ingenious clue to the cipher at the heart of this puzzle.

The entries appeared in the grid in *reverse* alphabet.

So, if *A*=*Z* and *B*=*Y*, and so on, then 'the greatest city in the world' was, obviously *LONDON*. Or, less obviously, *OLMWLM*.

But that was as far as he'd got, because as Pippa had also hinted at in her letter, question number one was more difficult than question number four, another clever nod to the reversal theme. Everything was back to front. It left Clayton completely confounded, but if anyone knew London, it was Nancy.

Her lips were puckered around her e-cigarette and, from where he was sitting, she was becoming increasingly obscured behind a thick plume of vape smoke. It smelled, and tasted, like pear drops.

T	K	U	T	Z	P	A	A	S	Y	B	V	O	Q	W	L	A	N	U	E
D	O	B	M	V	O	T	E	G	I	H	W	F	A	T	D	V	G	I	B
S	H	Q	U	U	Q	N	F	O	Q	Z	P	P	B	E	M	H	N	T	Y
F	W	N	O	R	A	T	Y	V	D	E	X	I	X	Q	A	E	A	C	H
N	O	V	Q	Q	Z	U	N	C	H	G	E	J	P	N	C	R	O	W	K
Y	S	K	L	F	N	P	V	N	G	U	B	Q	Q	U	V	X	K	I	Y
V	B	D	G	I	D	U	S	O	I	H	M	N	O	G	Z	P	G	U	Y
I	C	N	J	S	V	Z	I	J	L	G	M	V	W	Y	R	E	H	Y	D
P	I	F	W	L	Z	M	I	C	M	I	G	Y	P	C	K	Z	W	J	G
N	G	Q	B	N	X	I	B	T	T	L	V	S	M	C	K	K	L	D	F
K	L	M	T	H	U	R	U	V	I	H	N	X	H	C	W	X	I	R	V
Q	K	W	D	Y	V	D	P	C	L	O	M	L	B	I	A	L	I	Q	I
G	J	T	Q	N	A	W	Q	H	L	S	G	Y	T	T	Q	D	Z	N	V
Q	W	Z	L	I	M	L	G	K	N	L	I	Y	L	A	O	I	S	W	S
I	C	U	B	X	P	X	X	D	M	F	H	K	L	Z	D	M	O	J	R
B	L	X	T	X	Z	O	D	O	P	K	N	N	I	O	S	L	P	O	N
Q	N	E	U	L	X	G	W	Q	D	K	F	H	T	L	O	W	E	P	J
U	S	N	Z	Z	L	G	V	D	I	S	N	P	N	G	B	M	H	J	X
O	E	G	Y	X	J	P	R	Q	U	D	E	K	P	A	U	L	W	A	Y
F	G	C	H	J	J	K	G	M	N	S	W	S	M	Z	Z	O	I	B	B

Clues to the four entries in the grid:
1. S: Basement (10)
2. S: 87-135 (7)
3.W: Oratory, Uruguay, Bunch of Grapes (8-4)
~~4.N: The greatest city in the world? (6)~~

'Found the next one!'

Nancy raised her pink highlighter triumphantly above her head but before she could swipe it across the page, she bellowed, 'And the next!'

When she finally looked up, she still had the magnifying glass held right up to her face. Her eyes were as big as saucers.

'Nobody ever studies wrestling,' she declared, and Clayton – baffled – stared at her.

'I beg your pardon?' he asked.

'Noel Edmonds shaves weirdly!' she added, as if that cleared everything up.

He hadn't a clue what she was on about. It was like she was malfunctioning.

She was leaning forward now, eyebrows hitched above her pink-framed spectacles, looking at him expectantly.

'I'm sorry, Mrs Stone, I have no idea what you're talking about.'

Nancy sighed. 'Cardinal directions.' She passed him back the sheet.

'Oh,' Clayton replied. 'Like points on a compass? Never eat Shredded Wheat.'

'Exactly. That's what the letters in front of the clues reveal. The direction that the solutions are pointed in the grid. That makes it a little easier anyway.'

She handed him back the page, with the two additional words highlighted with her pink marker.

T	K	U	T	Z	P	A	A	S	Y	B	V	O	Q	W	L	A	N	U	E
D	O	B	M	V	O	T	E	G	I	H	W	F	A	T	D	V	G	I	B
S	H	Q	U	U	Q	N	F	O	Q	Z	P	P	B	E	M	H	N	T	Y
F	W	N	O	R	A	T	Y	V	D	E	X	I	X	Q	A	E	A	C	H
N	O	V	Q	Q	Z	U	N	C	H	G	E	J	P	N	C	R	O	W	K
Y	S	K	L	F	N	P	V	N	G	U	B	Q	Q	U	V	X	K	I	Y
V	B	D	G	I	D	U	S	O	I	H	M	N	O	G	Z	P	G	U	Y
I	C	N	J	S	V	Z	I	J	L	G	M	V	W	Y	R	E	H	Y	D
P	I	F	W	L	Z	M	I	C	M	I	G	Y	P	C	K	Z	W	J	G
N	G	Q	B	N	X	I	B	T	T	L	V	S	M	C	K	K	L	D	F
K	L	M	T	H	U	R	U	V	I	H	N	X	H	C	W	X	I	R	V
Q	K	W	D	Y	V	D	P	C	L	O	M	L	B	I	A	L	I	Q	I
G	J	T	Q	N	A	W	Q	H	L	S	G	Y	T	T	Q	D	Z	N	V
Q	W	Z	L	I	M	L	G	K	N	L	I	Y	L	A	O	I	S	W	S
I	C	U	B	X	P	X	X	D	M	F	H	K	L	Z	D	M	O	J	R
B	L	X	T	X	Z	O	D	O	P	K	N	N	I	O	S	L	P	O	N
Q	N	E	U	L	X	G	W	Q	D	K	F	H	T	L	O	W	E	P	J
U	S	N	Z	Z	L	G	V	D	I	S	N	P	N	G	B	M	H	J	X
O	E	G	Y	X	J	P	R	Q	U	D	E	K	P	A	U	L	W	A	Y
F	G	C	H	J	J	K	G	M	N	S	W	S	M	Z	Z	O	I	B	B

Clues to the four entries in the grid:

1. S: Basement (10)

~~2. S: 87 135 (7)~~

~~3.W: Oratory, Uruguay, Bunch of Grapes (8 4)~~

~~4.N: The greatest city in the world? (6)~~

Clayton tried to convert the latest entries Nancy had picked out as quickly as he could, using the back-to-front alphabet formula.

'Number three,' Nancy read out. '"Oratory, Uruguay, Bunch of Grapes." Any idea?'

He shook his head.

'Well, there's only one oratory in the city. The Church of the Immaculate Heart of Mary, otherwise known as the London Oratory. It's on the same road as the Embassy of Uruguay, and the famous Bunch of Grapes pub. So the solution is . . .'

Clayton lifted his finger to her, finally aligning the coded letters into their correct order in his mind. *YILNKGLM IZLW*, when you reversed the order of the alphabet was . . .

'Brompton . . . Road?' he said hesitantly.

'Bingo!' Nancy shouted. 'So what about question two then?'

Clayton glanced down at the sheet. Was 87–135 just a mathematical sum? A subtraction? He tried to decode *SZIILWH* but his brain was hurting with it all, and Nancy was on the edge of her seat, which only made it harder to concentrate.

He tipped his head to the ceiling as he ran the letters through his head, along a mental alphabetical scale, conscious of Nancy's slippered foot tapping impatiently in front of him.

'Minus forty-eight?'

Nancy spat out a laugh. 'No, Clayton. You're overcomplicating it now.'

'I am?' That was the last thing he wanted to do. Already his head was completely scrambled.

'Try putting clue two,' she said, 'in front of the solution to question three?'

Clayton looked down at the sheet.

'Eighty-seven to one-three-five . . . Brompton Road?'

'That's it!'

He squinted at her. *It was?*

'One of the most famous addresses in the greatest city in the world,' she declared. 'And Pippa's favourite shop in the world.'

'Harrods!' Clayton answered in a flash.

SZIILWH translated as *Harrods*. It all seemed so obvious now. But then, what was the final entry waiting to be uncovered?

Nancy reached over and took the sheet from his hands, tearing the lid off her highlighter with her mouth and running her pen along the middle of the sheet, in a southerly direction, before handing it back.

T	K	U	T	Z	P	A	A	S	Y	B	V	O	Q	W	L	A	N	U	E
D	O	B	M	V	O	T	E	G	I	H	W	F	A	T	D	V	G	I	B
S	H	Q	U	U	Q	N	F	O	Q	Z	P	P	B	E	M	H	N	T	Y
F	W	N	O	R	A	T	Y	V	D	E	X	I	X	Q	A	E	A	C	H
N	O	V	Q	Q	Z	U	N	C	H	G	E	J	P	N	C	R	O	W	K
Y	S	K	L	F	N	P	V	N	G	U	B	Q	Q	U	V	X	K	I	Y
V	B	D	G	I	D	U	S	O	I	H	M	N	O	G	Z	P	G	U	Y
I	C	N	J	S	V	Z	I	J	L	G	M	V	W	Y	R	E	H	Y	D
P	I	F	W	L	Z	M	I	C	M	I	G	Y	P	C	K	Z	W	J	G
N	G	Q	B	N	X	I	B	T	T	L	V	S	M	C	K	K	L	D	F
K	L	M	T	H	U	R	U	V	I	H	N	X	H	C	W	X	I	R	V
Q	K	W	D	Y	V	D	P	C	L	O	M	L	B	I	A	L	I	Q	I
G	J	T	Q	N	A	W	Q	H	L	S	G	Y	T	T	Q	D	Z	N	V
Q	W	Z	L	I	M	L	G	K	N	L	I	Y	L	A	O	I	S	W	S
I	C	U	B	X	P	X	X	D	M	F	H	K	L	Z	D	M	O	J	R
B	L	X	T	X	Z	O	D	O	P	K	N	N	I	O	S	L	P	O	N
Q	N	E	U	L	X	G	W	Q	D	K	F	H	T	L	O	W	E	P	J
U	S	N	Z	Z	L	G	V	D	I	S	N	P	N	G	B	M	H	J	X
O	E	G	Y	X	J	P	R	Q	U	D	E	K	P	A	U	L	W	A	Y
F	G	C	H	J	J	K	G	M	N	S	W	S	M	Z	Z	O	I	B	B

Clues to the four entries in the grid:

~~1. S: Basement (10)~~

~~2. S: 87 135 (7)~~

~~3.W: Oratory, Uruguay, Bunch of Grapes (8-4)~~

~~4.N: The greatest city in the world? (6)~~

HGILMTILLN. It took Clayton a minute or so, but eventually he got there.

'*Str… ong… room*? *Strongroom*?'

Nancy beamed, nodding. 'Pippa kept a deposit box in the strongroom at Harrods. For as long as I've known her, she stored her most treasured items in the basement there—'

'The key!' Clayton shouted excitedly. '*H* for Harrods! That must be what it's for, don't you think?'

Nancy grinned at him. 'So, I need to go to Harrods, unlock Pippa's safe, and find the next clue on her trail?'

'I imagine so,' she said, blinking. The venetian blinds in the window were casting a pedestrian crossing of sunlight across her face and Clayton felt an increasing affection towards the woman, and a feeling of melancholy that this would likely be the last time they were in each other's company.

'How would I get there?' he asked. 'From here to Harrods, I mean.'

Nancy looked at him a moment, then pushed herself gingerly out of her armchair. She moved into the hall and returned a few seconds later brandishing the keys to her cab. 'I'll drive you.'

A minute later and Nancy had grabbed her coat and darted up the stairs to check on her husband. Before Clayton had even managed to lace up his shoes, she was back in the hallway.

'He'll be fine for an hour or so,' she said. '*Pointless* is on.'

She pulled Clayton's coat from the mahogany hatstand and lifted her own wide-brimmed hat from one of its hooks. It was a crimson felt danby hat with a black velvet band wrapped around it and an arrangement of small, bright feathers tucked at the side, the kind a fly fisherman might use as bait.

Clayton's entire body went stiff as he watched her angling it jauntily on her head in front of the mirror. How hadn't he wondered about all the hats before?

Clayton counted nine, ten, eleven different pieces of formal ladies' headwear – cloche hats, bowler hats, bucket hats – all suspended from the stand. These were the sort of hats you might buy in a specialist shop. The sort of hats you might store in boxes. The sort of box he'd arrived in all those years ago.

Nancy turned and caught his eye.

'You all right, love?'

'Yes, yes, sorry. I was just . . . admiring your hat.'

Nancy looked surprised. 'Oh . . . thank you.' Her hand went to touch the rim. 'This one's donkey's old. But it's one of my favourites. You can tuck a lighter under the ribbon at the back, which is handy.'

Clayton smiled. 'You've got quite the collection.'

She turned to glance at him again. 'Yes, I wouldn't disagree with you there.'

'Where are they all from?'

'My father,' she answered. 'He was a milliner in the East End, had a shop, an emporium, actually.'

'Really?' Clayton's voice came out so high it was practically falsetto.

'Yeah.' Nancy looked at him dubiously. 'Hackney Hatters, it was called. I got some of the stock when my old man retired. There must be a hundred hats in my attic, all in their boxes.'

Clayton felt as if he might be sick.

Hackney Hatters.

H.H.

Minutes later and Clayton's bottom was clenched on the beaded seat cover of Nancy's passenger seat.

He had never attempted to break the human sound barrier before, nor had he hurled himself through a ring of fire as a human cannonball, but he couldn't imagine either experience being any less terrifying than it was to sit beside Nancy as she hurtled through London in her black cab.

They were only half a mile from her house and already he was feeling quite unwell. Nancy had put the heated seats on full blast as soon as she'd switched on the ignition and the beads of Clayton's seat cover were at an almost searing temperature. It felt like he was having a hot-stone massage he'd never asked for.

But it wasn't just the suffocating heat, nor the breakneck speed of the journey, or even the uncertainty about what he was going to uncover in Pippa's safe that was making him feel queasy. It was that he was sure he'd already discovered a clue that Pippa hadn't planted on her puzzle trail.

Nancy was linked to his arrival in a Hackney Hatter's hatbox at Creighton Hall. She had to be. There was no other explanation.

Could she be . . .? Was she . . .? The lady who'd abandoned him at the door? *His birth mother?*

'You all right?' she asked. 'Do you want me to switch the heaters off?'

'Please,' he said, pulling at his collar. 'It's getting a bit stuffy now, isn't it.'

The residual warmth from his seat wasn't helping. The whole area surrounding his bottom had an increasingly tepid, almost liquid quality. If he didn't know any better, he might have wondered if he'd wet himself.

Clayton focused on what was ahead of him, in search of more clues.

In the shadows of the footwell, a Tesco carrier bag contained a couple of well-thumbed novels he couldn't quite make out. On the dashboard was a bundle of purple wool wrapped around some knitting needles. Suspended from the rear-view mirror was a pair of pink fluffy dice, an air freshener – in the form of a cartoon llama – and a tiny photo frame dangling on a chain. The picture it held – about passport-sized – was of a distinguished-looking gentleman. His father? *Don't be ridiculous*, he thought, shaking his head. He couldn't focus on it long enough to decide anyway; it was swinging round and round and he could only catch flashes of the chap.

They were pulling up at the lights.

As the vehicle stopped, the man in the photograph spun round to reveal himself.

White cotton-wool hair. Military moustache. A ruddy complexion. He was in his early eighties, appeared friendly enough, and was handsome in his own way. Clayton was trying to decide if he could notice any resemblance when he felt Nancy's eyes on him.

'I know what you're thinking.'

He felt his heart sink.

'Either I've had a lot of work done, or my husband is old enough to be my dad.'

'Oh right,' he replied, laughing with relief, surprise and

embarrassment. 'Yes. I mean, no, I don't think you've had any work done.'

Nancy gave a kindly smile.

She kissed two fingers and pressed them against the photograph.

So far, Clayton had established only a few facts about the mysterious bedbound husband upstairs, but it took only the slightest expression of interest, as the car shot past Notting Hill Station, for the driver to open up about the man.

He was Pete Neenance. Pub landlord at the Old Queen's Head in Islington for over forty years, the final ten of those Nancy had hosted their weekly quiz nights. The pair had got chatting one evening, after years of knowing each other, and quickly realised they had so much in common. They were both die-hard Londoners for a start – born and raised only a mile from each other in the East End, but perhaps most surprising of all was that Pete shared Nancy's love of knitting. He was the only man she'd ever met who loved casting on as much as she did. Apparently, it was the one thing that calmed him after a busy night behind the bar.

'He even knitted the cake toppers for our wedding,' Nancy said. 'Two tiny figurines of us – they're in the downstairs loo.'

Clayton smiled. 'So, when you married, you didn't take his name?'

Nancy puffed out her cheeks. 'I take it that's a joke?'

'No,' he said, wondering why it would be.

'He's Mr Neenance. I would have become Nance Neenance. As if!'

Clayton smiled at nothing ahead of him, feeling his grip relax on the side of his seat.

'So he already had your name in his?' he heard himself say. 'That sounds like fate to me.'

'Serendipity,' she agreed. 'I've always believed in it.'

At the mention of the word, Clayton felt something shift in his stomach. He turned to look at Nancy, who seemed oblivious to the reference, instead examining herself in the fold-out mirror above her seat, pulling her forehead taut with both hands.

'I've been thinking about getting a bit of Botox, what do you think?'

'Oh no, I don't think you need it,' he replied.

'No?'

He shook his head. He'd never understood the obsession with ironing out wrinkles.

'Lines on a face,' he said. 'They don't just reveal your age, do they?'

'No?'

He shook his head again. 'They tell people that you've . . . lived, that you've seen stuff. You've survived.'

She was smiling fondly at him. 'Battle scars you mean?'

He tipped his head from side to side. 'More like when you cut into a tree, and you see the rings?'

He was beginning to wonder if the traffic lights were actually broken. They'd been sitting at a red for what felt like forever.

Finally, they flashed amber, and Nancy accelerated with the screech of a champion Formula One driver exiting the pit lane.

A few hundred yards from the Natural History Museum, she slammed her foot on the pedals at a zebra crossing. A procession of tiny rucksack-clad children scurried across the road like ants.

'For crying out loud!' She drummed her hands impatiently against the wheel.

They'd only left the house twenty minutes ago.

'I know how difficult it is . . .' Clayton announced, almost unconsciously. 'Seeing someone you love get ill like that, how worrying it can be.'

Nancy turned to look at him. 'Thank you,' she said softly.

Their eyes settled on the final few kids scuttling past and for a moment neither of them uttered a word. A weary-looking teacher eventually raised their hand in thanks and Nancy slipped into first.

She sighed. 'I suppose I've only got myself to blame.'

'Why's that?'

Another set of lights. She adjusted her hat so it sat more jauntily on her head. 'Let's just say . . . I've always been fond of an older gentleman.'

'*Right* . . . I see.'

Nancy's face was all naughty, a cheeky shimmer of a smile. 'So I guess, in some way, I knew I'd end up as a carer one day,' she added.

Clayton nodded. He knew how that felt.

Ever since he was twelve, he'd decided the direction his life was headed. He was going to remain at the Fellowship for ever, or at least until he was the last one standing, until there was no one else to care for. To care for, in the way they cared for him.

'I suppose that's the price you pay,' he mused.

Nancy shot him a look.

'When you love someone, I mean.'

'Right.'

'You'll do anything for them, won't you? You'll never walk away. You'll never abandon them . . .'

The remark had come out more pointedly than he'd intended, but he couldn't help himself. It was becoming very clear that Pippa's quest would never lead him directly to the answer he was looking for. No, what she was doing was inching him closer to the truth, leading him by the metaphorical hand, encouraging him to join the dots, to find his own answers. Clayton was the detective in his own mystery. He was in control of this quest, not her.

He glanced into the lady's eyes to see if there was a flicker of anything. Any glimmer of culpability, regret . . . shame, even. If she was the person who'd given birth to him then abandoned him all those years ago, he wondered what might have led to it, and why, after all these years, she'd never shown any interest in his existence, never considered stepping forward and announcing herself as his birth mother.

She *was* looking at him differently, he thought, her head tilted to one side, as if seeing him in a different light.

'You're absolutely right,' she said after a few seconds. 'And I wouldn't have it any other way. Plus, I'm lucky I get a few hours to myself each day. Neil's been an absolute godsend.'

At the mention of the carer, Clayton found himself sitting a little straighter in his seat.

'Yes,' he agreed. 'He seems very . . .' What was the word he was looking for: charming, thoughtful, handsome? 'Diligent.'

Nancy gave an agreeable smile. 'It's a shame you missed him today. He was asking after you—'

'He was?' The words tumbled from his mouth before he could stop them.

'Yeah.' She was looking at him as if she were about to say something further – lips slightly pursed – but in the end she just smiled, indicated left, and turned onto Brompton Road.

'It's funny,' she said. 'You two remind me of each other.'

'We do?'

'Nice lads, you know?'

Harrods was coming into view. The familiar forest-green canopies and the Union Jack flags mounted to the side of the building were in sight. The journey was nearing its end. It had been, Clayton realised, as enlightening as it had been exhilarating. There was something about being in a car, being in such close quarters with someone, but not looking them squarely in the eyes, that made it easier to open up, to raise the questions he might otherwise struggle to.

'What made you leave the Fellowship?' he asked.

They were turning into a side street, and these words hung between them in the car, lingering in the dry, stuffy air of the central heating.

'You disappeared the year I arrived, Mrs Stone. Where did you go?'

Out of the corner of his eye he saw Nancy briefly close her eyes, taking a breath.

'It was the toughest thing I ever did, Clayton, leaving my friends like that. You do realise that?'

He nodded, but it was more than tough, he thought. It was unthinkable, for him at least, to consider walking away.

'So why couldn't you stay?' he asked. 'What made you go?'

Nancy sighed. 'I was looking for something. Something I needed . . . for myself.'

'And what was that?'

She shook her head and smiled ruefully to herself. 'Love. I wanted to fall in love with someone, Clayton. I wanted it more than anything else. Sounds silly, doesn't it?'

'No,' he replied. 'No, it doesn't sound silly at all, actually.' If he was honest, it was something he'd also yearned for over the years. Although there wasn't much risk of that happening to him anytime soon.

'It was Pip who made me realise the clock was ticking on us all,' Nancy explained. 'When she told us about applying to become a foster parent.'

'Sorry?'

Nancy turned to him, her eyes widening in surprise. 'You didn't know about that?'

Clayton felt the colour drain from his face. He shook his head, lowered his gaze into his lap. *A foster child?*

'You know what she was like when she set her sights on something,' Nancy added. 'There was no stopping her.'

Clayton wasn't sure how to process this news. He wondered first where Pippa had got the idea of fostering from, then what had stopped her from pursuing it, whether it was his arrival that put a halt to her plans.

'Did you ever want children?' he asked.

Nancy shook her head quickly. 'No, that was never something I've craved.' She whipped into a parking space, with impeccable precision. 'But hearing Pip talk about chasing an ambition like that . . . an emptiness she felt, an urge she had . . . it made me realise . . .'

'What?'

Nancy switched the engine off. 'That it's never too late, Clayton, to find the missing pieces that make you feel complete. That there's nothing more important in life than pursuing the things you're hungry for, before it's too late.'

Crave, he thought. *A hungry desire*. Five down.

As Nancy glanced at herself in the visor mirror, he pondered what he most wanted out of life, beyond finding out who had been responsible for putting him on this earth. He wanted friends, and perhaps even to experience love of some kind, to find a new kind of Fellowship when the one he'd always known was no longer around.

Nancy turned and smiled, her face opening like a book. He was pleased he'd come to her for help, and he didn't want to say goodbye to her yet.

'Nancy,' he said quietly.

'Yes, dear?'

Clayton swallowed, unsure whether he was ready to ask Nancy the next question on the tip of his tongue. 'Do you . . . I mean . . .' He paused. 'Would you mind coming into Harrods with me?'

'Oh.' Her eyes went very big behind her spectacles.

'I'll be as quick as I can . . .'

She looked in the rear-view mirror and adjusted her hat, then took her keys out of the car. 'I'd be honoured, Clayton.'

A rush of wind whistled through the cab as she opened the door, ruffling Clayton's hair and flooding him with a renewed sense of purpose.

He smiled and opened his own door, stepping onto the bustling pavement of Brompton Road and heading in the direction of Pippa's next clue.

Chapter Thirty-Two

THE FELLOWSHIP OF PUZZLEMAKERS

MONDAY, 18TH MARCH, 1991

Although Pippa had promised everyone she would be in her office all day, happy to speak about anyone's objections to her fostering application, suddenly she had more important things to do.

She took the fast train to London, letting Angel know that the emergency plumber would be arriving while she was out. The gold-plated skeleton key was tucked safely in a hanky in her cardigan pocket as she left the house that morning. She'd put off her trip to Harrods long enough and the ceiling collapsing the previous evening had left her with no choice.

She'd been bequeathed a safety deposit box at the famous London department store as part of her twenty-first birthday inheritance. Stashed away in the vaults were precious Allsbrook heirlooms, almost all of which she'd started to auction – without anyone knowing – to clear the various debts she'd accrued. There was her mother's costume jewellery, her father's prized coin collection, her grandmother's Italian glassware. All gone.

Now, just one treasure remained.

Twelve months before her mother's premature death, and her own birth, Pippa's father had commissioned a portrait of his beloved wife, painted by a family friend who was a celebrated artist of the time.

As a young woman, Pippa had made a vow to herself. She would never part with it. It was the only remaining link to her past, and to the mother she'd never met. But she couldn't think of any other way to pay for the repairs and ensure that the Fellowship survived. She *had* to sell it.

Pippa returned from Harrods later that afternoon with the portrait wedged firmly under her arm. She rested the picture gently against her desk, making sure her mother's face – blurred behind a layer of bubble wrap – was looking away from her, then sank into her office chair.

Things would soon sort themselves out. Everything would be back on track before she knew it. She even had a potential buyer lined up. Edwin Dankworth – a close companion of Jonty's – was a major art buyer in the West End, and the two of them were already in touch. She hadn't told Jonty what exactly she was selling, but he had been more than happy to introduce them. It was being couriered straight to Edwin's shop for a valuation later that day. They just needed to agree on a good price, that was all. If it was worth as much as she thought it might be, then she'd be able to pay for the repairs and get back on top of the Fellowship finances without anyone suspecting they'd ever been in trouble. That she had failed them all.

She took a deep breath and closed her eyes, allowing everything to go dark for a second, before reopening them, as if resetting herself.

The sun was trying to make an appearance. Warm, glaring rays were bleeding through her lace blinds, illuminating her office as if she'd just installed new bulbs. And yet, despite the fact the rain had eased off and things were brightening up, Pippa couldn't shake the sense of melancholy hanging over her, like dark clouds were following her everywhere.

The leak had been stopped temporarily, that section of the hallway roped off, but investigations were ongoing and didn't sound great. Someone would be back in a few days to complete their diagnostics. Scaffolding was required. The house was unnervingly quiet. The social worker was still scheduled to arrive the following day. Pippa had been debating on the train what she should do. Cancel the visit at the last minute and hope they could rearrange a future date? Or press ahead and make sure their visitor didn't see the gaping hole in the hall?

Then she saw it. A cream envelope resting in the keys of her typewriter. On the front, a hastily scrawled *P* had been dashed off in green ink. Someone must have delivered it while she'd been out.

Pippa sought her silver letter opener from her top drawer, sliding the blade under the envelope's lip, releasing the tacky seal in a hurried swipe.

The document inside had been typed on official Fellowship headed paper.

FAO: Miss Pippa Allsbrook,

I am writing to officially record my objection to the proposal as outlined in yesterday evening's unofficial consultation (March, Sixteenth).

You were correct in highlighting the democratic values that we have all chosen to live by, here at Creighton Hall.

As per our residents' agreement, which we all signed and agreed to – yourself included, might I add – a unanimous vote is required for you to continue with this motion.

Please accept this note as a formal rejection to the plan and respectfully abandon the bid.

Yours gratefully,
A resident
The Fellowship of Puzzlemakers

Pippa felt sick to the stomach.

She assumed there would be one or two who had a bone to pick, though nothing serious enough that she wouldn't be able to talk them round. But for someone to deliver such a hard-hearted, lily-livered note like that? Without even the decency to speak to her in person? How cowardly, she thought. How callous and cruel.

Pippa turned the page over in her hands, as if scouring the words for any hidden clues. The fact it had been typed and not handwritten was no coincidence. Whoever had written this note didn't want to risk Pippa finding out who they were. There was nothing personalised about it. No distinguishing features at all. In fact, it could have come from any of them.

Anyone but Earl, of course.

The letter consumed Pippa for the rest of the evening, and that night she lay restlessly in bed wondering what she should do with it.

One thing was certain. She wasn't going to show it to Earl. He'd only encourage her to do the obvious thing and cancel tomorrow's visit.

No, it didn't take Pippa long to decide that she was going to press ahead with the house assessment. In fact, the letter had simply reminded her quite how much the opportunity meant to her. She folded it up and placed it out of sight under her pillow.

Pippa's mettle was simply being tested, that was all. At sixty-four years of age, nothing had ever stopped her doing anything – people and plumbing included – and it wasn't going to be any different now.

Chapter Thirty-Three

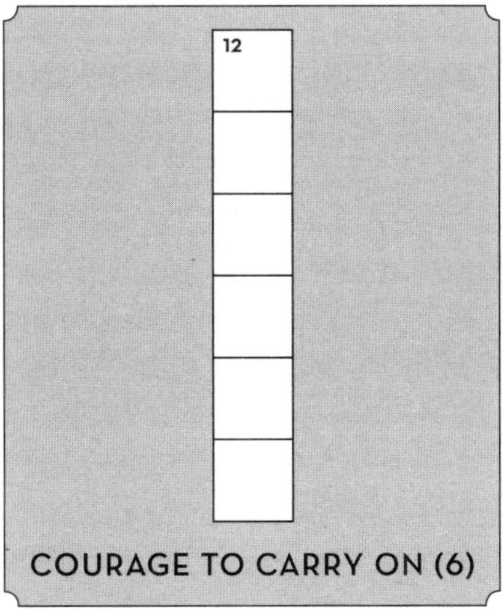

Clayton and Nancy were practically galloping to keep up with a wiry, moustachioed man from Harrods who was guiding them on a giddy helter-skelter course through the department store, whirling past Scarves and Gloves, then Hosiery and Lingerie, before sweeping through the grand Egyptian Hall.

It was as if Earl had designed the maze-like layout that comprised the seven floors of this place, he thought. It was a miracle anyone ended up finding what they were looking for.

Mr Stopford-Sackville, who had met them at the concierge desk and was now whisking them down to Pippa's safety deposit box, was the spitting image of Anthony Hopkins in *Howard's End*. His shiny name-badge on the lapel of his emerald-green suit informed them he was a Client Services Executive and At Their Service.

'But you can call me Julian.'

Clayton's nerves were jangling like the antique key in his pocket.

Julian was surprisingly sprightly for a man of his size, and no sooner had they entered the magnificent golden Egyptian Hall, than he had turned a sharp left into the Oyster Bar, followed by Chocolates and Confectionery. Perfumes.

Clayton was beginning to wonder if it was some sort of joke, whether this chap was simply seeing how much of the store he could get them to walk through until one of them cottoned on. Even Nancy – a walking, talking atlas of London – appeared to be finding the route dizzying. As Julian shepherded them into a rather snug elevator, tucked away in a discreet corner, she glanced over her shoulder, as if mapping the way back out.

The lift lurched suddenly, beginning their excruciatingly slow descent. Nancy shot Clayton a funny look as she stood beside him, both their backs pressed to the wall. Clayton noticed that she was gripping the handrail on the side of the lift as if her life depended on it.

'You all right?' he asked in a hushed voice.

She nodded, but her face said something else. The poor woman needed to get back, he thought. Her husband was waiting for her.

The lift finally juddered to a stop, a gentle chime sounded, and the doors slid open.

Julian ushered them both out into a long dark-wood-panelled room lit with great glowing orbs suspended from the ceiling.

Clayton couldn't help but pause to take it all in, and he was sure he heard a little gasp escape from Nancy's mouth.

'This is the oldest part of the store,' Julian announced, 'and perhaps the least visited . . .'

Because no one can find it, Clayton thought.

'It was built in 1896 and we have over three thousand safes – everything from small strongboxes to eight-foot-high vaults. If you head over to the desk there, they'll be able to assist you. I hope you find everything you're looking for.' He bowed his head dutifully, then stepped back into the lift and was gone.

A lady with tightly permed hair, wearing an emerald twinset uniform that matched Julian's suit, stood up from behind the huge mahogany desk at the end of the room. 'Good afternoon,' she said warmly. 'Welcome to the Safety Deposit Department. I'm Mrs Hecklesford and I'll be assisting you today.'

'Hello there. I'm Clayton Stumper.'

Mrs Hecklesford returned his smile, then flicked through the great logbook open in front of her on the desk.

'How strange, there's no Stumper listed here. Is it *your* safety box, sir?'

'Oh, no. It's not. I'm here for Pippa Allsbrook's box.' He thrust his hand into his pocket and presented the ornate golden key. 'She gave me this . . .'

The woman blinked at him, then leaned across the desk and took the key from his outstretched fingers. 'Let me see . . .'

She sifted through the book, dabbing her finger with her tongue every few pages. 'Ah, Allsbrook. Here we go.'

There was a brief pause as she read the details on the account. 'So . . . you were assigned Miss Allsbrook's proxy safe-holder in September last year, sir. Does that sound right?'

Clayton nodded, his eyes wide. That meant Pippa had meticulously planned everything six months before she died.

'Did you bring some form of identification with you?' the lady asked.

Clayton dug his hand into his other pocket and pulled out the passport he'd brought from home, just as Pippa had asked him to in her original note.

At least there would be no international travel required, he thought.

'Please take a seat. I'll just go and run a few security checks and I'll be back in a jiffy.'

As she left the room via a side door with a frosted glass window, Clayton wondered if Mrs Hecklesford had made her own assumptions about how he and Nancy knew each other. Whether she'd realised they were basically strangers, or if she had decided that they were relations, perhaps mother and son. Whether she was, in fact, right.

In the waiting room, Nancy had slumped into one of the red leather chairs, her eyes fixed on her hands in her lap, while

Clayton paced the carpet opposite her. He didn't want to sit down. He just wanted to unlock the safe, to see what was waiting for him. A silence stretched endlessly between the pair of them.

Eventually, Nancy lifted the strap of her handbag over her shoulder. 'I'm sorry, Clayton,' she said. 'But I shouldn't be here. I'm going to head off.'

'Oh,' he said, trying to hide his disappointment.

'It's not that I don't want to be here for you,' she explained, running her finger along the gold studs on the arm of the chair. 'It's just that, this is . . . personal. Whatever Pip has left behind for you here – and I promise, I'm no wiser than you – it's got nothing to do with me.'

'It . . . *hasn't*?'

She shook her head and for a second her eyes narrowed on him as if she were trying to read his mind.

Clayton returned her gaze. She was still wearing the hat with the feathers poking up at the side.

He was trying to decide if he believed her, if he *wanted* to believe this lady had nothing to do with bringing him into this world. The funny thing was, he was beginning to grow quite fond of her.

'This is your story, Clayton. It's *your* mystery to solve, no one else's.'

'But—'

'I think you ought to experience this alone, don't you? I think that's only right.' Nancy zipped up her quilted coat. 'You asked *why* I left the Fellowship. *Why* I couldn't stay.' When she removed her hands from her pockets, her right hand was holding a small velvet pouch.

Clayton felt a lightness in his chest as she lowered the little bag into his hands.

'I was gifted this a long time ago, by a man I loved very much. I want you to have it now.'

Looking down at it, he couldn't help but notice that the velvet was exactly the same shade as the lining of Pippa's coffin: a rich purple hue. The tiny bag, with its tatty drawstring drawn tight, held something small and hard and round by the feel of things. A ring?

'Love is more complicated than any puzzle anyone will ever set, Clayton.'

She was looking at him with such a deep intensity, he found himself riveted to the spot, as if under a spell.

'But the trick, young man, is to find the person who loves you the way *you* love them. The way you *deserve* to be loved. Because, in the end . . .' Her hands were clasped around his again. 'Love is all that matters.'

She stood up, straightened her coat, then went on tiptoes to plant a kiss on his forehead, before turning on her heels to leave. And just like that she was gone.

Alone once more, Clayton tipped the contents of the pouch into his hand.

An elaborate ladies' ring dropped out, settling into the folds of his palm. It was beautiful. But it was only when he examined it closely that he appreciated the complex design of the thing.

It wasn't just a ring, but two – one silver, another gold – both sliding together to form a finished piece. It was the ring she had shown him when they'd first met. The ring that Pippa had posted to her before she died. The one she'd left behind at the house. The interconnected bands were embellished with small yellow stones. Two halves of a heart that came together to make a whole. The lemony jewel – about the size of a garden pea – refracted on the strip lighting of the room and when he tilted it, he noticed a hidden engraving on the inside – a series of foreign symbols meticulously inscribed.

φιλία

The door swung open and Mrs Hecklesford bustled into the room, holding a leather binder. 'We're all ready for you, sir. If you'd care to follow me?'

Clayton stuffed the ring in his jacket pocket. 'Thank you.'

The lady glanced around the room, as if wondering if Nancy was ever really there at all.

'I'm afraid my friend has had to dash somewhere,' he explained. 'But I can handle this on my own.'

He was saying this to Mrs Hecklesford, but he was saying it to himself too.

He pushed himself up from the chair and allowed Mrs Hecklesford to shepherd him through another enormous door and into another chamber, where security cameras were angled in every corner.

As far as the eye could see there were individual vaults of varying sizes – the smallest about the size of an ice-cream tub, the largest somewhere nearer a wardrobe – all numbered with a gold engraved plate on the front. Portals of people's most valued possessions. A wall of hidden treasure.

'Number three-seven-two, sir,' Mrs Hecklesford declared, looking down at her binder. She passed him back the ornate golden key.

The safe Clayton had been taken to was of the medium variety – slightly larger than the dimensions of a standard hotel safe. About the size of an Aga oven.

As he held the key out in front of him, towards the box, he realised his hand was shaking. *Come on, Stumper*, he said to himself, thinking of another of Pippa's crossword clues he'd cracked earlier that morning. *You've got more* **mettle** *than this.*

'Allow me, sir,' Mrs Hecklesford said, pulling a tiny pocket torch from her blazer pocket and shining a beam towards the hole. 'These locks tend to be a bit stiff, so give it a good wiggle, won't you, sir?'

Clayton carefully inserted the key into the lock. He used both hands to angle it just so, to grip the long stem and rotate it ninety degrees. When he did, something inside clicked and the front of the safe flicked open.

He inserted his hand gingerly into the safe, started patting around inside, gripping the first thing his hands fell on. It was something long and flat and square by the feel of it. A picture frame? A painting? Whatever it was had been well packaged anyway, bound in brown parcel paper, reams of crinkling tape and something soft and plump underneath, presumably a layer of bubble wrap.

Clayton gripped the sides with both hands and hauled the item out into the dim light. There was a criss-cross of string holding the whole thing together. From that string dangled a brown tag. Clayton flipped it over.

Dearest Clayton,
Part three. You're getting there. I knew you would.
Love always,
Pip x

Not knowing what else to do, he held the item to his chest for a moment.

Mrs Hecklesford looked at the package in his hand, then at him. 'I take it you've found what you need, sir?'

Clayton didn't know what to say, because he wasn't exactly sure. He wasn't sure what he'd expected, and he wasn't sure what he'd found. Not yet anyway.

Back at the hotel, the late-afternoon sun cast a glow across Clayton's room. He was glad he hadn't opened the package straight away. Nancy was right – whatever was hidden inside was personal, possibly even momentous.

As soon as he'd got back, he'd set the parcel down on his extremely plush pillows, as if he were carrying a sleeping child and putting it to bed. On the bedstand sat Pippa's ashes in the hourglass that Hector had made. He liked having them close while he was sleeping.

He went to the door, flipping the cardboard sign on the handle so it read *DO NOT DISTURB*. At home he had something similar: a novelty Christmas gift from one of the residents. *QUIET, I'M NAPPING*, it said.

A doze in the middle of the day, as far as Clayton was concerned, was one of life's greatest pleasures. He excelled at it, too. Twenty minutes tops was all he needed. He could drop off anywhere. Not that he'd had much chance to indulge recently.

Clayton reached into his pocket and drew the Swiss Army

knife attached to his keys. He prised the inch-long blade out and pressed the tip in a corner of the parcel to make an incision, and then his fingers were clawing at it, tearing great strips off the paper, like a kid on Christmas morning.

He was through the outer layer in no time, then he was pulling the bubble wrap to pieces, the material going *pop*, *pop-pop*, *pop-pop-pop*, as he ripped it to shreds.

The moment he realised what it was, he instinctively pushed the thing away, took a step backwards, gripping the edge of the bed.

It was an oil painting in a gilt frame. It was a picture of a child sat on a wooden stool, beaming up at the artist. It was a picture of himself, as a little boy.

Clayton's hand lifted to cover his mouth.

It was unsettling, frightening almost, to be confronted with the gaze of your younger self like that. Because that was what he was looking at, he was sure of it. At least that was until he removed the final bit of bubble wrap. When he took a step back and considered the piece as a whole, he started to doubt himself.

The boy's hair – while still fair like his own – was considerably darker than it had been when he was that age. Clayton's used to be almost bottle-blonde. This child's was brown. The eyes were definitely right – a steely-blue – but the child in the picture had more of a squarish head; Clayton had always been round-faced, even more so when he was a child. He'd seen pictures where his head was as round as a bowling ball. And not only that but the clothes were completely at odds with what he'd always remembered wearing as a little boy. Pippa used to dress him in bright, infantile colours, which he fought against as soon as he was old enough to. But this child was wearing an immaculate white shirt, paired with smart beige trousers and navy braces he'd definitely never seen before.

Clayton didn't know what to think. Although this clue hadn't come with any instructions, it didn't take long for Clayton to decide what it was. It was a spot-the-difference puzzle. But if this boy in the picture wasn't him, then who on earth was it? And what possible part could they have played in his past?

Chapter Thirty-Four

THE FELLOWSHIP OF PUZZLEMAKERS
TUESDAY, 19TH MARCH, 1991

It was a few minutes to nine o'clock when a silver Renault Clio pulled up in front of the house, a full hour before Pippa had expected. She was sure the social worker had said ten o'clock.

Pippa watched a young lady clamber out of the car and lift a hefty pilot case from the boot.

She had the face of an exquisite porcelain doll, a fashionable blonde bob, and legs up to her armpits. Pippa couldn't help but feel self-conscious. Here she was, a woman in her mid-sixties, childless, unmarried, without even a long-term romantic relationship to her name, about to have her future determined by someone young enough to be her daughter. It left her feeling a tad chagrined.

Pippa hastily opened the front door and darted down the steps in her tatty silk slippers before their visitor could get anywhere near the front door.

In the entrance hall, where a few days earlier there'd been a crystal chandelier dangling above their heads, there was now an opening into the bright blue sky beyond. Not only did she have to avert her guest's eyes from this small calamity, but she also had to discourage her from engaging in conversation with the other residents. She knew at least one was staunchly against the visit.

'Good morning,' she called out. 'Thank you ever so much for coming.'

The lady wedged a clipboard under her spare arm and extended her soft, slender hand. 'You must be Miss Allsbrook? Lovely to meet you at last.'

She flashed the badge on her lanyard: *Miss Jasmine Knight*,

Social Worker, Child Services, Mid-Beds County Council.

'The pleasure's all mine, Miss Knight. Please. Follow me. I thought I'd take you via the garden, if you don't mind. Just so you can get your bearings. Do you like gardening, Miss Knight? I can't say I'm wild on it myself, but the smells in the rose garden at this time of year are charming . . .'

She knew she sounded as mad as a March hare but it didn't matter, she just needed to get the woman inside.

The young lady – with a hesitant grin – followed Pippa cautiously along the crazy-paving path that trailed the perimeter of the estate, having awful bother in her dainty kitten heels, especially in the alleyway at the side of the house where they were confronted with a series of puddles, which, to her credit, she gamely vaulted over like a racehorse.

On the rear terrace, Pippa could just make out Earl in his royal-blue gardening dungarees, digging out the trenches that would form part of his epic hedgerow maze. She gave him a cheery wave, but he was too absorbed in the task to notice her. Then her eyes went to the jigsaw studio tucked away in the trees. Hector would be in there painting his latest collection, alone this morning, as Angel had been tasked with prepping the house ready for their special visitor. She had been helping out in the studio almost a year now, and apparently had even started creating her own pieces. Hector claimed that her technique had really come on, that she had a definite gift, a natural aptitude for capturing light, mostly, but that her portraiture was rather splendid, too. Pippa was pleased for the girl. Angel had clearly found herself a hobby, something to get lost in. That was, after all, what the Fellowship was all about. Indulging in life's pleasures.

'You have a very beautiful home,' Jasmine remarked. 'It's like something out of a fairy tale.'

Pippa turned to look at the house: the turrets and the stone facades, the arch-style windows and the tall brick chimneys that sat slightly squiffy on the roof. She couldn't agree more. Living at Creighton Hall was, in itself, a kind of fairy tale.

'And I suspect a perfect place to raise a child.'

'Yes,' Pippa agreed, turning to smile at the lady. 'Yes, I really do hope so.'

They spent next to no time in the rose garden, for it was obvious Miss Knight had little interest in smelling their flowers. Still, Pippa had successfully navigated her to the rear of the property, and the back door to the conservatory, just where she wanted her.

'Come in, come in,' she urged. 'Please, don't bother taking your shoes off.'

Inside, Angel was frantically setting a table for tea.

Pippa gave her a hesitant smile.

The two ladies had almost come to blows earlier when Pippa had gone to inspect one of their vacated suites that Angel had promised to prepare for the social worker's inspection and found the bed unmade and the furniture covered in a thick layer of dust. She clearly hadn't touched the room in weeks. In the end, Pippa had donned her own pinny and given the place a proper spruce up herself.

'Miss Knight, let me introduce our housekeeper, Angel.'

'Please, call me Jasmine . . . it's a pleasure to meet you, Angel.' She set her bag and brolly under the wicker table. 'This must be a lovely place to work.'

The housekeeper gave a tight grin in reply, pulling out a chair for their visitor, then – even before her bottom had made contact with the seat – shoving it back under the table, making the poor young woman scream in fright.

Angel, mumbling her apologies, proceeded to dash out to the kitchen.

'Sorry about that,' Pippa said under her breath. 'She can be a little un-coordinated at times.'

Jasmine waved the apology away.

'I wish I could tell you she's new,' Pippa added, 'but she's actually been here longer than us.'

Angel returned a moment later with a three-tiered stand of breakfast treats. She set the wobbling tower of plates smack bang in the middle of the table. Salmon blinis, miniature pastries, tiny fruit tarts.

'Anything else you want?'

'No, that's all marvellous,' Pippa replied. 'Thank you, dear.' She nudged the stand to one side so she could actually see her guest.

'Gosh, what a treat,' Jasmine remarked. 'I'm lucky if I get a cup of tea at most people's houses.'

Pippa laughed. 'Oh . . . this isn't like *most* people's houses.'

Jasmine looked at her a second. 'Mmm, yes, I'm beginning to see that.'

She reached into her pilot case and pulled out a dizzying number of forms, explaining that the paperwork was always the most time-consuming part of the visit and something she liked to get out the way first, before carrying out the house assessment. 'Also, I wondered when I might speak with the other residents?'

'The *other* residents?'

'That's right,' Jasmine replied, looking confused. 'This is a . . . commune, is it not?'

Pippa pulled a face. 'You can call it a commune if you wish, Miss Knight.'

'But you wouldn't?'

'Well, Miss Knight, I've always thought communes were inhabited by . . . misfits. Screwballs. We're perfectly normal here. Just like any other family.'

'I see.'

'Why exactly do you wish to speak to the others?'

'Safeguarding,' she replied. 'It's part of our protocols. Everyone will have to go through the same checks, of course.'

Pippa swallowed nervously. 'Do you take milk?'

Jasmine nodded and Pippa lifted the vintage porcelain milk jug in the shape of a flying Chinese dragon – the creature's flared nostrils doubling as the spout. The monstrosity was a novelty gift from Larry Towles, who'd made a trip to Shanghai a few years back to the factory where his plastic cuboid puzzle toys were manufactured. He'd picked up the jug in a local market. It wasn't something Pippa would ever actually *use*, but in true Angel style it had found its way onto the table with their finest bone-china crockery.

As Pippa started on the forms, she tried to formulate an excuse as to why it would be difficult to speak with the other residents today. She was still racking her brains when Angel burst back through the door.

'Someone on the phone for you, Miss Allsbrook.'

Pippa sighed. 'I'm a bit tied up here, Angel. Is it urgent?'

The housekeeper shrugged at her.

'Did you get a name?'

'I think it was an Edmund. Or it might have been Edison. Or Edgar?'

Helpful as ever, she thought.

'Something about a painting you're selling?'

Pippa's heart stopped. *Edwin Dankworth.* She gripped the edge of the table. It was Jonty's friend, the art dealer, calling with his offer already. He'd valued the portrait in less than a day. Surely that could only be good news.

'If you need to take the call,' Miss Knight said, 'I really don't mind.'

'Are you sure?' Pippa asked, breathless with excitement as she pushed herself out of her seat.

'Not at all,' Jasmine replied. 'And perhaps now would be a good time to chat with the other residents?'

'Umm . . .'

Before Pippa could stop her, Jasmine had got to her feet and turned to their housekeeper. 'I was just saying how I was looking forward to meeting everyone.' She reached inside her bag. 'I have some forms, and some questions to run through, character references, that sort of thing. I wonder if there's a good space to do that in?'

'I could ask people to gather in the library?' Angel offered. 'If that would help?'

'No,' Pippa shot back. 'No, I don't think that will help, Angel, thank you.'

'Why not?' Angel asked. 'Most of them are in there already.'

Pippa gave their housekeeper an icy stare, but Angel just blinked at her, oblivious.

'Which way is it?' Jasmine asked, and Angel pointed towards the door.

'Just through there. I can show you.'

Pippa was trying to stop the housekeeper telepathically with her eyes, but it was all too late. Jasmine was already stepping out of the room, stepping towards the library, towards the entrance hall.

The entrance hall.

Pippa gasped and rushed to divert them, but it was too late. By the time she'd caught up with them, Jasmine's mouth was already gawping at the ceiling ahead of her.

'Good *God*.'

'Oh . . . pay no mind to that, Miss Knight. That's entirely cosmetic—'

'But the ceiling, Miss Allsbrook, it's entirely collapsed.'

'Yes, it does rather look like that, doesn't it?'

'It looks . . . *dangerous*. Are you sure you're all safe . . . living here?

Pippa had to bite her tongue. 'Quite safe, yes. So long as we don't dance underneath it. Do you want to step back a tad there, Miss Knight?'

The social worker – realising she was directly beneath the opening – made a shield with her arm over her head and took cautious strides into the corner of the hall as if cowering from an incoming missile.

Pippa turned to look at Angel.

The housekeeper had been standing helplessly between them, not saying a word. Pippa registered a haunted look on the woman's face and couldn't help but shoot her a kind, forgiving look.

As maddening as she was sometimes, Angel never meant any harm. She always tried her best. She just always seemed to get everything wrong. But this particular faux pas wasn't her fault at all. Not really. It was Pippa's mistake.

She smiled at the social worker. 'We'll have that patched up in no time, won't we, Angel?'

Angel looked doubtful.

'No time at all,' Pippa concurred with herself. 'Do you still wish to speak to people, Miss Knight or . . .?'

Five minutes later and Pippa had her ear pressed firmly to the library door while everyone gathered inside. It seemed Jasmine was still intent on continuing her investigations, curious as to who on earth might live in a house with an open-top roof.

She was going to probe them all, to find out what they made of Pippa's character, and her capacity to raise a child, and Pippa was unwilling to miss a single second of it.

She'd instructed Angel to tell Edwin Dankworth that she'd call him straight back.

She twisted the brass handle of the door very slowly and inched it open a fraction, wedging the tip of her shoe inside the door, angling herself to try and catch what was being said.

Inside, Earl was introducing Jasmine to the assembled group, explaining that she needed them all to fill in a form, and that she had a few questions for them all.

'And I hear you will be seeking character references,' Jonty's muffled voice could be heard interrupting. 'As part of the extensive checks you carry out?'

Jasmine offered something affirmative in reply.

'Good,' Jonty replied. 'Because it's important for you to know, Miss Knight, that what we're about to tell you isn't an isolated assessment of Pippa's character, certainly not one person's opinion. It's our collective view.'

Pippa's stomach churned.

'Pippa Allsbrook,' Jonty continued, 'is a total nightmare. She is prickly, cantankerous, stubborn—'

'Scary at times, too,' Larry piped up. 'You wouldn't dare get on the wrong side of her.'

'She really is a piece of work.' Jonty agreed.

The treachery, she thought. *The spinelessness of them all.*

'But . . .' He paused to clear his throat. 'She is unquestionably the kindest person I know. And it's my understanding, having spoken to Earl at great length on the matter, that this is something that Pippa wants very much indeed.'

'There isn't a bad bone in that woman's body,' Nancy piped up. 'Earl's right, she'd make a wonderful foster mother. I've seen over the years how she's nurtured us all, mothered us, really. Not that we'd ever let her know that, of course. It would only go to her head.'

Pippa smiled, tears prickling at the corner of her eyes.

'She looked after me when I needed someone most,' Earl announced next. 'When my wife passed away, she called me almost every day . . .'

Something inside her shifted, a warmth radiating through her whole body.

'. . . I'm not sure I've ever told her how grateful I was,' he added, 'for how she looked out for me back then. And for offering me a place here, a fresh start, a purpose. It's exactly what I needed. She knew that even before I did. So I decided I'd do anything to support her, to encourage everyone here at the Fellowship to get behind this final challenge of hers.'

'Miss Knight,' Jonty went on. 'We've discussed every possible eventuality, debated it till we were blue in the face, and we want you to know we're ready and prepared for whoever arrives at our door.'

'Pippa's more than capable on her own,' Nancy added. 'But with all of us here, all our combined experiences, I think you'd be hard pushed to find a better place to raise a child.'

'There's a thousand years between us all,' Earl declared. 'Did you know that, Miss Knight?'

At this, Pippa released the tip of her shoe from the door, until it secured shut in front of her. She could feel an expansion in her chest, the sense of affection she'd always had for her fellow puzzlemakers, one she had always felt was infinite, deepening somehow, almost overwhelming her.

She straightened her skirt, then pulled a handkerchief from her cardigan sleeve and wiped it under her eyes as she marched through the scullery, through the kitchen and into the conservatory.

Back at the table, she was halfway through the next form when she stopped dead, her pen hovering above the page.

The anonymous complainant who'd written the letter of protest must have made themselves scarce for the summit. There was only one person's voice she hadn't heard. One person conspicuous by their absence.

Hector Haywood.

Chapter Thirty-Five

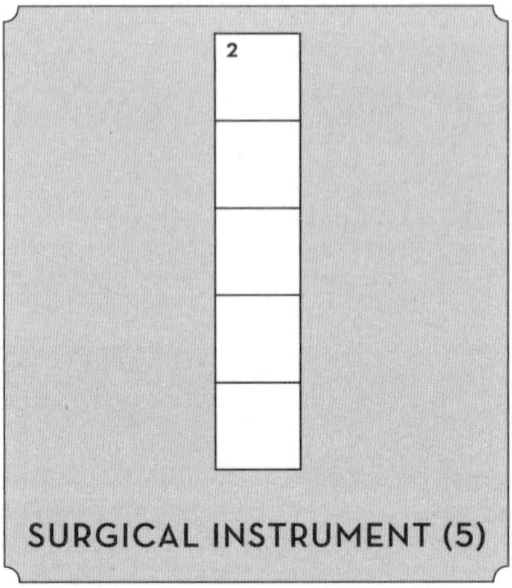

That evening in bed, Clayton studied the ring that Nancy had given him under the glare of the hotel's reading lights, running his finger over the strange symbols, wondering what they might mean.

As soon as he'd got back from Harrods, he'd taken the portrait of the little boy into his ensuite, wrapped it in a towel and put it out of sight in the bath. He would look at it again tomorrow. There was something about the eyes. It was as if the child were watching him.

Sometime around midnight, he reached over in his bed for the crossword, and his glasses, on the bedside table. He flipped over Pippa's ashes in the hourglass timer.

Two down, he thought to himself with his duvet pulled up to his neck. *Surgical instrument, five letters*.

Over the past few evenings, it had become a ritual of his to glance at the grid before climbing into bed, then allowing Pippa to count him down, as he tried to solve the clue with his eyes closed.

He'd never had any issues sleeping in the past, but ever since he'd been in London he'd barely got through a night without waking half a dozen times. There was just too much to think about.

Knife? he thought. *That could be a surgical instrument.*

Forceps? *No, that's six letters. Clamp*?

Suddenly he remembered that two down intersected with the third letter of one across, which he'd already solved – *appearance* – so unless he'd made a mistake, the solution he was looking for should begin with a P.

It was around this time that Clayton, with his glasses still on but his eyes closed, drifted to sleep, waking a few hours later with the answer in his mind.

Probe.

That sounded more like it, he thought. Pippa was never done noseying.

As he left the hotel the next day, he felt strangely light, like he was walking on air. It was a combination of drowsiness and a glimmer of excitement, too.

In the night, when he'd been unable to get back to sleep after cracking two down, he'd decided that he'd spent today paying a visit to one of his favourite places, the British Museum. But it wasn't to get lost in the Rosetta Stone or revel in the bust of Ramesses II, it was to probe the meaning behind the ring that Nancy had presented him with. He was certain the inscription was Ancient Greek, and if its meaning was behind why Nancy had left the Fellowship, then he was determined to find out what it meant.

He'd visited the British Museum several times over the years, usually for one of their special exhibitions and always with Pippa by his side. But on this occasion he was going alone.

He'd checked the museum's website and seen there was a daily tour at 12 p.m. of the Greek and Roman galleries, led by one of their curators. He wondered, if he asked nicely, whether they might take a look at it for him.

Clayton was striding purposefully along the edge of Hyde Park drawing up a mental timetable of the day when he stopped to glance at his watch.

A man on the phone pacing behind barged into him.

'Sorry,' he blurted out, but the chap had already moved on, cursing him under his breath.

Clayton was rooted to the spot. He still had a good few hours until the tour started.

Wondering how he might kill time, he glanced over his shoulder and felt a force not entirely his own pivoting him around so he was looking north, towards Paddington. In the direction he had last seen Neil.

And then, he wasn't entirely sure why, but he found himself crossing the road, moving in the opposite direction of where he was originally heading. To see if he could catch a glimpse of Serendipity.

I'll just take a quick look, he thought. To see if I might pick out the houseboat that Neil lives on. For curiosity's sake, if nothing else.

From the grey wash of the city came instant magic and brightness. Stepping into the tranquil oasis that was Little Venice, Clayton was reminded of Alice entering the colourful, enchanting Wonderland. It was like falling into another world.

Lush elm trees mirrored in the canal transformed the otherwise murky water into a vivid shade of lime green; the ornate bridges connecting the network of waterways gave pops of sky blue as far as the eye could see, and the distinctive boats were painted a rainbow of designs, with names stamped on the side in jaunty text that made Clayton smile as he passed. He particularly enjoyed all the puns. *Over the Hull. Vitamin Sea. Unsinkable II. She Got the House.*

It didn't take long for Clayton's gaze to land on Neil's floating home and the moment it did, he felt a sense of rising warmth inside him.

Serendipity was stationed between *M'Darlin'* and *Happy Daze.*

It wasn't as large or imposing as some of the others he'd seen, but with its wooden-crate flower boxes on the roof and shiny brass portholes catching in the midday sun, it had a definite rustic charm. The colours also added to its old-world quality. It was decorated in the classic narrowboat palette: forest green with primary red and yellow trim. Neil was obviously a traditionalist, like Clayton himself.

He took a seat on a bench overlooking the water and had

barely extended his legs out in front of him when he noticed a large tabby cat slinking its way along the roof of the boat. He was about twenty yards away but as the creature sauntered closer, he could tell from its enormous shaggy frame and long, furry tail that it was a Maine Coon. The gentle giant of the cat world.

It ambled from Serendipity to Great Escape – leaping from bow to bow – before bounding onto the towpath.

'Hello there,' he murmured.

As the cat approached, Clayton couldn't help glancing under the bench to see if there was a bird or squirrel cowering beneath him. There was nothing. She just wanted to say hello.

'Gosh, you're a friendly thing, aren't you?'

Its whiskers tickled his outstretched hand.

'Do you like head scratches?' he asked, running two fingers down the middle of the cat's forehead. Right between the eyes was Klotski's favourite spot.

The cat started to purr – a happy, bone-deep rumble – and Clayton felt a sudden pang of homesickness.

'My name's Clayton,' he whispered. 'What's yours?'

The cat looked up, blinked at him. Her eyes were the colour of marmalade.

He realised, returning the magnificent creature's gaze, that he'd actually lost his mind. Talking to a street cat, whatever next.

He was practically on his knees, and just as he was about to push himself up and get on with his day, he felt the unmistakable presence of another person moving towards him.

'Hello again,' came a voice. There was the sound of blood rushing in Clayton's ears.

As he spotted the scruffy trainers in front of him, his legs suddenly went liquid.

'Oh . . . *hello*?'

He tried to look surprised as Neil flashed his hand.

He was wearing a dark baggy jumper and skinny grey jeans, and a baseball cap obscured his eyes. 'Fancy seeing you here.'

Clayton's face burned. He didn't know what to say so just

laughed. It was a manic bark of a thing. 'Yes,' he eventually croaked. 'How funny!'

Neil took a seat beside him and there was a small silence that weighted the air.

Clayton ran a hand through his carefully combed hair. 'I completely forgot that you lived around here . . .'

'You did?'

He nodded, trying to avoid Neil's sharp gaze. 'It completely went out of my mind. I've only just remembered now. So your boat must be around here then.'

'It's right there,' Neil answered, pointing at the conspicuous fifty-foot vessel moored in front of them. '*Serendipity*.'

'Gosh. There it is.'

Clayton's cheeks were burning, like when he had his allergic reaction to shellfish; he could almost picture how red and blotchy they were going.

Neil had turned and was looking at him, which was only making matters worse. 'So go on then. Why are you hanging around Little Venice?'

'Oh,' Clayton replied airily, 'I just thought I'd come and explore somewhere new.'

'Right.'

'I've been meaning to scout out some new spots in London . . . expand my horizons.'

He could kill Pippa right now. This was all her doing. If she hadn't encouraged him, he might never have come and made an idiot out of himself like this. He'd learn for next time. Poking his nose in other people's business never did anyone any favours.

'I'm actually on my way to the British Museum.'

'Nice,' Neil replied. 'I like it there.'

'You do?'

Neil nodded. 'I'm a bit of a nerd . . . in case you haven't guessed.'

Clayton hadn't guessed. But he supposed he could be classed as a nerd too, if that meant being a bit non-conforming . . . not quite fitting in.

'Nancy gave me this ring,' he explained, pulling it out of his pocket. 'And it has these funny markings on it, which I think are Greek, so I thought someone at the museum might be able to help me translate them.'

'But why didn't you ask Nancy? Or just google it?'

Clayton, caught off guard by this suggestion, fell silent for a moment. Nancy had darted away before he could have asked anything but searching the web hadn't even crossed his mind.

'That's the thing about puzzles, though, isn't it?' he replied thoughtfully. 'The pleasure is in the solving, not in the solution.'

The cat had its paws on his knee all of a sudden. It let out a small enquiring meow.

'Looks like you've made a friend.'

'Yes,' Clayton agreed, thinking to himself, *and I'd like to make another one, too.*

Neil reached down and picked up the cat, holding it like a baby in his arms. 'This is Muriel, by the way.'

'She's yours?'

Neil nodded. 'Well, I wouldn't exactly say she's mine. I rescued her from a lady I looked after. I feel like she belongs to anyone she meets. Wherever I go, she roams from boat to boat, and everyone falls in love with her. She has no shame.'

'Good for her,' Clayton replied. 'We could all learn a thing or two from Muriel, couldn't we.'

'Couldn't we just. She's got a lot more friends than me. She's even on Instagram.'

'She isn't!'

Neil nodded, laughing to himself. '@Canal_Cat_Capers. She's got twelve thousand followers. Eleven thousand, nine-hundred and forty more than me.'

There was a brief pause as the two of them looked at each other, grinning.

'Twelve thousand more than me,' Clayton said. He'd never been one for social media.

'It's a smart-looking boat, by the way,' he added, pointing at his seatmate's home ahead of them. 'You never told me why it's called *Serendipity*.'

'No,' Neil replied. 'No, I didn't, did I.' He lowered his eyes to the floor. 'That's a long story . . .'

Clayton scanned the cheerful text inscribed in front of him, wondering what the significance behind the word might be. The notion behind it was lovely, of course. *Serendipity*. But nothing in life came about by chance, by happy coincidence. If he wanted something fortuitous to happen in his life, he'd have to make it happen. If he needed a bit of luck, he'd make his own.

'Would you like to come with me?' Clayton heard himself say.

'Come with you?'

He swallowed. 'To the museum, I mean. Only if you fancied it, obviously. I suppose you've got plans, it's a bit short notice, isn't it . . .'

Neil's feet shuffled awkwardly in front of them. He cupped the back of his neck with his hand. 'Yes. I mean, no, I don't have plans. Why not. I'll come with you if you like.'

Clayton smiled at the floor. The response made his heart rise and his cheeks burn.

Chapter Thirty-Six

THE FELLOWSHIP OF PUZZLEMAKERS
TUESDAY, 26TH MARCH, 1991

Pippa was alone in her dimly lit study, teasing an envelope marked *MID-BEDS COUNCIL* between her fingers, turning it under the glare of her banker's lamp, bracing herself for the outcome of her fostering application.

It had been a week since the social worker's visit. Since then she'd determined who the anonymous complainant had been and felt dreadful for even considering that Hector had been against her application. Of course, he'd been busy working in his jigsaw studio when the social worker had visited and oblivious to the fact she'd wanted to speak to them all. It was the miserable old dullard Eric Stoppard – the man who made whittled wooden games – who was forever reciting the residents' agreement back at her. He was a jobsworth, that was all, too spineless to address the subject in person, and so he'd delivered that nasty little letter instead. Pippa was certain of it.

The letter from the council had arrived on their doormat twenty minutes earlier, but she'd been reluctant to open it, to have her suspicions confirmed. Instead, she'd disappeared outside for a few steadying laps of the garden, anything to avoid the other residents in the breakfast room who kept asking why the repair works hadn't started, when the roof would finally be fixed, whether they were safe living in a house that appeared to be crumbling above their heads. *What exactly was the delay?*

Ever since the ceiling had fallen in on them, Pippa had been hit with one piece of bad news after the other. As she reached for her silver letter opener in the top drawer of her desk, she couldn't help wondering if that age-old proverb was true. Perhaps bad news really did come in threes.

First, there had been an update from the surveyors about the leaky roof. They'd completed their report and enclosed a quote for repairs. It was everything she didn't want to hear. The damage was *major*, the works *significant*, the cost to fix it all, *eye-watering*.

The second bombshell came from Jonty's art-dealing friend, Edwin Dankworth, whom she'd called back the moment Miss Knight had gone.

The treasured portrait of her late mother – the one she'd believed would get her out of all this mess – was, in fact, practically worthless. The artist had completely fallen out of fashion; the varnish had worn away and several layers of paint were missing from the piece. In fact, Mr Dankworth had been at pains to point out that the gilt frame was probably worth more than the picture itself. That's why he'd called her so swiftly. He hadn't wished to get her hopes up.

And then, thirdly . . .

Pippa slipped the knife under the seal of the council's letter, releasing it with one swipe. She peeled out the letter inside and her eyes went straight to the conclusive paragraph three-quarters down the page.

The accommodation did not meet required safety standards . . .

Pippa's body sank heavily into the chair.

A failure to satisfy criteria in relation to home-safety standards has resulted in your application, at this time, being terminated.

Even though she knew it was coming, it was still a shock to see it on the page. Right there in black and white. Her shoulders sagged in defeat.

She had fallen at the final hurdle.

The fostering dream was over. Miss Knight had determined that the Fellowship of Puzzlemakers wasn't a suitable place to raise a child. Not because of Pippa's capacity to parent, nor through a lack of support from the other residents, but due to something that Pippa had failed to address months ago, that now was beyond rescue. The house was unfit for human habitation.

Pippa closed her eyes, and took a deep, steadying breath.

It was time to face reality. Pippa was going to have to reveal all to the group. To open up about the financial situation. The bleakness of it all. To share all the unthinkable thoughts that had been swirling around her head these last few days. They couldn't keep living in a house with a roof they did not have the funds to repair. She had failed them all. They'd been scraping along for the last few years, Pippa oblivious – careless – to their bottom line, even though it had been there in black and white, and now they were at a point of no return. Now it was time to cut their losses. To wrap things up. They'd had a good run of it. *They came, they saw, they solved.* What else was there to do? She was going to have to sell Creighton Hall.

Chapter Thirty-Seven

11

UNCOVER OR DIVULGE (6)

At a few minutes to twelve, beneath the tessellated glass roof of one of the greatest museums in the world, a serious-looking lady emerged at the information desk, wrapped in what could only be a white king-sized bedsheet.

The costume was presumably meant to be an Ancient Greek toga, but the way it had been thrown together – with a gentleman's belt tied a little too snugly at the waist and a red silk scarf flung over her shoulder – gave the impressive of someone who, if Clayton didn't know any better, should be given a very wide berth.

'There's a lady over there,' Neil announced, 'dressed as a Greek goddess.' He had his hand buried in a bag of novelty sweets – Tutankhamun Treats. 'Do you think she's doing the tour?'

Clayton pulled a face. 'Either that or her wardrobe needs updating.'

Neil laughed. He was chewing the head off a jellied Egyptian pharaoh. 'Want one?'

'Why not.' Clayton dipped his hand inside the packet, helping himself to a strawberry sphinx. He tore off the rear end. It was like licking a battery.

'They're sour,' Neil explained.

Clayton's hand went to his mouth to stop himself spitting it out. 'How much did they set you back?'

'Four quid,' Neil answered, without batting an eyelid.

Clayton blew his cheeks. 'They saw you coming.'

From behind the information desk, the costumed lady cupped

her hands over her mouth. 'Tour of the Greek and Roman galleries begins in T-minus two minutes.'

The pair made their way over to her. A group of tourists were already gathered, scrolling through their phones, but as she started to do a head count, they sloped off, leaving just Clayton standing there with Neil, still gamely tucking into his sweets.

'Is it just us?' he asked.

The lady gave a tight grin in reply. 'I think I'll wait a few more minutes. In case there are any last-minute stragglers.'

Clayton decided to take the opportunity to speak with her about his slightly unusual request.

As much as he was interested in the Ancient Greeks, the myths and legends, and the brave Spartans, today he only really cared about one thing: the inscription on the puzzle ring secreted in his jacket pocket.

He explained to the lady that he'd recently come into possession of a piece of jewellery with a funny set of symbols etched on the inside, which he had reason to believe were letters in the Ancient Greek alphabet.

'So I wondered,' he explained, 'if you might be able to take a look at it for me? Perhaps tell me what the symbols mean? If they hold any . . . significance.'

The historian blinked at him. She extended her hand and issued a deep, put-upon sigh. 'Anyone would think this is the *Antiques Roadshow* . . .'

Clayton placed the ring carefully in the lady's palm.

She lifted it up against the enormous glass ceiling of the atrium, squinting at it with one eye. She studied it only for a few seconds, then handed it back without saying a word.

'Do you know what it means?' he asked impatiently.

She looked around, almost desperately, for other members of the public to join the tour. No such luck. She checked her watch again and Clayton did the same. Four minutes past twelve.

'Just you two, then,' she replied, adjusting her belt. 'My name's Julie and I'm going to be your guide today. Do you want to follow me to Europe and Pre-History?'

She turned and marched in the direction of the grand marble staircase, revealing a pair of well-worn slippers beneath the billowing bedsheet. They slapped noisily against the stone steps as the three of them climbed to Level Three. Neil grinned at Clayton, and they followed after her.

Together, they scooted through *The Americas*, across *The Middle East* and into a gallery signposted *Greece and Rome*.

'As you've come with your own . . . assignment,' Julie said, 'I thought we could begin the tour here. Might I suggest you take a look over there, sir, beside those stone tablets. Exhibit Four A.'

She gestured to a cabinet in the middle of the room. 'I'll wait here until you're finished,' she added with a tight, almost sardonic smile.

Clayton waved Neil forward and the pair moved towards a collection of nondescript stone blocks illuminated behind glass.

In front of them, on an information panel, a series of Greek symbols and their English translations were all laid out in a helpful grid. Clayton felt a sudden lightness come over him. There was the Greek alphabet on the left, the name assigned to each character in the middle, and to the right, its literal English translation.

He handed the ring to Neil, then grabbed a pen and reprinted the symbols as best as he could onto the back of the museum guide.

φιλία

Αα alpha = a	Νν nu = n
Ββ beta = b	Ξξ xi = x (ks)
Γγ gamma = g	Οο omicron = o (short)
Δδ delta = d	Ππ pi = p
Εε epsilon = e (short)	Ρρ rho = r, rh
Ζζ zeta = z	Σσς sigma = s*
Ηη eta = e (long)	Ττ tau = t
Θθ theta = th	Υυ upsilon = y, u
Ιι iota = i	Φφ phi = ph, f
Κκ kappa = k	Χχ chi = ps
Λλ lambda = l	Ψψ psi = h
Μμ mu = m	Ωω omega = o (long)

'Race you!' Neil said, and Clayton's eyes darted between the page and the board, his pen scribbling down the English translation as he went. Neil was doing the same, but all in his head, sucking in his breath every few seconds.

'I think I've got it,' Neil announced after a couple of seconds.

'Wait!' Clayton said. 'I'm almost there.'

Eventually he finished writing the five-character word on the page, and Julie the historian was standing over his shoulder, checking his workings.

'*Philia*,' he said slowly. '*P-H-I-L-I-A*.'

Neil nodded in agreement.

'What on earth does that mean?'

'I know,' Neil said, before the curator could say anything. 'I think so, anyway.'

'Go on.'

'It means *love*, doesn't it?'

They both looked to Julie, who was staring at Neil with her head jerked back as if seeing him for the first time.

'That's right,' she said. 'How did you know?'

'It was a question on *Mastermind* a few weeks ago. I've watched every episode since I was a kid.'

She smiled, then pointed her finger in the air. 'There's actually more to it than that.'

'Go on,' Clayton urged.

'The Greeks,' she began, 'were sophisticated in the way they talked about love. Far more sophisticated than we are today. In fact, they reckoned there were six different varieties of it.'

'Of love?'

'That's right.'

'This variety – *Philia* – describes a very particular form of affection. A deep, almost spiritual attachment. The love you might share with your closest friend. Your soulmate. An ally, even.'

'So not romantic then?'

Julie shook her head. 'Quite the opposite. *Platonic*.'

Clayton pulled back slightly. So the man who'd given Nancy this ring *did* love her, but as a friend, not as a lover.

'I thought it might have been a wedding ring,' he said, shaking his head. 'I don't know why.'

'It's a friendship ring,' she said. 'In its purest sense. Whoever presented it wanted the person to know they treasured their companionship, that they loved them, yes, but in this very special way.'

He stared at Julie. If the Greeks were correct, and love took so many forms, then how was it possible to tell the difference? How did the love of a deep friendship differ from that of one rooted in passion and sexual desire? Could one become the other, given a bit of time?

After Julie's tour finished – they had both felt obliged to do the full circuit with her – Clayton and Neil headed back out into the open air and sat on the steps underneath the great monolithic pillars, passing the remainder of the Tutankhamun Treats between them.

'I hope you don't think it's weird or anything,' Neil said, his cheeks visibly reddening. 'But I actually looked you up after we first met . . . on the internet, I mean.'

'Oh,' he replied, shocked. 'Why?'

'I was intrigued. I'd overheard some of the things that you and

Nancy were talking about, like the Fellowship…' He tailed off. 'I wasn't eavesdropping or anything! You'd left the door wide open.'

'I don't mind.' Clayton felt strangely flattered. 'What did you find?'

'There's a few articles written about you, aren't there?'

Clayton wafted his hand in front of him. 'It turned into a bit of a circus, really, when I landed on the doorstep.' He pulled his coat a bit tighter around himself, feeling a chill. 'I wouldn't believe everything you read, Neil. Most of what was written was fabricated. The journalists just got carried away, that's all.'

Over the years Clayton had lost count of the number of times he'd heard the story of the media scrum that had gathered in the days and weeks following his mysterious arrival.

The puzzlemakers were riding high when he first appeared. After a famously rocky patch, the Fellowship's profile was suddenly on the rise, and residents had woken up one morning to find photographers from the *Mirror* and the *Sun* camped outside the gates, trying to catch a glimpse of the mysterious baby rumoured to have been delivered in a hatbox outside the door. In the end Pippa had resorted to calling a few pals of hers – tabloid editors she knew via the lunches she attended on Fleet Street – asking them politely to rein it in. The child had done nothing to deserve this level of intrusion.

'So what's the truth? Did you ever find out where you came from?'

Clayton sighed. 'I still don't know.'

'You don't?'

He shook his head, then took a steadying breath.

It was time to come clean. After all, what was a friendship – even a burgeoning one – if not a chance to divulge your full self.

He was going to ***reveal*** all, to a total stranger.

And so, as they set off back the way they had come earlier that day, Neil listened as Clayton disclosed everything. About the puzzle trail he was trying to follow, the series of clues that had been set by someone who had raised him as her own, someone who had also left behind a crossword that was forcing him to confront all sorts, to experience things that he might not otherwise, including this confessional chat right now. How the first clues on the trail had led to him turning up at Neil's employer's house a few days ago. How he'd wondered if Mrs Nancy Stone might have been his birth mother, especially when he'd seen all the hats in the hall, and she'd revealed the name of her milliner father's shop. Hackney Hatters. How that tallied with the etching on the top of the hatbox he'd arrived in: *H.H.* How Nancy had helped him locate a portrait of a young boy, secreted in a strongroom at Harrods department store, who looked weirdly like himself, but actually wasn't him at all. How he wasn't sure what to think really. How he was back at square one.

By the time he'd confessed all, the light was beginning to fade. Clayton had walked considerably further than he needed to once again. The turning for his hotel was several hundred yards away, but he was enjoying himself too much to care.

'Put your phone away.'

'Sorry?' Clayton was just about to show the picture he'd taken of the child's portrait when Neil finally opened his mouth to speak. 'What did you say?'

'I *said* put your phone away. Now.'

In front of them, two tall figures emerged from the shadows of a pedestrian bridge wearing what looked like ski masks.

Neil had gone stiff beside him, even increasing the gap between them so they were a shoulder width's apart marching towards the men.

'If they ask for anything,' Neil said under his breath, 'just give them it. You don't know what they're carrying.'

Chapter Thirty-Eight

THE FELLOWSHIP OF PUZZLEMAKERS
WEDNESDAY, 27TH MARCH, 1991

Creighton Hall was eerily still. Even the steady tick of the antique grandfather clock in the corner of the boardroom sounded more sinister than usual.

Pippa had summoned everybody at short notice at 9 a.m. sharp. She knew everyone would guess an emergency summit was unlikely to be called unless she had something very good or very bad to share. And given that she'd been avoiding them for days, she knew they would assume the worst.

'I'm not sure how else to say it,' she said, trying to keep her voice light and even, trying to hide the fact she was close to tears. 'But, the truth is, we've been scraping by for quite some time. The reserves are running dry. And I fear we've reached the end of the road—'

Bonnnng.

The clock chimed its hourly bell, cutting into Pippa's speech, allowing her to turn away from those gathered before her. She was finding it hard to look them in the eyes.

Bonnnng. It was as if the bells were signalling something other than the fact it was nine o'clock in the morning. *Bonnnng.* It was the beginning of the end.

'One more storm,' she went on, 'and the entire roof could cave. Someone could get hurt. It's just not safe, it's not sustainable. I wish there was a magic money tree. But there isn't. I've tried everything, really I have, even selling off heirlooms – paintings, jewellery, anything of value – but that's no solution. There just isn't enough coming in. I've run out of options—'

'But what are you trying to *say*?' Nancy said, stubbing out her cigarette into the glass tray in front of her. 'How are you suggesting we . . . *fix it*?'

She was unusually sat as far away from Jonty as physically possible, both of them taking opposite ends of the long table. Whatever had happened between the two of them, Pippa was yet to determine but she couldn't help noticing that her friend was no longer wearing the puzzle ring Jonty had given her on Valentine's Day. The two of them had seemingly parted ways. It was the last thing Pippa needed to deal with.

She closed her eyes, took a deep breath and returned the gaze of her friend.

'I'm afraid, it's over, Nance.'

'*Over?*' Nancy echoed, her face contorted with confusion.

Pippa nodded.

All the life had been drained from her; she barely had the energy to answer. 'The game's up, everyone. I'm terminating the Fellowship of Puzzlemakers.'

They looked like a Renaissance painting, she thought. There she was, standing in the centre of the long, polished mahogany table, and her disciples, her devoted puzzlemakers, were all gazing up at her: pale, panicked, pleading for some reassurance.

Jonty lifted his hand in the air.

'Go ahead, Jonty.'

He cleared his throat. 'Do you mean to say that the money we've earned . . . the capital we've *collectively* raised, has all been . . . squandered?'

Pippa lifted her finger to stop him. 'Not squandered, Jonty. Just spent. I never imagined how expensive this place would be to maintain. It's a total cash drain. The money comes in, and then it goes straight out again.'

'But surely there's a contingency pot. A sinking fund?' Earl looked at her with kind, pleading eyes, but Pippa was struggling to hold his gaze.

'I wish I'd thought of that, Earl. It's obvious now, isn't it? I'm afraid I've let you all down.'

'Sorry.' Hector shook his head. 'So, we can't repair the roof? There's nothing in the bank?'

'A couple of thousand. Tops.'

'What if we made cutbacks?' Nancy asked. 'Borrowed some money from the bank?'

Pippa shook her head. 'We're still paying off the interest on a few loans, and I've been auctioning anything I've personally got of value, just to keep us ticking along. I've been doing that for years, trying to get on top of it all. I didn't want to panic anyone, you see.'

There was a collective headshake, which made Pippa's insides ache. Nancy's eyes were creased with contempt at her. At the other end of the table, Eric Stoppard – the somewhat reserved wooden-puzzle maker seldom seen outside the workshop – scraped his chair behind him and exited the room in disgust.

'Does anyone else have anything to say?' Pippa asked.

Geoff Stirrup, the mild-mannered numbers man, had his arm up. 'I'm sorry. Can I get this straight. Are you really telling us, Pip, that the Fellowship is winding up. This is . . . *it*?'

'Surely not,' Earl said. 'You're not saying that, are you, Pip?'

Pippa felt as if she might be sick. She could see it in all their eyes: they were not only furious with her, but heartbroken at the prospect of this family breaking apart. And Earl – who'd been here only a matter of months and was back to being his old self again – was about to have his life upended once more.

'I'll take the brunt of whatever happens next,' she said. 'Don't worry about any of that. The house is officially in my name. Any debts will be, too. I'm the one who's failed to make the money work. I'll face the consequences.'

'But why the devil didn't you show *me* the balance sheet?' Geoff slammed his hand against the table, making everyone rear back in surprise. 'I could have crunched some sums. I was an accountant for forty years, for crying out loud!'

The fury that lingered in the silence was so profound it was practically audible.

Pippa could see the cogs in people's minds turning and the enormity of the situation registering in their eyes. She felt a sense of shame so great she wanted nothing more than to disappear into thin air. She drew her scarf a little tighter.

This was all her doing.

Her own stubbornness, her own selfishness, her own superciliousness. She was to blame for all of it.

'The end of mirth is the beginning of sorrow,' Jonty professed.

'Enough with the riddles.' Nancy cut in. 'We don't need it right now, Jonty.'

'So that's it then?' Earl asked. 'It's over, is it?'

'Listen to yourselves!' Hector said, suddenly on his feet. 'That's . . . *it*?' he echoed. 'Of course this isn't *it*! I think we're forgetting something here.'

As he made his way to the top of the table, everyone's attention turned towards him, hoping, no doubt, that he had the answer after all.

'With respect, Philippa, the Fellowship doesn't belong to you, does it?'

Pippa shook her head.

'It's all of ours. You don't make the decisions. We're a commune, remember?'

'We *are*. You're absolutely right.' The second she heard the words come out of her mouth, she realised how hypocritical they were. She had tried to make herself indispensable, that was the trouble. She had tried to prove to them all that there was nothing she couldn't solve, nothing that would defeat her.

A room full of extraordinary minds. Imagine what we could achieve together.

That early proclamation from their inaugural pub session rang in her ears. She'd allowed her fear of failure, her reluctance to share her problems and to expose any weakness, to get the better of her, and to jeopardise the very thing that she'd been fighting to protect.

'We started this adventure *together*,' Hector said. 'And we'll continue it *together*. Is that clear?'

'But I've tried everything,' Pippa said pleadingly. 'I've left no stone unturned, Hector. Really, you must believe me—'

He lifted his hand to stop her. 'You're talking about *yourself* again, Philippa. This isn't on *you*. It's on *us*.'

Pippa nodded shamefully at the floor. He was right. If the Fellowship's downfall had been her *own* doing, then if it stood any chance of being saved, it would be down to them *all* to save it, not her alone.

'*To go further, go together*. Remember that?'

It was meant to be a motto the Fellowship lived by, but the notion was one she'd all but forgotten in recent years.

'We're puzzlemakers, aren't we?' Hector said. 'We *solve* things. So let's consider it our next challenge. If we can't crack this, then nobody can.'

He turned to a fresh sheet on the flipchart in the corner of the room and pointed at Pippa with a marker pen. 'How much?' he asked. 'How much do we need to raise to get ourselves out of this mess?'

Pippa rubbed the back of her neck. 'Twenty,' she replied, so quietly even she could barely hear herself. 'Twenty thousand pounds will pay for the new roof and wipe our debts. A clean slate.'

Everyone shook their heads in disbelief, but Hector barely flinched. Of course, the Fellowship held even more significance to him than most.

Pippa was reminded of the lugubrious figure she'd discovered living in a campervan all those years ago; the awkward, tortured artist whose life had seemingly gone off the rails after some awful family tragedy she'd never got to the bottom of. One thing was certain though: Pippa and her puzzle club had saved Hector Haywood from going down a very different path in life. It was clear he couldn't imagine his life without the Fellowship.

He jotted the extortionate figure down on the page and encouraged everyone to shout out their best money-making ideas.

'You're our biggest earner, Hect,' Les Dobson shouted out. 'How about you create the biggest jigsaw the world has ever seen? One hundred thousand pieces! We could invite the public to sponsor a piece. A pound a pop! We'd be quids in.'

'What about our optical illusions?' Nigel Bentham said, more sensibly. 'They always go down well. Is there an installation we could build? To make them interactive?'

Geoff raised his hand. 'I'd be happy to host a jigsum-athon.'

'And my maze isn't far off,' Earl chipped in. 'To be honest, I'm so pleased with it, I reckon we could charge admission.'

They continued throwing around all manner of suggestions for a few minutes until Hector, who dutifully added everything to the page, paused to make a steeple with his hands.

Pippa's eyes locked onto him.

'I've got an idea,' he announced.

'Go on,' she urged.

'A fayre,' he said, almost in a whisper. 'A spring fayre.'

Pippa froze on the spot. 'What do you mean? Like . . . an open day?'

'Exactly,' he replied. 'We throw open the doors to puzzlers nationwide, for the biggest puzzle event in all of puzzledom. We can flog products direct to solvers themselves, charge admission fees for the house and gardens, sell tickets to Earl's maze, organise tours of the workshop, run speed-solving jigsaw competitions, Geoff can run a jigsum-athon, you could host crossword-setting masterclasses . . .'

The room practically buzzed with excitement as everyone nodded and murmured between themselves. It was genius. So simple and yet so clever.

Nancy was the one person who wasn't giving much away; she had angled herself away from everyone, looking pensively out of the window.

Pippa would have to speak with her afterwards, see if there was anything she could do to make it up to her. To show how sorry she was.

But, Hector was absolutely right – they'd only fix this if they came together as one. She'd created a problem too big to solve herself. Now, she needed them all more than ever. She watched him draw a big circle around *SPRING FAYRE* on the paper, nodding fervently at them all.

'It's our final roll of the dice,' he declared. 'What have we got to lose?'

Chapter Thirty-Nine

10

WINDOWS TO THE SOUL (4)

Clayton's body was shaking like an old washing machine.

Only an hour earlier two masked thieves had wrestled him to the ground before robbing him of a fistful of notes he'd stuffed into his wallet that morning, and then his mobile, before throwing it straight back at him, no doubt realising the device had little resell value.

Still dizzy from the ordeal, he was shambling along the towpath like a drunkard, dragging one torn trouser leg in front of the other, with Neil dutifully at his side.

'One step at a time . . .' his friend said. 'There's no rush.'

They were only just done giving a statement to the police. Neil had said he was lucky. *Lucky!* That he shouldn't have put up a fight. That you didn't know what people were carrying these days. Clayton dreaded to think.

'We're almost there,' Neil said. 'Just a bit further . . .'

He wasn't used to being fussed over. But that was exactly what Neil was doing. Fussing. He couldn't say he wasn't enjoying it.

He felt his friend's hand tuck around his waist, ushering him towards the houseboat.

'Mind your head . . .'

Clayton stepped aboard Serendipity, one hand gripping the top of the boat, the other holding a cold compress against his throbbing lip.

He'd be lying if he said he wasn't pleased to get a glimpse inside Neil's home, but descending into the body of the vessel, Clayton was overwhelmed by the charm of it all.

The space was tiny – barely bigger than the scullery at home – but it had the feel of somewhere much larger and grander. It was almost as if he'd stepped back inside the Fellowship and been transported to an entirely new dimension at the same time.

'Sit down here and don't move.' Neil guided him towards a reclining armchair as if he were an invalid. 'Are you sure you don't want to go to the hospital? I'll come with you if you like?'

Clayton didn't answer. He was too busy taking in his surroundings.

The walls – though they were spinning slightly – were adorned with similar veneered-wood panels that they had at the Fellowship, and, mounted to them, brass paraffin lamps, emitting a similarly dreamy, almost magical light to the ones on the wall in the library.

There were other pleasing nods to Clayton's home: a whistling kettle sat on a two-ring hob in the tiny galley kitchen and a duck hatch opened not onto the scullery like the one in the dining room at Creighton, but straight onto the water. It was clear that, much like the Fellowship was to Clayton, Serendipity was Neil's sanctuary, his haven from the outside world.

Clayton slumped into the chair – a recliner pushed up against the wall – and suddenly had a feeling that, by simply sitting down, he was taking up too much space, that he was invading Neil's world.

'I'll be fine in a moment,' he said. 'Don't worry about me. Once I've caught my breath, I'll be out of your hair.'

There was the metallic taste of blood coating his mouth and his throat was bone-dry. What he wouldn't give for a proper cup of tea.

'I'm putting the kettle on,' Neil said. 'Milk, one sugar, isn't it? Or shall I give you two? Might help with the shock?'

As Neil opened a cupboard door and pulled out a box of Yorkshire Gold, Clayton felt his eyes swimming.

He wasn't sure if it was the sight of his favourite tea that was making him well up, or the simple gesture of someone offering to put the kettle on – to take care of him for a change – but whatever the reason, he pressed his hands over his eyes as if pushing the emotions back inside.

'You OK?'

'Mmm.'

'Sure?'

'Mm-hmm.'

When Clayton eventually removed his hands, Neil was crouched down in front of him. He was holding up both hands, seven fingers extended.

'What can you see?'

Clayton squinted at him. 'A handsome young man who's fussing unnecessarily.'

Neil's cheeks instantly flushed and he pushed himself up, walking away.

Clayton clenched his jaw.

He wasn't sure why he'd said that, but he had. And he meant it. He fancied the man. He had from the moment he'd first set eyes on Neil. There. He'd admitted it to himself for the first time.

'Now I *am* worried,' Neil said from the galley. 'You're . . . *seeing things*.'

Clayton smiled. He opened his mouth to speak, then changed his mind. He'd put his foot in it enough as it was.

For years, he'd got used to dodging the questions surrounding his sexuality, for no other reason than he wasn't quite ready to answer them. The residents would continually quiz him on when he planned on getting a girlfriend, but there were just two people who never raised the subject. Pip and Earl, the two who knew him more intimately than anyone, never pushed him on the matter. They must have known, somehow, that his interests lay elsewhere.

The awkward silence was interrupted by the stovetop kettle whistling like a small steam train.

Neil went to pour the tea while Clayton continued studying the place, looking for further clues as to who this man was, why he felt such a strange connection to him.

He realised the boat was just like one of Hector's quaint jigsaw paintings. The longer you studied it, the more it revealed. Like a picture within a picture within a picture.

On floating shelves dotted about, science-fiction books were lined up by colour, and down the far end of the saloon, several computer monitors were mounted above a desk, a wall of white light flickering from the screens like the Starship Enterprise.

'I told you I'm a bit of a nerd.' Neil had noticed where Clayton's gaze had landed. He was carrying two giant Sports Direct cups and a packet of shortbread.

Clayton felt the corners of his mouth lift into a contented grin.

While the tea was brewing, Neil had thrown a few sticks of kindling on the little stove and it was kicking out a surprising blanket of heat. It crackled faintly like popping candy in the corner.

'Lovely tea,' Clayton said, with both hands curled around the giant mug. It really was excellent. Neil obviously had plenty of practice making tea for his clients.

'Just sit tight, I want to have a look at that cut.'

Neil disappeared into the back and returned with a first-aid kit. He fished out some cotton pads and a bottle of TCP and came right up to Clayton's face to examine the cut above his eye.

'Can you tip your head back?'

Clayton did as he was told. He felt Neil's warm hand gently cupping the back of his head and a shiver went down his spine.

'That's it.'

'Ouch.'

'Sorry. Try and keep still.'

The stinging was tempered only by the view. Clayton tried concentrating on Neil's face, on the creases in his furrowed brow, the dark bristles of his immaculately maintained beard, the slightly furry trim around his ear lobes.

'You've got green *eyes*,' he blurted out, before he could stop himself.

Windows to the soul. Ten across. He'd been looking into the **eyes** of everyone he'd met all day.

Neil continued dabbing the wound but was stifling a smile.

'Quiet.'

'But you have!'

They were beautiful, he thought. Like the emerald-coloured marbles in the solitaire set at home. Perhaps that was why he was drawn to him.

Neil took a fresh cotton pad and doused it with antiseptic.

'I think they're more green-grey actually.'

'They look quite green to me.'

On second inspection they were very green, almost startlingly so. 'Only two per cent of the population have green eyes . . . did you know that?'

'I didn't.'

'Something like that, anyway. It's the rarest eye colour in the world, so they say. And the most attractive. Officially speaking, I mean.'

Neil laughed. 'Who says that then?'

Clayton wasn't actually sure. 'Science, I assume. It's how we're all genetically inclined . . .'

'Is it?'

'Yes, it is.'

'And so . . . you find me . . . attractive, do you?'

'I do.'

Neil offered a brief, tight-lipped smile. 'That's good then, isn't it.'

'Why's that?'

He turned and disappeared down the back of the boat, reappearing a few seconds later carrying cushions and blankets, with a sheepish look on his face.

'Because I'd like you to stay here the night.'

Clayton felt an unfamiliar sensation in the pit of his stomach.

'Just so I can keep an eye on you. In a medical sense, of course.'

It wasn't nerves but something similar, he thought. A sort of flutter, like a little bird was trapped inside him.

They beamed at each other.

Chapter Forty

THE FELLOWSHIP OF PUZZLEMAKERS
TUESDAY, 2ND APRIL, 1991

Pippa's typewriter chimed as she reached the end of a line.

She was desperately typing up the final batch of invitations for their spring fayre, scheduled in just five days' time, but was having trouble concentrating.

On the window seat behind her, Nancy was in a hazy cloud of cigarette smoke, silhouetted against the bright midday sun.

'I just don't *get it*,' she announced, her hands extended in front of her as if she were about to catch an invisible beach ball. 'Does he really think I'd want a friendship ring? At my age? I'm not eleven, for crying out loud.'

It had come to light that the ring presented to her at the Valentine's do was a ring that symbolised love, just not the sort Nancy had especially wanted.

'Jonty's sixty-nine, isn't he?' she asked. 'So there must be, what, thirty years between him and Angel?'

Pippa took a deep breath. As if things couldn't get any worse, it had also come to light that Jonty and the housekeeper had taken dinner together the previous evening.

'There's thirty-five years between them, actually,' she answered. 'He's almost double her age.'

Nancy made a retching noise behind her. 'Can't we sack her?'

Pippa sighed. Even though the thought had crossed her mind once or twice over the years, in truth, she wouldn't dream of it.

'I'll pretend I didn't hear that. Angel is as valued a member of this family as anyone else, and you know it. Plus, she hasn't done anything wrong!'

'But Jonty is a pensioner!' Nancy fired back. 'It's an abuse of power. We can't allow Angel to become his mistress.'

Pippa spun her chair round, rolling the castors noisily against the hardwood floor towards her heartbroken friend.

'They had lunch at the Beefeater, Nance. A carvery, that's all. Hardly a night at Claridge's, is it?'

Ever since the spring fayre had been proposed by Hector a week earlier, the residents had been more productive than ever, turning over as many puzzles to sell at the event as possible. There was a new energy about the place and a boundless zest had taken over everyone. Everyone that was, except Nancy, who to Pippa's surprise and slight concern, seemed more consumed by her failed relationship with Jonty than the threat of the Fellowship's closure.

'The thing is,' Pippa went on, 'how do you know Jonty doesn't wish to pursue a friendship with Angel too? Perhaps they're just mates.'

'What *man* wants to just be *mates* with women?'

Pippa looked pensively over her friend's shoulder. *A gay man*, she thought. A gay man might want just that. But she daren't risk saying it aloud so pushed the thought to the back of her mind.

'I'm so sorry, love. I know you were fond of him.'

Nancy nodded into her lap, entirely dejected.

'I don't suppose you two ever . . .' Pippa was struggling to find the words. 'Were you two ever . . . *intimate*?'

Nancy looked up, blinked, then gave the smallest of nods.

'You *were*?' Pippa was shocked at her friend's admission. The two of them shared everything together. 'Why in Heaven's didn't you tell me?'

Nancy raised her eyebrows, outraged. 'That's rich, coming from you! You've been keeping secrets from me for months!'

Pippa immediately averted her gaze, embarrassed by her own hypocrisy. 'You're right. I can hardly talk, can I?'

Seconds later and Nancy was experiencing a fresh wave of despair. She sunk her head into her hands, and Pippa, not knowing what else to say or how to comfort her, offered a hug, pulling her friend right up to her side.

'To be honest, Pip,' Nancy finally said, 'I wanted to forget that night ever happened. The sex was hardly earth-shattering. I think we were both out of practice, you know? It didn't exactly . . . conclude.'

'Well . . . yes.' Pippa felt terribly uncomfortable all of a sudden. 'Nothing to be ashamed of, dear.'

'Jonty had a bit of trouble, with his old—'

Pippa waved for her friend to stop. She didn't need any more details.

'Pip, when was the last time *you* had . . . you know . . .'

Pippa found herself squirming on the seat. After a few seconds she said, in a quiet, old-maidish voice, 'Frankly, Nance, I wouldn't know where to begin, it's been that long. I'd need to consult an instruction manual.'

There was a faint laugh and Pippa felt her shoulders drop, hearing her friend's familiar cackle in her ear, the scent of her own perfume lingering in her nose.

'Any news on the fostering?' Nancy asked as the two of them separated.

Pippa didn't say anything, just pushed herself up from the seat and rolled her chair back to her desk with a fresh sense of bitterness foaming inside her. Eventually she gave a quick shake of the head over her shoulder. 'That ship's sailed, love. It was a no.'

'Oh, Pip, I'm sorry.'

Pippa forced a grateful smile, then turning back to her desk, splayed her expert secretarial hands over the keys, and proceeded with the invitations.

Everyone was busy preparing for the fayre. Next door in the library, Jonty Entwistle was finalising his riddles for The Great Puzzle Quiz, which Nancy was meant to be overseeing, while mathematician Geoff Stirrup was working on some equation-setting for his jigsum-athon. Throughout the day, all of the Fellowship's bestsellers would be available to buy at discounted rates, plus they were doing live demonstrations of their newest releases, including Sudocubes, Sphere Today – a natty little invention from Eric Stoppard – and Jubble II, an update on their popular tiled letter game with beautiful glass tiles, rather than stone.

Pippa had only managed to type another two invitations when Nancy opened her mouth behind her.

'If I could give you a child of my own, I would.'

Pippa's fingers were an inch above the keys. Her whole body went stiff. 'What did you just say?'

'You'd be a terrific mother, Pip. We all know that.'

'Well . . . thank you, but—'

'I'm not sure I want children, Pip, to be honest,' Nancy continued. 'But then, we're all after different things, aren't we?'

'What do you mean exactly?'

Nancy batted the question away with her hand, then turned to Pippa with a grave look on her face. 'I guess . . . the ring . . . it's made me . . . question things.'

'Question *what* exactly, love?'

'My future here,' she answered, and suddenly her voice was so sober, so calm and considered, it made Pippa give her an anxious stare. She couldn't possibly mean it. She couldn't leave the Fellowship, certainly not now, before they'd even secured its future.

Nancy blinked at her.

'Oh, don't talk such nonsense!' Pippa eventually replied, realising this was just her friend's usual histrionics. It would soon blow over in a few days. 'Imagine this place without you!'

It was less than a week until the fayre and Pippa was darting across the lawn towards the jigsaw studio. It was barely 7 a.m. and she was carrying a breakfast tray out to Hector, still in her nightdress and with her curlers cooling in her hair. Ribbons of cloud were forming in the sky and beneath her rubber-soled, slippered feet she had left a silvery trail across the dew-tipped lawn, like a giant snail's.

It was Pippa's idea to prepare a special treat for all the residents that morning. Coddled eggs, granary toast, tropical fruit salad.

It was the least she could do, given how hard everyone had been working and how forgiving they'd been. All except her loyal, long-standing deputy, who, from the moment she'd confessed to her financial failings, had thrown himself into his work and barely looked at her.

Pippa was ashamed of herself for letting him down so badly, but there was something else playing on her mind. She was the only person who knew that, if they were forced to sell the house, it wouldn't be for the first time that Hector found himself without a home.

That morning, Hector had been tucked away in his studio since the crack of dawn putting the finishing touches to some new works he was displaying at the fayre.

The Spring Jigsibition, as it had been playfully dubbed, would be one of their main events – the largest display of jigsaw art to be hosted anywhere in the world. Not only would it showcase Hector Haywood's epic back-catalogue, but also his latest collection: *Companion Pieces. Six Brand-New Works Celebrating Fellowship in All Its Forms*. Pippa couldn't help but note the timeliness of the theme.

The tips of her slippers were sodden as she made it to the foot of Hector's hideout.

The studio was tucked behind a few sycamores at the south side of the lawn. It looked, from certain angles at least, like the world's worst treehouse. In fact, it was a large potting shed on stilts, elevated ten feet in the air on an old rickety platform made from scaffolding planks.

The whole thing was a death trap, she'd been saying so for years, and yet, as she approached this quiet corner of the grounds, and gingerly made her way up to the steps, Pippa couldn't argue that the set-up looked rather quaint.

On the decking, at the foot of the steps, were a couple of planters, made out of two rusty tin baths, with spring bulbs emerging from the soil like tiny green swords. There was a whiskey barrel repurposed as a rainwater butt and, dangling from the roof of the studio, a collection of wind chimes fashioned from old tins of tomato soup and clanging silver spoons – all designed to stop the birds from nesting on the roof.

'Hector, love, it's me. I come bearing coddled eggs.'

A peace offering, she thought. *An olive branch, at least. Give me a chance to make it up to you, will you.*

'Couldn't get the door, love, could you?' she called out, balancing the silver breakfast tray in the crook of her arm.

Without a spare hand to knock, she resorted to butting the side of her head against the glass instead.

Knock, knock.

Nothing.

Eventually, she contorted her grip on the tray and managed to grip the handle, letting herself inside.

It was much like any other artist's studio: a mess of paint pots and palettes, brushes, easels, and canvases strewn all over the place. As Pippa inched her way inside, stepping over various paraphernalia on the floor, she finally caught sight of Hector in the corner, obscured by a canvas lit by an anglepoise lamp behind him. He had a paintbrush between his teeth and headphones over his ears and his eyes were narrowed in concentration on whatever was in front of him.

Pippa lifted her hand. 'Yoo-hoo!'

He jumped out of his skin the second their eyes met.

'Only me.' She made her way towards him as he switched off his Walkman.

She had just put down his breakfast on a stool, when she sensed a shadow emerging behind her, something big and broad and forbidding. Without a moment's thought, she spun round, knees bent, arms out.

'Dear God!' she cried out, pressing her hand to her heart.

It was only Angel.

'You frightened the life out of me, love.'

'Oh.' Angel made a face. 'Sorry!'

Pippa waved her apology away, embarrassed by her outburst. 'What are you doing here anyway, dear?'

'I've been helping Hector. I have been for months.'

'I *know* you have,' Pippa sighed. *It was my idea.* 'But at this unholy hour?' She glanced at her watch. 'You don't usually start till nine?'

Angel shrugged. 'There's lots to do before the fayre, Mrs Allsbrook. Many hands make light work . . .'

'Well, that's true,' Pippa replied.

She realised the young woman was still in her own clothes, yet to put on her uniform. As she stepped into the light, Pippa took a second to observe Angel's outfit. It was a baggy khaki-green boiler suit, not unlike an RAF uniform, as if she were about to jump out of a plane.

'You will fill in your timesheet, though, won't you?' she added. 'Make sure you're getting paid for all the extra hours?'

Angel nodded gratefully and Pippa smiled back at her.

They could scarcely afford it at the minute, but she hated the idea of Angel not being recompensed for her extra work. She moved to where Hector was standing, behind a large canvas where, beneath it, a wastepaper basket was filled with a mountain of jigsaw pieces.

'Is this what I think it is?' she asked.

Hector nodded, with an electric glint in his eyes.

'Marvellous.' Pippa felt a jolt of excitement pulse through her veins.

A Masterpiece of My Heart was to be one of the fayre's surprise showstoppers.

The special limited-edition mega-jigsaw would be composed of Hector's favourite jigsaw scenes from over the years, which, once complete, would form the largest commercially made puzzle in the world.

'All forty-five thousand pieces,' Hector said, bending down and grabbing a fistful of pieces, allowing them to fall between his fingers.

Pippa beamed at the man.

It had been costly to make, and the product had a very limited market, so they'd agreed on producing just one special edition of this unique puzzle for their most ardent solvers. With any luck, it would be sold at the fayre to the highest bidder.

'And you're sure you'll have all the artworks ready for your exhibition?' she asked. 'We've only got five days to go.'

'I'll do my best.'

'I know you'll *both* do your best,' she corrected, shooting a look between Hector and Angel. 'I never doubted that.' She gave the housekeeper a wink, conscious not to leave her out. 'We're all hugely grateful to the pair of you. Truly.'

It was nice to be able to compliment Angel for a change, rather than correcting her, Pippa thought.

She was about to leave when she turned on the spot at the door, clicking her fingers triumphantly in the air. 'Oh, I almost forgot.'

'Yes?' Hector asked.

'Guinness World Records . . . they've confirmed their attendance at the fayre.'

'Oh,' he replied, his eyes going very big for a second.

'So at least we're guaranteed one visitor!'

'We're getting an adjudicator then?' he said. 'It's all confirmed?'

She nodded. 'And with any luck, Mr Haywood, you'll be making it into the record books. How about it, eh?'

Pippa's buoyant mood was instantly dashed the second she got back in the house.

A group had gathered in the hallway and the mood was solemn, panicked even.

'*There* you are!' Earl cried, still in his dressing gown. 'Did you know about any of this?'

Pippa, sensing the hysteria in the air, folded her arms across her nightdress. 'About what?' she asked. 'What's going on?'

'It's *Nancy*.' Earl looked on the verge of tears. 'She left in the night, Pip, before any of us could stop her.'

'What are you talking about?'

Earl gripped her by the arm, as if steadying her from a fall.

'Nancy's packed up and gone back to London, Pip. We've just found these letters.'

Pippa's entire body went cold.

Nancy had gone? Without even saying goodbye? She felt her arm reach out for the letter marked with her name, before ripping it open, hoping her friend had a very good excuse for herself.

Chapter Forty-One

18

_______ONE'S STUFF (5)

Clayton was wearing a pair of Neil's pyjamas. Brushed cotton. Soft as anything. He couldn't remember the last time he'd stayed up this late. It was a quarter to three in the morning.

The conversation aboard *Serendipity* had been gentle but forthcoming, accompanied by the faint crackle of the wood-burning stove. In the last few minutes, he'd learned that Neil had grown up in Tring in Hertfordshire, that his mother died suddenly when he was young, that he was raised by his grandma, Maureen, from the age of seven until he was nineteen, when she also passed away. Every now and then he would say something like, 'I should let you sleep,' or, 'You must be tired,' but then would carry on speaking anyway, and Clayton really didn't mind, even though he was exhausted, because he'd be happy staying up all night if that's what Neil wanted.

It was pitch black through the portholes, creating the impression that they could be anywhere. Occasionally the noise of late-night revellers stumbling along the towpath reminded Clayton where he was. He was bobbing up and down on the Grand Union Canal, in the greatest city in the world, fifty miles from the Fellowship. He was spending the night on board a boat owned by a man he barely knew but was really starting to like very much.

They'd discussed hobbies, Neil revealing his lifelong passion for computer games, particularly the Xbox and *Gears of War 4*. They discussed their mutual love for classic cinema. And while Clayton confessed to being a foodie, Neil admitted he was a hopeless cook and incredibly picky when it came to what he ate. All of these revelations were aided, induced even, by their sharing a bottle of Madeira. It turned out they were both fond of a fortified wine.

'So let me get this straight.' Neil put his drink down and reached for Clayton's phone. 'The cryptogrid led you to this painting at Harrods? Of a boy you don't know, but looks just like you? And now you're at a dead end?'

'That's right.'

They were sitting opposite each other in the saloon of the boat, Neil at the dinette table, on the padded bench, Clayton on the armchair that, when reclined, would become his bed. The topic of conversation had moved on to his quest, the puzzle trail.

Neil pinched in on the photo. 'Was there anything on the back?'

'The back?'

'Of the painting? On the frame or the canvas?'

'Umm . . .'

Clayton wasn't actually sure. He'd been so troubled by the little boy's gaze, so lost in their likeness, he couldn't remember.

'I'm not sure, to be honest. I'll have to check when I get back to the hotel.'

Neil handed him back his phone. 'Might be an idea.'

There was a creak as the boat drifted from the side of the bank and back again.

'Who's that?'

On a ledge behind Neil's head was a photo frame that had caught Clayton's eye. He'd been scouring the boat for any photos, any clues to whether he had a girlfriend . . . or a boyfriend. From where he was sitting, the picture appeared to be Neil standing in front of a gaggle of young women at a party. Friends?

'Oh . . . nothing.'

'Go on,' Clayton urged. 'Who are they?'

Neil reached round and took the picture, placing it out of sight in his lap. 'Don't worry.'

'Are they your mates?'

'Sort of . . . but no, not really.'

He sheepishly got up and handed Clayton the picture.

In the image was Neil standing in the centre of frame with his arms around a gaggle of young ladies all done up to the nines in slinky tops. When he looked up, Neil was blushing.

'Don't judge, OK? But . . . I'm a super fan.'

'Oh . . .' Clayton replied, pausing to look again. So they were famous? Popstars? 'So I should know them then?'

Neil looked appalled. 'You don't know who Girls Aloud are?'

'The name rings a bell,' he lied.

'Alexa!' Neil bellowed, making Clayton jump out of his skin.

'Who's Alexa—'

Neil lifted his hand to stop him. 'Play my favourites.'

At once, the opening bars of a song were being blasted from an invisible speaker somewhere, the twang of a guitar, the blast of drums.

'Alexa,' Neil shouted again. 'Turn it *up*!'

Suddenly he was up and whipping Clayton to his feet with warm, clammy hands, and the second Clayton stood he realised quite how drunk he was, and how drunk Neil was, too, judging by the way he was waving his arms in the air like he was drowning.

Strut *one's stuff.* Eighteen across.

Clayton wasn't sure if he was going to get the opportunity to fulfil this one, but within a few seconds, he found himself with his arms in the air, too, following Neil's lead, the pair twirling in and around each other, in a space barely bigger than the telephone box at home, occasionally knocking into one another like spinning wheels.

The song was so catchy. The more it went on, the more Clayton realised he was enjoying it. The lyrics were interesting too. Something about the sound of the underground. He could feel the sweat forming on his forehead, but he didn't mind that much because Neil had a bit of a shine going on too.

As Clayton continued to dance with this handsome man on this charming boat at this absurd hour, he felt an unfamiliar sensation, something warm, almost electric, surging through him. It was more than just the Madeira they'd been quaffing, he was sure of it.

'Alexa . . . stop!'

It went silent all of a sudden as Neil collapsed on the padded bench of the dinette. 'I'm knackered.' He sighed. 'I should sleep. I've got work in . . . five hours.'

Don't, Clayton thought. *Let's have a nightcap at least.*

'Yes,' he replied sensibly. 'I suppose I ought to as well.' Clayton fell into the armchair and cranked the recline lever on the side. 'It's well past my bedtime.'

Neil moved over to him, squeezing his shoulder, before stumbling down the back of the boat, raising his hand drunkenly above his head.

'Night, Clayton.'

'Night, Neil.'

What felt like only a few hours later, Clayton woke with the most awful head. The pain was so sharp and his vision so blurred, it took him a moment to remember where he was. For a second he thought he was back at home. Neil's cat, Muriel, had appeared sometime in the night, curling up with him just like Klotski used to when she didn't struggle with the stairs.

It was the first time since he'd arrived in London that Clayton had slept so soundly.

He rubbed his eyes.

Through the porthole, a sheer mist blanketed the water, turning it to frosted glass, and the leaves of the overhanging trees, the wildflowers and the grass verge were wearing last night's rain.

Lifting himself out of his reclining chair-bed, he folded his blanket in a neat pile and draped it over the arm.

Moving into the galley, he noticed their glasses from last night drying on the rack. The empty bottle of Madeira poking out the bin.

He'd promised to cook breakfast and was thinking about doing eggs, but wasn't sure if Neil had any, or how he might like them, remembering how fussy he said he was.

It was only when he went to look inside one of the kitchen cupboards that he spotted the note on the worktop.

Morning, Clayton.
I'm heading to work. Help yourself to anything for breakfast. When you're off, the door's on a latch, just pull it closed behind you. Good luck with the puzzle! I hope you find what you're looking for.
Neil x

Clayton felt an instant crush of disappointment.

Glancing at the blinking time on the boat's cooker, he realised it was eleven-fifteen in the morning. He'd overslept, missed his chance to thank Neil, to say goodbye. Or even to ask him out for a drink sometime. A trip to the cinema, perhaps. Or to see Girls Aloud, if they were still touring.

Clayton got dressed into yesterday's still-damp clothes that Neil had tried to wash and gathered up his bits, folding up his borrowed pyjamas and leaving them on the side, before giving a final stroke to the cat, and disembarking.

Back at the hotel, he lay on his bed ruminating.

Thoughts swilled around his head about last night's close call with the masked robber, about the two of them strutting their stuff on the boat, and the way Neil had squeezed his shoulder goodnight, and the kiss he'd added to the end of his handwritten note. He supposed everyone put kisses on messages these days. He shouldn't read too much into that.

But there was something else he was chewing over, too.

Neil's instincts were right. There was something on the back of the portrait. As soon as he'd arrived back, he'd retrieved the portrait of the little boy from his en-suite and spotted something glaringly obvious on the back: a sticker in the bottom right corner, with a name he'd never heard before and an address that meant nothing to him.

CLAYTON,
IT'S NEVER TOO LATE TO FIND YOU,
WITH LOVE, PIPPA.

Mr Jonty Entwistle.
Wilde House Nursing Home
Vauxhall Pleasure Garden
London
SE11 5HL

A few hours later, pulling up outside the address in a black cab, Clayton was instantly comforted by the sight of the nursing home in front of him.

It was a nursing home, but it wasn't how he expected a nursing home to look. He assumed they were all the same: drab, characterless institutions with concrete wheelchair ramps and ugly support rails and safety locks on the windows, but this one had a violet awning over its entrance, cheery bedding plants in each of its window boxes, and a well-maintained front patch of lawn, all encased within iron railings and a very well-manicured privet hedge. The ramp leading up to the door was red-carpeted. On first impression, it looked more like a boutique hotel.

Clayton stepped out of the cab and fumbled for his change to pay the driver. He'd been working himself up and his legs had that slightly numb, jellylike quality.

Approaching the carpeted ramp, he pressed a steadying hand against the brass rail and made his way towards the entrance. From the intercom came a lady's voice.

'Hello?'

'Afternoon,' he croaked. 'I'm here to visit a . . . Mr Entwistle. Jonty Entwistle?'

There was a buzzing sound and the door clicked open.

Inside, it was a rainbow of colour: yellow floor tiles and orange leather tub chairs, and a forest of lush green ferns pressed against deep indigo walls.

To Clayton's left, behind a glass-fronted reception, a girl with pink hair looked bored stiff. She was twirling her hair around a biro.

'Is he expecting you? Are you on the visitor's list?'

'Umm . . . possibly.'

'Are you a relative of his?'

'I'm not sure, to be honest.'

'What do you mean, you're not sure?'

'Well . . . it's just—'

'Does he know you?'

'I think so,' Clayton answered. 'Yes, I'd say there's a good chance he does.'

The woman blinked at him. 'Sign in, please. I'll have to check your name against our records.'

Clayton scribbled his details in the book and, while the lady dug around in some files, he moved towards the waiting area.

Settling into his chair, he reached for a magazine from the red Formica table, briefly distracted by two elderly ladies making their way across the floor in front of him. They were clinging to each other like their lives depended on it.

Clayton didn't have a great feeling about all of this.

Of course, he couldn't just rock up at a nursing home and expect to see one of the residents without approval. His visit would need authorising. He could be anyone. But then, just as he was flicking through the pages of *Saga Magazine*, the receptionist reappeared in front of him, smiling.

'You're on the visitor's list,' she said. 'Looks like you were approved earlier this year. Do you want to follow me?'

As they moved towards the elevator, Clayton couldn't help marvelling at Pippa's impeccable planning, the way she'd put this whole thing together for him.

He followed the girl to an apartment at the end of a corridor on the second floor.

She knocked loudly on the door then stood to one side and, almost an entire minute later the chain rattled, the latch clicked, and the door peeled open.

Clayton found himself looking straight into the eyes of a thin, wizened man wearing a brown tweed suit with a silk cravat tied beautifully under his chin.

'Hello.' He gulped. 'I'm Clayton. Am I right in thinking you were expecting me?'

There was a brief pause before the man flashed a glittery smile and, without saying a word, waved him inside.

Chapter Forty-Two

THE FELLOWSHIP OF PUZZLEMAKERS
THE MORNING BEFORE THE FAYRE

The gates of Creighton Hall were set to be thrown open to all of puzzledom in less than twenty-four hours and, somewhat inevitably, rain was forecast, threatening to wash out the most important day in the Fellowship's history.

Final preparations were ongoing, and there was a definite buzz about the place, as people bustled about the house and grounds, getting their puzzles ready for the public.

And yet, despite the surge of activity, Pippa was struggling to fully engage.

She found herself alone, rummaging through her friend's abandoned possessions in the newly vacated Trivia suite, not knowing quite what to do with herself.

Nancy had left behind a few old jumpers, a couple of hats and – somewhat unsurprisingly – Jonty's friendship ring. Pippa had tucked it safely in an envelope and left it in her bedstand in case she ever wanted it back.

The various goodbye letters she'd left for each resident gave only scant details of her rash thinking – that she had made the decision very recently, that they shouldn't worry, and that she might not be in touch for a while, until she'd settled and knew she wouldn't be tempted back.

Pippa was worried sick, desperate for her to ring, to let them know she was at least safe, that perhaps she'd changed her mind and was heading home.

'Oh, Nance,' she said under her breath, settling on the end of her friend's bed. Her shoulders slumped, as if collapsing under the load they were carrying.

She peeled out the crumpled letter from her cardigan pocket, in case, on one further read, she might be able to glean something from it.

Dear Pip,

I hate to leave like this, but I'm afraid I don't have much choice.

If I'd have spoken to you, I know you would have convinced me to stay. You're so good at that. I hope one day you'll forgive me and understand why I had to go. I'm doing it for myself – just like you've always encouraged me.

Wishing you the greatest luck for the fayre. I hope with all my heart it secures the future of Creighton. I've enclosed a cheque with the proceeds of my last quiz night. Please add it to the pot.

"I came, I saw, I solved."

With lots of love,

Your friend,

Nancy xx

Pippa folded the note back into quarters, running a hanky under her eyes.

Nancy was right. She would have tried to have convinced her to stay. But perhaps that would have been a selfish move on her part. Perhaps she was selfish, sometimes, always wanting what was best for her, not what was necessarily best for others. And perhaps this was the best thing for Nancy, to start a new life on the outside, to find herself a partner, someone she could share the rest of her life with.

But what if there was something else going on, Pippa thought. Something more than just a woman too scared to say goodbye, for fear of being dissuaded, or seeing how much it would hurt the people she was leaving behind. In the dead of the night, Pippa had considered every possible scenario, including one that left her cold.

What if Nancy had found herself pregnant? She had said something peculiar to her only a few weeks ago, Pippa realised, something about giving her a child of her own, if she could.

But if she *was* carrying a child, and Jonty was, presumably, the father, then, judging by her friend's appraisal of the experience, the whole conception wasn't just miraculous but almost immaculate. Still, it was an option.

Pippa tried to push the thought to the back of her mind.

She spent the next few minutes surrounding herself with little pieces of her friend, treasured memories of their time together. In a corner of Nancy's wardrobe, she found a battered leather box with gold studs tracing the hexagonal lid.

A hatbox.

It was one of several, similarly sized boxes she remembered Nancy arriving with at the house all those years ago. Hatboxes were perfect for storage, her friend had insisted, and because of her family's millinery business, she'd accumulated quite a collection of them.

Pippa prised the lid off the box.

It was full to the lip with old cushions and blankets. Not knowing quite what to do with herself, she started pulling them out, one by one, unfolding and refolding them in a pile next to her on the floor. At the bottom was a chunky chenille throw in custard yellow, its woollen links as large as an industrial steel chain. She remembered it instantly and, with a slight nip in the air, wrapped it around herself, pulling it up to her face, burying her head in its smell. Nancy had started knitting it on the coach home from Creighton, and, later, once they'd all moved in, had continued in the evenings, each night the blanket pooling around her growing bigger and bigger, taking up the whole chesterfield in the end so no one could squeeze in beside her.

Pippa would take the hatbox and the blankets and she would give them to Hector. He was always complaining about feeling the cold in his studio.

She moved towards the window, peeling back the curtains. She'd been trying to keep an ear on the telephone box outside, hoping her friend might ring. But the trouble was, the phone had been almost permanently engaged ever since Nancy had left. Suddenly, Jonty Entwistle was never off the blower.

He was out there right now, tucked inside the red booth, the receiver glued to his ear. Perhaps Nancy had given him a number? Perhaps he knew exactly where she was and for whatever reason, perhaps even at Nancy's insistence, wasn't telling them?

Pippa had an inkling something was up, and she was determined to get to the bottom of it. She was going to confront the man herself.

As she made her way down the carpeted central staircase of the house, gripping the polished banister as she went, Pippa tipped her head up to make herself as tall as she could.

In recent weeks, she'd had the wind knocked out of her sails somewhat. The whole affair with the finances and the wretched leak wasn't just embarrassing but, on a deeper, personal level, quite diminishing. Telling everyone she'd come unstuck, watching them realise she'd let them all down, that she'd lied. And worst of all, admitting that she'd failed. It was her worst nightmare.

She was pacing through the entrance hall, skirting around the roped-off section where the chandelier had fallen, when she bumped into Angel by the cloakroom.

'Are you off somewhere?' she asked.

She was wrapping herself into a black hooded shawl, like a cloak.

'Just into town. Won't be long!'

'Oh?'

Pippa couldn't help glancing at her watch. Unless she was mistaken, it was the middle of the working day. They had a rather important event on in the morning in case it had slipped her mind.

'Shamanic sound bath,' Angel added breezily, as if that was a perfectly fine excuse.

'I see.'

'I'm getting my spirit recentred.'

'Right.'

But there were rooms to prepare, Pippa thought. Windows to

clean, floors to mop. She was about to put her pinny on and get stuck in herself.

'Well, good luck with that. I hope the shamans are . . . on your side.'

Angel looked at her without expression.

'And that the cosmos brings you everything you need.' Pippa didn't know quite how it all worked, but she wanted to sound encouraging.

Angel gave *her* a wide-eyed look, as if *she* were mad, then lifted her hand airily above her head and darted towards the door, slamming it shut behind her.

For a moment, Pippa found herself staring into the space where the housekeeper had just departed, thinking nothing profound, but distracted all the same.

It wasn't the first time their housekeeper had popped out for a touch of spiritual nourishment that week.

On Tuesday morning, when usually she'd be changing everyone's beds, Angel had popped to Newport Pagnell to get her chakras aligned. And on Thursday, a rather hefty parcel had arrived for her, carrying a kilo of quartz crystals, all the way from Guatemala, no less. God knows what the girl was up to, but right now Pippa hadn't the capacity to think about it.

An enormous cloud the colour of a bruise loomed over Creighton and as she picked her way across the striped lawn, a fierce breeze whipped through the rustling trees, the temperature plummeted, and she felt a chill over her arms and neck.

A marquee the size of a circus tent had appeared at the rear of the grounds, almost like magic. The white plastic walls of the temporary venue rattled against the steel poles in the breeze, as Hector scuttled from the studio to the tent carrying his canvases, ready for his first-ever Jigsibition.

As she made her way towards the telephone box, she could just make out Jonty's muffled, waspish tones, and found herself stalling, trying to listen in.

It sounded as if he were reciting Shakespeare in there. His usual verbose ramblings.

But the voice was faint and, and against the sharp wind, it was impossible to make out, so she went round to the front and waved at the man inside.

'Quick chat?' she mouthed through the door.

Jonty pointed at the phone in his hand, as if she hadn't realised he was engaged in conversation.

Eventually, after realising Pippa was going nowhere, he mumbled some excuses down the receiver and, returning the handset, made his way out of the booth.

'How may I assist?'

'Answer me this,' Pippa blurted out. 'Where is she?'

He tilted his head. 'Nancy?'

'Yes.'

'I can assure you, Pippa, I haven't the slightest notion. I adore the woman immensely, I really do, but clearly not in the way she desired . . . or deserved.'

'*Is she pregnant?*'

He reared back. 'I beg your pardon?'

'I know that you two have been . . . *intimate*,' Pippa said. 'And I figured that might be one reason she's gone, because she's carrying a child she doesn't want?'

Jonty took a step back, his face pale with shock.

'I'm her best friend, Jonty,' Pippa added. 'And I'd do anything for her.'

As the silence stretched endlessly between the two of them, she watched the corner of his mouth start twitching as if he were on the verge of spilling something important.

'It is of my firm belief,' he eventually announced, 'that Nancy simply wished for a clean break. I'm sure she'll notify us when she's ready to talk, when she knows you'll have . . . calmed down. And when she's less enraged with me after the tête-à-tête we had last night.'

Pippa felt something inside her shift. 'What tête-à-tête? What are you talking about?'

'Well,' Jonty began, his voice full of regret. 'I fear I've rather gammoned her.'

'Gammoned?'

It wasn't often that a word left Pippa stumped.

'Deceived,' he explained. 'Diddled. Duped.'

'Go on.'

He shifted his weight from one foot to the other.

'I tried giving her clues, Philippa . . . the puzzle ring, for instance, but nothing seemed to do the trick. And even when I forced myself, I couldn't love her the way she wanted. It's just not in me.'

Pippa's heart sank.

It dawned on her, once again, that the notion she'd had all those weeks ago, that Jonty's affection for the ladies of the house, that his theatrical way of expressing himself, and his impeccable sense of style were perhaps all clues to his repressed sexuality, might in fact be true. She'd once thought of him as a ladies' man but perhaps she'd got him wrong completely. Nancy obviously had too.

She shook her head at the whole sorry affair.

'Life is short and time is swift,' Jonty declared. 'If anyone exemplifies that, it's you.'

Pippa frowned slightly.

'The way you go about tackling things, I mean.'

She folded her arms around herself.

The fostering application, she thought. It had clearly set them all thinking about what they craved in their life, what their missing pieces were.

'It's never too late, is it?' Jonty declared, 'to find ourselves?'

Pippa folded her lips into a weak but well-meaning smile, then turned on her heel and headed back to the house when Jonty called out to her.

She turned slowly.

'I was just conversing with my . . . friend . . . Edwin. The art collector I introduced you to?'

She nodded.

'Would you object if he joined tomorrow? Only, I've decided . . . To thine own self be true!'

After a brief pause, Pippa nodded, realising he was quoting from *Hamlet*. She felt a warmth spreading throughout her chest at the idea of this man finally finding himself, realising where he slotted into the crossword of life. She hoped the two of them would be very happy together.

'Of course,' she replied. 'Everyone's welcome at the fayre.'

Chapter Forty-Three

A FAINTEST NOTION NOT TO BE IGNORED (7)

A cup of tea with Mr Entwistle was proving to be a form of divination.

At least, that was how it was beginning to feel for Clayton, who'd been sipping an Earl Grey in the man's sitting room for ten minutes when he suddenly thought to take out his jotter and start making notes.

He was in a very low wicker lounge chair in the corner of the room. The snooker was on the television and there was the faint sound of balls knocking into each other, the monotonous drone of the commentator. His host sat bolt upright in a luxurious red armchair with his feet plunged in a bubbling foot spa. When he spoke, his legs routinely shot up and out of the water, making a right mess all over the floor.

'It's a wise child that knows his own father,' Jonty bellowed. 'A wise child indeed.'

'My father?' Clayton asked breathlessly. 'Do you know who that is, Mr Entwistle? Do you know who my father is? My mother?'

The words slipped off his tongue and hung heavily in the air.

'I'm trying to work out why I'm here, Mr Entwistle. I guess it's because you know something or can help me in some way?'

Jonty immediately lowered his gaze and Clayton wondered if the man had failed to hear him or was simply ignoring the question.

After a brief silence, there was a *tap . . . tap . . . tap* on the linoleum of the hall.

He glanced over his shoulder to see another elderly chap entering the room.

This gentleman was of a similar age to Jonty, and leaning over a gold-plated walking cane, moving towards them with such an awkward gait he couldn't help but push himself out of his chair.

'Would you like a hand?' he asked.

The gentleman craned his neck to shake his head, then continued to shamble across the room, eventually slipping into another armchair beside Jonty's.

It was only as he prepared to sit back down that Clayton clocked the enormous, framed portrait hanging behind his chair.

There was art plastered all over the flat – on almost every surface available – but until now he'd missed the striking picture of Jonty, which, to his untrained eye at least, shared definite similarities to the one Pippa had left for him at Harrods.

There was something about the muted tones of both pictures, the abstract daubs of colours and dappled brushstrokes. They had been created by the same artist, he was almost certain.

Clayton adjusted his grip on his pen, glancing down at his notes. 'I'm so sorry . . . did you say "wise child" a second ago or "wild child"?'

Jonty gave a shrill cackle. 'Ask me no questions . . . I tell you no lies.'

'Nope, sorry, Mr Entwistle, I don't know what that means

either,' he replied, trying to hide his frustration. 'Could you say it once more?'

'Pull up your chair, dear boy!' Jonty bellowed, waving him to come closer. 'I won't bite!'

Clayton forced a tight grin and scraped his chair a few feet closer.

He'd actually been quite happy with the distance between them. Up close, Jonty was nothing short of startling. His eyes were enormous, deep-socketed and shrewd, his cheeks hollow and pale, his jowls lavishly whiskered. And there was something about his thunderous voice and cryptic turns of phrase that was unnerving.

Half of him was beginning to fear that everything coming out of the man's mouth was just gobbledygook. Either that or perhaps he had some form of dementia. So far, he had scribbled down:

IT TAKES A VILLAGE TO RAISE A CHILD.
THREE (THEE?) MAY KEEP A SECRET.
WALNUTS AND PEARS YOU PLANT FOR
YOUR HEIRS.
A WISE CHILD KNOWS HIS OWN FATHER.

The other chap in the room offered nothing but a friendly smile. Clayton wasn't sure who he was, but he didn't appear to be going anywhere.

'I suppose what I'm trying to ask, Mr Entwistle, and . . . Mr . . .'

'Dankworth,' the mysterious man answered. 'Edwin Dankworth.'

Clayton smiled in response. 'Do either of you know anything about where I've come from? Can you help me in any way at all?'

He glanced first at Jonty, who suddenly had his hand inside a packet of Cadbury's chocolate eclairs, and then Edwin, who was fumbling with his cuffs, avoiding his eye entirely.

For a while there was silence, save for the sound of the water gurgling between Jonty's feet and the rustling of sweet wrappers.

He thought he'd try a different tack.

'Jonty,' he began. 'Tell me how you knew Pippa. Am I right in guessing you were a Fellowship member? What was your specialism?'

Leaning forward in anticipation, Clayton noticed the long lashes floating above Jonty's eyes, unusually dark against his pale complexion.

'Chief Lexicographer,' Jonty replied.

Clayton smiled, pleased to have finally got a sensible answer. So he was a wordsmith. That explained his verbose turns of phrase, at least.

'And what's your favourite word?'

'Pragma.'

'*Pragma*?' Clayton asked. 'Sorry, but I'm not sure I know what that word means?'

Jonty had closed his eyes. For a split-second Clayton panicked that the old man had expired in front of him, but then he emitted a wheezy breath, and it was clear he'd just dropped off.

In the corner, Edwin gave a sympathetic smile.

'I'm not very bright, clearly,' said Clayton.

'No, no,' Edwin replied. 'It's not English . . . not really. It's an Ancient Greek word.'

'Oh.' Clayton felt a tingling at the base of his neck. Just like on the ring, then.

'It means love,' Edwin explained. 'A particular type of love.'

Clayton found himself gripping the arms of his chair. He knew the Greeks had several ways to express love – *Philia*, referring to friendship, and *Storge*, symbolising parental love, and now *Pragma*, which presumably meant . . .

He watched Edwin reach over and drape his hand over Jonty's cardiganed arm. So they weren't friends, but lovers. Romantic lovers.

'Nothing worth solving is ever easy.' Edwin declared.

Clayton nodded pensively at the couple, and even though the man was supposedly sound asleep, he could have sworn that Jonty's lips lifted into a tiny smile.

Moments later and Edwin was levering himself out of his chair and asking Clayton to follow him.

'There's something we were asked to give you,' he said as they moved towards the hall. 'Something that arrived in the post.'

Clayton felt his insides vibrate with anticipation as he went towards the door.

Another parcel from Pippa, he thought. The last one, surely.

Before trailing Edwin into the hall, he shot a final look at the portrait of Jonty behind his chair and darted towards it, skirting around the chair to get a better look.

If there was *a faintest notion not to ignore*, it was this one. He'd solved six down earlier on and had set about his day determined to follow his nose, to listen to any **inkling** he had. Scanning the picture for any clues, Clayton felt an expansive feeling in his chest. Tucked in the bottom-left edge of the canvas his eyes landed on the artist's signature. A barely decipherable name, scrawled in white paint. Bert E. Wangles.

Clayton had never heard the name before in his life, but as he dashed out of the room, he felt a rush of something flood through his body.

He was met by Edwin leaning into a mid-century sideboard, fumbling for something inside.

'We've been keeping something for you,' he explained, eventually pulling out a shallow, lidded box roughly a few inches high and fifteen inches long, wrapped in brown paper. 'I hope it's what you're looking for. We haven't opened it, of course, but there's a note on the front from someone I think you know.'

Clayton glanced at the parcel, realising his hands had started to tremble.

'Dearest Clayton. Never forget... puzzles bring people together. With love, always, Pip x

'Thank you,' he said softly, tucking the box under his arm. Already he had a clue what it might be, just from the size of it. 'Will you say goodbye to Jonty for me?'

'I will,' Edwin replied, leading him to the door. 'And you know where we are if you need us.'

Clayton shook the man's hand, which, despite his obvious balance issues, was surprisingly sure and steadying, and as he left the flat, he repeated the name of the artist over and over in his head.

Bert E. Wangles.

Bert E. Wangles.

Bert E. Wangles.

Chapter Forty-Four

THE FELLOWSHIP OF PUZZLEMAKERS
MORNING, THE SPRING FAYRE

Pippa's stomach felt all twisted, like a Gordian knot puzzle.

Today was the day. Everything was set. The gates were opening in forty minutes.

It was no coincidence she'd opted to wear a pure wool jacket by Mansfield that morning with the most excessively padded shoulders. She knew it made her look a little ridiculous, but perhaps it might conceal the heavy burden she felt. The pressure of it all, weighing her down.

She was in the conservatory with Earl, watching the last few residents dash between the house and the marquee, making final preparations. Miraculously, the weather had cleared, and sunshine was forecast, which was one less thing to worry about.

'All this brouhaha is giving me the ab-dabs,' she remarked.

Earl looked at her baffled.

'The jitters!'

She'd just got back from helping Jean – the Fellowship's lead trivialist – set up the admissions table out the front. They had a number of associates RSVP already, but for the public, tickets were available on the door. She had lent Jean the cash tin and given her change from fifty pounds, broken into various numerations, which she was sure would cover it.

In the distance, she could just make out Hector and Angel lugging a bucket of pieces into the tent, towards Jigsaw Corner. This was where the Jigsibition was taking place, and the world's largest jigsaw puzzle was set to be assembled. There was a tangram of trestle tables – eight of them slotted together to make an enormous oblong – on which they would encourage visitors to help them construct the thing. It had been deliberately positioned next to the tea urn. Hector was confident that, with enough people volunteering a hand while having a cuppa, it would be complete and ready to be signed off by the adjudicator from Guinness World Records before Earl's grand unveiling at six, when everyone would be invited to get lost in a sunset maze session.

In between those headline acts, Geoff Stirrup – lead arithmetician – was set to host a series of numerical games in the marquee (he always demanded complete silence when running any maths tournament, so his jigsum-athon was taking place in a smaller tent at the back of the site) while Jonty was hosting a live Riddle-Me-This masterclass in the bigger tent.

Meanwhile, in the house, Angel was leading guided tours of the communal rooms while Pippa was set to invigilate two crossword tournaments in the library. Quicks at two, Cryptics at four.

She downed her coffee – her third that morning – and turned to the mazemaker. 'Can I share something with you?'

He gave a small, trusting smile. 'Of course.'

She found herself gripping her wobbly middle again. 'I feel awfully responsible, Earl, for all of this. It's eating me up.'

Earl shook his head. 'Of course, you should feel responsible, Pip, but you shouldn't feel *guilty*.'

'How do you mean?'

'Look at what you've created, you should be proud!'

Outside, through the window of the conservatory, Geoff, Jonty, Eric and Martin had gathered outside the marquee to open a bottle of fizz and the sight of it tugged at something inside her, reminding her of the very first session all those years ago.

She'd been reflecting a lot on the Fellowship's inception recently. It may have started out as a puzzle club, but it was so much more than that now.

'Fellowship,' Earl said, tipping his head to the window as the group raised a toast. 'You were never going to rescue this place alone, Pip. But together we will. Just you wait.'

Pippa swallowed the lump in her throat. Earl always knew exactly what to say.

Fifteen minutes later, she was busying herself at the refreshments table, filling the urn and unboxing all the pale green teacups they'd borrowed from the local church, when Earl reappeared, dashing into the tent with a rapturous look in his eyes.

'Pipster! Come and look. Quick!'

Before she knew it, he'd grabbed her by the hand and whipped her out of the marquee, and the two of them were bolting across the grounds together.

'Earl, what the dickens has got into you?'

When they reached the terrace, Earl ushered her down the path by the side of the house and pointed ahead of them. 'Look!' He struggled to catch his breath. 'Look out there, Pipster!'

As she angled herself to get a view to the front gate, Pippa felt her hand go to her chest. She couldn't believe her eyes. Behind Jean's lace-cloth-covered admissions table, was a line of people, the likes of which she had not seen since the last Harrods January sale. They went as far as she could see.

'Puzzles,' he said, throwing his arms around her. 'Isn't it what you always said, Pip? They bring people together!'

Tucked away at the side of the house, the pair clung to each other just like they had on Valentine's night, and Pippa, allowing her head to fall on Earl's shoulder, felt a rare sense of ecstasy come over her.

Jean's going to need more change, she thought to herself.

Pippa spent the next forty minutes at the opening of the marquee, greeting the long line of attendees traipsing up the carpet as if she were the Queen.

Among their acclaimed guests were all the crossword editors from the broadsheets and tabloids; several local and national journalists looking to write pieces; Alan Bailey, the current national Scrabble champion; several legendary chess masters, and, to Pippa's best estimate, at least two hundred and fifty members of the puzzle-loving public. In ticket sales alone they'd already raised several thousand pounds.

The next in line was the esteemed art collector, Edwin

Dankworth, a handsome man immaculately presented, not unlike the image Pippa had conjured in her head.

'Pleasure to meet you at last,' she said, extending her hand.

He was accompanied by a radiant Jonty Entwistle stuck to his side. The two chaps were in matching tweed suits. They looked the perfect couple.

'The famous Philippa Allsbrook,' Edwin declared. 'Or do you still go by your nom-de-plume, Squire?'

'Pippa's just fine,' she replied.

It had been a while since anyone had called her by her pseudonym.

'I feel I owe you an apology, Edwin,' she said. 'For wasting your time with that portrait I sent you . . .'

He waved her words away. 'Not at all, Miss Allsbrook, I just wish I could have given you better news. Something tells me it might hold more sentimental value than anything.'

Pippa gave a consenting smile. She had decided that, rather than returning the painting to the vault at Harrods, she would display her mother's picture prominently in her bedroom instead.

'There was me thinking it might be worth a few bob,' she said, shaking her head. 'Shows how much I know. Still, we've got our very own spring Jigsibition which might be of interest. Do make sure you speak to our artist, Hector, if you head over. He's terribly talented.'

Edwin shot a look over his shoulder then leaned towards her. 'In actual fact,' he murmured, 'I've been meaning to commission a portrait of someone . . . rather special to me.'

'Oh?' Pippa said.

Jonty, overhearing this, went beetroot. He was turning seventy later that summer. It was listed on the Fellowship's birthday calendar.

'I don't suppose Hector's open to commissions?'

Pippa hadn't a clue, but the man clearly had cash to flash and if he was in the mood for spending . . .

'Oh, I'm certain he would be,' she answered. 'Once the fayre's out the way he'll be as free as a whistle. Why don't you ask him?'

Edwin promised that he would, then planted a kiss on each of Pippa's cheeks and went on his way, Jonty on his tail as if being pulled on a lead.

Fifteen minutes later and next in line was a middle-aged lady clutching a clipboard to her chest as if her life depended on it.

'Valerie Keeling, how do you do,' came the voice in front of her. 'Guinness World Records.'

'Oh!' Pippa replied, thrilled the lady had made it, though a tad surprised to see her so early.

She shook the lady's hand. 'So you're the adjudicator?'

Valerie nodded. 'And I believe you have the world's largest jigsaw for me to verify?'

'Umm . . .' She felt her heart plunge. 'I think we're still a *little* way off.'

'Oh?'

Pippa took a breath, trying to hide her panic. She had forgotten to give the lady a time. Her fault entirely. 'Do help yourself to a tea, though, Valerie. And there's plenty of cakes and biscuits.'

'I'm coeliac.'

'Oh, I thought you said you were Valerie?'

'I *am* Valerie. But I'm coeliac.'

Pippa shook her head with a wry smile. She thought she'd said she was *Celia.*

'I'm with you now. Well, hopefully you can stomach a rich tea, at least. They're only thin, aren't they?'

She thanked the lady for coming all this way, then, glancing around the marquee searching for Hector, dashed outside.

If he stood any chance of getting in the record books, and if the Fellowship were going to benefit from the publicity, they were going to have to get a wiggle on. There were forty-four thousand pieces still to find their place in the picture.

Chapter Forty-Five

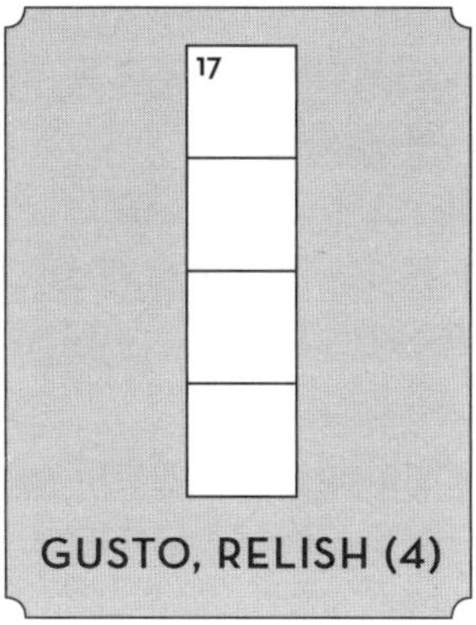

Clayton was hurtling through the backstreets of Paddington in a cab, with Pippa's latest parcel sitting in his lap.

Leaving Jonty and Edwin's fifteen minutes earlier, he'd opted not to go back to the hotel with it but head somewhere else instead. As the note on the box suggested, puzzles were meant to bring people together, and he knew this one would be far more fun to solve alongside someone else.

The taxi shot past Paddington Station and he felt the bubble of nerves rise inside him.

'Anywhere around Little Venice is fine,' he called out to the driver. 'I can make my own way to the canal.'

The sun had dipped to nothing as Clayton stepped out of the car.

Tucked under his arm, Pippa's final clue was bound in reams of brown parcel paper, just like the portrait at Harrods had been, but it was the noise that the contents made when he shook it that really gave the game away.

Whenever the cab went over a bump or sank into a pothole, the box in his lap rattled. It was the unmistakeable clatter of interlocking cardboard pieces, probably a thousand or more.

A jigsaw.

The towpath was quiet at this hour, and he felt that familiar tingle, the fluttery sensation in his stomach, as he let himself out of the cab and made his way towards Neil's floating home.

As soon as he clocked *Serendipity* moored up ahead, he found himself stalling, wondering if this was such a good idea.

It was seven in the evening.

The lights were on in the portholes of Neil's boat. What if he was having his tea, or had a visitor? By the time Clayton was teetering down the steeply sloped cobbled path to the water, he realised it was too late to back out.

He'd managed to pick up a bottle of port and some crisps in a corner shop near Jonty and Edwin's and was wondering where exactly he should knock.

The thing was, Neil had already shown his cards. By inviting him to stay the night on the boat, by looking after him when he was attacked on the towpath, he'd already revealed that he cared for him. Now it was Clayton's turn to show he felt the same.

'Neil?'

He tapped lightly on one of the portholes, not wanting to scare the life out of his friend.

'Neil, it's Clayton. Sorry to turn up like this.'

His hands didn't know what to do with themselves. His fingers ran through the stubble on his chin, then scraped his hair, before settling in his pockets where they landed on his atomiser, and before he could stop himself, he was applying a quick spritz of Paco Rabanne.

He moved to the rear of the boat where he gently rapped his fist against the paintwork.

A few seconds later and there was the sound of a door opening and out popped Neil on the stern, wearing nothing but a blue fleece dressing gown and a surprised look on his face.

'Oh . . . Hey.'

'Hi.' Clayton gulped. 'Sorry to turn up like this.'

'That's all right.' Neil adjusted his robe and inadvertently flashed his bare torso. 'Everything OK?'

'Oh, yeah . . .' Clayton blustered. 'Yeah, I'm feeling pretty good actually.'

Neil grinned. 'Good. I'm pleased to hear that.'

The two men looked at each other a moment.

Behind them, a coot broke the silence, battering its wings on the water, gliding a few inches above the canal, the white tips of its wings causing deep ripples in the brown soup below.

Clayton lifted the carrier bag. 'I've brought treats. And a puzzle!'

'Oh, right . . . so do you want to come in?'

Clayton didn't need to be asked twice. He already had one foot on board the boat.

'Alexa!' Neil bellowed as they settled opposite each other at the dinette booth. 'Play my favourites.'

The music instantly made Clayton's heart rise. He'd been listening to a little Girls Aloud on his phone these past few days and within a few bars of this particular song – 'Something Kinda Ooooh' – his shoulders were rocking.

As he started to peel away the paper from the box, he realised Neil's gaze was directed under the table, towards his feet.

'Have you always worn brogues?'

Clayton subconsciously tucked his shoes under the bench. They'd been tapping against the hull of the boat without him realising. They're not brogues, he thought. They're Oxfords.

'Umm . . . why's that?'

Neil shrugged. 'Just curious, I suppose. They're kind of smart. I like them.' A tiny smile was creeping into his face, a knowing, impish grin.

It was then that Clayton felt something inside him shift again, a pang of some kind. He folded his hand over his navel to try and staunch it.

When he eventually ripped off the brown paper to reveal the jigsaw box below, both their faces dropped.

'There's nothing on the front,' Neil commented.

Clayton took a deep breath.

'So I guess that means . . .' He prised open the lid of the box.

'This one's a blind jigsaw.' He grabbed a fistful of pieces inside, trying to make out what was on them, but it was impossible to see. 'There's no picture to work from, Neil. It's the hardest jigsaw of all.'

'How many pieces are there?'

Clayton chewed his bottom lip as he examined the box.

He could tell just from looking that there were significantly more than the standard one thousand pieces; it was probably a two, even three thousand piecer, possibly even more.

'Oh, I don't know, probably a thousand or so.'

Neil shook his head. 'I think there's a lot more than that, and you know it.'

Clayton grinned.

'Shall we do it together, then?' he asked, itching to get started. 'I could show you some tricks of the trade if you like. It shouldn't take too long, particularly if we join forces.'

Neil smiled, pulling his robe a little tighter around himself, exposing his chest once again.

Clayton tried to avert his gaze. 'Why don't we start with the moon?' he suggested, moving to pick out several grey, cratered shapes he'd already spotted in the pile. 'And, while you're at it, keep an eye out for any straight edges . . .'

Neil nodded and a smile lit up his face.

As the two of them set about building the image – while jiggling in their seats to the greatest hits of Girls Aloud – Clayton realised this was exactly what Pippa meant when she spoke of squeezing the pips out of life. Puzzles or pop music or anything else that made his heart rise. *Gusto, relish. Seventeen Down.* This was the **zest** for life she wanted him to find.

'Alexa!' he shouted. 'Turn it up!'

Chapter Forty-Six

THE FELLOWSHIP OF PUZZLEMAKERS
AFTERNOON, THE SPRING FAYRE

'Introducing the Fellowship's latest prototype,' Eric Stoppard declared from the demonstration table in the marquee. His voice was uncharacteristically loud and assertive. 'Sphere Today!'

Pippa watched the shy craftsman dip his hand inside his jacket pocket and dramatically pull out a polished wooden sphere, about the size of a grapefruit, which he'd been working on for months. From where she was standing, she could just make out the series of hairline cuts drawn across the wood, where one segment became another.

He lifted the ball above his head in front of the assembled audience, twisting it like a lightbulb, and it practically glistened like an orb in his hand.

There was a chorus of caught breaths and Pippa stepped away, making her way towards Jigsaw Corner where another flock of puzzle enthusiasts were in raptures. The Jigsibition had been a huge hit and almost all of Hector's works had sold out of their limited-edition run. But it was the mega-jigsaw construction that had really captivated people.

It had become the talking point of the whole event. Ever since word had got around that someone from the Guinness World Records was in attendance, there had been an enormous uptake in volunteers and people of all ages gathered to offer a hand, grabbing a fistful of pieces from the bucket before taking their seat at the table. It was a place where people could enjoy a cup of tea and biscuit and catch up with old friends while playing their part in a piece of international puzzling history.

Any moment now, the world's largest jigsaw would be complete. The image – an amalgamation of Hector's most popular works, mostly vintage British scenes – had emerged across the trestle tables over the course of the afternoon and now they were less than a hundred pieces away. They were filling the shelves of a traditional sweet shop. Rhubarb and custards. Cola cubes. Milk bottles.

Pippa went and positioned herself next to the man responsible as he surveyed the operation with his usual militant eye.

'Well, well, well, Mr Haywood,' she declared. 'Can you believe it . . .'

Hector glanced at his watch, smiling. 'Less than fifty pieces to go now, Philippa. Bang on schedule.'

She was thrilled for the man.

This entire event had been his idea and, judging by the figures she'd been accumulating from the sales tables throughout the day, it was very likely going to save the Fellowship from closure. Or at least buy them a decent period of time to get their finances in shape. She wasn't sure how she'd ever be able to thank the man.

Pippa folded her arms around herself, feeling a chill. The sun was disappearing, and the temperature had dropped noticeably.

Thankfully, Valerie, the adjudicator, had stuck around and was standing by with her tape measure, ready to sign it off. Pippa couldn't help noticing she already had her coat on and handbag slung over her shoulder, and appeared to be the only person in the marquee not to have had the most marvellous day out.

There was a smattering of applause from the other side of the tent. Eric must have rolled his wooden ball until it fell away into pieces, ready to be put together again.

'Won't be long now, Valerie,' Pippa called out to the woman with the clipboard, who turned to her with a face like thunder.

'Jesus. What a doom merchant that one is,' she said under her breath.

Hector rolled his eyes at her in agreement. 'Some people just do not know how to enjoy themselves, do they?' he replied, and Pippa, shaking her head, helped herself to another Hobnob from the table.

'Where were you earlier anyway?' she asked.

Hector glanced at her. 'What do you mean?'

'When Valerie arrived, you were nowhere to be found.' She had to stop because her mouth was full. 'You were missing for over an hour.'

'Oh. I was just,' he waved his hands airily in front of him, 'talking to someone about something.'

Pippa made a face. 'That sounds very *mysterious*.'

'Well, it was private. It's . . . personal.'

She looked at him aghast. Since when was her deputy so into keeping secrets?

'Who were you talking to?'

Seconds later and Hector let out an impatient breath. 'Jonty's . . . companion, if you're so desperate to know. Edwin. He's after a painting, that's all.'

'*Oh*.' Pippa was slightly disappointed it wasn't something more interesting. 'I knew that already.'

She returned her gaze to the jigsaw table, wondering why Hector was being so cloak-and-dagger about it all, and why the conversation had to happen outside the marquee, in private. She was about to ask him but was interrupted by a commotion around the table.

'What's going on?' she called out.

Suddenly, there was a frantic searching of various surfaces, followed by the timid voice of a man at the jigsaw table, pointing at the almost-complete image in front of them.

'There's a hole,' he said. 'We've got a missing piece.'

What followed next was surely the most dramatic twist in any jigsaw solving that had ever taken place anywhere in the world. Even Valerie perked up.

'Nobody move!' Pippa bellowed, as if they were in a heist movie.

She made her way towards the table with a wide gait in case she stepped on the thing.

After checking every flat surface within a bobbin's throw of the table, she didn't know what else to do. The piece – the lid of a jar of cherry bonbons – hadn't walked out of the tent by itself. It must have got caught in the folds of someone's clothes, she decided.

'Gentlemen, I'm going to pat you all down now. And I don't want any of you to think anything of it. OK?'

Fifteen minutes later and with no sign of the missing piece anywhere, Pippa was at a loss.

'I'm afraid I have to leave now,' Valerie said, hugging her clipboard.

'But . . .'

'If you want to reapply at a future date, Miss Allsbrook, you can contact our offices.'

Before Pippa could stop her, the adjudicator flashed her hand at everybody and marched out of the tent. She turned to the crestfallen figure standing over her shoulder.

Hector looked completely and utterly devastated. Her heart broke for the man.

Moments later and with the sun beginning to fade in front of their eyes, there was no time to waste.

'You're all set with the maze?' Pippa asked Earl. 'Nothing you've forgotten?'

Earl shook his head, taking a swig of champagne from his mug. There were a dozen bottles to go round, but they'd run out of flutes so had resorted to reusing the teacups from the church.

'And you're certain there's a route to the end, aren't you?'

He laughed.

'People aren't just going to get trapped in there, are they? I have visions of us ringing the fire brigade . . .'

The sound of his rollicking laugh always pleased her, and she felt her shoulders drop after the tension of the last hour.

Of course, Earl's maze was always going to be a triumph. She'd known that even before he did.

It was his most elaborate creation yet, measuring several hundred square feet, with a route that actually spelt out a single word. No one had yet to discover what this word was because Earl was yet to let anyone inside.

Earl stepped forward in front of the assembled crowd, where a ribbon stretched over the entrance of the maze. The secateurs in his hand flashed as they caught the low evening light.

'Before I officially declare the maze open, I believe a toast is in order.'

He lifted his mug of fizz to them all, and Pippa could sense he was about to congratulate a crushed Hector on his epic jigsaw creation, but before he could say a word there was a collective gasp from everyone gathered before him.

'The missing piece!' someone shouted. 'There it is!'

'It's under your cup!' Jonty shouted.

Pippa pushed her way to the front of the crowd. '*What*?'

Underneath Earl's green teacup, extended loftily above his head, was the vanished jigsaw piece taunting them all. The lid to the jar of cherry bonbons.

Earl's eyes suddenly went very big.

He necked the remainder of his bubbles before peeling the missing piece from the bottom of his cup. It must have got trapped underneath when people were having tea at the table.

Pippa joined everyone in turning to glance over her shoulder, where the adjudicator had so recently departed.

'VALERIE!' they bellowed in unison.

And then, before anyone could stop her, Pippa hitched up her skirt and legged it across the lawn, accompanied seconds later by several other members of the public, who charged in a single stampede towards the poor woman like a scene from the Battle of Agincourt.

'VALLLERRRIIIIEEEE!'

They caught her just in the nick of time.

'Please, Valerie,' Pippa pleaded, gazing at the woman through the windscreen of her Fiat Panda. She had launched herself on the bonnet just as she was reversing out of the drive. 'It won't take a second, will it?'

Moments later and the largest jigsaw in the world was finally complete. Hector was now a world record breaker and the Fellowship now an even greater part of puzzling history. They would be in all the national papers the following week.

Chapter Forty-Seven

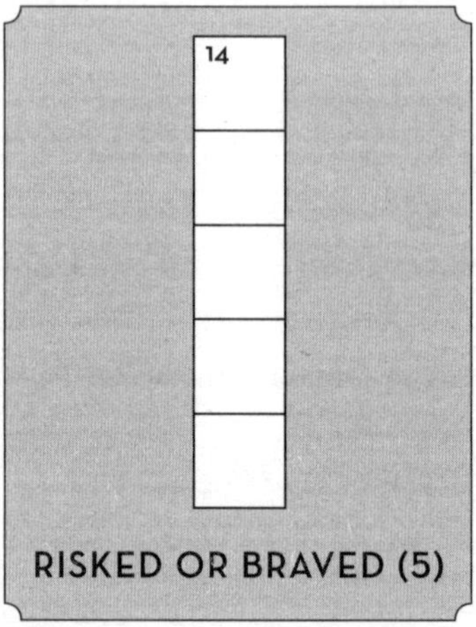

Clayton couldn't remember time passing by so quickly.

The gentle spittle of rain tapping the portholes of Serendipity sounded like the rolling boil of a kettle and as the hours passed, the intimidating mountain of jigsaw pieces had reduced to a more reasonable mound, waiting to find their place in the picture.

'You're picking up bridge, Neil, not moon. Look for the textures. The textures will guide you. You can't be led by colour alone.'

'Right,' Neil replied, straightening in his seat, and flicking a few solid grey jigsaw pieces back into the box. 'So you're sure there's a bridge in this jigsaw then?'

Clayton pointed to a small heap of cobblestones he'd assembled in front of him. 'Either that, or a winding road leading somewhere. It looks like Europe to me, don't you think? It has that sort of feel. My guess is Venice or Paris. I've definitely never seen this one before, though.'

Clayton knew the Fellowship's jigsaw portfolio like the back of his hand. But one thing was certain, this particular design had not come from Hector Haywood. It wasn't his style at all.

He had no idea yet what on earth Pippa was hinting at, where she was pointing him to, but he couldn't help remembering that she'd asked him not to forget his passport. He'd needed it to prove his identity at Harrods. But maybe there was another reason he'd been asked to bring it along.

Clayton pushed the thought to the back of his mind, not wanting to be anywhere in the world other than right here. Moments later, Neil disappeared to the galley and returned with a bottle of cognac and two tumblers. He watched as Neil took his seat and rummaged through the box again, pushing to one side the yellow glow of streetlamps, and what appeared to be glistening water of some kind – a lake, or river, perhaps.

They'd already assembled the majority of the sky, working outwards from the celestial-studded atmosphere down to the coloured rooftops that made up the horizon.

The pair had started to sway in perfect sync with each other, lost in the task at hand, the music of Girls Aloud, and each other for company. There was a glare from the reading lamp above them, a soft light cast over Neil, which was making it difficult for Clayton not to look at him.

On a few occasions he found himself deliberately picking up a puzzle piece from a section he knew Neil was working on, just so he could tip his head and watch him out the corner of his eye. The urge was growing, becoming harder to ignore, more tempting to indulge.

'I'm moving the boat tomorrow,' Neil announced, and Clayton, surprised at this revelation, found himself glancing up at the helmsman with a slightly panicked look. 'I'm a continuous cruiser, so I have to find a new spot every few weeks. To save me paying for permanent mooring.'

'Right.'

'You can help me if you want? I could show you the ropes. I'm leaving at two o'clock. Come over if you fancy. You could ride Serendipity yourself.'

'I will,' Clayton replied, beaming. 'I definitely will.'

It sounded like a date to him.

An hour later and – with just a handful of pieces left – a romanticised tableau had taken shape in front of them, one they'd both decided captured the city of Amsterdam in the Netherlands.

Clayton wasn't sure what to think.

It was the houses that caught his eye at first, with their elegant façades and ornate gables, their steep steps and shutter-clad windows.

But there was one building that stood out among all the others in the centre of the picture.

It was a pink house with an impressive clock face glowing beneath the apex of its roof. The long hand of the clock hovered, ready to strike midnight. It was larger than any of the other buildings it surrounded; grander too, and something about the way the artist had captured it – right in the centre of the frame, the colours more saturated – suggested it held significance somehow.

There were only four pieces remaining. Clayton pushed them towards Neil so that he could complete the puzzle, while he wondered what it could all mean.

Neil carefully inserted the final shape into place and the pair of them stared down at the picture, beaming, until their eyes locked onto the small, gaping hole in front of them.

The central house in the scene – the one with the giant clock face – was incomplete.

'Oh, you must be joking,' Neil said, frantically patting his lap and running his hand across the table.

Clayton's eyes scanned the jigsaw. The hole was where the front door of the pink house should be. A missing piece.

Suddenly Neil was crouching on the floor, running his hand across the carpet of the boat.

'It's got to be here somewhere.'

Clayton did not join in.

Instead, he remained firmly in his seat, running his hand over the conspicuous hole in the picture. Of the four or five thousand pieces that they'd found a home for, the one that was missing was one that featured the front door to the central property in the picture – the pink house that Clayton had been drawn to all along.

It was a sign – a clue in itself.

Pippa was leading him to the house in the picture. To Amsterdam. The missing piece had been withheld on purpose. He was sure of it.

'This is just another a clue,' Clayton announced, and Neil banged his head under the table.

'What?'

'The missing piece is *the clue*,' he repeated, certain of it now.

Side by side at the dinette table a minute later, with their faces just inches from each other and their knees brushing, Clayton **dared** to do something he'd never done before.

He leaned over and folded his hand against the back of Neil's head, until their two heads were coming towards each other, their lips pressing together.

When they eventually separated, Neil dropped his gaze and Clayton felt an instant flush creeping across his face, and he wondered if he'd done something wrong, wondered how something that felt so right could possibly be wrong, until he felt Neil's fingers lifting his chin and their lips touching once more.

They remained like that for quite some time.

Chapter Forty-Eight

THE FELLOWSHIP OF PUZZLEMAKERS
THE MORNING AFTER THE FAYRE

Pippa couldn't remember the last time she'd pulled an all-nighter.

Of all the ways she had imagined the fayre might conclude, watching a grown man on his hands and knees at four in the morning rescue a ladybird was not one of them.

'Come here, you little blighter,' Earl said.

The pair were in the centre of the maze and only just beginning to sober up. Earl was perhaps an hour or two behind her.

'What on earth are you doing, Earl?'

'This little fella here . . .' He had it on the tip of his finger now. 'He's going to get crushed if he's not careful.'

She smiled, admiring how gentle he was being, sending the creature on its way with a light nudge of his fingernail.

Eventually he clambered back onto the bench and Pippa turned to him.

'I'm so happy for Hector, aren't you?'

He nodded. 'If ever someone deserves an accolade . . .'

She couldn't agree more. 'But do you think he's . . . happy?'

Earl tipped his head from side to side. 'Difficult to say, isn't it? He's never out of the studio. Have you seen how much time he spends in there?'

'He's always been a workaholic,' she replied. 'He's been busy preparing for the fayre, that's all.'

Earl shook his head. 'This is different. Recently . . . it's been different. Don't you think?'

Pippa squeezed her eyes at the sky trying to decide.

She supposed she'd been too caught up in her own dramas to notice, but now she thought about it, they had definitely seen a lot less of him in recent months. In fact, she couldn't remember the last time they'd enjoyed their morning eggs together, which had once been a daily ritual for them both.

'I can't help feeling the man's hiding something,' Earl continued, 'something dark lurking in his past . . .'

Pippa felt a sudden chill and wrapped her arms around herself. 'How do you mean?'

Earl shrugged. 'I'm not entirely sure . . . some kind of tragedy. Perhaps he lost someone? Perhaps it's something he's never been able to speak about.'

Pippa was immediately reminded of the speech Hector had made all those years ago when Creighton was a hotel, and the three of them had been sat at the bar. Earl had just shared the news about his wife and Hector's reaction had been more than conversational, or even sympathetic. It had come from a much deeper place. She'd always remembered that.

And then there was the incident with the campervan, many years before that. Hector had been homeless for a while and, despite the fact she'd offered him her spare room and the two of them had become housemates for a while, she'd never understood how he'd ended up living like that. She'd never told a soul about it either.

'I have a funny feeling one day it'll come out,' Earl declared, raising his finger conspiratorially in front of him. 'His head is elsewhere because his heart is elsewhere. If anyone should know about that, it's me. One day, when he's ready, I'm sure he'll tell us.'

With that, Earl leaned his head on her shoulder and started to nod off.

She shook her head and allowed her eyes to close, too, to tune out all the noise in her head, to focus on nothing but the birdsong.

The fayre had been a greater success than she could have dreamed. They would count the money in the morning, but she was confident they'd exceeded their targets. It would be enough to pay for the emergency repairs, and perhaps there'd even be some spare to put aside. It had already been agreed that Geoff would take over the Fellowship's accounts. Pippa was surprised to find that she was actually relieved by this change of guard. Numbers had never been her strong suit. She wasn't afraid to admit that now.

'I don't know about you,' she said, stifling a yawn. 'But I'm shattered.'

'Truly sozzled,' Earl mumbled next to her, rubbing his forehead. 'And my head is bursting.'

For a while they were both silent, and for Pippa that was absolutely fine. She glanced around at the green walls that surrounded them, feeling a rare sense of calm and contentment, allowing her weight to fall gently on Earl's shoulder. Earlier that evening they'd agreed to plant a tree in the centre of the maze, immediately behind where the bench was. A weeping willow would be a nice addition, Pippa thought. The drooping branches would provide a nice bit of shelter from the elements.

'It's a marvel, this maze,' she said. 'You know that, don't you? You've outdone yourself.'

'Thank you.'

'I mean it.'

'No, I mean thanks. For twisting my arm. For encouraging me to move in . . .'

They were both looking at each other now, their faces just inches apart. 'You can be so persuasive when you want to be. There was no way I'd be here now if it weren't for you.'

Pippa beamed.

'Tell me, Earl, do you believe in destiny?'

'Are you talking in a romantic sense?'

She thought about it. 'Perhaps.'

'Then no.'

'No?'

She felt a pang of disappointment. 'So you don't think there's someone that's meant just for us all? That any aspect of our life is . . . predetermined?"

Earl shook his head.

Pippa couldn't help but feel disappointed. 'It's funny, sometimes I wonder if the universe has . . . ideas. I know that sounds a little nutty.'

She thought straight away of Nancy, the alchemy of their

chance encounter on Westminster Bridge all those years ago.

'If mazes have taught me anything, Pipster, it's that in life there is often more than one route to the end goal.'

'So there's no path to happiness?'

'Of course there isn't,' he replied. 'That's what mazes are for.'

Pippa sighed.

'In real life, you just have to keep moving forwards or backwards, sideways even. Whatever feels right in the moment. You'll find whatever it is you're searching for eventually.'

Pippa gave a contented smile. That was a lovely idea.

A minute later and she felt Earl tap her on the shoulder, whispering in her ear, 'Did you work out the word?'

'Hmm?'

'The word that's hidden in the maze?'

'Oh.' She rubbed her eyes, sitting up. In truth, she had forgotten all about it. 'I'm a cruciverbalist, Earl. You know I'm hopeless with mazes.'

'*Try*.'

She shook her head. 'I'm too tired, Earl.'

'Give me your hand, then.'

Earl's hands were getting cold. He took Pippa's index finger, gripping it by the sides like a pen, and started drawing the course they'd walked invisibly on her knee.

Pippa was concentrating as hard as she could to follow where the line was going. *Up, down, left, right, right, down, up, left.*

As he got to the end of the word, she could almost see it carved into her leg and felt her heart lift, rising with such intensity, it almost forced her out of her seat.

'It's what this place was built on . . .' Earl said. 'It's why we're all here, isn't it?'

Before he could finish, Pippa's hand was cupping the soft folds of his cheeks and she was moving her face towards his and the two of them were about to kiss for the very first time.

'It's been a while,' he said, closing his eyes in anticipation.

Pippa laughed, trying to decide which way to angle her head. 'You're telling me . . .'

Chapter Forty-Nine

7

ZILCH AT WIMBLEDON (4)

Clayton had never felt like this before. Whatever it was, was consuming him. Lying exhausted on his hotel bed, the morning after the kiss, he found himself bouncing between giddiness, jitteriness and blind euphoria.

He'd spent the past hour at St Pancras International Station where he'd bitten the bullet, purchasing not one, but two tickets to Amsterdam from the Eurostar terminal. They were only thirty-nine pounds. Departing first thing in the morning. He hoped Neil might consider joining him.

He supposed he could have bought them online, but ever since he'd got back from the boat, he'd been restless, not knowing what to do with himself.

He'd barely slept a wink, staring at the ceiling, ruminating on the evening, going over and over it in his mind, trying to recall how their kiss had started, exactly how long it had lasted. It wasn't a fleeting peck, that was for sure. They'd been at it for a couple of minutes.

Clayton glanced at his watch.

He was counting down the hours until he saw Neil again. Still two and a quarter hours to go until they'd be riding Serendipity together.

He hoped Neil would be up for joining him tomorrow. If the last few days had taught him anything, it was to put himself out there a bit. You got so much more out of life when you let people in.

Blessedly, there was time for a nap.

As Clayton got under the covers, he was careful not to disturb the neatly ironed clothes he'd laid out on one side of the bed. Navy Cuban-collar shirt, zip-up jacket, grey cords.

He reached for his phone charging on the bedstand and set the alarm. Forty minutes would do him. He'd wake up feeling like a different person. He knew he would.

He allowed his head to slump into what was surely the world's plumpest duck-down cushion and, within seconds, was dead to the world.

When Clayton eventually stirred, it wasn't because of the alarm function on his phone – which it turned out he'd set to a.m. rather than p.m. – but the knock on the door from the housekeeper entering his room to carry out the evening turn-down.

Clayton went into panic mode.

He scrambled to his feet, telling the lady not to worry, that he didn't need his bed turned down, thanks very much. Before he'd even seen what the time was, he knew something deeply regrettable had happened.

He'd slept for four and a half hours. And to make matters worse, he didn't have Neil's number to let him know he was running late.

Twenty minutes later, Clayton reached the familiar stretch of canal in Little Venice, exactly where he should have been three hours earlier, breathless and in a complete flap. A fizz of excitement came over him as he raced down the cobbled slope next to the bridge.

This feeling was only fleeting, though, because the second he clocked the empty expanse of murky water ahead of him there was a dropping in his heart.

Between M'Darlin and Happy Daze was a forty-two-foot gap where Neil's boat had always been moored. Neil must have thought he'd been stood up.

Serendipity had gone.

★

The following morning, with the tickets paid for and no way of contacting Neil, Clayton was left with no choice but to venture to Amsterdam alone.

He packed up his things and went to check out of the hotel, not before lifting a postcard from the reception desk.

Dear Neil, he dashed off. *Sorry about last night. I can explain. I did something stupid, that's all. Where did you end up heading? I'm going back home soon, just paying a visit somewhere first, though. Hope we can hang out again another time?? Apologies again. Take care. Clayton x*

He regretted the double question mark, but he wasn't going to cross it out now. Instead, he added a second kiss, then a third for good measure, before writing his phone number in large digits at the bottom of the card.

The receptionist in front of him was obviously watching him write every word, but he didn't care.

He addressed the postcard to Nancy Stone – the only way he could think of reaching Neil, a man of no fixed address – and with *31 Cheviot Street* still imprinted on his brain like the wax seal on Pippa's letters.

'I can post that for you, if you like,' the receptionist offered.

'Are you sure?'

'Of course, Mr Stumper,' she replied with a kindly smile. 'It seems rather important.'

He felt his cheeks colour. 'Thank you. It is actually.'

Clayton took a cab to St Pancras International Station. Whenever they passed any stretch of water, he couldn't help but shoot a look out of the window, wondering where Neil had gone.

It wasn't as if he hadn't tried to find him. He'd spent an hour looking for Serendipity but kept losing his bearings, kept stumbling into shady characters on the towpath who appeared like ghosts out of thin air, just like the chaps who'd robbed him a few days ago had. In the end, he'd panicked and, feeling more alone than at any other point in his life, ran back to the safety of the hotel where, in a moment of sheer fate – or even serendipity – he received a call from Cilla Millington.

She hoped he didn't mind but she hadn't spoken to anyone in

a few days and wondered if they could have a quick chat before she headed off to bed? She was so pleased he'd added his number to her birthday card. She hadn't known who else to ring.

Clayton had sunk to the floor of his hotel room, swallowing tears. Of course, she hadn't realised that he needed the conversation as much as she did.

Five hours after departing London, Clayton stepped out of the Centraal Station into the bright afternoon sun of Amsterdam, feeling oddly buoyant.

On the train, he'd been reflecting on the quest, how it was meant to reveal his past, but so far it had taught him about nothing but his future.

From Cilla he'd been reminded of the power of human connection and how sometimes, a single conversation with a stranger could change everything. From Nancy he'd realised that friendship, while a critical part of anyone's existence, sometimes wasn't enough on its own to sustain a person, and that it was OK to chase something else, to look for something more. Neil had given him hope that one day this might happen for him, while his exchange with Jonty had given him nothing but a headache – though his relationship with Edwin had inspired him to follow his heart and, ultimately, make a move on *Serendipity*.

If seven across was something Pippa wanted him to experience outside of the Fellowship, then in their own way, they'd all contributed to this clue.

Love.

Friendship, community and romance – in the last few days, Clayton had witnessed it all.

On the Herengracht, he held up the image of the unfinished jigsaw on his phone to a series of vaguely similar views on the other side.

He'd decided to commence his search here, in the south-east of the capital where, according to the guidebook he'd picked up at the station, some of the richest merchants and most influential regents and mayors of the city had lived.

There was something undeniably charming about the quaint lanes and the rows of skinny canal houses, which all looked like something out of a Golden Age painting. He could see the appeal of the place.

The trouble was, no sooner had he perused one quaint street than he found himself walking another. The houses – all wonky and gabled – looked identical, the endless canals, all similarly brown and lacking in any defining features.

As the heavens opened, and with nothing over his thin jumper other than his waterproof cagoule, Clayton realised he'd brought entirely the wrong coat. Amsterdam was unseasonably cold and whenever he was near the water, it was bloody freezing.

He wondered about popping into a café until the weather cleared, but decided to press on, lifting his hood, keeping one eye on his phone and the other desperately scouring the buildings in front of him.

Heading towards the Keizersgracht, leaving the Herengracht behind, Clayton realised what an enormous task he'd set himself.

Another endless expanse of water stretched ahead with countless properties on either side. He was determined not to be overwhelmed and as he pulled up at a bridge a few hundred metres along the canal, his spirits instantly lifted.

There – a few hundred feet ahead of him – was an imposing house with a pink exterior that bore more than a vague resemblance to the one in the jigsaw. In fact it was the perfect shade.

Clayton felt a rush of something shoot straight to his head.

He crossed the bridge without looking, narrowly avoiding a cyclist who sounded his bell and shouted something he could only assume was an expletive.

Approaching the steps to the building moments later, Clayton glanced up at the place and could feel his pulse throbbing in his ears.

He found himself stalling, his feet suddenly heavy against the tarmac, as if not wanting to be dragged any further. There was something about the potential of what might lie ahead, the enormity of it all, that was suddenly overwhelming.

He took a few considered breaths, allowing his pulse to settle, before ascending the stairs.

With his face inches from the door, he rapped his knuckles gently against it before he could change his mind.

A few seconds passed and the door gingerly opened, and a gnarled lady of advanced years glowered at him.

'*Zich Voortmaken!*' she bellowed from the front step.

She had a wild look in her eyes and a wooden broomstick in her hand, which she angled at Clayton as if they were in a jousting match.

'Get away, young man! Private property!'

Clayton lifted his hand in apology and darted clumsily back down the steps, finally pulling into a dingy, dead-end alley at the side of the house.

He pressed his back to the cold brick and took a few steadying breaths.

This was all a mistake, he realised. In fact, it wasn't just a mistake but an embarrassment, travelling out here on his own, in search of a house he thought might be intrinsically linked to his past, simply because a missing piece in a jigsaw, gifted to him by a man with dementia, had told him so. On closer inspection the house wasn't anything like the one in the jigsaw. It might have been the same colour, but this one had six windows, not eight like the one he was searching for.

He would find a basic hotel to stay the night and send a quick text to Earl to let everyone know he'd failed in his mission, that he was putting this whole debacle behind him. Whatever Pippa was trying to steer him towards, whatever the point of this quest had been, he would have to put to the back of his mind.

Clayton tugged at the hem of his jacket and stepped out of the alley, realising that was never going to happen.

He blinked into the harsh late-afternoon light and moved in the general direction of the train station, losing his footing on a kerb and finding himself up to his ankles in a puddle.

A tram was approaching and he pulled into the shelter, shaking his leg dry. At least he wouldn't have to walk back. His brogues, now squelching with every step, were also starting to rub at the heel, and he could feel a blister forming.

Beside him, a young mother was hunkered over a pushchair, pulling silly faces and mouthing a foreign nursery rhyme at the baby inside. The sight was such an everyday one, and yet Clayton couldn't help but avert his eyes. It was as if the universe were taunting him.

As the tram hissed to a stop, he reached into his travel purse for his all-day ticket.

Most of the seats were taken but Clayton found a spot in the middle of the carriage, opposite the conductor, who was positioned behind a futuristic information desk – just like Spock on the Starship Enterprise. He even had the fringe.

Clayton realised the man was looking at him. He had his head tipped quizzically to one side and was smiling as if they knew each other.

He returned the grin, out of politeness more than anything, then continued idly watching the city sliding past him.

There were people on bicycles everywhere, weaving in and out of the traffic as freely as if they were strolling through a park.

It didn't take long to feel the conductor's eyes on him again.

'*Ben je verdwaald?*' the man called out.

Clayton glanced over his shoulder, wondering if the man was talking to someone else.

'You've been going round in circles, haven't you?' the man added, realising he was English. 'Are you lost?'

'No, no, I'm good. Just getting my bearings, that's all.'

'But I've seen you pacing along the Herengracht at least six times now.'

Clayton felt his cheeks flush at the idea of being watched all afternoon. 'I'm not too familiar with the city, that's all. And I've a dreadful sense of direction. Couldn't find my way out of a paper bag.' He spat out a laugh and turned back towards the window, wishing the man would leave him alone, or at least mind his own business.

'Are you sure?' the inspector asked. 'I've been doing this job for almost ten years now. I know the city like the back of my hand.'

Clayton paused as he took in the man, caught off guard by his directness.

A few seconds later, he reached into his pocket and retrieved his mobile, swiping the screen until he located the photograph of the jigsaw assembled on Neil's dinette table. He pinched in on the gaping hole in the middle of the image, pushed himself out of his seat and moved towards the man.

'Does this scene look familiar?' he asked, handing the device over. 'That great big house right in the middle. The pink one. That's what I'm looking for.'

The chap examined the picture, angling the phone this way and that with his brows furrowed. 'Hmm.' He tugged on his earlobe. 'Is that the Wittineburg?'

Clayton shrugged. 'I haven't the foggiest; it's just somewhere I'm keen to track down. What's the Wittineburg anyway?'

The man patted the inside of his jacket for a pen.

'No, no, it's not. I tell you where that is. That's the old Salmon House. I'm almost certain. I can tell from the way the trees are bending. What do they call that place now?'

He drummed his fingers on the desk, then struck his hand down.

Clayton watched him scribble something on the back of a ticket stub before handing it over.

Het Kunsthuis
Oostenburgergracht 73

'Get off at the next stop, and jump on the C12, heading east,' he explained. 'You're looking for Kadijken Station. Then Oostenburgergracht is two streets on your right. There's a flea market on the corner. You can't miss it.'

Clayton took the slip of paper. 'Thank you,' he said, touched by the gentleman's kindness. 'And what does it mean?' he asked, running his finger along the address. 'The name, I mean.'

'Het Kunsthuis? It means the Art House. It's a boutique hotel – quite nice inside but I don't think it gets great reviews. Apparently, the woman that runs it is a bit . . . as we like to say . . . *hoofd in de wolken*.'

Clayton looked at the man confused.

'She has her head in the clouds . . .'

Clayton passed by the crowded stalls at Waterlooplein Market without stopping. He had been mouthing the name of the canal the Pink House supposedly overlooked – *Oostenburgergracht* – as he went, hoping it was as charming as the word suggested.

He crossed a steep cobblestone bridge where a lady was selling tulips by the dozen in a rainbow of colours, and another a little further up that was adorned with glistening steel padlocks catching on the sun setting behind. Love Locks, they were called. He'd read an article about them once in the *Telegraph*. They were all emblazoned with lovers' initials, declarations of undying affection and, on one that he examined as he passed, a note from a couple on an anniversary trip: *Ann & Andy – 40 Years Together. I hope we get another 40!* Clayton paused to consider the Dutch barges parked along the canal. The names were mostly indecipherable, but the colours were pleasing to take in, and similar to the ones on the Grand Union. He was instantly reminded of the gentle rise and fall of Serendipity. Of Neil. He tried to think of something else.

Further along, as he made his way towards the street that he had spent all day looking for, he began to stall.

Once again, it was as if his legs were trudging through mud, trying to slow him or to stop him from progressing any further.

To be out here, all on his own, on the cusp of discovering something so fundamental to his existence on this earth or, in fact, finding nothing at all. A dead end. He wasn't sure what would be worse.

The street the Art House belonged on was wide and long with elm trees, tall and primeval, lining both sides. Clayton weaved in and out of them as he made his way along, passing a coffee shop called High-Drated, which sold *The best coffee in Amsterdam* and *Very Special Brownies*.

It was only when he turned his attention to the houses opposite the café that he finally caught it: the flash of shell pink he'd been looking for.

THE ART HOUSE, BOUTIQUE HOTEL

5-STAR LUXURY, WORLD-CLASS CONTEMPORARY ART EXHIBITED.

PAINTING WORKSHOPS AND COURSES.

The black-carpeted steps leading up to the hotel were immaculate, the gold banisters polished to a sheen.

Clayton allowed his eyes to close for a second, for the breath he was holding to come out, before he tramped up the steps and peeled open the heavy door.

A bell signalled his entrance but inside there was no one to greet him. After a few seconds came a shrill woman's voice.

'Mind yourself!'

Clayton froze on the spot. He looked around the lobby but there was no one.

'I've just polished the floors!'

He took slow strides into the lobby, realising that the floor hadn't just been polished but waxed to such a shine, it was practically an ice rink. He skated across the floor in his leather-soled shoes.

'Hello?' he called out. His voice bounced off the walls. 'I wondered if I might be able to speak to the manager?'

To his left was a glass cabinet with branded hotel merchandise for sale: 'Art House' sketchbooks, tins of 'Art House' liquorice sweets, 'Art House' watercolour paint sets, pencils and brushes, and behind those, to Clayton's disbelief, a familiar-looking jigsaw box, this time with the completed image on the front and its name. *The Art House Hotel.*

Eventually a lady popped up in front of him, as quick as a jack-in-a-box. 'What is it that you're after? A room?'

She had unnaturally dark, cropped hair, an intense, unblinking stare, and a frighteningly pale complexion.

'Umm . . .'

'One night? Two? And is it a single, a double, a suite?'

'I . . . actually . . . umm . . .' He couldn't get his words out. He didn't know what he was looking for, not really.

'Card or cash? How will you pay?'

He fumbled for his debit card in his wallet. 'One single room, one night,' he heard himself say. 'I'll pay by card.'

'Name?'

'Stumper,' he answered. 'Clayton Stumper.'

The woman's face changed in an instant and suddenly they were both looking at each other and neither of them were saying a word, but they didn't have to because Clayton knew, somehow, exactly who this woman was.

Before he could do anything, she dropped a key on the desk, then brandished an envelope from the counter, sliding it towards him, before turning and dashing away, fast as lightning.

Clayton felt as if all the air had been punched out of his lungs.

So the woman had been expecting him? The letter had been prepared in advance, ready for his arrival.

He staggered towards the mahogany check-in desk and reached for the envelope. Like all the others he'd received over the past few weeks, it had his name on the front, though it had clearly not been dispatched by Pippa. He could tell by the handwriting. And the type of envelope. This time, she hadn't written whatever was inside. He was as certain of that fact as he was about the significance of the lady who'd just checked him into the hotel.

She was his mother. He was her son.

Chapter Fifty

THE FELLOWSHIP OF PUZZLEMAKERS
THURSDAY, 18TH APRIL, 1991

It was a little over a week since the fayre. Though things were beginning to settle down at Creighton and their finances finally stabilising – thanks to record sales at the event, a wave of new contracts, plus Geoff's shrewd accounting – Pippa had spent the past thirty minutes of her morning in a fit of despair, dashing from room to room, getting increasingly distressed.

It had come to her attention that Angel, hot on the heels of Nancy, had packed up and gone in the night.

Outside, she tore across the lawn towards the jigsaw studio, to the only other person who she knew was awake at this hour. It was barely seven in the morning.

'Angel's quit,' she shouted at her deputy.

The man turned at the top of the stairs, pointing a water pistol at her. He'd been firing at the pigeons on the roof again.

'What do you mean?'

'She has vacated the premises, Hector! Abandoned us! Deserted! Another one disappeared without so much as a goodbye.'

For Pippa, hearing the words for the first time hang in the morning air, made her blood boil and the back of her throat clam up. She wasn't sure if she was about to fly off the handle or burst into tears.

'Right,' Hector said, scratching the side of his head. 'I see. That's something, isn't it.'

Pippa couldn't believe her ears.

She had just informed her deputy that the woman who had been at Creighton longer than they had, the woman who'd driven them around the bend for years, had departed from Creighton, and yet his response was so . . . subdued. As if she'd just told him they'd run out of milk.

'Are you not going to come and help me sort this mess out? Do you not care?'

'Of course, I bloody care!' he finally snapped. 'Jesus Christ, Pippa. I care!'

She froze on the spot.

He hurled the water pistol to the ground, where it smashed at her feet, then disappeared inside his studio, slamming the door shut behind him with such force that the whole structure quivered in front of her.

Pippa's mouth opened in disbelief.

In all the years they'd known each other, she'd never once witnessed the man raise his voice.

She paused for a moment, trying to decide how to respond and then, before she knew it, started ascending the steps, one at a time, until her hand was gripping the door and she was letting herself inside.

Pippa was immediately thunderstruck at the scene in front of her.

Hector was sitting hunched on a stall, his head in his hands, and it was clear from his pose, from the way his shoulders were slumped and starting to shake in front of her, that he was crying.

Pippa felt her hand press to her chest, as if it had just been punctured.

It wasn't just the sight of Hector so visibly distraught that was making her insides ache. It was the painting he was sitting in front of, which wasn't one of his usual jigsaw pictures at all, but a portrait.

A portrait of a little boy.

She averted her gaze, feeling that she was intruding in Hector's space.

Eventually, she made a few cautious steps towards him and, sensing the man was on a knife edge, lowered her voice to barely a whisper. 'Did you know, Hect?' The floorboards creaked beneath her silk slippers as she got closer. 'Did you know she was leaving?'

Without glancing up, he lifted his hand, pleading for her to stop.

She got down to his eye line and finally he looked at her.

'Where has this painting come from, Hector?'

'Angel painted it.'

Pippa took a deep breath, trying to keep her voice entirely level. 'I see.'

'She's got a gift, Pippa. A rare gift and I've encouraged her to pursue it. That's why she's left.'

For a moment, a heavy silence infused the paint-fume-filled air and the two of them just stared at each other.

'Will she come back for her things?' she heard herself ask.

Hector shook his head. 'She has everything she needs apparently. She wants to start over.'

'But—'

'She took a hatbox,' he explained. 'She doesn't own a suitcase.'

'A hatbox?' Pippa echoed.

'The one you gave me the other day. Nancy's one. With the blanket in it? That's all she wanted, with a few essentials.'

'Where has she gone?'

'Travelling,' he replied. 'She's never been out of the country, Philippa. How could I stop her? She's thirty-four years old and she's never left the country. She wants to see Europe. To go to art school. To see if she can make it as an artist.'

Pippa, while comforted at the idea of Angel pursuing a new vocation, felt her body go cold at the thought of their housekeeper alone in the world.

Wherever she ended up, she hoped she would find happiness, that one day she might consider returning, even for a flying visit.

She turned to the portrait of the child staring back at her, wondering with growing concern, and increasing certainty, whether the boy belonged to Hector, whether this was the tragedy that had been lurking in his past all along.

Chapter Fifty-One

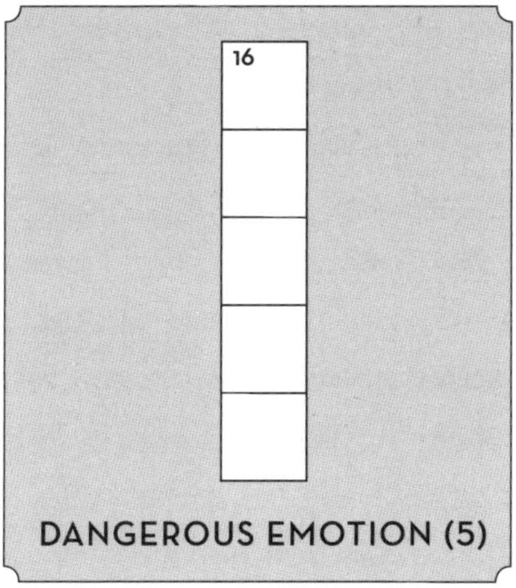

Clayton had located his room on the first floor of the Art House and was perched on the end of his bed, pushing down on his knees to stop them from shaking. He pulled out a letter from the envelope.

> *Dear Clayton,*
> *Hector here. I expect you've had enough of questions. Now you want answers, and I will endeavour to provide some for you. You deserve them, of course you do.*

He paused, a tightness building in his throat. Hector Haywood?

> *It begins with the child in the photograph enclosed. His name was Lucas. He was my son. He was a quiet, sensitive boy who was supremely kind-hearted, much like yourself. He had an excellent ear for music and loved his piano lessons. I lost him in a road accident when he was six years old, along with my beloved wife, Elizabeth.*

The pain I experienced during that time, Clayton, was not something I believed I'd survive. I spiralled, ended up living out of my van, for a period. That was when the puzzle club came into my life. When the Fellowship saved me. When I found a new family.

I promised myself I would never love again the way I loved my wife and son. And I must admit, I never did. Not quite the same anyway. But I experienced something like it when I acquired an assistant in the studio. She was our housekeeper really, but she showed a keen interest in the arts and before long was turning out impressive pieces herself, nothing like my own. We developed a certain kinship, which developed into something else entirely.

I'm sure you must feel hurt, Clayton. Betrayed, angry even. I hope that one day you might see it in your huge heart to forgive me.

When you are ready, just dial O for Reception downstairs.

With great admiration and love,

Hector Haywood.

There was a faint knock at Clayton's hotel-room door thirty minutes later.

It had taken all that time for him to pluck up the courage and dial 0 on the phone next to his bed, to catch his breath and feel his legs again.

He peeled open the door to the strange receptionist who had greeted him downstairs, *his birth mother*, and felt an overwhelming flood of emotions as the pair locked eyes once again.

'Come this way,' she murmured.

Clayton nodded and followed the lady along the corridors, feeling as he did like he was floating, not quite dreaming but not far off. He tried to contain the heat he could feel building inside him, the unusual sensation of fire pulsing through his veins with such velocity, he wasn't sure what he might do with it.

Anger.

Of course, he should have guessed that this trail would end in heartbreak. The stakes were too high to bypass that.

The lady led him to a wrought-iron spiral staircase at the centre of the hotel that showed no sign of ending, and then her large, sandalled feet clanged against the metal steps. Up and up they went, as if climbing to the moon.

They passed a sign which read: *Sky Parlour – This Way* ↑ / *Hemel Salon – Hierheen* ↑ and perhaps he was still in shock, but Clayton felt a strange sense of calm come over him as he made his ascent.

No more games. All he had to do was ask the questions. It was time for answers.

Over the years, he had heard countless tales about Creighton Hall's former housekeeper. *Angel Webster.* Although this woman sounded eccentric, even by the Fellowship's standards, people always spoke of her with quiet admiration. It sounded as if, in her own unique way, she had kept the whole place together. Just like he did. She looked after them all, without fuss or fanfare.

Residents often touched on her matronly manner, her formidable work ethic, her spiritualism, and her unique ability to turn a simple task into a much less straightforward one. That seemed to be the joke: Angel being a nightmare. Fixing a leaking radiator would turn into a full-scale plumbing disaster, polishing the china was bound to result in some accidental breakages, and once, when climbing onto the roof to do a spot of tiling, she'd famously taken a fall before she'd even reached the top rung of the ladder. She'd dislocated her knee and torn a ligament in her ankle. They'd been without clean sheets for weeks.

'We have a life class starting soon,' Angel explained as they reached the top. 'But one of these rooms should be free.'

The Sky Parlour was, in fact, several interconnecting art studios in the attic of the hotel, divided by a series of blue velvet curtains.

Angel whipped back one curtain and they were greeted by the bare buttocks of a man, bending down to smother oil over his spectacularly ripped and endowed body.

'Excuse us, Klaas.'

Angel turned puce and dashed away, leaving Clayton to steal one last glimpse over his shoulder.

Now, they were in a bright, paint-splattered room with exposed floorboards and several art easels positioned in a semi-circle. On the back wall, a collection of striking portraits were hanging slightly squiffy on the wall. There must have been a dozen or more, all in elaborate gilt frames, just like the one Hector's son had been presented in.

As Clayton stepped forward to examine the pictures, he noticed several had been signed with that familiar name: Bert E. Wangles. This mysterious name wasn't the lady's pseudonym but an anagram of her name. Bert E. Wangles was Angel Webster.

'Why did you use a pseudonym?'

'That was when I was starting out,' she explained, coming to stand beside him. 'Pretending to be a man in the fine-art world. It opened all sorts of doors. Bert E. Wangles – I thought that was quite good, no?'

Clayton couldn't help but smile. He was fairly sure Pippa had done something similar when she'd started compiling crosswords – at least she'd gone by a name that everyone assumed belonged to a man.

'I tried googling the name,' he said. 'But couldn't find anything.'

Angel gave a satisfied grin. 'I paid someone to have it wiped. I go by my own name now.' She gestured to the collection to her right, which Clayton guessed contained her more recent pieces, all signed *Angel Webster*.

Angel ushered him over to a table in the middle of the room. 'Take a seat.'

Clayton pulled out a chair that wasn't directly opposite the woman.

'I bet you have plenty to ask me.'

He grimaced.

Above them an enormous skylight roof was making him squint. There were vapour trails of two aeroplanes streaking across the sparkling blue sky like the lanes of a swimming pool.

'Did you ever plan to keep me? Were you ever tempted . . .'

'No,' she said firmly. 'No, I knew exactly where I should take you. I never had a single doubt where you belonged.'

The directness of her reply, the speed at which she answered, took Clayton aback.

'Why couldn't you keep me?'

This time, Angel pressed her back to the chair, let out a faint breath.

'Because I knew there was somewhere better for you.'

Clayton couldn't help but shake his head.

'It sounds trite, doesn't it, but it's true. I knew they'd be able to love you far more than I was ever capable of loving.'

'We're *all* capable of love,' he said. 'All of us.'

'Yes, but . . .' She was looking at him differently, her head inclined to one side. 'In different ways, I think.'

Six ways, Clayton thought. According to the Greeks, anyway.

'That maternal, parental feeling . . .'

'*Storge*,' he heard himself say.

'Sorry?'

'That's what that type of love is called. I found out the other day. The Greeks called it *Storge*.'

'Right . . . well, that's not something I've ever experienced. Or desired, even. And besides, I was about to begin a new life in Europe. I had found my gift, something I was actually very good at, and I knew the universe was calling for me to apply myself, to use my talent to forge a new life . . .'

Angel was suddenly learning forward, her face now just inches from Clayton's, completely fixed. 'Don't move.'

'What is it?' he asked.

'This *light*.'

She clicked her fingers airily at the light filtering through the window above. Clayton went to look up, but Angel lunged at him, her fingers gripping the sides of his head, twisting it back to where it was.

'I'm going to take your photograph, OK?' she said, more as a statement than a question. 'And one day I'm going to paint you.'

Before Clayton could gather himself, the lady lifted an old-fashioned film camera from the pocket of her smock dress and was pointing it at him, her legs sprawled out like a rugby player about to enter a scrum.

'Stay *exactly* where you are.'

Clayton froze on the spot. He gathered his cagoule together without looking down. 'Does my hair look all right?'

Angel pulled a pained expression from behind the camera, then stepped forward and licked the palm of her hand, slapping it with some force on the top of his head, flattening his quiff.

'That's better.'

After taking a single photograph and stashing her camera away, Angel slumped back into her seat opposite.

'Are you into astrology, Clayton?'

He shook his head.

'Then you're missing out.'

'I am?'

'The stars are there for us all. And the day I left the Fellowship, the universe was telling me what I should do . . .'

Up close, he realised they had the exact same bump on the bridge of their nose.

'. . . It was a few weeks later that I realised I was carrying a child.'

'*Me,* you mean.'

Clayton couldn't help but correct the woman. 'Do you ever read my stars?' he asked. 'Ever wonder what I'm up to?'

'Sometimes,' Angel answered, and then, leaning forward and looking at him with a strange intensity, she continued. 'Right now, Clayton, I know that Mars is moving into Capricorn in your ninth house, so you're finding answers and taking charge through discovery and adventure.'

Clayton sat a bit straighter.

'Am I wrong?'

He shrugged, feeling weirdly exposed.

'And over the next few days, with the new moon in Cancer, you're going to have a personal and spiritual breakthrough of some kind – a rethinking of who you are.'

Clayton's insides lurched.

'Plus, romance is on the cards. It looks like you'll be given a second chance by someone. Are you seeing anyone at the moment?'

He shook his head, gripping his stomach which was suddenly doing somersaults.

'Well, *that's* soon going to change,' she added. 'If you want it to, of course.'

Clayton adjusted himself in the chair, not knowing how to feel.

'More than enough time yet, young man. To get whatever it is you want out of life. To find yourself.'

Clayton nodded.

That was exactly the notion that united everyone on this strange quest, he realised.

Nancy found herself in the devotion she had for her husband, and cabbing. Jonty found it in Edwin, while Hector found it in the Fellowship – a place that had saved him, given him purpose again. And then there was Pippa. She had found it in the family she'd created all those years ago in that room above the pub and the son she had gone on to raise. She had found it in him.

'Hector's on his way . . .' Angel announced, pushing herself out of a chair. 'He wants to talk to you. To explain himself. Up to you of course.'

Chapter Fifty-Two

GNAWING PAIN OF CONSCIENCE (7)

The morning after, at the bandstand in Amsterdam's Vondelpark, Clayton found himself shaking hands with Hector Haywood, a man who suddenly seemed incapable of looking him in the eye.

'Hi, Clayton.'

'Hello, do you want to . . .' He nudged his head towards the expanse of green behind them, hoping they could walk.

'Yes,' Hector answered quickly. 'Yes, that sounds like a good idea.'

Clayton smiled at the ground. It was odd – as if they were meeting for the first time.

Wandering through the manicured lawns, passing dog walkers and pram pushers, skaters and cyclists, he wondered if people might know from looking. Two men walking in step together. Fifty plus years between them. Both in waterproof cagoules. Father and son.

'Have you not got a warmer coat?'

'No,' Hector replied, digging his hands into his pockets. 'I didn't think it would be this cold, to be honest.'

'Me neither,' Clayton said. 'We can go inside if you like. I think there's a café just over—'

Hector shook his head. 'I think it's good for us to walk, don't you? Walk and . . . talk.'

Clayton nodded.

They continued walking but neither seemed ready to talk. Instead, the silence stretched endlessly between them and Clayton didn't worry about filling it.

He allowed his mind to drift, to wonder where Neil had ended up on Serendipity and whether Nancy had passed on his postcard. Whether they might get the chance to see each other again, as Angel had predicted so definitively yesterday.

Hector folded his arms behind his back and sucked in a breath of air.

'How are you feeling?' he asked. 'If that's not too vague a question.'

Clayton shrugged. 'I'm not sure yet,' he lied. 'Still . . . processing, you know?'

The truth was he felt everything and didn't know what to feel first.

He was angry to have been kept in the dark for so long and embarrassed to have been fooled; he was happy he would never again have to wonder, yet sad for all the wasted time. And he was proud. Proud he'd got to the bottom of it all, with a little help from some new friends.

'I guess, my first question is . . . *why*.'

The words caught in his throat and he was worried he might cry. Clayton bit the inside of his lip. '*Why* couldn't you tell me, Hector? *Why* has it taken so long?'

The jigsaw artist took a deep breath and suddenly his eyes closed, as if he were in **pain**.

15			

FRENCH BREAD (4)

'There is no easy answer . . . but the truth is, the day you arrived, you were as much a shock to me as you were to everyone else.'

Clayton turned to look at him, wondering how that could be.

'So you didn't know Angel was expecting? You had no idea until . . . I arrived?'

Hector shook his head. 'And even then I tried to convince myself I couldn't have fathered you. That you must belong to someone else. But before long it became obvious. To me at least.'

'How?'

'You looked just like him,' Hector answered, his voice cracking with the emotion. 'You looked just like Lucas . . . when he was young.'

They continued walking for a while in silence and Clayton's fingers curled around the skeleton key in his pocket, comforted by its solidness in his hand.

'Why didn't you confess to being my father?' he eventually asked. 'In all the years we've lived under the same roof . . .'

'They loved you from the moment you arrived,' Hector replied. 'It would have changed things if I'd have claimed you as my own.'

Clayton knew immediately who he was speaking of.

If the Fellowship were his extended family, it was always Pip and Earl who were his parents. They would forever remain that too, despite what he was beginning to uncover.

'I know what it's like,' Hector said, 'to love a child the way they loved you. I couldn't risk spoiling it for them. Never in a million years.'

Clayton swallowed hard as he led the way across a narrow bridge, leading to a bandstand in the centre of a pond, surrounded by tulips.

'And so,' Hector continued, walking by his side, 'the two of us made a pact. Pippa would raise you as her own, and we would keep the secret between ourselves. Then, when the time was right, I would give you all the answers. But I insisted it would never impact on your relationship . . .'

'So you decided to wait . . .' Clayton said.

They both sat down on a bench in the middle of the pavilion and Hector nodded. 'Until whichever one of us died first. And as soon as Pippa started to go downhill we started setting the trail. She wrote the letters. I sorted everything else. We thought you deserved your own adventure.'

If a *gnawing* pain *of conscience* was something Pippa wanted him to experience, or at least reflect on, then he was doing that right now.

Remorse.

Here was a man he had known his entire life and yet had never really known at all. If Hector's biggest mistake had been fathering him out of wedlock, and not admitting to it until now, then surely his sentence was worse than the crime. Out of loyalty to Pippa, and to the Fellowship – a place he had always felt indebted to – he'd stuck around while Clayton grew up in front of his eyes, looking just like the son he had lost.

That was why there had always been an air of tension between the two of them. Every time Hector looked at him, he'd been reminded of Lucas. The thought of it made his insides churn.

'I'm so sorry to hear about . . . the accident,' he said. 'I can't even imagine.'

'Thank you.'

At this, they both looked into each other's eyes and Clayton couldn't help but register that familiar stony gaze looking back at him, something he'd always thought was antipathy, but now realised was something else entirely. The light had gone from Hector's eyes. He was still grieving.

They agreed to meet for a coffee in the morning, before catching the train back home together.

As they made their goodbyes and headed back over the bridge, Clayton felt a strange lightness come over him. It was beginning to rain, but he didn't mind; it was only drizzle, and it would soon clear. His phone vibrated in his pocket and before he had even reached for it, he had a feeling who it might be.

> Hey Clayton. It's Neil. Thanks for sending your number. I wondered where you'd got to. Xx

Chapter Fifty-Three

THE FELLOWSHIP OF PUZZLEMAKERS
12 WEEKS AFTER THE FAYRE

Pippa absent-mindedly swirled the sugar into her tea that midsummer morning, feeling lost. The day had dawned crisp and clear, but her head was all fog, like she was looking through frosted glass.

Ever since she'd spoken to Hector, she'd been consumed by the conversation, haunted by the secret heartbreak in his past, and riddled with concern for Angel, wherever in Europe she had ended up. They still hadn't heard a peep from her.

She had learned during that revelatory chat in the jigsaw studio that Hector's trauma had all stemmed from a devastating episode in his life eighteen months before they'd first met at the pub. This was the catalyst for his life spiralling, for him living out of his van.

'What happened?'

'Car accident . . .' he said, in a low, furtive voice. 'The three of us were on holiday in Devon. We were driving back from dinner. Elizabeth and I had just decided to try for a second . . . a second child, you know?'

Pippa's heart plummeted.

'And I can't remember feeling as happy as I did then, Philippa, to be honest. I really can't. I was drumming my hands against the wheel, feeling so . . . blessed.'

Pippa shook her head in disbelief. It was the stuff of nightmares.

'Minutes later and we were all lying in a ditch. Literally minutes. A chap in a Mercedes was to blame. Four times over the limit he was. They didn't suffer, Philippa. It was instant. On impact, you know?'

She closed her eyes for a second, stunned.

'And what about you?' she asked. 'Were you not injured?'

'Unscathed,' he answered, with a touch of rage. 'Only a few scratches on me. Doctors said it was a miracle.' He spat out a laugh. 'That's why I don't drink, by the way. I've never touched a drop since. Out of respect for them.'

Suddenly Pippa remembered where she was and proceeded with her morning tea.

'That milk's on the turn,' she muttered to herself, sniffing the inside of the glass bottle. She poured a dash into her cup, dropping in an extra sugar cube to compensate. 'Won't kill me, will it?'

In between her quiet murmurings, Pippa hummed the theme tune to *The Archers*. She peeled open the fridge and returned the sour milk and butter dish.

She was just about to top up the urn when Hector appeared behind her. He was in his usual painting shirt and dungarees, about to head out to the studio.

'I've been thinking,' he said, placing his cup under the spout. 'If it's all right with you. Everything I told you about . . . Lucas and Elizabeth . . . and Angel . . . will you keep it between us? Can it be our secret?'

Pippa pressed her hand to her heart. 'Of course, Hector.'

She'd hoped it went without saying. Not everything in a commune needed sharing, after all.

Hector slurped his tea and they both turned to look out the window.

'Don't mind me!' came a voice from behind.

Earl hobbled into the room holding the small of his back, blowing his cheeks as if he'd just completed a marathon.

He'd just returned from Mawdley Castle, a National Trust site in Shropshire. He'd spent the past week up there overseeing not just one hedgerow maze, but four of them, dotted across the formal grounds to form a family treasure trail. After a week of heavy labour he'd put his back out, and took every opportunity to make it known how much pain he was in.

'I'm heading out to the studio,' Hector announced, clearly in no mood to listen to him.

'It's actually worse today,' Earl remarked. 'It's kind of a sharp, shooting pain all the way down to my leg. I'll try a hot bath later on.'

Pippa murmured something vaguely supportive under her breath and watched through the window as Hector traipsed across the lawn towards his studio.

It was frosty out but the most perfectly bright day, like someone had turned the colour up on the television set. A piercing blue sky made everything appear sharper, more vibrant.

Earl poured himself a tea and blew on the cup. 'There's something at the door by the way.'

'What is it?'

He shrugged. 'A big box of some kind. I couldn't bend down to pick it up. Because of my back. Are you expecting something?'

'No,' she replied, wondering what it could be. They didn't usually get deliveries on a Saturday. 'I suspect it'll just be more canvases for Hector, or it might be toner for the printers or . . .'

She stopped trying to guess, she was boring herself.

Before Pippa could think of what to say next, Earl had reached out and folded his hand around the sleeve of her cardigan. 'You're miles away. Is everything all right?'

Ever since their kiss in the maze, the pair had been spending more time together, and Earl had become that little bit more tactile with her, especially when they were alone.

She nodded, forced a smile. 'Oh, yes, I'm all good, just not sleeping very well at the moment, that's all. I've been to the doctor's, got myself some tablets. Should be right as rain in a few days.'

Earl gave a concerned look but didn't say anything.

'Shhh. Can you hear that?' Pippa asked, a moment later.

Earl froze, angled his ear at where her finger was pointing. 'No, I don't think so. What is it?'

'Listen,' she hissed. 'It's like an alarm going off. A piercing sound? It's been driving me mad all morning.'

'I can't hear a thing, Pip. You've got better hearing than me whatever it is.'

'It comes and goes,' she replied, waving her hand airily above her.

'Are you sure it's not tinnitus?'

'Stop it.'

Earl gathered up their plates and went to the sink while Pippa headed towards the door, ready to crack on with the day.

'Don't forget the delivery,' he shouted.

'What?'

'The box at the door?' he reminded her.

Pippa let out a sigh. 'Leave it to me. I'll grab it now.'

Five minutes later and standing on the front step, with the front door pulled behind her, Pippa's heart was in her throat.

She lifted the hatbox, and its bundled contents, and carried it immediately in the direction of Hector's studio, wondering what on earth they were going to do.

Chapter Fifty-Four

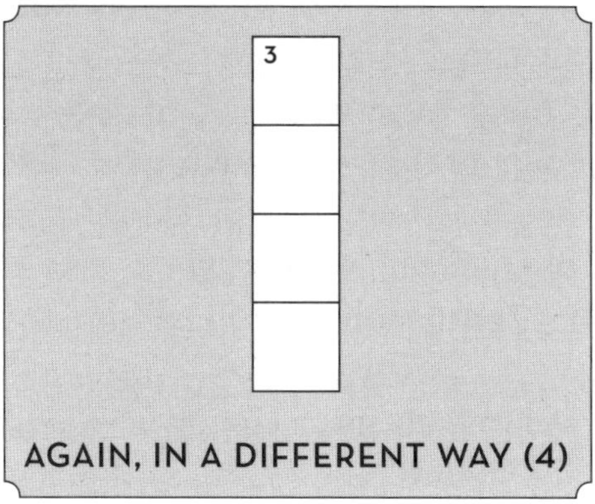

Again in a different way was the motto of the Fellowship's twenty-fifth annual Puzzle Fayre.

Clayton had attended countless fayres in his lifetime, but this one felt different, and not just because it was taking place in the autumn, rather than the usual spring.

It was a cool, blue-skied, somewhat breezy day and inside the centre of the hedgerow maze, a cluster of leaves were taken from their branches by a sudden gust of wind. The wispy, elongated strips – coloured from red to rust – cascaded to the earth like ticker tape.

The tree that Clayton had grown up with inside the maze – now a fully mature weeping willow – had recently been adorned with a small silver memorial plaque.

It read:

In loving memory of Elizabeth and Lucas Haywood.
Gone too soon.

Ever since Clayton had returned from Amsterdam with Hector, things were beginning to feel different. And while he wouldn't go as far as saying it was a happy ending – given the personal tragedies involved – Clayton was beginning to think of it more as a hopeful beginning.

For a start, he was beginning to see the world, and himself, **anew**.

He wasn't so much of an enigma, he'd decided, but more of a riddle. A dichotomy of things. A walking paradox.

He was a young man who liked drinking brandy and wearing old-fashioned brogues but these days he also enjoyed playing real-time strategy games on the Xbox and listening to Girls Aloud.

Clayton turned to their special guest, who earlier that day had hosted one of her famous pub quizzes in the marquee.

'I still can't believe it,' Nancy said. 'I'm back!'

For the first time since she departed twenty-five years ago, Mrs Stone had returned to the Fellowship. It had been a sold-out session. One of the biggest hits they've ever had at any fayre.

She was sat beside her old friend, Earl, and the Prince of Pieces, Hector.

'You're not getting cold?' he asked. 'Because if you are, we can go inside?'

'I can barely breathe, I'm so warm!' She unwound the woolly scarf Clayton had insisted she wear.

'Do you know,' Earl said, 'if anything, I'm *too* hot in this thing.'

Hector helped him unzip his old sheepskin jacket which Clayton had also insisted on.

'I just don't want any of you getting ill, that's all,' Clayton explained.

'I'm going back inside,' Hector announced. 'I've got to cash up. It was another busy one, wasn't it . . .'

He briefly touched Clayton's shoulder before disappearing into the maze corridor. It had become their thing. He would never be a great one for hugging, like Nancy was, but Clayton understood that he showed his affection by gently pinching the top of his shoulder.

'We're actually in the warmest spot in the garden,' Earl said, once Hector had gone. 'Inside these green walls.'

He was right. It was a fortress, Clayton thought. They were properly insulated from the outside – it was why he'd always enjoyed spending time in here.

Nancy reached into her purse and sparked up, blowing a perfect ring of smoke above them. 'We've got you to thank for this, Clayton. Bringing the old gang back together.'

Clayton smiled. Inside, among the hundred other guests, Jonty and Edwin were getting reacquainted with everyone. Even his friend, Cilla Millington, had made the trip.

Earl turned and beamed at him. 'The man who solved his own mystery.'

Clayton shook his head. 'Stop it.'

'I still can't believe it,' Nancy said. 'That all this time, you and Hector were . . .'

'This place was built on surprises,' Earl explained.

'And secrets,' Clayton added. 'I just wonder if there's any left.'

'No,' Nancy said. 'It was never about secrets, not really. It was always about Fellowship. And parties! We used to have so much fun.'

Clayton smiled and turned his eyes to Earl, who was studying him with a curious new gaze and mumbling something to himself.

'What was that, Earl?'

'*All these extraordinary minds*. It was something Pippa said, in our first session, in that room above the pub all those years ago. *All these extraordinary minds . . . imagine what we could achieve together.*'

'She said that?'

He nodded and the two men looked at each other for a moment.

'You're the best thing we ever produced. You know that, son, don't you?'

Clayton felt a warmth expanding through his chest, just as Earl lifted his hand to his heart.

'What is it? It's not your angina playing up, is it?'

'No,' Earl laughed, and took Clayton by the hand, pressing his palm hard against Earl's woollen jumper, where the breastbone stuck out.

'Feel that?'

Clayton shook his head.

'That's pride, son. I'm bursting with it.'

A few minutes later, there was the sound of feet crushing gravel. Clayton angled his ear, waiting to see who would appear, knowing full well who was approaching. He had that familiar tumble in his stomach, the one that indicated something new and good in his life.

'Do you need a hand?' he called out, trying to swallow his laughter. He nudged Earl, who snorted a little. Nancy beamed at him with her finger pressed to her lips.

Seconds later and the feet continued to scuffle, stopping abruptly again.

'Will I come and get you?' he shouted. 'You're lost, aren't you?'

'Don't you dare,' Neil called back, with mock indignation. 'I'll work it out for myself, don't you worry. I'll get there eventually.'

It took a few minutes and when Neil eventually appeared he looked utterly dazed, as if he'd just cracked the Enigma code.

Clayton pushed himself up from the bench and draped his arm around his shoulder.

'Perfect timing,' he said.

'Why's that?'

'Because we're all going back inside. I forgot my big coat and I'm bloody freezing.'

'Will you lead the way, Clay?' Earl asked.

'Of course, I will,' he answered. 'We'll only get lost otherwise, won't we?'

'Cheeky bugger,' Nancy said, and they all shared a laugh.

'Follow me, everyone. It's this way.'

HET NED

ANSWERS

1 A	P	2 P	E	3 A	R	4 A	N	5 C	E	
		R		N		L		R		6 I
	7 L	O	V	E		8 L	E	A	R	N
9 R		B		W		I		V		K
10 E	Y	E	S		11 R	E	V	E	A	L
M				12 M		S				I
13 O	O	14 D	L	E	S		15 P	16 A	I	N
R		A		T		17 Z		N		G
18 S	T	R	U	T		19 E	G	G	S	
E		E		L		S		E		
	20 A	D	V	E	N	T	U	R	E	S

ACKNOWLEDGMENTS

When people ask, I usually say that I started writing this book three years ago, but now I think about it, it's been a lifetime in the making. There are so many people to whom I am eternally indebted.

In my TV career, I've been fortunate enough to work under some magnificent storytellers. I'd like to thank Jim Allen, Nick Hornby, Tina Flintoff, Beth Morrey, Jack Bootle, Eliana Capitani, and, of course, the Bracket to my Hinge, Teresa Watkins, for everything they've taught me and for all the laughs over the years.

Most of us can name a teacher who's had an impact on their lives, but I'm fortunate enough to have three. Becky Dawson, Sarah-Jane Kelly, and Sarah May, thank you for championing me and my creativity at very different stages of my education.

I'd like to pay tribute to some of my older friends. First, another beloved mentor of mine, the late Mira Hamermesh, a trailblazing filmmaker, artist and writer I was lucky enough to assist whilst at film school. Secondly, my telephone friend, Cilla, whose conversations are always a tonic. And how can I forget the residents of Whiteley Retirement Village who were gracious enough to allow Dani and I into their homes, to tell their stories, all those years ago.

The Fellowship's founding members were inducted at the Faber Academy back in early 2020 and I'll always be grateful for the Class of COVID's early encouragement and feedback. Thanks to Andrew Hulse, Anna Slater, David Bullock, Frances Salter, Heather Twidle, Lauren Grest, Nicola Moyne, Phillip Williams, Rachel Ricucci, Tania Cagnoni, plus my lockdown buddy Marija Bračkovi , and the obscenely gifted Andrew Davis who, in a bizarre twist of fate, ended up designing the most beautiful cover for this book. It makes me smile every time I look at it.

A special mention must go to Anstey Harris and everyone who attends her Zoom Writing Club, especially you Maureen, for being there to celebrate the deal; plus, my literary sage Hannah Griffiths; coaching extraordinaire, Katy Loftus; and the wonderful Jessie Burton, who encouraged me to keep going at such a pivotal point. An extended thanks to my friends at the London Library – my second home – and to the brilliant people behind London Writers' Salon, Writers' HQ, and to booksellers and bloggers across the country who do so much to champion debut writers like myself. You're all a joy.

Thanks to my best mate, Caroline Mitchell, for the deadline snacks and dinners out; to my long-suffering brother, Jon, and his girlfriend Shan, for cheering me on from the sidelines; to my very special nan – May Carey – who has waited far too long to get her hands on this book, and my other nan, Jeanne, who sadly will never get to read it, but influenced elements of this story all the same; and to my partner-in-crime, Thomas Carson, whose unending kindness and positivity inspires me every day. Tom, you're as old in your soul as I am in mine and I'm so proud to have you at my side on this new adventure.

I'm lucky enough to have the best team behind me and my agent, Hellie Ogden, the dream-maker herself, has masterminded the entire thing with such grace and good humour throughout. H, thank you for believing in me and this book right from word go. I'm so grateful to have you in my corner. A huge thanks to my agency WME, and the original team at Janklow & Nesbit, especially Nathaniel Alcaraz-Stapleton, Ellis Hazelgrove, Maimy Suleiman, Kirsty Gordon, Ma'suma Amiri and Janet Covindassamy, for sending this book out into the world so skillfully and with such passion. Thanks also to Emily Hayward-Whitlock and Rhiannon Davies at the Artist's Partnership, for seeing the potential in this story beyond the page. I can't wait to make our exciting announcement soon.

To my brilliant editors, Charlotte Mursell at Orion and Caitlin Landuyt at Anchor, crikey, where do I even begin? Thank you for seeing my potential, for pushing me, and for telling me when to stop. You've contributed so much to this story and its success is yours as much as mine. Also, eagle-eyed copy editor, Suzanne, I feel I owe you a drink one day.

Before I finish, I'd also like to thank you, the reader, for picking up *The Fellowship of Puzzlemakers* in the first place. I really hope you enjoyed it and that it perhaps got you thinking about what your missing piece might be. If you end up writing a short review online, recommending it to a friend, or posting about it on social media, I would like to offer a thanks in advance here. It really makes such a difference.

And last but not least, the final acknowledgement is reserved for my parents – the greatest you could ever wish for. Mum, you may not be 'in this book' in a literal sense but your warmth and kindness are embedded in every page, and Dad, your wit, wisdom and sheer bloodymindedness is, too. You've both supported me in every aspect of my life and this novel is entirely for you. Thank you.

CREDITS

Samuel Burr and Orion Fiction would like to thank everyone at Orion who worked on the publication of *The Fellowship of Puzzlemakers* in the UK.

Editorial
Charlotte Mursell
Snigdha Koirala

Copyeditor
Suzanne Clarke

Proofreader
Clare Wallis

Audio
Paul Stark
Jake Alderson

Contracts
Dan Herron
Ellie Bowker
Alyx Hurst

Design
Jessica Hart
Andrew Davis
Helen Ewing

Editorial Management
Charlie Panayiotou
Jane Hughes
Bartley Shaw

Finance
Jasdip Nandra
Nick Gibson
Sue Baker

Marketing
Lynsey Sutherland
Lucy Cameron
Jennifer Hope

Publicity
Leanne Oliver
Frankie Banks

Production
Ruth Sharvell

Sales
Jen Wilson
Esther Waters
Victoria Laws
Toluwalope Ayo-Ajala
Rachael Hum
Francis Doyle
Georgina Cutler

Operations
Jo Jacobs